By the same author

NON FICTION

All Of Us There
History of Fashion Photography

FICTION

The Far Side of the Lough

DORA

or

The Shifts of the Heart

POLLY DEVLIN

ARROW BOOKS

Author's Acknowledgements

I owe a debt of gratitude to Diana Michener and Suzanne Lowry and thank Wendy Stevenson, Penny Krinski and Anne Reynolds, for their invaluable help.

I wish to acknowledge the hospitality of the Hawthornden Castle International Retreat where a section of this book was written.

Arrow Books Limited
20 Vauxhall Bridge Road, London SW1V 2SA

An imprint of the Random Century Group

London Melbourne Sydney Auckland
Johannesburg and agencies throughout the world

First published in Great Britain in 1990 by Chatto & Windus Ltd.

Arrow edition 1992

1 3 5 7 9 10 8 6 4 2

Printed and bound in Great Britain by
Cox & Wyman Ltd., Reading, Berkshire

ISBN 0 09 991210 4

For Daisy Garnett

ONE
The Island

I

'To begin with the old rigmarole. In a country there was a county and in that county there was a townland and in that townland there was a house where a baby had just been born. She was one of many babies born in that same house within a remarkably short space of time and she was baptised, without much ceremony, in a small Irish church by an Irish priest who was hardly sober and who poured more water over his own feet and the godparents' hands than over her head. She was christened Nora.'

So far, so good.

The sun was beating at the rattan slats in a way that Dora had never known the sun could do. It was like something alive, thickset, yellow at the gates. Her gauze top was sticking to her body. She imagined herself in cooler climes.

'When she was sixteen she changed her name to Dora: not in any legal sense – she wouldn't have known how to go about it, nor would anyone else in the remote country district in which she lived, nor would she have had the nerve, or what the neighbours would have called the conceit, to do any such thing. She changed her name by stealth and cunning. She had begun the process that led to the annulment of her baptismal identity in her own mind, years before, in the compositions of yearnings and fantasy. From the moment she became a self-conscious girl, Nora seemed to her a most unsuitable name. Many adolescents believe this about the name they have been given and indulge in flights of fancy as to the names their parents might have given them, if they, ordained mundane and prosaic by their very nature as parents, had been able to discern the extraordinary creature they had nurtured. Then surely these genetic necessities would have reached into richer coffers for a name to suit their miraculous progeny and instead of the Joans, the Susans, the Janes and the Josies, would have found monikers such as Esmeralda and Daphne, Grizelda or Amaryllis. So at one point in her continuous starveling rebellion might adolescent Nora have thought. But Nora's change of name was not of this conviction nor born of such resentment. She sought a shield and entry into another world, sought a name that would be a habit, like those the nuns wore which rendered them sexless and anonymous, strange, destroyed women.

She felt rather than thought – for from earliest times Nora was not a great thinker, though she was a champion of instinct and feeling – that since they had eschewed everything which was womanly and fruitful they ought not to be subject to gestatory functions. It was not fair that they should accrue so much merit from despisal. She feared them and their rejection of the world and the way their curves were revealed when the long straight scapulars that fell from their neck to their feet blew away from their bodies in the wind. She stopped eating and made a show of it and began to waste away. The headmistress, a bony bad woman called Sister Scholastica, took her into her study and said Nora, Miss Nora, this is how we treat notice-boxes especially those who break the fifth commandment, and slashed her hands with a rod.

Nora was taken away from that school not because of the beating across the palms of her hands, which had given her great satisfaction since she was indeed a notice-box (and which, as no one had ever been beaten at the school before, meant that she was noticed with a vengeance) but because her parents could no longer afford the boarding-school fees.

She was to start at a day school in September and that summer she changed her name to Dora.

It was not just that the name seemed generations, countries and classes away from Nora – that is to say, she thought that it was Edwardian, English and something else, something vague, imponderable, which she couldn't name but sensed as existing and which in a conversation years later she first heard formalised, but also that

Nora was so old-fashioned in its least chic sense, Irish, unglamorous, what James Joyce had called 'country-cute', though of course Nora, like her earlier namesake, had not read Joyce when she was sixteen and thought that Joyce was a girl's Christian name like Evelyn. When she was older and learnt a little German and the meaning of Freud she smiled, did Dora, whose sentimental education left little to be desired. She was put out to find that Evelyn Waugh was a man.'

I say, of course, Dora noted, because, of course, no Irish person reads Joyce until they have encountered and in some wise accommodated another country.

'Nora knew little of the cluster of associations behind the name Dora. She had read Dickens and knew of the child-wife whom David Copperfield adored. "Dora! What a beautiful name! She was more than human to me. She was a Fairy, a Sylph, I don't know what she was – anything that no one ever saw, and everything that everybody ever wanted."

At that time Nora thought it a nauseating description of a silly babyish creature, for even then Nora had learnt that Irish habit of absolving men and blaming women. In her more ideological days Dora regarded her namesake as a betrayer of her sex for she was susceptible enough to Dickens's art to forget that she was only a creation of a writer's imagination. Of the other Doras she knew little, though in her later life she collected what she didn't call Dora-isms. She had not heard of Freud and his famous patient, she had not read of Dora Carrington who had hated her name and, being a woman in equal measure, she had not heard of the German prison camp of the Second World War, had not read Kilvert's diaries and his talk of the woman he loved, nor had she heard of Dora Russell, though she had bought the paperback version of her husband's autobiography and still means to read it. She had never heard of the Defence of the Realm Act and when she did was irritated at the misuse of the acronym for such legislation. Every other time she came across the name or the acronym she felt it verified her choice save when she read Tennyson's "Dora" and found an anti-heroine. She defused her dismay by learning some stanzas of the poem the better to savour its piteous whimsy and take note of its moral lessons, if only to practise the opposite of what it preached. It was obvious that Tennyson's meek Dora was as plain as a pikestaff and *that* Dora did not intend to be. "The more he looked at her, the less he liked her" was one of the lines she declaimed with most success, and "But Dora lived unmarried till her death." Not for me, she thought, not for me.'

Looking back, in the heat of the island, Dora realises the importance of her new naming, undertaken with the desperate affectation of the young. Having once assumed the name, it became as close a connection as her own skin. It became her integument. In naming herself she incarcerated Nora, and with her assumption of the new name, such a tiny change, one consonant, she believed herself to be lifted above her earlier, defined, and limited identity, which, she felt, had been so hooked into her relationships with her family, her school mates, her teachers that she could never escape the prison of the shame of childhood.

She knew that however she turned and struggled on the hook of her existence the truth was she had to live in some kind of tryst, or treaty, with Nora. She could not gainsay continuity with the child she had been. Yet she felt if she did not smother Nora under some cloak, she would have to sit like a hare in the middle of a field held by an invisible snare of pain, encircled by the hidden eyes of watchers.

So the child who had been Nora was put into a state of stasis. Like the cherry-cheeked virgin in her glass coffin, adored but beyond response, who never changed but never rotted, who lay protected from the hot hands and demands of dwarfs, Dora thought that Nora lay suspended in the transparent resin of memory, and that as she made her pilgrim's progress through life she could, if she so minded, hurry back and check on her, the disgraceful creature, lying there uncracked, amberised, waiting.

'The child who was Nora put an end to her childhood, left her name to the living effigy, rechristened herself and set out, tabula rasa, on her journey to death, or to life, if that is a better way of putting it, for those of you with tender sensitivities and an optimistic bent.

You may ask what Nora's honest and complex parents thought of her change of name. They accepted it, without protest and apparently without puzzlement or curiosity, as they accepted so much, and from the day she announced the change they tried never to call her anything but Dora.

Sometimes, when she went back to her original place, an old person or a school contemporary called her Nora and though at first she was alarmed by this it came to mean nothing. At times she still thought there was nothing she would like more than for someone to greet her as Nora and, further, that she would be able to react unaffectedly, spontaneously, but that, she believed, would be impossible. If she could resurrect Nora then she would have discovered the secret of growing up or growing old, and Nora is for ever young.

For years Nora was her hidden, protected child who was too stunned and too fragile, too full of shame, to live in the world that Dora apprehended lay in wait for her. Looking back Dora wants to think that she devised the stratagem so that Nora could abide in her own country while Dora lived in exile; wishful thinking. What is true is that for years Nora lived in Dora's head, as in a crystal ball which she could shake and watch the dust settle, and there would be Nora who with a bit of luck was weeping, so all could be deemed well. We all have our little ways. Such times are past for Dora. She does not look forward or back or towards Nora now. She looks to herself.'

There was a knock on the door. Dora rose and was about to open it when she noticed in her reflection how the sweat on her body made the thin white muslin stick to it. She pulled a bathrobe around her. Someone knocked again and the handle turned. She opened the door quickly. The young man who did room service was standing outside.

Dora was wary. The day after her arrival she had found him at her dressing-table, holding her amber necklace against his brown throat; he had put it down slowly almost languidly, looking back at her through the mirror, undismayed. She had seized the necklace up and left the room afraid to speak. Now he was smiling with something more in his smile than Dora liked. She told him she had not rung, he must be mistaken and closed the door and looked at what she had written. She had once defined her own occupation as that of an interpreter trying to be a scribe, and it was said with the anger and irony that coloured so much of these scrivenings.

Perhaps only when she went back and chipped Nora out of the glass cage, glass that wasn't glowing and transparent but amber with the suppressed glowering of sadness and rage, and united her with Dora, whoever she was – a lost Irish woman, a spoiled English wife, a person in exile, who was all the same, quite at home in her new country, a creature of comfort, a human in pain – could she look to herself and be whole; she remembered various definitions of wholeness, when Io and Jupiter merged and the heavens ceased to exist, and thought on: perhaps not wholly to be desired after all. As Dora well knew, division could be expedient; separation had its uses.

She shuffled her papers into a folder and showered in cool water and went out into the brazen sun. She walked past the palm trees across sand so fine it seemed pulverised, to the edge of the water. The hard-faced woman and her besotted husband were in the water wading ashore. As she walked past the pig-scraping tree she wondered whether it was feasible that a child of sixteen could employ such a device, changing her name in order to predicate her life so that she could always have alternative beginnings.

The boy from room service was standing by an old boat. He was in shorts, a turquoise polyester shirt. She turned back but he came up behind her and said, 'Can I be of service? I give very good service.'

'No, thank you,' she said, politely refusing his message, determined to think well of him, or at least well of herself, to keep the murderous rage under the trapdoor. 'I don't need anything. It's kind of you to ask.'

Encouraged, he moved nearer, and she hurried on, he lunging after, so that she could no longer give him the benefit of the doubt. Yet she could not bring herself to humiliate him though she felt herself humiliated. He would be back on room service tomorrow; how could she scream at him now, hurl loudly her rejection of his assumptions (and where had he learnt those assumptions if not from Western women on his beaches) and have to deal with the aftermath, the whole ambivalent scene, the avoiding of eyes, the surliness on the morrow. She turned back to the hotel and into the prickly heat of her bedroom.

Any single woman alone invited it; she corrected herself, did not invite it, became prey. She thought of the men on the beach who looked at her covertly. No woman would accost them. The men might joke about the possibility, wish coarsely that it would happen, exhibit with enjoyment their lack of imagination about the condition of women. Yet, if a woman did make an advance, her name would be bandied about between them, like a hot little bundle, and then the story told to their womenfolk who would never dream of doing such a thing.

She remembered once how she had told a man on a terrace in Greece that she fancied him and he had fled and she knew he would have related the scene, as an example of his own desirability, never for a moment considering it rose out of a kind of ardent desperation on her part. Afterwards she had been ashamed of herself, especially since she had not fancied him; but she was in her thirties and alone as she so often was, as she chose to be, fleeing her family, and it was a warm scented night and she wanted a man's body, any man's, wanted it enough to cry for it. Men could pay for sex, solicit it, accost for it. A single woman could not venture to ask for it without making a pariah of herself, without being labelled dirty, greedy. Caveat emptor, married women.

She went inside and sat down at her dressing-table and looked into the mirror, a mirror stained with shadows that reflected the windows opposite so that it looked as though there were a double image, a shadowy outline around or behind her occupying the place where she should be alone, an image with hair like tussore, looking at her across the room, frail, foxed, as though buried under pourried years.

In the heat she felt foundered and she rose and pulled the blinds up with force, so that they hung at strange angles and the sun battered in under them; she screwed up her eyes so that she saw only herself in her anonymous room, in a different hemisphere in a new beach hotel – opened only two seasons before but already wearing a scuffed look – in a room with fans that often did not spin, a mosquito net that was inadequate, and a wireless that did not work, while across the world her own house hummed, without a tremor, in its grooves.

Her skin was burning (although how badly it was burnt she did not yet know) and she scolded her reflection. Scolding was second nature to Dora, complaint third. Both traits she believed she inherited from the outline she feared she glimpsed in the mirror.

'You're going to peel and the quicker you tan the quicker it will peel and turn a grisly grey,' she said to herself, her lips moving and then aloud, enunciating the words carefully, 'and you'll get skin cancer.' She listened to the words and ducked her head as though to push the thought away, in case she brought the cancer down on herself in a slow drift from heaven. A nice idea of heaven there, she thought, and wished again that the child beneath the womanly appearance had not been reared in quite such a didactic and mad dispensation. She lay down on the bed and looked at the ceiling where at night lizards clung and scuttled, like visitations from a crack in the transparency.

At this time, Dora was in her mid-thirties, if she was telling the truth which was then unlikely. At times she became confused as to her age, a deliberate confusion, and had even altered her age in her passport by the judicious use of a cross stroke, a cross stroke which she believed was against the law. Cross stroke she said to herself when she matched up the inks for the careful forgery, well-said, I am indeed cross and not just about age but about everything.

It was the nineteen seventies and where she lived was caught in the glaze of ice and snow of a northern mid-winter, but she was marooned on a blisteringly hot island where she had gone not just to find the sun but to try to come to her senses. For years she had headed for the sun for two weeks as a matter of habit, and since money was no object she went to the other side of the world each time, as though she might find her Ultima Thule. And to go to the sun was an imperative. For almost two decades, that pale bodies should have an all-over tan was a sign of success and desirability, an essential, as though such bodies could only be restored to their owners – whoever they might be – by being roasted almost to a nice piece of crackling; and even as she lay under the sun Dora thought what a strange practice it was, as strange and archaic as using lead on one's face, which pursuit of beauty killed many an eighteenth-century beauty. Dora was not hoping to have her body restored to her, since she felt she had never had it in the second place. (The first place was somewhere else again.) She was getting a tan so that if she had to be undressed by others she would look better although she would have been indignant at this explanation. Yet why else would one burn one's skin if not for someone else, or to wear a white swimsuit better? 'Turn me over,' said St Lawrence, 'for I am well enough done on this side.' Talk about imagination, thought Dora, he did it for the love of Jesus.

At this time, Dora still thought of herself as a girl though she knew that if she were found dead, murdered or drowned, newspaper reports would say that the body of a woman had been recovered. But, though she felt that the spirit which informed that body was too young for womanliness, Dora was womanly through and through and had been since she was young. She has never been girlish. She looked untouched and occasionally a look of innocence shone out when she was off-guard.

Dora thought of herself as young, not through any self-delusion or calling back of youth, nor through any blindness to the quality of her skin tone, nor in order to deceive herself (although certainly to deceive others) but because her life, although in a disarray that frightened her, was just beginning to make a kind of sense, and her chronology was somehow linked to this sense. Until this new awareness had hesitantly arrived, unsure of its welcome, she had believed that she propelled herself on her own energy through the active universe. Now she has gone to the other extreme and thinks that she has always been passive, and the circumstances and events of her life (which no doubt she, in some ways, precipitated), have arbitrarily happened to her because she was there as, say, meteors hit the earth, or as human beings evolved quite by chance, not because the ancestor rearing itself out of the primeval slime was the fittest, but was, rather, mutatis mutandis, the luckiest.

Dora felt that her new awareness about her condition marked the beginning of the end of her odious and painful adolescence and that she needed more time before being able to take on the burden of being a fully paid-up woman. The price seemed too high in terms of yielding certain attributes which she thought made life easier. She remembered something she had once read, perhaps in Joyce, something about the ancient Romans believing that the age of seventeen marked the divide between childhood and adolescence, and that thirty-one was the beginning of inventus. If she was remembering rightly, which was to be doubted since everything seemed to be such a smattering with her, this meant she was being lapped by younger women in her creep towards maturity. She felt she would never reach that state and would find senility first, bypassing the wise stage altogether.

At night in bed, or when she went out on solitary walks, she tried to think what this new awareness, sprung from two paradoxical insights, meant, in terms of her future. The insights were arrived at, she assumed, by age, attrition and paid help, and one was contingent on the other. One was the realisation of her own personal insignificance in the scheme of things; it hardly mattered whether she lived or died. The other was the realisation of her own personal significance, the fact that her life was momentous because she was there, and occupied an important place in the scheme of things. She would tussle with this for a while and then would try to sleep, or hit out at the nettles with her stick, feeling lonely and worthless and angry, and would as a last resort remember the people who thought she was above and beyond any value, priceless in any negotiation. To them, at that time, she was the ideal mother.

Mother or lover, wife or friend, in all of these positions she knew who she was by reflection, but her own value as a person and her merits were neither clear nor dear to her. She could not make her value or merits worthwhile or negotiable, and the admissible modest and ordinary realisation that she had merit and value had come to her only in the guise of revelation and was thus to be doubted. She needed more time than she thought she had, to bring her awareness and ideas into a working part of her life, hence her altering the age on her passport in order to defeat official time. Dora learnt as she grew older and calmer that those caught up in passion and hectic turmoil often believe that time is running out more quickly on them than on anyone else.

She rubbed some cold ointment into her seared skin and went back to her dressing-table and took up her pen and added some lines to a letter.

'It is because I can see you accepting my behaviour and not rebelling, that I go on behaving badly. You give me permission through silence, and then wear a martyred air.'

She left down her pen and thought about the boy at the door and on the beach. Perhaps she was transmitting some horrible vibration of need and sexuality which was meant for her lover Theodore's ears only and it was picked up by other antennae, a kind of Hilversum of love. The letter was to her absent husband, Simon, a letter which she would not post, as she articulated sounds in her throat when she was with him which she did not utter, though God knows anyone listening would have thought she never drew breath. She kept the undertones silent, and destroyed these missives because she thought she was not so far gone as to inflict gratuitous wounds. She could inflict those in the course of an ordinary day with so little effort it seemed pointless to sit down and compose them. And his behaviour, after all, was not martyred. It was good. It was, to the casual observer, impeccable behaviour and he got credit from such onlookers as could be bothered.

Dora was not casual – indeed was inclined to the obsessive – nor an observer, though she had always thought of herself on the outside of things, looking in and thus observing. In fact she participated, and precipitated whilst pretending ignorance of and responsibility for both activities, and tried to control everything around her whilst professing and occasionally practising timidity. The thing she feared was that Simon's behaviour arose out of his religious beliefs, an idea of sacrifice, of virtue being earned like a moral salary. If it was so, then he would never make a move, since the worse she behaved and the more he bore, the more his good marks accumulated, gold stars in heaven.

She resented the idea that she was a tribulation to be borne, a means for her spouse to achieve greater spiritual growth. Torturers might be necessary, she reflected, however extravagant an idea in the human scheme of things, if only to bring the saintliness of martyrs and saints to the surface, for their goodness to be noticed; and she did not wish either to be a torturer or a weapon with which her husband could scourge himself. His goodness in putting up with her, was, she was sure, noticed. Certainly she noticed it.

In the groves bordering the beach she had seen a pig run its neck up and down an edge of sharp bamboo until it bled. It apparently liked doing it. Martyrs, she reminded herself, chose their conditions. They were not victims.

She abandoned this line of thought since it seemed to lead towards murky waters in which she would find herself pitying torturers for the role in which they found themselves and decided that the reason she did not send the letter or shape the sounds was because she was frightened of what might happen when he received the letter or heard the noises. She discarded this explanation. Fright betokened interest or power and Dora chose not to believe that she was much interested in her husband or that he had any power over her. Playing for time she might have said, as another explanation for her silence, if she hadn't become wary of using expressions like this, since her friend Stella did a flying tackle on the words Dora used and made her listen to what she was saying.

'Nothing one says is inadvertent,' she often said. And so: 'Playing for time is it? So it's just a game? Or a gamble?'

If it was, Dora thought miserably, it was a death-game. Indeed, increasingly life had begun to seem like a dark game to Dora, with everything pulling her towards the underworld. The shadow of Hades seemed to fall around her wherever she went. Outside, the whole of an exotic island bloomed and scented itself but she lived in the gloom and squared her shoulders and tightened her mouth and looked towards the shadows as though there were an invisible jury watching her daily navigation towards some version of the truth.

She feared she was a trial, certainly she had been told so often in her childhood and perhaps the patterns had been set too far behind for her to be able to change them. She remembered how much of a trial her own mother had seemed to her as she and her sister Iris had sat mute, silenced by the hostility of their mother's shoulders, squared against the encroachment of their presence on the brown leather seat in the back of the old Riley. They had wondered even then, young as they were, why it would have been such a calamity to have yielded herself into being pleased by anything.

Now Dora believed that for her mother to have allowed her tight face to slacken with the curve of a smile, her body to ease into a sense of pleasure, would have meant the lowering of too many defences, a broach in the dykes she had built up which would have allowed pain to rush in and take over. Dora feared that she, too, in time would become frightened of pleasure, of being pleased, and for years had worked to make sure she had a spontaneous reaction ready whenever it was called for, to have joy or gratitude at her fingertips. They rarely were, they remained just out of reach, although captured in abundance when the moment had passed, but all the same she proffered them remorsefully, and Simon took them with generosity, as though they had been given with grace when they might have been. He had never made her feel empty-handed. Her mother, Dora felt, had driven gratitude and joy out of her own life because it would have been too painful to have allowed them in; but now Dora knew, too, that her mother's hands had been fully occupied, and though she had struggled to remove herself from the totemic position, she had had to watch as everyone else walked away while she held up the sky. She did her best, Dora thought, and I thought that her best, like mine, was not up to much, and I knew nothing.

II

In coming to this island Dora has left her lover behind, and a loving husband, Simon, who lives in their family house in Suffolk, a battlemented, elaborate edifice which he has inherited, and which is called, Dora decides for the purpose of writing, Keep Hall. Her lover teaches at a college in Cambridge called New Court, a name that is near enough the truth, and echoes the cross-overs that happen in life where names deliver messages, and coincidence becomes synchronicity and Dora-isms abound, in all of which Dora finds verification of what she wants to believe. These Halls of Residence are connected by her, the go-between, as are the men who live in them but she isn't fool enough to say this to either of them and in any case Simon knows nothing about New Court and its teaching staff. Or is not supposed to. Or pretends not to. Who knows. Certainly not Dora.

She got off the bed and went over to the mirror and tried to banish all the nonsense, to look straight at her reflection, at the singular person looking back. The sun made the glass dazzle. As she peered, her eyes narrowed, she resurrected certain details of her mother's lost face. The soft loose skin around her pinkish brown upper lip like a delta from which a hundred little tributaries ran with a reverse flow: whenever she applied lipstick it seemed to melt and float upwards along these backwaters, channels of coloured chemical grease. It was partly to avoid her ever getting these lines, partly to avoid ever knowing that her own children would sit watching her own implacable and unforgiving back from the back of any car that Dora sought to dismantle her life in order to try to build its future in another shape. A fool's game, she thought, which suits me well. She was also working hard on a flanking rearguard action by turning her shapely self into shapelessness, as though she could physically parallel the guilt and pain which had thickened into a salted aspic around her emotions.

She picked up a strange piece, a fragment of memory and pain which once fitted so snugly into place that she didn't even know it was there. She had no idea where it should go, or how to deal with it, and she turned it over and over to try to see a pattern.

The new figure who had burst through the pattern of her life a little while before, leaving, like Desperate Dan, a hole his size in it, had knocked the routine and shape of the life she and her husband had built for themselves, right out of true. Indeed, in the past few months, she had sometimes thought it would be easier to die than to deal with what was happening but she knew, fundamentally, she was not serious. She made little stabs towards the idea, and told Stella so.

'See,' Stella said, triumphantly. 'Listen. Little stabs, you don't mean to do yourself much harm. Hara kiri only works with big stabs.'

Dora's little stabs included twisting her ankle, straining her back, hurting her wrists and most of all losing or mislaying things. Keys, books, large dishes, children's clothes, overcoats, scarfs, cars and always, always, the jewellery that Simon gave her which, for as long as she had it, she treasured. She used to pray, each time he replaced something she had lost, that this time she would not lose it, her lips moving in an atavistic invocation to St Anthony. Equally, as she sat cramming food down her gullet, like a gannet, she would pray to St Mairead, who starved herself to death to prove her love to God, to intervene, to stop her eating. Mairead never bestirred herself.

Almost the first time they met, Simon gave her a gold necklace which he had brought back from Peru. Its heavy links were hammered and engraved with an intricate feather pattern. Dora liked it more than anything she had ever owned, though she thought he was mad to give it to her since she was resolved never to see him again. Nothing there to interest her.

Some time later, he took her to the South of France and one day, walking alone through a field of lavender, she was taken short and ran, thighs pressed hard together, across the stony dry field with its scratchy, pungent crop towards the ruin of an old house, and there in one of the tumbled rooms open to the Provençal sky, she hunkered and peed. As she did so, the necklace parted, she felt it open at the back of her neck, stealthily as if a small reluctant animal or snake which had been trained and forced into ornament, its mouth grasping its tail, had suddenly seen a chance for freedom, unloosened itself and tried to slide away. She watched it while it slid between her breasts, negotiated the bottom of her bra, and then casually grasped it before it sank into the water leaking into the ground at her feet.

She put it to one side while she hitched up her knickers, and she walked on. There was hardly a day for the next twenty years when she didn't think of the little pile of gold marking the place where she'd squatted. When she went back twenty years later to pick it up, the ruined house had been transformed into another kind of ruined house, a villa with enormous plate-glass windows. The turquoise sheet of a swimming pool lay where she had laid her spoor.

Later Simon gave her an emerald ring, surrounded with diamonds. It was from India, and had belonged to his grandmother and soon after he put it on her finger, Dora joined a health club in Mayfair. On her first visit, she was intrigued by the other women there, so suspicious, so bright-eyed, their hair puffed-out, their clothes expensive but tacky, their lips outlined with a dark pink and filled in with a paler colour. They were quite unlike any of the women she knew or had ever known. She put the ring in her locker along with her clothes and went through to the gym and the exercises, using ungovernable machines and when she came back, walking like a pouter pigeon, the ring had gone from the locker. No one at the club would take responsibility.

Dora didn't need a Stella to tell her what she was doing in losing her valuables. But no matter how well she explained herself to herself she could not stop it, since to Dora self-esteem was not a matter of mind over matter. For Dora at this time, to matter was unforgivable and the person who made you matter had to be punished or put into oblivion. Such behaviour and her droppings made Dora grieve and feel guilty, and her lack of self-esteem was further nourished. Not a very constructive circle you may say, but not an uncommon one.

Dora, scratching out her mark, far away from home, alone, has children being looked after by other women. When she thought of this aspect of the affair, she felt momentary guilt and wondered why. The fathers of her acquaintance had their children looked after by other women constantly and appeared to feel normal and happy with the arrangement. Dora, when she was at home, looked after another woman's child as part of her own family. She felt responsible for him in more ways than one. Sometimes it seemed to her that by so passionately wanting all the children in her charge to lead a happy life, whilst herself leading an unhappy one, she was tempting fate to bring the opposite onto their small heads. But she could not stop hoping for their happiness, no more than she could stop casting her shadow over their small shadows. A pulse beat of love for all of them underwrote every moment of her day.

And Dora grieved for them, for no good reason, although they seemed strong-willed enough to resist vicarious grief, endless interference and the constant monitoring of love. While Laura, her first-born, was an infant, Dora could hardly look at her pottering about, without wishing her back within, where she was protected by Dora, and protected from her.

Once in Paris, Dora had gone to an old acupuncturist. It was the fashion in the seventies. The treatment room was high, silent, filled with grand and ugly pieces of French furniture, made with a lot of ormolu and inlay, large Chinese porcelain vases, and a modern chaise-longue. The doctor looked like a fantastical drawing of an Oriental, almost a caricature, with his long moustache, his slit eyes. He was wearing a conventional grey suit but the effect was of a mandarin's robe. He stuck a lot of long needles into her as she lay on the chaise-longue and she yelped with pain. She had rarely felt anything so sharp and disagreeable.

'You must come often,' he said, 'to calm these terrible orages. You are full of orages.'

She never went back but felt calmed by the very naming of the turbulence and storms she felt raging within her. 'Orage,' she murmured, 'orage. I have an orage coming on.' And the incantation sometimes even arrested them. Not often. Dora was a martyr to her temper.

She abandoned the scolding letter to her husband, Simon, and continued the one to her lover. 'Today I uncorked a bottle of essence and it was the stale one I had taken by mistake, and I was nostalgic because the last time I was wearing it, and smelling like that old pharmacy, we were together. I watched a couple on the beach, he was younger than she was, or looked it, and she looked hard and shaven. But alone, among all the other couples, he kept touching her flesh, stroking it, checking that it was near, and his desire for her was as living as anything else on the beach, a third party between them, and watching them I yearned for you.'

She thought of what she had not written. The ordure on the beach, in the dawn, the rank smell, the women sweeping the beaches early before the guests came out, so that it looked as though the beaches were naturally clean; the fact that on the island she felt like a parasite who had taken over the host. She envisaged any one of the many men on the beach who looked at her, touching her, and felt not a kindle, not a stirring of her flesh, save perhaps towards the man who was so absorbed in his wife.

She compared her behaviour on other earlier beaches and thought this longing for her lover must be some kind of valediction but wondered if there had been one lone attractive man on the beach would she have felt so inclined to keep aloof. She feared not, and her fears sprang as much from the suspicion that her old habits were only suppressed and avidly battening on themselves, to thunder out later, as from her superstition that if she slept with a stranger it might do something irrevocable to herself and to her lover. To her, the proof of her passion was that she hardly glanced at any man.

Dora was nothing if not analytical, although her theories (she was inclined to think of them as answers) were arrived at through what her lover said were intellectually-suspect methods. She had always suspected her own intellect so his suspicions seemed further proof of his superiority. She believed that he was all the things she was not, or thought she was not – logical, rational and brilliantly clever – partly because he had persuaded her to believe so, partly because he was so and mostly because she wanted him to be so. Dora knew she was not clever because she only had insights and made suggestions when confronted with a problem and saw connections throughout daily living. Her lover did things immediately and arrived at conclusions. When Dora examined her suggestions she usually found she had already acted on them. Her lover concluded that the insights which Dora arrived at were a matter of happenstance, crazed thinking, haphazard conjunctions, luck and the fact that she was Irish. He despised, admired and dismissed her abilities whilst he made use of the results to adjust his perceptions and further himself.

'Protect us all from female intuition,' he would say with scorn as though it were an inferior malady which struck at women. Dora wondered how much better the world might have fared if the male had had such an attribute and was somewhat upset by his attitude because she had come to regard her intuition as one of her few assets. It struck Dora that he might be jealous but she felt that this was a disloyal line of thought. She lifted a clean sheet of paper and began again.

III

Dora learnt to regard her intuition as an asset soon after she first came to London and moved into a flat belonging to a friend called Henrietta. It is Henrietta's child Thomas whom Dora has adopted. Thomas was left to Dora in Henrietta's will and he is the son of Dora's first serious lover, or rather since he treated her with inherent frivolity, the first lover she took seriously. From the beginning of their friendship, Henrietta had remarked on this intuition with such particular if ambiguous admiration that Dora had feared it would become self-conscious and rear up and leave her for ever. Her insights had become so much a part of her equipment and form of self-reference that they no longer seemed either attributes or a matter for conjecture, or even for doubt, which was perhaps a pity.

Nothing ever happened accidentally to Dora. This was what she believed. Cause and effect were as one and this refusal to admit of accident in a life which seemed full of accident and unrelated happenings, made Simon impatient (he had only to think of all the jewellery accidentally lost), her lover furious, and caused some of her friends to think she was almost unhinged. Cause and effect. To these friends she behaved in an unhinged way, she could see it happening but couldn't control it: they made their philosophy fit her facts and vice versa. She would fall over their doorstop or the glass would break in her hand or she would watch open-mouthed as her handbag fell upside down, spilling everything into the street; once while she was driving alongside a bus in the Cromwell Road, whose driver she thought was bullying her, she swung the car hard, bashing the bus and battering the side of her car.

'That will teach him,' she said to her friend Pamela, who got out as soon as possible, and walked to the nearest tube station.

Among Dora's friends, and she did not have that many, since she was a difficult woman though she had little idea of this (she thought everyone else was difficult), were Pamela and Stella. Pamela was a film-maker, and in a world where no one else seemed to get anything done, was always busy, making films funded by obscure organisations, about ethnic walkers and weavers living in tents. If they were shown as parodies, Dora thought, as she sat in small dark cinemas in Wardour Street at the private views organised by Pamela, and stared at wobbly shots of goats crossing a mountain stream, you could admire them as classics of their kind. Once Dora was amazed to hear that Pamela had broken right out of the hairy tent ambience into that of a chic intellectual salon in Paris. Three monstres sacrés, two French, one American, had agreed to be filmed discussing events of literary importance. Dora was astounded – and no doubt jealous – at Pamela having obtained an entrée to such a circle, akin, it seemed to her, to floating up in space and bumping up against, say, Turgenev looking for Dante and Beatrice with an incompetent recording angel trying to follow events. When she saw the finished film she sat in the back row of the little room, trying desperately not to laugh hysterically, unforgivably. The three talkers whirled at the edges of the screen as though spinning out from a centrifugal force, their hands like ectoplasm in corners, the boom swinging about their heads as the camera lurched and tilted.

'I was so nervous I got drunk,' Pamela said, without the least embarrassment – 'but I had to keep going.' The film was a great success in Paris where critics analysed the methods by which Pamela had broken down the innate reverence of the camera towards its subjects.

Lately Pamela had taken to talking obsessively about babies. Whenever she came to stay in Suffolk Dora's children behaved as dream children or angels might. Once Pamela was out of sight, they reverted to their natural baddish behaviour. Dora could not imagine how they knew to behave like this. She was shocked and pleased by this deviousness which seemed to be instinctive, inherent. Surely not inherited from me, she thought, and wished it were. So much for the insight.

'It's become the time,' Pamela had said, the last time she had come to visit, 'for me to have a child. I just need a baby.' And to that end had brought a man whom she believed might do as a putative father.

Dora thought of old Mother Nature grinding away and wondered what she would be like were she childless. If she were single and approaching forty she would certainly be muttering a countdown of the biological clock and putting out saucers of milk to lure stray males. She remembered Virginia Woolf's sad comments about the symbolical quality of the childless couple, standing for something united (whistling in the dark, that was) and then, later, in her deep depression, the memory of her sister Vanessa's children, springing unbidden into her mind, and the surge of warmth and life that children bring to a house and to a life. She had written, 'I might have had a child of ten by now,' and Dora imagined she must have had an abortion to have calculated like that, to have had the thought.

The symbolical quality of the childless couple was another way of looking at what other ages and generations had called barrenness. Calling it a symbol was a redemption of what must gnaw at your soul – no, not your soul, Dora corrected herself, it gnawed at your body.

She had once seen fabric being pulled towards enormous rollers to be printed. The wheels turned, the stretched fabric inched forward, nothing could prevent it from being sucked into those weighty slow-moving rollers unless the whole system ground to a halt or someone wielded terrible shears. Once through, the fabric went on its way, printed and stretched, slackening towards its final folding. Dora grimaced. She knew there was no point in making discouraging noises to Pamela, saying you need money, time, love, patience, a desert of love that sometimes is not watered at all and a vast back-up organisation, resources or friends, if you are to have and hold a baby, in its proper secure station, till late adolescence doth you part. Most of all you need, she thought, but did not say, you need a husband, since to listen to Pamela was to believe that she had scouts out all over the world behaving like collies, shepherding potential spouses towards Pamela's fold.

'I don't want to wait until I'm in my forties to have a child,' Pamela said. 'Besides, the statistics would make me think twice. I want one now. What I love about Meredith is when I said this to her she didn't raise an eyebrow. She said, "Oh great, Pamela, I'd love to have one too."'

Pamela's voice was bland. Dora hardly dared look at her. She thought of Meredith, on her third divorce, with a certain rancour.

'What age is Meredith?'

'Forty-three, forty-four?'

'And she wants to have a child?' Dora said genuinely astonished.

Meredith was keen on the idea of psychic illnesses and listened to her body as though she had hidden a bugging device in it and wished to eavesdrop on the worst; Dora had understood that her ovaries had closed down permanently.

'Oh, she doesn't mean it,' Pamela said impatiently. 'It was only – it's why she's such a marvellous friend, always encouraging one, entering enthusiastically into what you want to do, so life-enhancing, so sincere.'

'Sincerity is a dubious emotion,' Dora said, determined, since she couldn't be life-enhancing, to be honest, or difficult. 'A very suspect quality. I use sincerity for my own ends.' Pamela took no notice. Unlike Stella, she hardly listened to a word Dora said. Pamela subscribed even more heartily to the idea of connection than Dora and they verified each other in the meantness of things, which led to some ugly scenes later when Dora did something that Pamela never meant at all like nicking Pamela's lover. Pamela often brought evidence of how fate worked in wondrously connected ways and laid it out like so much jetsam, which, if she could only assemble it, might make a raft to save her life, or at least, her sanity. Dora concurred with this, and discussed Pamela with Stella, Dora's other Best Friend who disliked Pamela, and kicked the jetsam apart. Stella was a painter and not one for dissembling and she became more successful as the years rolled on and life began to match up to her spectacles which were not at all rosy-coloured.

Occasionally Stella came to stay with Dora in the country, when she wanted to get away from London, or a husband or a lover, but she made no bones about finding the country boring, never mind Simon. For his part, Simon treated Stella with a courtesy which masked his mistrust. Stella professed to dislike Dora's way of life in Suffolk, the rituals, the walks, the dinner parties, the ancient help tottering around which, Stella said, Dora must surely rent from rejects from *The Archers*, the acquaintances who congregated for drinks with their big rigid voices and hairy clothes. Stella observed their jovial good-will towards herself, this pale-faced, black-clothed, kohl-eyed, fluid-voiced female who made tart and sardonic comments which, she thought, went over their heads. They were not interested in Stella which she found the most boring aspect of it all. She considered it their loss.

Stella always helped Dora towards some version of the truth, Stella's version, no doubt, but it seemed to Dora a lot better than her own. Dora believed in Stella. And since Stella believed – not for nothing has she been for years in Jungian therapy – that as humans share a similar basic anatomy, so their mental and psychical foundations are much the same, and her cognitive leaps would be as relevant to Dora's condition as her own. It worked both ways of course and Dora learnt to give tit for tat. In almost every conversation Stella almost casually picked up on the choice of words in an answer, or remarked on the tone, or pointed out the hesitations, and these observations generally led to something else, something Dora didn't want to face or had hidden from herself. Sometimes they led nowhere but the diversion gave them both satisfaction, made them feel they were philosophers of a kind.

'What are you going to do?' Stella asked her, soon after Dora realised that, because of the advent of her lover into her life, what was happening to her was no longer an adventure, but a grim pursuit in a labyrinth, with some sort of death at the centre.

'I don't know,' Dora had said miserably. 'I can't move.'

'I'll come and visit you,' Stella murmured and Dora drove back to her house in Suffolk, trying to ignore a pain in her back which increased as she drew nearer home. The next day she was in bed with what the doctor, looking vague, said was probably a strained ligament and which, whatever it was, rendered her incapable of movement. Stella came down to stay for a couple of days.

'A strained ligament,' Dora said scornfully. 'It's what they say when they haven't a clue. Like the word virus.'

'But you did bring it on yourself,' Stella said as she sat in Dora's bedroom looking down, with a certain amusement in her eyes, on the black sheep grazing beyond the haha. 'I've said often enough, you must watch what you say.' Dora looked at Stella's mouth to see the trick and resolved never to say anything like 'I'm mad about that' or 'It will be the death of me' in case she prophesied something only waiting to be named to come alive.

In Stella, Dora confided the emotional itinerary of her life though, as she talked, she was ashamed to hear herself bemoaning her fate when she knew she had so much good fortune.

When Dora was trying to resolve what was happening, she was often stricken in mid-sentence by the feeling that she had been given so much that it was wicked of her to ask for more. One of the stories she read to Laura and Alice at night, while Thomas snuffled into his pillow, concerned a greedy boy ('Greedy,' Laura murmured, pleased at the badness of it, 'greedy, greedy boy') who, finding himself in a cave filled with jars of treasure, plunged both his hands into the jar of gold to try to grab as much as possible, and found that his hands were stuck and came away with nothing. Lucky not to have his hands hewn off, Dora thought.

Stella helped Dora to go on by telling her she was not asking for more, she was asking for different. Dora was grateful. At the beginning of their friendship Dora had thought of herself as much cleverer than Stella, but now Dora knew that Stella in the course of her life had learnt how to be wise, to deal with conditions that seemed beyond mending, to make connections to see signifiers and talismans in everyday happenings. For all Dora knew she could cast spells. Dora felt somewhat put out that this advancement of learning appeared to have happened to someone who did not deserve it, since she felt that Stella had not paid her full dues of misery. Dora was vague about what these dues were but they did not include being married many times, having many lovers, dealing profitably in property and being a successful painter. Perhaps, in other words, Dora was jealous.

Over the years, Dora and Stella telephoned each other daily to check on pulses, heartbeats, temperatures, the state of the day, and whenever Dora was in London, which was often, since she always kept up her work as an interviewer, they had lunch together, usually at Stella's house. Over the years Dora, following Stella's peregrinations, has acquired a knowledge of London's postal districts which a taxi driver might envy. Stella, married or single, with every change in income bought houses in unfashionable areas and then moved on, making money every time. Dora has lunched with her in Camden Town, Clapham, Notting Hill, Highbury and these days makes her way through the by-ways of Ladbroke Grove, towards the mighty hinterland of north Kensington.

In the time before her flight to the island Dora found it increasingly hard to get herself out of the house to see anyone other than her lover. It was as though she were in hiding and to go out would reveal herself to the scare. To keep an appointment, to do an interview, to go to a library or office in connection with her work, even to see Stella required an amount of energy which Dora, whose energy had always been limitless, now found inordinate. She took on less and less work, found herself turning down assignments, cancelling appointments, and felt as though she had to summon a Krakatoa from her innards to get her out of her door and into the outside world.

She made lists. Lists of what she must do before she could leave; lists of what she must do when she came back; lists of what should be done whilst she was away; lists to Betty (who helped her with her children) which lists, Betty, who had forgotten more about children than Dora would ever learn, pinned up on the nursery notice board and never looked at again; lists of food and useful hints to her housekeeper; lists of the things she must not leave without, as though she were Edmund Hillary starting out on the last stage of Everest. Before she left her house in the country she checked her keys, gloves, the car key, the diary, taking them out of her bag to make sure they were there, and when she shut the door, left at least one vital item behind. Having said her final goodbyes to the children, kissed their tear-stained but resigned faces, having been almost pushed out the door by Betty, who had to restore normality and sequence to these children, the door would burst open and Dora would come flying in, hands waving, pretending not to be there, to pick up the purse, the passport, the ticket, the list, and would rush out again, leaving a vacuum, movement and the promise of excitement far away from home as her legacy.

Yet when she went to visit her lover, she danced out of the house like a vagabond, leaving everything behind, like the young man in the Bible enjoined to follow Christ. When she remembered that injunction, to leave all and follow me, she understood that Christ was demanding that those who followed him must fall in love with him, nothing less than total infatuation. Heaven in that case, thought Dora, must be a kind of marriage where one finds that the young prophet you followed will reveal his real self. King of all he surveys, just like his old dad.

IV

All the same, Dora always managed to make it to Stella's house, though rarely as a single excursion. She gathered up her energies and collected up her things and contrived to set up the day so that dates more or less dovetailed: to chuck one date would be a useless avoidance and to chuck them all, more trouble than it was worth. Stella thus became a port of call, a fuelling stop on the way to recording an interview, or going to the library, or the aromatherapist or to the hairdresser. Dora sometimes wondered what Stella got out of the friendship, until she worked out that Stella got friendship out of it.

Almost always when Dora arrives at Stella's house she is late, or thinks she is late. Stella does not mind since she allows for Dora's games, and has always adjusted Dora's estimated arrival time to a realistic level. At the beginning of their friendship the adjustment meant more time for the pre-prandial drink or more drink for the pre-prandial drink so that Stella was well away before Dora turned up. Because Dora did not drink spirits at all and wine only rarely, it never occurred to her to question the amount that Stella drank. In the middle years of their friendship when Stella was married to a painter it was Stella herself who first used the word alcoholic to describe herself, much to the astonishment and disbelief of Dora, who thought alcoholics were down-and-outs, or the sad-eyed furtive men who waited outside the pubs of her childhood for the doors to open and who left at night carrying bottles to get them through till morning. Now, years on from the establishment of these lunch meetings, Stella no longer drinks alcohol at all and goes on working at her easel or her table until Dora arrives. Stella professes to know by the way Dora walks into her room what size burden she is humping along. She said this once to Dora who replied, to tease or even pre-empt her, 'I'd be lost without it.'

'You're not going to be lost today,' Stella said on this particular day as Dora came in, looking as though she were a parachutist whose backpack has turned out to be filled with stones. Dora knew she must get away or spill out all over everyone's life, drowning them in acid. She felt that, if she were not given time and space and a chance to breathe without pressure, something terrible would happen, some explosion that would blow apart everyone she loves.

'I was talking to Simon over breakfast,' Dora said, 'and we seemed to be getting on well. I mean, anyone observing the scene would have seen the archetypal happy couple, he reading bits from the paper, me laughing, and then I got up and went over to the breadboard and sliced the top of my finger off.'

'Did you go to the doctor carrying it packed in ice like everyone seems to do?' Stella asked, pouring the mineral water. 'The roads of England are jammed with people carrying severed arms and legs and fingers, apparently quite stoically, for microsurgery.'

'Not literally sliced off,' Dora said. 'But enough to have to put elastoplast on. So I must have been furious about something.'

'Or perhaps you're just careless with a knife.'

'Hardly,' Stella said.

'Do you remember saying that one day I would be caught in the vice of passion?' Dora asked.

'Thank God I gave up the business of prophecy,' Stella said, 'and not vice surely? I think passion's a virtue.'

'And I simply didn't listen. I was above all that. I thought I was more mature than you.'

'I think you are,' Stella murmured. She looked at Dora and began to laugh.

'It's no laughing matter,' Dora said, trying to be cross. 'It's not like a grip at all. It's as if a huge cuckoo fledgling has shoved into my body until there's no space left for me. Perhaps it's hysterical love like hysterical pregnancy and doesn't exist at all.'

'You realise,' Stella said, 'that he is the monster you've tried to avoid meeting ever since you started to grow up. You can't simply leave the castle and run into the woods.'

'I know,' Dora said, though she didn't know why. But how was she to explain any of this to her lover who dealt only in rationalities and saw her indecision as symptomatic of her irrationality, her fluctuating moods as lack of character, not as the discernible tips of an enormous submerged iceberg of fear that seemed to her to constitute her life. She felt angry, helpless, tossed like a cork and yet she knew herself to be a strong-willed ambitious woman. In God's name, what had happened to her?

She watched Stella set out the lunch. She knew she was seeking permission from Stella to go away and would have to justify herself all through lunch to give herself courage and to accustom herself to the idea.

'Have you said anything to him?' Stella asked.

'To Simon?' Dora asked, ingenuous as ever. 'Not yet. There hasn't been a chance. He avoids everything he doesn't want to know. We were driving home from an appalling evening last week – increasingly I become defensive and prickly the moment I set foot outside my own territory, I have only to cross someone else's threshold for my hackles to rise like a mad dog's so that the horses and people back away and no wonder – and I started a row, a horrid trivial row about nothing, about a wireless or wet shoes or something and I listened to myself going on and on like a fishwife and he wouldn't react, or rather, reacted so nicely, so calmly, *he* apologised, that I finally took a hold of myself and said, "Look Simon, this has nothing to do with a wireless, or shoes, or whatever, it's to do with something far more important." And he said, "I know. I know you haven't been happy for some time, and I wish I could do something about it. All I want is your happiness and the children's happiness." "And what," I asked, "about your happiness?"'

She got up and stood in front of Stella's easel, and stared at the old face looking back.

'He said,' Dora swallowed, Stella put a glass into her hand and Dora kept her face still, 'He said, "I know it irritates you when I say things like this, but all the same it's true, – I find it easy or much easier than you to be happy. What would make you happy?" But he chose his time well to ask the question,' Dora said, looking wildly and accusingly at Stella. 'Because by now, we're trapped between two bloody juggernauts and can't see a thing ahead. So I said – oh the courage – "This isn't a conversation you can have while you're supposed to be concentrating on driving."'

'It was your conversation,' Stella said. 'You chose the time to bring it up. And he did take up the challenge. It was you who ducked out.'

'He won't shout you know,' Dora said. 'I've never heard him raise his voice. If the telephone rings and I'm up at the top in the workroom, he'll come up. Same in the garden. I'll be miles away and I'll see him come out of the garden door but he won't shout, he'll plod the whole way, his lips moving. It drives me mad. I bellow at him, "Shout!" but he won't.'

'You're complaining? About a man having manners?' Stella asked. 'Every man I've taken up with not only shouts for me, he shouts at me. I could well do without being shouted at ever again.'

'If he shouted I'd know where I was,' Dora said miserably.

'No you wouldn't,' Stella said. 'You'd just be able to blame him more.'

'What am I going to do?'

'Don't take any major decisions till you come back from this holiday,' Stella said. 'And when you come back you could begin to compromise. For a start, why don't you move to London?'

Dora held tighter onto her glass and pushed the fear away. 'Well, hon, that's pretty radical,' she said. 'Simon couldn't leave Keep Hall, it's his life, his family have lived there for, well you know, Stella, I just couldn't.'

'I didn't mean Simon move,' Stella said. 'You move.'

Dora could hardly countenance what she had heard. 'You mean leave Simon?'

Stella said, 'Well, I didn't say that. You did. It does happen, you know. I meant you have somewhere in London and spend less time in the country. Simon's rich enough.'

'But it's so beautiful there,' Dora said. 'I couldn't, suddenly, demand a house in London – there's no reason for it. There's everything that you could want there.'

'What are you talking about, Dora?' Stella said. 'You've made yourself ill trying to say that you can't live the way you're living and now you're saying you've got everything you want in Suffolk. Choosing involves choice, you may remember, and transformation involves suffering.'

Dora wanted no part of transformation if it involved suffering. She feared change, feared suffering, feared shriving. Shriving was a monkish word that had nothing to do with her own rich life and nor did she want it to have. If she had to be transformed, then she wanted it to be at the touch of a spangled wand.

'I can't just leave one house and run to another and start all over again,' Dora said. 'I don't see how anyone could.'

'Speak for yourself,' Stella said. 'It's perfectly easy once you try. And lovely as Keep Hall is, it's like incarceration down there. If you ask me, once you start putting biscuits in boxes on guests' bedside tables you're done for. I don't know why you gave up that flat of Henrietta's. It would have been perfect for you now. You could easily have kept it on. You had tenure on that for life, you know.'

'It's easy with hindsight,' Dora said. 'But you don't start off marriage with fall-back positions already established. Anyway, we couldn't afford to keep it on, even if we'd wanted. We were all much poorer in those days.'

Stella looked at her, a sideways covert glance.

'Do you think much about those days?' she asked.

Dora thought about it. 'I never do,' she said. 'There's no call for it. In Suffolk I don't know anyone who knew me then. I'm just Simon's wife there.'

'You always say you never fell in love before you met this one,' Stella said, 'but you were in love with Tony.' Dora began to protest but Stella looked at her. 'Why do you always deny it?'

'I don't always deny it,' Dora said. 'I just wasn't, and anyway we don't often talk about it, Stella. I'd never met anyone or anything like him and I may have loved him but I certainly wasn't in love.'

'Might you have married him?' Stella asked. 'Adopting Thomas – don't you sometimes look at him and wonder?'

'What I felt for Tony,' Dora said, 'in an odd sort of way didn't affect me.' She saw Stella's face. 'I admit,' she said hastily, 'it changed me, changed my way of life and living. But the thing I hate about what's happening to me now is that it affects me like an illness, all the time, I can't escape, I can't think of anything else, I wake up and within a second he's there in my head, my daily life is like a dream, I'm only real when I'm with him, and I know that can't be right. That's why I want to go away.'

Stella went across to a cupboard and took out a brown bottle which she handed to Dora.

'Take this with you,' she said. 'It's a wonderful remedy when you're down.'

Dora held it up to the light. It was thick and dark.

'I used to wonder why holiday places were called resorts,' she said. 'I'm beginning to know. Last resorts more like. What is this?'

'It's just herbs,' Stella said.

Dora was trembling with fear at the idea of sending herself off on holiday, at her nerve in tempting fate to get rid of her and her mess once and for all by slinging her out of the sky, still attached to her seat by her safety belt, tumbling around and around until her lungs collapsed, or perhaps falling straight down, her entrails pushing up out of her open mouth, like a curly vapour in the stratosphere, writing some last apocalyptic message, *mene, mene, tekel upsharsin*, or *the bitch deserves to die*.

When the time came to go, she left him and the children with a heavy heart, although she surmised it was no heavier than his who held her in his arms and said suddenly, surprisingly, so that she had to turn her head away, refusing an expression she would find unbearable, 'Do come back Dora. I want you to know that I love you under any circumstances.'

She hid from the words, their underlying meaning. She did not want such guarantees, such declarations, they gave her a power she despised. She wanted suspicion, punishment, ultimatums. She muttered a rosary of imprecation and superstition as she drove out past the ruined lodge at the end of the avenue, turned up the small hill that led to the main road, and consoled herself with panaceas about how, when she came back, she would make it up to all of them, that whatever happened she would let nothing damage the children's needs. She stopped, switched off the engine and looked back at the house as though she might never see it again, or if the gods were kind and she lived, then never see it in the same guise, the place where she and Simon had lived in a kind of harmony.

Taking a longer perspective, years later when she is long home from this holiday and has finished with the scribbling, she sees that she was as much shipped off by her husband, to separate her from her lover and to allow her perspective, like a headstrong heiress in a Heyer story, as she was driven by her own volition. But at the time she thought Simon had no inkling about her lover and that he was the fatal secret. She had thought that what was happening to her was unique and deadly, as she had thought that the plan to go away was a conspiracy with herself, to get herself away from the arena where, goaded by the intolerableness of her life, she might burst out with what she took to be the truth, in a torrent of anger; or worse, get up and leave.

Dora had always thought that if she once let loose her anger it would scorch and blast her world. It is not only hard for angry people to realise that anger released is often only a gust of hot air, it is diminishing to their idea of themselves. Anger, Dora remembered, is precious when it seems the most powerful thing you've got.

Dora's erstwhile harmonious life had taken place and shape in Keep Hall which lay in a fold of land, under the great curved cup of the sky over Framlingham. Dora knew the moods and colours and shapes of Suffolk as well as, say, she knew her own body which as we may have discerned, is not all that well. She kept them at a distance, the shapes of land and body.

When she first moved to Suffolk, after her marriage, she was astounded by the size of the skies and the length of the horizons, coming as she did from a place where horizons lay in the next field and the fields were measured in roods. Simon's house lay in a wooded fold. In any other county the declivity would have been unremarked. Here the slopes looked like a hill, its trees like a deep wood.

Simon was a modest man, surprised by how successful his business had become. His family had always been rich, though, if pressed, he would have said only that they were well-off, and even admitting that would have made him uneasy. As his company became more successful he did not tell Dora how much money it was making, which was a great deal. He explained later, when she spoke of settlements, that talking about the amount of actual money in his company, about turnover, or, worse still, profit, especially profit, gave the wrong impression, since money was an asset, to be ploughed back into research and development. Money, to Dora, was a commodity good for one thing only. To be spent. The first time that Dora heard her husband called a millionaire, or rather read it in the business section of a newspaper, she had what Betty called a real turn. The label changed the way she looked at him. Money had always mattered to Dora. How much money he had was among the criteria necessary for her to find a man interesting and when she first met Simon she had thought him poor because he did not behave in the way she thought rich men must. He did not own a flashy car, did not drink or send back vintage bottles of wine with a sneer, did not take her to expensive restaurants or dress in smart clothes. One day, though, when they were driving up St James's he stopped outside a Dickensian-looking shop and asked if she would mind waiting while he picked up some shoes that were being mended. She thought it a very odd place to find a cobbler and came with him into the shop, and entered another age. Long-laced boots were displayed with certain erotic overtones in glass cabinets. All the shoes and boots looked made for Edwardian feet. A man in a leather apron came out from behind what looked like a forest of fungi but was, she saw, any number of lasts, greeted Simon by name and produced his shoes. The man, who was surprisingly young, showed Simon the work and they murmured with pleasure. Dora waited for Simon to pay, but no money changed hands.

'You wouldn't think it would be worthwhile to put it on account,' Dora said when they left, 'mending shoes.'

They went into another shop almost next door, a cavernous wine shop, again like something from Edwin Drood, where once more Simon was greeted by name. As he gave his order, the street door ricocheted open and a small rotund man cannoned in, past the old counters and down a flagged passage, bumping without apparent damage into anyone or anything he encountered on the way.

'Only Master Johnny back from lunch,' the young man taking Simon's order murmured. While Simon and he looked at wines, Dora went out of the shop and back to the shoe shop.

'How much,' she said without preamble, 'how much does it cost to repair shoes here?'

The young man said, 'We only repair our own shoes, madam.'

'And how much is a pair of shoes?'

He looked pained.

'We would have to make your last,' he said.

She interrupted. 'Roughly how much, please?'

'About one hundred pounds,' he said. Dora's weekly salary was twenty-two pounds. She became nicer to Simon.

Now that Dora is rich, what constantly surprises her is how puritanical people are about rich women. They can forgive transgression, bad behaviour, unhappiness but being rich, without its being an issue, is unforgivable. Rich women, Dora realises, have to be bitches or brats or stout-hearted lasses who have eschewed love and clawed their way to the top; or else must be princesses or hide a guilty secret; and they must always be punished. Most of all, rich women do not do ordinary things and lead ordinary lives. They are expected to flaunt their money, behave blatantly and look every day as though they were setting out for Ascot or from a satin-covered bed. In fact it seems to Dora that her early misconceptions about how rich men behave are still held by many people about rich women.

In Suffolk, or when she goes to stay in Sussex or Gloucestershire, Dora is surrounded by rich women who behave, she thinks, in a perfectly ordinary fashion, but are more comfortable and generally seem to have a nicer time than poor women. This doesn't necessarily make them happy.

Simon was by way of being a sailor when he was not at his business and was in his element when he was in or on the water. Dora disliked and was afraid of the sea, she found it an alien place, and always swam sideways to the shore, afraid to go out of her depth. When she watched Simon handle his boat with a competent contentment, saw it skimming across the water, away from her on the shore, she felt something different from the gratitude and affection which was as much as she could muster for him about this time. She felt pride, as though she had some hand in his skill, in his craft, but this pride disappeared when he stepped on shore and became a landlubber, a prosaic, kindly man without vanity, without any sense of self-importance. Dora without acknowledging it, admired her husband. Admiration is a potent ingredient in a marriage, as much as affection, and whilst it remains, there is hope, which is why Dora did not acknowledge it. What she did acknowledge was that she was bored by him and excited to fever by her lover. Nothing new in that.

The truth was that before she met her lover Dora had become accustomed to living her life in a state of boredom, anxiety, and obsessive love for her children, a cocktail of some potency and one, she felt, that many women drank daily. After a day's inbibing of these spirits, husbands might well wonder why their wives were not themselves, the young, nubile nannies they thought and hoped they had married. No one, Dora thought, could get through the violent tedium of young, daily married life, without becoming angry, so that the very way a husband ate a meal could become a matter for thought-murder. She wondered how many husbands found their wives lovable and exciting after they had borne their children. Life as a single parent is the daily state of many married women and their husbands become interruptions. She imagined thousands of husbands seeking each night among the bedclothes and the duvets for the bodies they once found so exciting and coming instead upon the stony thighs of the women they find they have married.

There was no doubt if Dora was being honest that before she met her lover she was up on some crow's nest in the structure of her life, on the lookout. Dora knew that at certain times in any woman's life, the treasure chest that is her femininity, her sexuality is battened down, and Nature, sly old brute, pretends to be quiescent, to be soothed. You might as well be a block of wood as be a woman, thought Dora. She looked at the other women of her age with young children whom people in shops called dear and whose husbands, at certain kinds of gatherings, were asked what the wife did. Then one day, when the children had become less demanding, having grown out of the stage where their well-being was a biological imperative, the same young women, well not so young now, sent out a message, just the faintest signal, hardly discernible one might think, that famous bat squeak, the merest whiff of musk, and the men came, dropping out of the trees or from behind the wheels of their cars or from behind their office desks or their dry martinis, hairs on the palms of their hands or their buttocks, swarthy or white-skinned, crew-cut or curly-haired, appearing like the annunciation with no sense of their own ridiculousness, from all kinds of unlikely vestries, certain, so as far as Dora could see, of their welcome, all of them, no matter how dunce-like, or complacent.

Dora watched. At work, at parties, at gatherings, she saw that the woman would almost certainly know more about the verities of life than the person who moved across the ground towards her, but that would not occur to him. The odds are that she would even be grateful for the approach of the male creature as he sidled up. At least in the decades of the sixties and seventies, Dora's time for these observances, this all seemed true, though it also seemed to Dora in her older age that things hadn't much changed, and that wise, good, young women were as foolish as ever. And the truth, she had to admit, was that the young man had not sidled up to her – he had come running across her garden like Mercury, and she, intoxicated by his speed and her own upsurge of adrenalin, had welcomed him.

Since her lover's arrival, though, terror and passion filled her days, and time either so imploded that one day vanished before she caught hold of it or else elongated into an enormous hank of hours, slicing her energy as it unfurled. The speed of each day depended entirely on him. She remembered how her daughter sometimes asked how long it was until a promised treat, and how her face fell when Dora said three hours, or days, or weeks, and Dora knew now what her daughter felt: that the hoped-for event would never happen because time was stuck. In Dora's case, clogged by the terrible, slow-moving charity of marriage.

Her idealisation of and infatuation with her lover made her see everything about him in high relief and she looked constantly in his direction, even when he wasn't there so that the persons in the foreground were out of focus, as if viewed by someone with glaucous vision. Her husband seemed always cloaked in a good grey mist like a nun turning a corner at the end of a corridor, and even her children, the most solid things in her life, even-keeled as ducks, barred with a balance point for dabbling, all pertinent when the wind blows four quarters at once, seemed to her to be in danger of disappearing and were running hand in hand through her sunny house, into the shadows.

Her lover was called Theodore and he was not boring or not so far. Everything about him excited Dora including his name. She could never get over its felicity, as if he had been christened solely to assert his love for her. She was attached to him in a way that astonished her since she first felt the bond and when they made love she felt as though she were soldered to him. Sometimes, especially after she had had her sexual fill of him, she thought he was no longer important to her, indeed felt a kind of repulsion, and was appalled at her habit. Each time she found he was not a habit but an addiction and that she was never sated. Day by day when she was away from him, time gnawed at her, fraying her mind so that every thought became a tendril curling towards him and she could think of nothing else.

It was partly Theodore's monstrous clarity, his sharp edges, the high visibility quotient of those glowering eyes, that made her so engaged with him, though it made her frightened too. Where Simon moved there were blurred edges, lost trails, dimnesses, so she didn't know where his goodness ended and emptiness began, and she was afraid to test too far in case she fell.

Part of the reason for her precipitate flight under the guise of holiday was that Theodore had begun to plot and plan for her to leave Simon and to marry him and had delivered several terrible ultimatums, in a voice like Ivan the Terrible's. Dora believed that not only was he completely serious, but that he was dangerous. So did he. The prospect of leaving Simon filled Dora with a blank dread. She knew well that part of her attraction for certain men had always been that she was profoundly married. For Dora marriage was not just a contract and never a matter for expediency. The dogma that marriage is a sacrament, a mark on the soul that can never be erased or annulled, was dinned into her as a child and the dogma itself became a sacrament that was not to be gainsayed. Among other such indelible sacraments she remembered, were ordination and baptism and though, even as a child, Dora had thought it violent that a baby without any choice in the matter should be marked for ever, inducted into a creed, in a kind of celestial press-ganging, it took her a long time to work out that marriage could be made to seem the same. The fact that Dora regarded marriage as a sacrament did not deter her from roundly abusing it. In any case, she had forgotten what the definition of a sacrament was. Something about an outward sign of inward grace; and all she felt was inward turmoil, passion and violence. The outward signs were exemplified – her skin was burning, blistering – she could almost feel it beginning to peel away. She had roasted it on purpose.

With Theodore's arrival, she discovered that there are other stronger imperatives than the moral one, including the call of her own nature, the nature of which she thought she was beginning to perceive. She did not like what she saw. She tried to look at it straight on but the sun, even with blinds down, dazzled her.

As she sat in her room weighing scratches and strategies, Dora felt that the eddies of her going were just now reaching her and she put her head on the dressing-table and let the ripple that had started with her departure a world away widen out and pulsate against her skin, in an instant's negotiation with the past, and then flow out and away. She felt so tired that she didn't want to stay awake any more. But only in vigilance could she see what was coming. She rose to her feet and walked out of the room and down to the palm groves.

From the day it began, Dora's marriage was the central point of her existence. When she went to the altar she entered, or so she was told, into a solemn and binding contract which brought with it moral imperatives. In fact on her wedding day she was angry and distraught and could have been entering into a contract to live like rhubarb under a bucket for all she cared. All she wanted was for it to be over and done with.

Since it happened, Dora had followed her moral imperatives, that is, she knew on which side her bread was buttered. Not that Dora had much to do with bread. It was all cake. She had it and ate it and the signs were on her, although at times it seemed to her that the cake was coated in bile. To any outsider Dora appeared to get what she wanted, although the fact is that no one can know what anyone else really wants. Certainly Dora seemed blessed with what the world had to offer, and she, from time to time, was truly grateful. She took little for granted. Grants are the conferring of rights and Dora was never quite sure that right was on her side or that it even knew she existed.

Two or three things prevented her from accepting that what she had was as much as most women would dare to crave. One, she wanted more; two, she deserved nothing; and three, knowing the ways of the world or the habits of fate, the odds were that those things she loved the most would be the first to be forfeited, in the game of fortune that she appeared to be winning, but which could at any moment reverse into disaster. Things, you understand, being a shorthand way of describing her children.

In earlier days to divert the predator who stalked her and who was either Lucifer the angel of light, or God, the deity of darkness (both presented as demons in the pantheon of her religious upbringing), she surrounded herself with anything she could lay hands on. The diversions did not work, the predators still hovered, and a gap remained which nothing seemed to fill. She set about eating, to plug the black hole, and got fatter but was insatiable. She set about sex and got thinner but with the same end result.

Her travels through the Kingdom of Sex left her untapped and, she thinks, unscathed, save for two small bald patches on her head that only she knew about, since they were hidden by her mane of hair, and were made when her first lover, Tony Flaxmeyer, pulled her out of a bath and halfway across a room, demolishing a good deal of her pretension on the short and violent journey.

What was odd was that her daughter Laura had two small round bald spots on her head, known only to Dora, since they were now covered by Laura's rich red mane, and Simon, if he had ever noticed them, never mentioned them. Dora had gazed at these round spots with rapt and fearful interest, as Cain might have peered at his mark, and thought that it proved something, perhaps something to do with Jung and his theories, or with witchcraft and old wives' tales, like eating strawberries and bearing a child with a strawberry birth mark. She hoped it didn't mean that she and her daughter were two of a kind.

Before she was married, if a man professed love, or worst of all, need, for Dora, she walked out of his life, sometimes immediately, climbing out of his bed and gathering up her clothes and leaving him, hoping never to meet him again. Need sickened her, talk of love tightened her heart into hardness. Indeed, she thought of falling in love as rather like breathing in an infection. She never considered that perhaps she wore a mask of fear and that in filtering the fall-out of love she was stopping other nutrients from reaching her soul. She thought such behaviour on her part showed a maturity, an ability to resist the kaleidoscopic ephemeral loves that hung about waiting to be contracted like consumption; and perhaps she was right.

She knew there was a monster ahead, or perhaps he lay in wait behind her, a monster she had long sought to avoid, the prince, or dwarf or giant crashing through the forest, swinging along the wisteria to scale the ramparts. She thought about the creature he sought, hiding in fear, hoping to be found, not knowing what was arriving and whether he would chop down the hedge around the castle, or swing across the rafters like quicksilver to scoop up the treasure or insist on the naming of things. He lay in wait, in the shadows, a step ahead, or under the surface of the waves, to the left of the patch of moonlight on the ceiling. Until he appeared, the threat lay with every man. Sometimes she felt she had been living scared witless, and had put on layer after layer of flesh to protect herself.

Those many affairs before her marriage seem now, to Dora, to have been diminishing adventures into strange territory, like a tourist who travels into the interior of a country but misses its heart and perceives only what pertains to his own needs and discomforts, discombobulation, and occasional gratification. When she met Simon, the monster put on a human face.

That hunger that she tried to stuff into abeyance persisted. It was nothing to do with fidelity. It was a question of needs. Simon gave her everything she wanted but none of it seemed enough or permanent. She felt as though she lived within a mirage so that if someone tried to walk towards her the angle of existence would disappear and she would vanish. She lived in terror that something would happen to her children. Even the bricks and mortar of their centuries-old house seemed transient and she walked around its gardens feeling that the whole place was a separate state to which she did not have citizenship. The litanies and supplications would begin and she would think, if I could get back to Ireland perhaps I could come to rest, but knew it was sentimental nonsense, Irish moonshine. All the same with such whines and threnodies, such broken lances, did she try to keep misfortune, which waited to pounce on her, at bay; and she tightened her mouth, and her shoulders, lest she should ease herself, muscle by muscle, into any kind of comfort.

TWO
The Main Land

I

In the year of Dora's first pregnancy Stella was married to a man who liked to see his wife in the kitchen and Stella at that time was happy to comply. There was no other kitchen like it, with its black and white floor and herbs and bunches of flowers and Victorian oleographs, statuettes of women and greyhounds straining at the leash, and plates with painted mottos like 'a good mother makes a happy house' on the big dresser.

Stella was always in the forefront of fashion, not particularly in clothes (though she looked good in whatever she wore, she resented spending money on clothes) but in movements, trends, currents, decorations. Ideas, styles, looks that often became preoccupations with the general population years later, were simmering and bubbling in Stella's mind, talk, and behaviour a decade before and by the time they became generally available she had discarded them. Dora met her as she met so many of her friends, when she went to interview her, a young woman artist with an exhibition in a prestigious gallery, at a time when such events made news. Her show was a success. Dora saw in the arts column of a popular newspaper, underneath a photograph of Stella with black-rimmed eyes and painted white cheekbones and nose, the headline 'Pretty as a Picture and She Can Paint'. She occasionally quoted it at Stella as a tease, but Stella no longer cared.

In Stella's house Dora heard, for the first time, discussions about sex, men, money, women, morals, money and, most shocking of all, mothers. Dora had been reared in a society where mothers looked like monolithic carvings from the Cyclades and the very word mother had its own resonance. She remembered, as Nora, writing out a laborious and illuminated acrostic, a kind of testimonial, using the letters of the word mother for each line and beginning, M is for the many things you gave me, O means only that you're growing old, T is for the Tears you shed to save me, H is for Heart of Purest Gold; halfway through she had stopped. Purest bleeding pinchbeck and she had never seen her mother cry in her life.

When Stella had said that her own mother was common, Dora was amazed. It was the first time Dora had heard anyone criticise the sacred cow, as well as being the first time she had heard the word common used in its pejorative sense. It was not a word used in Ireland, one more thing to that country's credit.

'People are always shocked when I say that,' Stella said. She sounded complacent and could afford to.

'I'm not shocked,' Dora said, lying through her teeth.

'I can see you're not, you're so bloody grown-up,' Stella said. 'You're the most grown-up person I've met for ages.' She didn't seem too pleased about it.

'A bit of childishness would come in handy,' Dora agreed. As far as she remembered she hadn't said anything about her mother then, still grappling as she was with the idea of being allowed to view her adversely. There was nothing to say, or she couldn't find the words or more likely didn't want to start facing up to something that was far far beyond her. 'God we women are a miserable lot,' Stella said, 'but it's true. My mother was a really common little woman.' She spoke clearly with a weight on each word, smiling as she said the words, nodding with emphasis on each adjective. 'Not that she was all that little but she thought of herself as being minute. She was always saying how little she was. I remember her coming down in the morning once, screaming that there was a big spider in the bath frightening poor little her. And she always used to tell me how hard it was for her, me being born, because I was such a great big baby and she so tiny. Silly bitch.'

She gave the jugged hare a furious stir and poured in a dollop of liquor from her glass. Dora was pregnant and the smell of the jugged hare made her feel she might vomit horribly all over Stella's tiled floor.

'Where did you get those tiles?' Dora said.

'It's a bit grand isn't it,' Stella said. 'I've just always loved that look. I know it should be with slate and stone and all, but it looks all right with vinyl here. Relatively speaking.'

'It's lovely, I love things to be black and white,' Dora said and the smell of jugged hare hit her nostrils again, and she thought here it comes. But it stayed down just below her gorge.

Stella looked at her. 'Sermons in stones,' she said, 'or tiles. Be sure and tell me if you aren't feeling up to eating this. I love hare but it is a bit gamey and I won't be offended if you can't handle it.'

'It smells amazing,' Dora said. Her stomach stirred in affront.

'You've got much thinner,' Stella said. 'Except for your tum, of course. Your arms and legs.'

Dora patted her stomach. 'Have they?' she asked. 'I think perhaps I'm bearing a bear, and it's hibernating in there. It's the most constructive diet I've ever been on – as soon as I eat a meal I sick it up again. Isn't it extraordinary how you'd do almost anything rather than vomit. Yet once it's over you feel much better.'

'Speak for yourself,' Stella said. 'And are you sure you want to eat? I don't like the turn the conversation is taking.'

'I'm absolutely sure. It would be nice after the baby if I stayed as thin as this. The doctor said that I'm the only person he has treated who weighed less at the end of pregnancy than at the beginning. I shrink as it grows.'

Stella looked startled. 'Is that good for the baby?' she asked.

'Oh, yes,' Dora said. 'He says that it's Nature's little way, to let the baby take priority whatever happens to the mother.'

She would have been happy if the baby consumed as much of her as possible. She envied Stella her thinness, her little stick arms, their vulnerability; she couldn't think of anything nicer than to have arms that looked like Stella's as though they could tumble off the shoulders, so finely were they hinged. Dora's arms were round and plump and secure, like the arms of women in saucy Edwardian photographs.

'You'd look like Worzel Gummidge if you were thin,' Stella said.

'That's consolation talk,' Dora said. 'It just doesn't work.'

'Well you'd be horrible if you were thin,' Stella said again and then, seeing Dora's face, 'I know people are always saying that to you but hasn't it occurred to you that it might be true?'

'No,' Dora said.

'Well, actually, now that I look at you, I see that it might not be,' Stella said. 'If you don't look at the baby, her, him or Bruin, you actually have become amazingly thin and it suits you. Look at your legs.'

Dora stretched out her leg. She had lengthened her skirts but even at six months' pregnant she was wearing a skirt four inches above her knee. Later, when she looked at photographs of herself, she realised that she looked like a pitched tent on stilts. She had to admit that above the knee there was a hollow where before there had been rotundity.

She wondered why this concave shape was so much better than convex. She thought of the models who were her mentors, skinny asexual waifs with all the charm of paper-clips and of the designers, men, who were prone to announce that they only dressed women who looked like adolescent boys. Men, my foot, Dora thought, things in men's clothing.

'What masochism makes us accept the image of Twiggy as something admirable?' she asked Stella. 'What madness makes us pour money into the coffers of men who call our breasts bumps and like us better the flatter we are?'

'I don't,' Stella said. 'And women collude. They don't have to go along with it.'

'They do, in a way, if they're not to be ignored or discounted,' Dora said. She could never understand people who were thin and who weren't also glamorous. She often thought that if she were thin she would be the most glamorous person ever. She would always look wonderful, as Stella did now, in a long brown grubby dress slit at the sides. She wasn't wearing tights, Dora could see, and very likely no knickers. Certainly no bra and she had a cartridge belt around her waist, with cigars instead of bullets, in the belt.

'What a marvellous idea,' Dora said. 'Don't they get crushed?'

'They do a bit,' Stella said, 'but at least I can find them. Better crushed than lost.'

'I don't know,' Dora said. 'At least when it's lost it's gone. Crushed you keep trying to smooth it out.'

'Like my face,' Stella said. 'I look in the mirror and ask who are you and what have you done with Stella?'

'Oh, Lord,' Dora said, 'I'm becoming such a bore. I read the other day that in all fruitful marriages part of you had to be abandoned and die, and I thought, if anything, that was rather cheering – at least it made me think that my marriage must be fruitful because certainly something in me has atrophied. I used to dread married women droning on to me about how awful it was being married and having children and I'd think, Oh, Christ, why don't they do something about it, but now I'm exactly like those women myself.'

'The trouble with you,' Stella said, 'is that you hate living in the country.'

Dora looked at her appalled. 'I wish you hadn't said that,' she said. 'I never even thought that I don't like Suffolk. Or maybe I don't want to admit it. If I did, then I'd have to do something about it.'

'Exactly,' Stella said, 'and I think you might have agrophobia.'

'Is that a fear of being aggressive?'

'I didn't mean that,' Stella said doubtfully. 'I meant a fear of going out.'

'Oh agoraphobia,' Dora said. '*Agoraphobia*, you mean – it's from the Greek word for market-place, I think.'

'A bit of childishness *would* be handy,' Stella said crossly.

'I quite like going out,' Dora said. 'I mean here I am with you, if I had agoraphobia I wouldn't be here, would I?'

'Yes you might,' Stella said. 'A mild form, I mean. It's a lot of effort for you to go out, isn't it? You really have to build up to it. Put things out and count and check them, over and over. All that. Am I right?'

'Well, yes,' Dora said. 'But then you've seen me do that. And not wanting to go out is laziness as much as anything else. Not wanting to make the effort. I'm a slob at heart. Plus heaving this great lump about makes you just want to sit with your legs wide apart like those old women in buses.'

Stella started to laugh. 'I must say one thing for you, you don't have any shit. I'd never admit it was laziness even if it was. I don't think it is laziness. I've got agoraphobia. I find it hard even to go out shopping.'

'Really?' Dora was most surprised. She looked around the

kitchen, filled with things from shops all over London. 'But you're always . . . ' she stopped, 'you're always on the move.'

'Ah yes,' Stella said, pouring herself another drink. 'But I don't like it, it's an effort. I have to be very rational about it and talk to myself, and Pete helps a lot. It is only a mild form but it could get out of control if I didn't work at it. And *yours* could too.'

It consoled Dora that all that was wrong with her was a dislike of Suffolk and an incipient fear of going out. All the same the combination seemed to add up to a fairly insoluble problem – the only solution to which was living as a recluse in London.

'The truth is,' Dora said, 'I'm just not ready to be a mother. I haven't finished being a daughter.'

'Oh, if you were ready to be a mother it would be too late,' Stella said, throwing some small black things into the casserole, 'the biological time-clock would have stopped ticking. You're only ready to be a mother when you're a grandmother.'

'I think it's because I'm pregnant,' Dora said. 'All the hormones have run amok.'

Dora remembered everything in that particular kitchen with fondness. Stella was on her second marriage then. Dora had not met her on her first but she knew that every time Stella remarried, she started from scratch and created a new environment depending on what she had married for, what she intended to make of it and whom she had married. The more she married, the less she cooked. There were two freezers at that point, Dora remembered, full of green beans. But then in those days any woman worth her salt froze a ton of green beans every year, blanching and cooling and labelling in order to eat two packets of coarse green squares in March or April. And there had been herbs, bottled and dried and packeted, and mushrooms hanging on lines like dead bats, and pottery mugs of mustard, opening which broke every knife in the house.

Stella was cooking from Arabella Boxer's *First Slice Your Cookbook* and Dora remembered how she had fallen on it, amazed at its cleverness and had bought it, and put it on a par and on a shelf with Carrier's *Great Dishes of the World*, her first excursion into gastronomy, which had contained a recipe called 'My Colcannon'. She had thought My a French or Greek word, and was open-mouthed with astonishment to discover that Colcannon was simply what she had known as cabbage and champ, and that the most basic dish in the Irish culinary repertoire (not at that time large) was a great dish of the world; and further that My was the possessive pronoun.

It was all taken so seriously then. Perhaps it still was, Dora thought, but the delicious lunch she'd been unable to eat at Stella's house years later on the way to the island in the sun had been, Dora guessed, from Marks & Spencer. She herself kept a good table by the simple expedient of keeping a good cook. Perhaps simple was not the mot juste she thought. It was an expensive and complex operation keeping a good cook, never mind keeping her – or him – happy.

She remembered, after her first eye-opening, mouth-watering meal in Stella's kitchen, flogging home from Berwick Street market with two enormous carrier bags filled with ingredients for coq au vin, or some variation on chicken stew. She'd peeled twelve little onions – she'd never seen such stunted vegetables but the recipe said twelve so she'd bought twelve, had gone up and down the market to get every ingredient without deviation – and then spent hours cooking it. It was soon after she came to London and stray friends from her student days on the loose had eaten it without noticing, except one, Denis from Northern Ireland, who rolled a pearl-like onion around his plate.

'What's this footery wee thing?' he said, and Dora gave up on the cooking.

Stella dished up the jugged hare. Dora lifted a forkful to her mouth and ran from the table to the lavatory and vomited till she thought the baby would come through her mouth. In fact it was born through her skin by Caesarean a week later.

When she came back Stella was solicitous, apologetic and only a touch reproachful.

'I thought you looked a bit odd,' she said. 'Why on earth did you have it?'

'I thought I wanted it,' Dora said. It would take too much effort to explain that having seen Stella pore over its entrails and stir it like something out of *Macbeth* she could no more have said she didn't want it than she could have taken off her clothes and pranced around naked in the kitchen singing bubble bubble toil and trouble.

She put her reluctance to tell Stella the plain truth – that she couldn't under any circumstance eat that potage of hare – down to her tender sensibility. And doubtless both her own and Stella's sensibility or touchiness played their part in the sham. Dora's sensibility then was so raw it seemed as though it was screaming, but her silence was also to do with fear, and gratitude, fear of offending Stella, fear of causing her pain, fear of being scolded, fear of being thought difficult; gratitude for being asked to lunch, gratitude for being talked to; gratitude for being cooked for. She didn't even begin to think of telling her the more profound pagan reasons: that the hare was a magic animal and to eat it would be to undertake a cabalistic rite.

She remembered seeing, as a child, old men on their rickety carts turning back from a journey, if a hare crossed their path and even going to bed for the day. She was not going to devour one for anyone, not even Stella.

'Well, what *will* you have?' Stella asked and then without waiting made her a dish of mashed potatoes and vegetables. It tasted like the most delicious kind of baby food, and Dora, suddenly famished, sucked at it, and as she did so something shapeless and predatory began to move in the tarn of her mind and began to glide upward towards the surface. The displacement raised a bubble of agitation, visible only for an instant, portending something dreadful, then it slipped from her inward vision, the agitation sank, the surface calmed. She sucked at her spoon avid for more.

II

In the early years of her marriage, when her children were just out of babyhood and she was still feathering her nest, Dora listened to her friends, talking of love and pain and passion and adultery (though no one ever called it that), with interest, envy, fearfulness and a certain derision. She felt, if the truth be told, a contempt for those who fell ill of love. She believed that feelings like these were a matter of choice and that she had forsworn the choice. But if she, however tentatively, ventured this opinion to those of her friends currently infected, they stared at her as if she were mad, or implied that she was of the species of accusers who say that women who are beaten or raped have chosen to be victims, and pointed out impatiently that if one meets or is in the power of something stronger than oneself then one can easily be rendered helpless.

'You just keep away,' said Dora. 'Don't put yourself in the position.'

'Hark,' Stella said. 'You just wait till you're in the grip of passion. Don't come running to me.'

Dora thought it sounded as though love were a kind of King Kong that would one day make off with her up the side of life and Stella's accounts of her turbulent love affairs between and during her marriages, verified this vision. For years she fell in and out of love, plummeted into passions and off balconies, banged herself around, sprained her ankle, scraped her hands, escaped over walls, behaved in fact as the swash-buckling lover in farce behaves.

Lunchtime was more dramatic then as she recounted her adventures, hands crossed over her stomach as though to keep the pain and fever from blurting out. Dora was jealous and Stella listened patiently when Dora whined about the choice she had made.

'Not that there was a choice,' Dora informed Stella in all seriousness as though she had been manacled and led into marriage. 'I forfeited passionate love because I didn't want to know about it. I forfeited it for a mate, for a provider, for security. I never was in love with anyone. Being in love,' Dora said warming sententiously to her theme, 'is a thing for contemporaries to do together. And I couldn't possibly love a contemporary. I couldn't trust anyone the same age. I knew so much more than anyone else, you understand. I knew nothing. Nothing. Nothing. And now I know less. I wish I knew what it feels like to fall madly in love.'

'No you don't,' Stella said. 'Most of the time it feels appalling.'

'I'm incapable of grand emotion,' Dora said with a certain complacency. 'I settled for security and comfort and no danger. I'm stunted.'

'I'm not at all sure that's true,' Stella said and Dora wondered whether to take offence then or later. 'Perhaps it's a sign of your maturity.'

'Well I think it's better for your soul to have loved and lost than never to have loved at all,' Dora said.

'Don't you believe it,' Stella said. 'That's an old wives' tale.'

'I am an old wife,' Dora said. 'And anyway it was Tennyson.'

But Dora was a silly, young, unhappy, damaged woman who yearned towards the limits of human emotions and she truly believed that she had not married for love, or certainly not in its romantic guise. She had not married to cure an insatiable itch which would soon be sated by familiarity, nor to quell the greedy ache of infatuation or the panics of passion. She entered a system that had obtained for centuries and still obtains in tracts of the world's social systems. She made an arranged marriage and married for life. She, of course, made the arrangements.

'I married a husband, not a lover,' she said speaking in a meek voice to show she meant no harm. She tried to fathom Stella's expressions but Stella refused to look back at her. Stella, amoral, unshockable by any deviation or perversity or malignancy in human behaviour, was not shocked by what she heard as Dora's cold-bloodedness, but bored by it.

Dora, thinking lack of response was moral outrage, made shift to deal with this by quoting from unassailable authorities.

'I believe in marriage as a sign of love,' she said with an air of knowing a lot more than she was letting on. 'And you cannot give a sign a wrong meaning. We all know that.'

'I don't,' Stella said. 'I'm forever following signs that promise one thing and deliver another, or send me in quite the wrong direction.'

'You're talking about signposts,' Dora said. 'We're not looking for the road to Chipping Sodbury here, you know. I'm talking Wittgenstein and gestures.'

'Sod Chipping Sodbury,' Stella said, 'and more often than not, gestures are all hot air.'

She told Dora a story that seemed beyond belief – of renting a room opposite where one particular lover lived and crouching for hours below the level of the window-sill so that she could watch his comings and goings. 'His comings mostly,' Stella said. 'God he was unfaithful to me.'

'And then you wonder why I've not married for love like that?' Dora said.

'I don't wonder,' Stella said. 'I know what you're married for.'

Dora listened to the emphasis on the preposition and treasured it in her heart against Stella. She did not ask her to expand. She did not want to hear it spelled out.

Dora did not wonder why her husband wanted to marry her. Many men had asked her to marry them. It appeared that she was the marrying kind and thus it seemed natural that he would want her too. In the early days of their marriage, Dora had thought him lucky to have secured her; in the latter days, she sometimes felt downright sorry for him, shackled to her.

She did not wonder why she had married Simon. It seemed both arbitrary and inevitable. And if, as Stella said, she had married him *for*, then her friends seemed to have married *because*. Because there was no choice, because they were in love, because of their passion. She believed that she had married for security, for self-esteem, for an entrée to a world in which she could perhaps bail herself out of her own worthlessness. She married him, as she thought, for credentials. In this she is as mistaken as she is in, say, the belief that Nora is lying waiting for an inspection.

She married because she knew he would be the perfect mate, who would die at the mouth of the cave rather than have his mate endangered. When she thought this, the image of the MGM Lion would pop into her head, roaring his steadfast comfortable roar. Anything further from Simon's rather light, modulated Old Etonian voice could hardly be imagined. She had spun a web for herself, as she thought, and only when she found herself in a new entanglement did she see that the web she lived in was one they had both woven and that he was at the centre of her life, immobile, listening to every twitch. She married, did she but know it, for love.

She had never actively used the word trust in connection with Simon. It seemed a small, relatively unimportant word and one whose meaning she had not pondered. It had certainly not occurred to her that it might be the only hinge for a way into the future, since she did not realise that she mistrusted everyone. It was only as she got older that she began to realise that trust was the rarest ingredient of all in life, or certainly in her life.

So she married him and settled, so she thought, for a kind and loving husband, who put up with her in a way that, as this story progresses, may make the cynical reader wonder at his motives, and the innocent one acclaim him; and which led Dora to the meaning of the word.

All the same, now, years later, she hated his immobility and believed it showed a lack of comprehension. If only he would not be so easily deceived, she thought, if only he would come out of the shadows and assert himself; if only he would make some move so that she should know in which direction to run away: if only he would raise his voice so that she could shout back and Theodore would hear her call and come to rescue her; instead of which he stayed at the edge of her vision, shadowy, cloaked, unresponsive.

She thought she despised him for the way he had flattened himself into the background of her life but she avoided looking at him straight on, and chose to view him in that half-light, a chiaroscuro which served only to eliminate rather than illuminate. The more she refused to look, the more she felt that she was living her life in semi-darkness. Even the sun beating at the windows at this other end of the world did not reach its corners. Her rooms lit up only when her lover entered them. Indeed one of the things that perpetually astonished her about Theodore was that he appeared to view her in the full light he brought with him and was not dismayed. Not that Dora trusted his vision. She thought he might be like Titania caught in a thrall, and that at some point he would awaken repelled, and when he saw what she really was, fall back, his hands to his throat gurgling with horror.

She remembered a story from her convent days, from the *Lives of the Saints* with which, with evident relish, Sister Scholastica had regaled them. These stories came from the top shelf of Religious Literature. There was St Lucy with her breasts cut off, proffering them to onlookers like two fried eggs on a plate; or Maria Goretti chopped up into pieces; St Catherine broken on the wheel; Pelagia, the belly dancer who dressed in men's clothes and lay inert in a cave; and St Marina who lay equally inert but in a coffin dressed in an iron girdle and a crown of thorns; the one with whom Dora felt the most sympathy was a beautiful saint, whose name she had forgotten, who grew a beard when men looked at her. St Hirsute no doubt. It was one way out. She fingered her chin and sat down on the blistering sand and stared at the sea, until her eyes watered.

There was a machine on the farm where Nora grew up, a machine which lay ever ready in the corner of the room of her dreams. It was a spiked nozzle, which was used to separate the skin from the flesh in veal calves. Dora felt that while she had been sleeping in some trance or fugue her skin had been lifted from her flesh and, in the livid space between, sensations and pain and feeling inserted to rub raw against each other. She felt that only Theodore by touching the surface of the skin could reach that layer below and soothe her pain and connect herself with herself all the way through.

She awoke with a start. A man from the hotel was standing above her. 'The sun is very hot,' he said. 'You will certainly be burned more badly if you persist.'

She thanked him and went back up the garden and into her room, where she crossed to her dressing-table and looked at Stella's tonic. Carefully she took the glass stopper out, as though her lover might come wisping out of the bottle, an enormous genie, there to do her bidding and love her to distraction. The image of the pharmacy in Cambridge sprang to life, its tall glass bottles, the blue and white painted misericordia jars, the contrived paraphernalia of the instant heritage business. In such places had she and Theodore laid down their ancestry. She put the stopper back in, and looked at herself straight on, determined not to see an ectoplasmic aureole. A smooth brown face looked back. Her shoulders were somewhat hunched, her nails a trifle bitten, the skin on her body burned, otherwise there was no external clue to what was going on inside.

In trying to look at her life Dora was put in mind of a film sent back by the space-ship Voyager, showing Io, one of Jupiter's moons, eternally trapped between the orbits of its massive master, and those of its sister moons. Io's shape was in perpetual turmoil, it whirled in a perfect ferment, straining one way, then the other, locked into dilation and contraction, becoming an orb when one attraction was the stronger, then being stretched into an oval as the other attraction went into the ascendant. The two sources of power were unyielding, and the powerful unstoppable excitations had melted Io's core, its thin skin was punctured so that its innards spewed out in a ferment of steam and heat and lava. Orb, oval, oval orb, poor Io.

Sitting in her hotel bedroom Dora felt frightened. She wished there was some way in which she could obliterate from living memory all traces of her knockabout progress through life so that everyone connected with it would drop like flies, and as each person disappeared and with them their fragment of unsignified knowledge, she would be able to push-start herself out again, this time as an amiable and easy woman rather than a difficult and neurotic one.

She pulled her notebooks towards her and went on writing. She hoped something would spring out from under her pen and illuminate her life, or better still, cure her; or, failing this, that something might push up and out, a disembodied hand, perhaps, which would trace a livid message on her wall, a message from the spirits giving her the answer, to do what she wanted. But such messages were no use since the old question remained. She wanted to know what she wanted.

III

Dora first came to London when she was nineteen. She brought with her all her worldly trappings. A small suitcase, the promise of a job, and a handbag which contained her passport, three pounds in notes, a packet of Du Maurier cigarettes and a box of matches, a stub of Love-that-Pink lipstick, some dark brown eye liner and black mascara. As soon go without food, no, not food, mustn't exaggerate, but something important, as go as without the eye liner. In Dora's pocket was the key to her future, the address of a school acquaintance who already lived in the immense and complicated world of London and who had that most glamorous of jobs – an air hostess on BOAC. The acquaintance had earlier agreed that Dora could come and temporarily share her flat and Dora telephoned from the Cromwell Road Terminal which was a little black and red prefabricated building and listened to instructions on how to find Putney. In the six months after Dora's arrival they moved flats three times. It was easy to find furnished flats, and they moved from Parsons Green to West Hampstead to Hammersmith, the fringe places of bed-sitter land.

Dora hated them all. They were unhinged places, tacky, smelling of transience and poverty, full of ugly furniture. Their landladies lived on the premises and made Dora feel guilty for using the front door. Dora never knew where she was, she had an address, but no way of pinning the address to the earth. Indeed, London as a whole had no geographical reality. It was a series of red, blue and green lines and dots and circles, learnt off the tube map, without any corresponding anchoring to the conglomerations of buildings and streets and squares above. Her real London was a city of her imaginings, a place culled from books, a literary city, a place of allusions, and poetic habitations.

Soho was the capital of Bohemia, a region of narrow streets and garrets and literary romances, and Fitzrovia a realm of turrets and tournament pubs where knights and poets jousted with words. When she found herself on Hampstead Heath she was filled by excitement. That this blasted heath over which Coleridge had roamed and moaned was also available to her, put her in mind of Browning's question about seeing Shelley plain.

When a girl in the office where Dora worked asked her to share her flat in the centre of Bloomsbury she was delighted but unsurprised. So should life be, she thought, full of magic and unjust rewards. The girl, Henrietta, was much senior to Dora, and had had little truck with her before the surprising offer. But Dora was still so untutored in hierarchies that Henrietta's seniority meant little.

In Bloomsbury Dora began to feel that she had arrived at an actual place rather than a stopping-off point, a place that had a climate and a reality and a past and a soul and the smell of poetry, like the Heath. None of this was apparent but literature had put its imprimatur on the place and that was that. Before she moved in, Henrietta warned her that there was no security of tenure, the flat was shortly to be demolished to make room for an extension to the British Museum, but after Dora's many flits of the past six months and since she felt that never in her life had she lived in anything other than a hand-to-mouth way, this potential lack of security caused her neither surprise nor worry. It would not have occurred to Dora to look into anything other than the immediately foreseeable future, a characteristic which she took to be one of the few useful results of her upbringing under the feckless régime of her father whom she also took to be the most gallant man on earth.

The flat was a warren, furnished by Henrietta, and Dora moved in and felt she had come home. After some time she was astonished to discover that Henrietta was fascinated and shocked by Dora's behaviour. It had not occurred to Dora that anyone would observe or discuss or remark on her in any way. She thought she was so outside the circles she kept bumping up against that no one inside these enchanted rings would or could notice her, never mind make her a topic for discussion. The idea of any kind of criticism was anathema and she was alarmed at the notion of her invisibility being breached. When she told Henrietta this, somewhat tentatively, Henrietta was amused.

'You have the highest visibility quotient of anyone I know,' she said. 'One can't take one's eyes off you.' She said it without rancour, or admiration.

Having once broached the barriers of intimacy, Henrietta advanced further. It transpired that she knew, or believed that she knew, a lot about Dora. She had observed her from the day she had arrived. 'So bouncy,' she said, 'so confident, so unhampered. And you seemed so artless.'

Dora listened aghast and amazed. 'Artless?' she said. 'Confident? Are you sure it was me?'

'Well, you give the impression of being so which is much the same thing.'

'And unhampered by what?' Dora said. 'That just means I haven't got anything.'

'Convention,' Henrietta said. 'I'm so dogged, ridden by convention.'

'Well, walk away from it,' Dora said crossly, 'and count your blessings.' She thought that what she would really like would be to know the conventions. Life seemed so much easier if you did. Convention was another word for privilege in Dora's book.

Henrietta further told her that part of the fascination and shock lay in Dora's mixture of trust and aggression, her odd way of behaving. 'What's so odd about it?' Dora asked. 'I don't behave any differently from anyone else.'

'Completely differently,' Henrietta said. 'You're an operator.'

Dora was angered by what she took to be cruel misapprehension.

'I don't operate,' she said, 'whatever that means. You said I was artless. I act entirely by instinct.'

Henrietta looked startled. 'That might well be true,' she said. 'I think what you've said is just what I mean. Or it begs the question. Operators cruise on instinct. The thing is how can your instincts have remained so near the surface?'

'Because I'm not educated out of my mind,' Dora said, very cross.

Henrietta had the grace to laugh. 'What I do envy,' she said, 'is your very good instinct about people.' She enlarged. It seemed to Henrietta that Dora could in a split second sum up a situation, a person, however complex, and produce an almost instantaneous composite three-dimensional character picture of the person before her who was as often as not presenting quite a different façade or set-up altogether. Although Dora's defensiveness sometimes distorted her analysis, the psychic identikit she produced for Henrietta after a cursory meeting with Henrietta's boyfriends, past or present, and her acquaintances, seemed to Henrietta to be almost clairvoyantly accurate.

Dora never appeared to put this knowledge to any use. The truth was that Dora had not yet learnt how to do so. She had not learnt to use her judgement. Well, she had no judgement, and the use of power has to be learnt through opportunity. All the same, her scanning system acted as a powerful protective system saving her from risk.

'What defensiveness?' Dora said and Henrietta laughed again. 'What risk?' Dora was now alarmed at the idea that risk was in some kind of holding position over her head just waiting for the all-clear to drop down on her.

'You're the most defensive person I ever met,' Henrietta said. 'If you're not on the attack.'

It seemed a frightful epithet to Dora to be placed on a knife edge between retreat and advance, and she wondered how one got to the middle ground and how to set about taking risks at a safe distance.

At first, Henrietta appeared to Dora to stand four-square to the wind. Where did she get it, this glorious confidence? She was no prettier, no cleverer, no more charming, if anything rather less of these things than Dora. Yet she behaved as though the world were there for the taking. Of course Dora was haunted by this misapprehension in later life. One of the things that puzzled Dora when she was mourning her, was why Henrietta had never questioned Dora's impressions of Henrietta. Now Dora believes that it was because she could not bear to listen to anything that might upset that tightly constructed persona. What price your intuition then, Dora thought, but she recognised that it was hard to see past that polished surface, that high-nosed face, the impeccable vowels, the manners which seemed to be the chief blessing of an expensive education. Dora would have yielded the useless academic knowledge that she carried around – the ins and outs of the Schleswig-Holstein question, the war of bloody Jenkins's ear, the rainfall of the Ozarks – for a few of Henrietta's social accomplishments or her gift for languages. Dora thought that she had no gifts, and dismissed the attributes which Henrietta lauded as talents. Her abilities in the art of living seemed simple common sense, and her intuition an ersatz kind of intelligence, spurious, without credentials. There was no degree called Doctor of Perception, there was no money in it.

She listened to Henrietta going on about Dora's antennae for nuance, to her best friend Alice, who dressed in blue gowns and was wispy and upper class, although Dora did not recognise this socio-economic grouping, since she knew nothing of class, save what she had gropingly discerned in Jane Austen's books. Alice died, not much later, in a clinic in Harrow having entered too far into changing perceptions. On first hearing of Dora's clairvoyance she had looked at her suspiciously and avoided her, though, not long after, dressed in embroidered skirts, flowing scarfs, her page-boy haircut changed by some alchemy into a cloudy mass of curls, she had sought Dora out. By then Dora could not look at her, knowing – presumably through those instincts – that Alice had already gone under, beyond the reach of any hand.

Dora's memory was another object of curiosity, speculation and amazed comment for Henrietta and, she said, for many of her friends who, because of their polish, thought Dora, must be much cleverer than she was. Dora's tendencies to over-estimate these women and to denigrate her own abilities was fostered by Henrietta's ambivalent admiration which Dora took, as was her wont, to be condescending. When Dora did an interview or attended a press conference or briefing she took no notes. When she went back to the office she sat down at her typewriter and reproduced the conversation exactly. Henrietta was sceptical at first and went with Dora to a press conference. She taped the speaker and later compared the transcript to Dora's text. They matched. Thomasina, their boss, was not so impressed.

'You must take notes or appear to make notes,' she told Dora, 'for at least two reasons. One, taking notes establishes a professional basis for what you are doing and makes it clear you are not just having a conversation. And, more important, one day someone will say that he never said what you say he said and will cite that you did not make a record of the conversation, and we will lose a lot of money. It's called libel.'

Twenty years later, when computer-speak came into general use, words to do with searching, storing, finding, Henrietta might have used them to illustrate what she meant by Dora's assimilation and storing of data to produce a print-out, though she would still have been as puzzled as ever by where exactly Dora got her information *from*. Twenty years later, though, the mansion block in which the flat was tucked, on the third floor, still stands, quite unchanged, Henrietta has gone, disappeared for ever and it seems to Dora that her famous memory has gone as well, has quietly leaked through some drain in her brain-floor. Henrietta was pleased when Dora agreed to move in. It saved her the trouble of advertising for a flat-mate. Dora for her part couldn't believe her luck. She could walk to work and, at last, she was living in a part of London already lodged in her imagination. Dora believed that Henrietta was even poorer than she was, a belief based on the fact that Henrietta tried to pay for her groceries at the little corner shop with luncheon vouchers and entered the duration of each phone call she made into a little red book. Dora later discovered that Henrietta ate expensive lunches in places where they had never seen a luncheon voucher and so had to use them up in other ways and that the meticulous records of the phone calls were a prudent necessity for her income-tax returns to her accountant.

Dora also supposed that Henrietta was her official landlady merely because she had got there first, and that she had originally moved in as a flat-mate to some previous incumbent, as Dora was now moving in with her.

Dora's belief that Henrietta also had to eke out her life on the lamentably low salary paid by the magazine (on the grounds that anyone who worked there could afford to work there), was partly based on how much she talked of money or the lack of it, partly on how much she exclaimed over the price of everything, but wholly because Dora knew of no other way of living. Dora, on her meagre salary, was as extravagant as she could possibly be but she might as well have been trying to cup a kingfisher in her hands as keep her money in her pocket or the bank. One of her father's more frequent bon mots had been 'The only money you have is the money you spend' and, naturally enough, Dora believed this to be a dictum.

She spent every penny before she got it, and paid interest, but thought she managed to get away with it because her bank manager was interested in her. He asked her out soon after she had opened her account there.

Dora was too much in awe of anyone in authority, and especially with authority over money, to refuse but after two almost silent dinners in a lugubrious bistro in Kensington she began to put him off with excuses. Every so often he made an appointment for her to call in to his office, when he would go through her cheque-book stubs. She found this almost as dismaying as if he had gone through her laundry basket and exclaimed on the state of her gussets. She began to write fictitious names on the stubs rather than have him know how much she had spent at Tuffin and Foale or Annacat and the more she invented the more he became interested in her fecklessness. She would never have countenanced sleeping with him, even had he suggested it. Anything that involved gain apparently precluded Dora's collaboration and she feared in any case that he was trying to make an honest woman of her.

One morning in the flat, Henrietta, leafing through a binder of papers that had arrived in the post, began to moan gently about its content, about what on earth she was going to do. Dora, knowing that Henrietta did not have a bank manager who fancied her, assumed it was much like the letters she got, only angrier, made Henrietta a cup of coffee and commiserated. Glancing at the binder she saw the legend *I.C.I. Company Report*. Henrietta explained rather haltingly that she had some shares in the company. Dora looked at her with amazement; she couldn't think what she was talking about, couldn't reconcile having shares with being poor; shares were something you heard about on the wireless.

Henrietta, seeing Dora's face, dropped the subject, stopped moaning and Dora went off to work pondering on what she had seen. Later that week, holding the ICI folder, Henrietta brought up the subject of money again. Her accountant, she told Dora, had suggested she should buy a house since there was some spare money slopping around. Dora began to laugh. 'Here we are,' she said, 'borrowing luncheon vouchers from each other and you're talking about a house. I should sack your man.'

'I have got a little money,' Henrietta said, looking sideways at Dora, 'but not anything like as much as some people.'

'How much?' Dora said. The idea of having anything in the bank seemed riches beyond imaginings. She wanted to hear round figures. Henrietta didn't want to talk at all.

'I was brought up not to talk about money,' she said.

'So was I,' Dora said. 'But that was because there wasn't any. How much?'

Henrietta looked shifty.

'When my grandfather died, my grandmother sold his business, to ICI actually,' she shook the folder, 'and she gave all the grandchildren a certain amount.'

'A certain amount?' said Dora. 'How much?'

'About a half a million pounds each,' Henrietta said, and then, seeing Dora's face, added, 'but it's all tied up and entailed and looked after by trustees, honestly, that's why I actually never have any cash. And it's not much compared to some.'

Dora did a quick calculation. She thought, if I worked for four hundred years without stopping, without spending, I would have what Henrietta now has and thinks little of. She never thought of Henrietta in the same way again and she could not look at her without seeing a sterling sign hovering over her, like the Holy Ghost

– the spirit of money whence, she was beginning to learn, all good things flow. A flicker of awareness reached Dora that, perhaps, anonymous everyday people could be rich, a man in the street or the girl at the next desk, that there need not be flash and glitter, *Tatler* and William Hickey coverage attached to the possession of wealth. In the dispensation in which she had been brought up, the word millionaire was spoken with bated breath, with the same overtones and meaning as say dragon, or griffin or unicorn, a mythical beast that might well exist, somewhere on the outskirts of the known but distant world. Her father sometimes sang in a voice that hovered over the notes, a few snatches of a song about a man who broke the bank at Monte Carlo. As he walks along the boulevard with an independent air, You can see the people stare, You can hear them all declare, There goes a millionaire, He's the man who broke the bank at Monte Carlo. The fact that you could have half a million pounds and not have it emblazoned all over you, indeed behave no differently from someone with a pound to last them a week, quite put Dora out. She clutched the pound in her pocket and determined to get some of her own quickly. Then she would see how things could change.

After the conversation with Henrietta, Dora suddenly began picking up signals which, for all her famous perception, she had not been receiving before. No equipment. Signals not just about money and class but a new word, grand. One day Dora heard that Caroline, a secretary in the office, was leaving. Dora, when she had first noticed Caroline, had looked at her with speculation and then, as observation deepened, with another blend of emotions to which Dora could not quite put a name; not exactly envy, not exactly derision, not exactly wonderment, not quite admiration, not puzzlement but something of them all. Every day Caroline appeared to be dressed in the same clothes yet every day they were different. It took Dora a long time to work this out. She saw shoes with gold chains on their heels, always shiny, always unscuffed. Only over months did Dora realise that Caroline must have twenty or thirty pairs of such shoes. She began to look at Caroline's feet as she came into the office, to make note of the subtle variations, the flat bows, the leather trim, the linked rings, the green and red petersham, the strappings.

Back in those days Dora's shoes were a sight to be seen, gold and purple and strappy things; she teetered along in them, inches high, with no hint of liberation; the more enchained her feet were, the better she felt, and she looked down on Caroline's little pumps with pity.

She observed Caroline's skirts and sweaters and realised that the word sweater would not figure in Caroline's vocabulary which was, Dora also began to realise, fairly limited. She wore round-necked cashmere jerseys with cardigans to match and neither garment ever had a crop of little furry balls of wool grazing over them as Dora's three sweaters had. The only constant in Caroline's unchanging outfit were her pearls and at one point in Dora's fascination with Caroline's appearance she thought that perhaps these too were changed daily; she hovered around the back of Caroline's desk staring at the nape of her neck until Caroline became uneasy. Dora was relieved to see the clasp was always the same.

Caroline's vocabulary may have been limited but Dora lacked more important vocabulary, the vocabulary of tribal signals, and it was some time before she worked out that Caroline was wearing a uniform. In her country childhood she had once observed a flock of yellow hammers pecking another yellow hammer to death. Its stripe had been only marginally smaller but it had tried to edge its way higher up the pecking order. When the time came, Dora by-passed the flock altogether, something easily enough done, since in the flock she passed, more money made for a bigger stripe. Back in those days, when Caroline was tripping around in the chained heels, Dora often had to go to the financial manager of the company in the middle of the month to ask for an advance on her salary, which foray made her blush with shame, much the same blush she had effected when the bank manager had first scolded her, and then asked her out. The accountant made her feel like the unwise virgin where the bank manager had made her feel like a slut but she was so accustomed to being grateful that she felt no rage that he should take a high moral line for advancing company money. As a result of paying back the loan she was always even poorer for the following months. Looking back on those days, Dora was inclined to be impatient at her naivety and honesty, and angry at the meanness of the company who used her talents to the full but never paid her a living wage. But most of all she resented the religion of her upbringing which had so infected her with the disease of gratitude and devalued her sense of herself that she was grateful to have a job at all. It would not, could not, have occurred to Dora to ask for more money for the astonishing amount of work she did. In employing her she felt that the company was doing her a favour and she behaved like a child who keeps quiet so as not to be punished even when she has done nothing wrong. Not that that had ever saved her from the blows which rained throughout childhood.

Caroline did not tell Dora herself she was leaving. But after all, secretaries came and went and there was never a shortage of young pretty women in the office. It was a prestigious place to work before making a good marriage, though again Dora was not too bright about prestige and had never considered marriage as an option. She only recognised fame. And in her book a good marriage was one where the wife was stuck at home, and she wanted no truck with that kind of goodness.

The art department made Caroline a funny card with a play of words on her surname, Paine, and they all signed it and dropped a contribution into a box for a present, a contribution Dora made with a mental sigh for, though she was generous by nature, what she gave away was her bus fare. Dora had liked Caroline, what she knew of her, not just that polished easy way she looked, but her diffidence, her English voice; she'd even begun to like the little gold chains on her heels, the big fat hair bands on her small thin head. What a Paine seemed an ambivalent salutation, or farewell.

Henrietta had *The Times* delivered every morning and, some weeks later, Dora, surreptitiously glancing through it, before Henrietta emerged from her bedroom, saw the name leap out from a Court Circular about the doings of the Duchess of Kent. She had travelled in an aircraft of the Queen's Flight: The Lady in Waiting in attendance was Miss Caroline Paine. The name danced in front of Dora's eyes. It was as significant as the conversation about money. A world that had been unknown to her was suddenly revealed, a door opened up, that door in the low grey wall that had stirred her in her adolescent reading. Dora instantly longed to enter the domaine that lay behind.

She wholeheartedly admired the reticence, the lack of boastfulness that Caroline had shown, in not mentioning her new job, but was puzzled by it. She mentioned this to Henrietta, who, with a certain tact, conveyed something subtle to Dora. To put it crudely, which Henrietta didn't, the fact was that Caroline could not be bothered to mention it to Dora. Caroline talked in code and lived according to a code and Dora knew none of the ciphers. Dora thought there must be a short cut to learning to decipher it, which she must find. She needed the language if she were to conquer the world she now lived in or, more realistically, come to terms with it. What it took her a long time to realise was that the English were a foreign breed to her. And what she never came to terms with was that they, this foreign race on whose soil she lived, were inherently patronising.

She had read in a nineteenth-century biography a message from a mother to her daughter advising her to say to herself the moment she awoke in the morning, 'I am an Englishwoman. I was born in wedlock. I am on dry land.'

When Dora murmured the mantra to herself, substituting 'I am an Irishwoman,' it did not have the same ring and Nora in the glass coffin stirred; Dora knew there could be no breaching such misplaced arrogance.

For all her putative artlessness, Dora had energy, ambition, a gift for flattery and a ruthless streak that surprised her, but surprised even more those against whom she used it, including her several consecutive lovers. It was only when she met the man whom she regarded as her first real lover, and in him met someone more ruthless, and more careless of feelings, that she was stopped in her impetus and, confused, began to look for directions and into the future. He knew the language and the ways of the world into which she was peering through the chinks; he knew it from both the inside out and the outside in, though he did not wholly belong. He introduced her to another parallel world and so forwarded her sentimental education, rubbed down her edges and did all of it in a hurry. She never admitted, never agreed and never allowed that he could teach her anything. To owe anything to him was, she felt, to be in his power and her instinct warned her that to be in any man's power was to give the lie to her life. Naturally enough she searched for powerful men, the better to live the slander.

IV

Years later Caroline and her current husband came to one of Dora and Simon's dinner parties. It was still the decade of dinner parties. Caroline and her husband were staying with mutual friends in the neighbourhood and when Dora asked them to dinner and they mentioned they had guests staying, Dora included them in the invitation. Caroline did not know Dora's married name and when Caroline saw her hostess her surprise was so manifest as to be almost rude. Dora's pleasure at her surprise was not so evident since she had been forewarned. Times had indeed changed when it was Dora who was making-up for someone else's naivety. Dora was all that was gracious and, at the large and long table, put Caroline on Simon's right. She placed Pamela, who was staying with her, beside Caroline's new husband to see how he would manage with that little feminine arrangement. That Pamela was staying was not in itself unusual, nor that she had brought with her another new man. What was unusual was that Dora had felt her heart shift when he made a flurried arrival into her garden. She decided to snub him and avoid him, and put him next to her on her right. Simon watched from the top of the table.

Standing with Caroline earlier that evening, with their backs to the yew hedges of the garden, which spread like a living quilt of colour around that quarter of the fortified house, Dora had observed Caroline's curious glances, listened to her politic probings, her ploys to try to work out how Dora had got to this position, and had felt not exactly a sense of déjà-vu but more a feeling of reversal into a place she hoped she had left behind her until it was time for her to make a formal visit back. She did not wish to go there inadvertently. The narrow paths which led out of her childhood and from which she had hurried like a rat to water were still too near and real for her not to fear she could easily get lost in them again.

This setting might be taken for granted by the woman beside her, in the evening dress equivalent of pleated skirt and twin-set and pearls – no doubt the same pearls – but it could never rest easy with Dora. She saw clearly enough the routes which had led to this setting so far removed from any connection with her early life, or with the young woman she had been, arriving unequipped, into a world where Caroline had always been at home.

As she stood looking back up at the house, she felt herself again at the centre of a mirage, floating over a void, and wished that it wasn't quite so easy to collect possessions of every kind save the one that she most craved. Self-possession she had learnt was not for sale, it was a gift. The problem, of course, was that if you hadn't got it, it was hard to pass it on. She thought of her mother shrinking from life and her children advancing to meet it and thought with gratitude of Simon and his quiet self-possession. Just as well. It was the last time she was to think of him for some time.

To some the house that Dora created in her efforts to make herself at home might have seemed an attempt at paradise, to others a place of incarceration, or a house for a Rapunzel without long hair. It all depended how you looked at it. Dora wanted it to be a fortress where she could live in comparative safety with her family though she felt that much of her time was spent in a waking dream. In this fortress she could hide from imaginary knights and poets and dark men who stamped their feet and demanded that she guess their names so she was much put about to find that it was occasionally insubstantial, that the doors swung open at a certain touch.

She left the house constantly, ostensibly to work or to go on those errands of beauty and pleasure and to see Stella but also hoping somehow to find that these imaginary creatures were real and might bar her path. She returned empty after each foray but with hands full, stuffing ever more objects into a house already filled with a surfeit of things.

Pictures, trunks, paintings, prints, Worcester and Crown Derby china, anonymous ceramics of dogs, lambs, lions, bocage; ducks, flowers, fabrics from every corner of the globe, from as far back as she could find them, some of them only held together by fragile silken threads, glass of every kind, Roman, Bohemian, Waterford, Lalique, decanters and jelly moulds and doorstops, rummers and candlesticks and funnels; globes, books, baubles, indoor bowls, shells, croquet balls, old wooden bowls, mugs and loving cups engraved with initials, not her own, furs, porcelain, delft, oak, walnut, watercolours, rosewood, mahogany, box, silver, spelter, bronze polescreens, the gatherings of a gambler who gambled on acquisition rather than loss, filled every room.

When she moved in it was already quite full enough with the accumulations of Simon's admittedly somewhat austere Quaker forbears but changing it and cramming it gave her hardly enough time to call her own. When she was supposed to be working or her children wanted her she would make them wait while she put another bunch of flowers into a vase, or put another stitch in the needlepoint, or painted a box, or tucked a counterpane or twitched the fringes of a paisley shawl wrapped around a mahogany pole so that it would hang the better.

It had taken many years to make the house look as it now does and she felt sometimes as she walked through the crowded rooms that she was moving through a treacle, which was her life. At other times she saw the house as a series of enormous guy-ropes holding her and her life down to earth and thought that without the ballast of clutter she would go weightlessly bumping into space.

But mostly she felt as if every room with its countless objects was a stage set against which she hoped to act out her life, which was drifting by, beyond her reach. She did not know where her real life was; the part that had been written for her seemed to have fallen out of her hands, if it had ever been in them. She scolded herself. If she could get off stage where would she be, she wondered. Back in old Ireland where she had no possessions? Back being Nora again? She lifted the local gazette to see if there was an auction she could go to for the staunch of another acquisition.

Tony Flaxmeyer had once said, watching her look around his apartment with disapproval mixed with amazement at the sheer extravagant effulgence of the place, 'Stop looking so po-faced. I like my ball and chain of clutter. I like kicking it ahead of me. I own therefore I am.' And Dora who owned nothing save for the contents of the suitcase, some knickers, a few frilly blouses, a couple of bras, her pairs of strappy purple and gold shoes and two or three mini-skirts, was stupefied, and supercilious. She felt there was something more moral and pure in her own bare life than there ever could be in luxury. Necessity and envy make their own righteousness. Now she looks back with regret on the houses in which Tony lived and wishes she had memorised every felicitous detail.

*

He'd come breezing into her editor's office one morning, dark haired, half-bald, his stomach billowing into a blue and white striped shirt, such thick expensive stripes, so that looking at his torso was like looking at a handsome helium balloon, or a porridge bowl, anchored by narrow and short legs which for all their shortness were nimble and fleet as Ariel's. She'd seen him go down the corridor, energy coming off him like the sparks from fireworks.

He hurtled in a trajectory of his own, tugging people along, catching them up in his slipstream. He was shrewd, cynical, exuberant, unscrupulous, with an enormous pride in his Jewish heritage which he said he could actually see behind him, as solid rows of solemn, clever, bearded rabbis, watching him, and stretching back to the crack of doom, or the birth of Judaism. He felt their breath on his shoulders and it spurred him on. He had, he said, a taste for comely blonde nordic women.

'Brunnhilde of course,' he said. 'I ought to be ashamed of my taste.'

'Thanks a bunch,' Dora said. 'And what do you mean by comely? When men use that word they always mean big, comforting and medievally obedient.'

'Big, beautiful, comes easily, and nothing middle-aged about them,' Tony said. 'It's all I ask for in a woman. Though obedient could be the favourite.'

It wasn't all he asked for, as Dora soon found out, but for the nonce she answered.

Flaxmeyer lived half the year in a rambling house in Ireland and the other half in London or around the world. He was a painter, no more and no less he said, than an itinerant journeyman or pedlar keeping up the traditions. His work was fashionable, though ahead of him were the lean years in terms of reputation when he fell out of fashion as the pop heroes drew their zappy pictures and wielded airbrushes and he laboured on with palette knives and brushes which a friend brought back from a certain town in India. He was too engrossed in leading the life of a rich man to be either wholly successful or taken seriously, which were synonymous for him, but he had a waiting list of what he called seriously rich clients. She did not know of his bravery as a very young man at the end of the war until years afterwards (by which time she had had enough of heroes anyway) but in the course of her connection with him she found him to be a man of paradox, moral, corrupt, kind to people, though he did not believe that anyone ever acted in a disinterested way. Everyone had their price. His gaze, so disconcertingly clear could as easily become opaque and never could anyone turn so blind an eye when it suited him. He knew exactly what he was doing and it was always expedient, frequently bordering on the criminal. When Dora found this out, she was most surprised. She had been brought up to believe in sin; venial sin she could countenance. Mortal sin meant death of the soul. Yet Tony dealt merrily in mortal sin and suffered no ill-effects at all, whereas Dora, afraid to err, felt herself punished at every turn.

When Dora first encountered him he was in Thomasina's office showing her some photographs. The sparks were still flying in the air when Thomasina called Dora in and did an introduction of sorts, that is to say she looked at Dora over her glasses and said, 'Darling, you know Tony.' With cries of pleasure she passed the photographs over to Dora as though for verification, though Dora had no idea of what constituted a good photograph and in any case thought photography a trivial pastime requiring no gift save self-importance. She had no problem with these photographs – they were merely photographs of a portrait of a grand old man, a man whom she knew of as a cigar-smoking bon-viveur, famous for his looks, his courage, an emblem of English integrity. What Tony had painted was a mendacious creature, the definition of a politician, a man with a weak greedy hole for a mouth, eyes that refused recognition. A bird perched on his broad old shoulders. Their beaks matched and his rocky face had the mean semblance of a smile.

'Wonderful portrait Tony,' said Thomasina. 'But does he like it?'

Dora handed the photographs back.

'He hasn't seen it,' the Tony man said, 'but he's so vain he only sees what he wants to see. The person I have to worry about is his daughter. She's appointed herself his guardian and when she's drunk she's liable to do anything. Look at Winston's wife and Sutherland – that great portrait. Destroyed. The Philistines are upon us.'

'She wouldn't,' said Thomasina.

'She would,' Tony said. 'Given half a chance.'

Dora tapped her foot and Tony looked at her.

'So this is the genius?' he said to Thomasina.

'The Dora herself,' Thomasina said. 'Darling, we're going to use Tony's portrait in the next issue and we need words. Tony will tell you all about Lord Bibury. We're going to call it "His Eye is on The Sparrow".'

Dora knew exactly what Thomasina wanted. The painter would ramble on about his sitter, Lord Bloody Bibury and Dora would have to turn his egocentric memories into peerless prose, while skirting the sycophantic.

'Dora's Irish too,' Thomasina said.

'I didn't know Lord Bibury was Irish,' Dora said shaking the photograph. 'He never had a good word to say about us.'

Thomasina looked at her over her glasses. 'I never know whether she's deliberately misunderstanding or not,' she said.

'I've never heard of anyone in Ireland being called Dora,' Flaxmeyer said. 'You ought to marry a duke with a name like that. Dora Connaught or Dora Leinster. Where do you come from?'

'I come from Ireland,' Dora said, 'the same place as you apparently.'

'What part?'

'People always ask the Irish that,' Dora said. 'They never ask the English.'

'Touchy,' he said to Thomasina and then to Dora: 'They do, they do, only they do it county by county.'

Thomasina said, 'It's true darling. There are terrific differences between Gloucestershire and Essex. Never mind Northumberland.'

When she got back to her desk, Annabel, who now sat at Caroline's desk, and had blonde streaky hair where Caroline was dark but was otherwise identical, said, 'I saw him in the corridor, what's he like?'

'Who?' Dora said, deliberately obtuse.

'Come on Dora,' Annabel said. 'Anthony Flaxmeyer to you and me.'

'I only spoke to him,' Dora said. 'Do you know him?'

'Everyone knows him,' Annabel said. 'My sister had a walk-out with him. She was besotted with him.'

'About *that*?' Dora said, and as she said it, saw Flaxmeyer look over the partition and beckon her. She rose, and followed him. It seems to her now, looking back, that she never looked back.

'If we're going to work together we'd better start now,' he said. 'Get your coat.'

'I'm busy,' she said.

'No, you're not,' he said.

He took her at a fast trot to a gallery in Bond Street where she looked at strange spiky pictures of snakes. He bought her one. It cost thirty pounds. She was overcome by pleasure. He saw her staring at the subject perplexed, though her pleasure at the acquisition was manifest.

'Words, yes,' he said. 'Visual sense, no. The Irish don't have any visual sense at all. Or not any more.'

'It atrophies under poverty,' Dora said. 'But how would you know.'

'Look at the glories of the Book of Kells and the early artefacts and you can see a visual sensibility second to none,' he went on. 'I dread going home after any absence, there's always a new violation on the landscape, houses like a plague of shingles. Give the Irish two things to choose from and they'll choose the ugliest each time. God, the houses they're now building to replace their cottages. No, I wouldn't have wanted to live in the old ones,' he said seeing Dora's face. 'Don't be so boring. I don't want people to suffer to feed my susceptibilities, but they don't need to move into things that wouldn't be out of place in a derelict mining village. They appear never to have seen a garden. Every house is plonked in the middle of a field with a cement surround or else in the middle of a midden. Yet look at their heritage. Ireland was covered in beautiful houses, I know, Dora, I know, we are talking of the Anglo-Irish, the money, the alien culture, I know it all Dora, I do, I live there, the Irish are even more boring about their past grievances and how they was robbed than we are. I know all about the Anglo-Irish and your hatred, I know to the point where my boredom is exquisite, so don't climb on your high horse with me. Anything you can do, the Jews can do better in terms of suffering, if you want to play that game.'

'One minute you're Irish the next minute you're Jewish,

whichever whinge best suits your story,' Dora said. She was surprised that he was Jewish, and that he said he was.

'They are not mutually exclusive,' he said. 'That's one of the good things. Jews are not a race. You can be any nationality and remain Jewish. Unlike the Irish who think if they don't proclaim it the whole time their cocks will fall off.'

'There are women in Ireland, too,' Dora said, prim; and he said, 'Exactly who I'm talking about and please look at this picture.'

She was flummoxed but only for a moment.

'Anyway the native Irish don't get on high horses, as someone said, and the English have no great famous visual sense. If you go to deprived areas of England you won't see many houses built in the charming vernacular. Have you ever driven through the docks of Liverpool? Or Oxford for that matter? Ireland was a deprived area of England for four hundred years. When did you become Irish? I don't hate the Anglo-Irish. I admire them. I want to be like them.'

'My, my,' he said. 'We are sophisticated.'

'No, we're not,' she said. 'Perhaps it's racial self-hatred. Or it's because they're richer than we are, or because they look better. They speak better than what we do, and look down their noses better.'

'They've got noses to look down,' he said. 'That's why your upper lip tilts up – it has to reach up to catch that thing above it which one must suppose is a nose.'

He leaned over and, in full view of the man at the big desk under the paintings, traced the outline of her lip with his tongue.

Her mouth fell open, weak with a new emotion. She pursed it back into line.

'You can't say the same for yours,' she said. 'Your lip hasn't room to breathe with that hooter looming over it.'

'And your lip will get you into trouble. Come on. Let's eat.'

'What about my picture?' she said.

'We collect it at the end of the show,' he said. 'Stop the fretting.'

They set off up the street at the same tremendous clip.

'It's not a fashionable creed,' he said, 'to want to be Anglo-Irish. I don't think I've heard anyone profess it before. Aren't you afraid of being called a Quisling?'

'You're not very sophisticated,' Dora said. 'You're shocked. And who would call me a Quisling? Who cares? Perhaps I'm secure enough not to have to proclaim my Irishness at every turn.'

'I rather think not,' he said, 'since it seems to be the sole topic of your conversation. Would you become a Protestant – don't you have to be Protestant to be Anglo-Irish?'

'Joyce was asked that question once,' Dora said.

'And what did he say?'

'He said that he had lost the faith but not self-respect.'

'Do you feel like that?'

'No,' Dora said, 'but Protestantism has not had a pretty history in Ireland. It was called the Church of Ireland and it had ten per cent of the population. Something called The Irish Society tried to convert the people to Protestantism by giving them scriptures in Gaelic. If anything would make me want to stay a Catholic, and nothing does, it would be to show solidarity.'

'Solidarity with whom?'

'Solidarity with the Irish,' she said.

'But if you want to be Anglo-Irish,' he said, patiently, as though to a child, 'then you're not showing solidarity to the Irish.'

'You are a dunce for all you're so clever,' Dora said. 'The Anglo-Irish were not a race either. They were a class. That's what the envy and rancour is all about. They had the attributes of the ruling class and to have a ruling class you've got to have underlings. I want to be an overling. But I would show solidarity with the Catholic dead who were so good, so brave, and who are owed at least the last respect of my respect for them.' She began to laugh. 'I'll say it before you do. I would have my cake and eat it.'

They turned into a restaurant Dora had often passed, a place of marble and fern and splashing water which looked more like the entrance to swimming baths than an eating house. A man in a dinner-jacket greeted her companion with little Italian cries of joy and he responded in what appeared to Dora to be the same idiom. They were led downstairs to a room full of flowers, and pink tables and people. Hundreds of people it seemed to Dora, the women chic, the men shiny. They sat at a table near the stairs. When they were settled she went on with the conversation as though they were still walking down the street.

'Have you ever heard of a man called George Tyrell?'

He shook his head.

'He was born a Protestant in Ireland. Not grand but the Tyrells, like the rest of their breed, thought themselves a cut above everybody else, meaning me and the likes of me.'

'Not you,' Tony said. 'Before your time surely.'

'He became a Catholic,' Dora continued, 'which was much the same to the family as eating horse for supper, and all his mother had to say was that that a son of hers should go to Mass with the cook was the most sensible sting she could feel.'

'It doesn't sound very sensible to me,' he said.

'Sensible in the old-fashioned sense,' Dora said. 'Acute feeling.'

'Not old-fashioned,' he said. 'French. And sensible by all means,' he said, 'lots of acute feeling,' and put his hand under the table between her legs, so they opened of their own accord, as her mouth had done when his tongue probed it. It seemed to her that she scarcely closed them again in his company.

They ordered a meal. He made no attempt to ask or influence what she wanted to order. She hated it when men explained what the speciality was or raved on about some obscure part of a beast cooked in some obscure way. As their lunch grew later many of the people leaving the restaurant stopped to greet him, and he smiled cursorily or made a quick agreement to talk, to telephone. He allowed no one to linger and made such quick introductions that Dora could hardly catch their names. Many of those she did, she recognised. She scoffed after one particularly elegant man and woman had departed, the man as catatonic as the woman was vivacious.

'Hope Lash?' she said. 'Hope Lash and Mungo Wiltshire? Who do they think they're kidding? Must be nom de plumes, they've got to be, can you imagine Mr and Mrs Wiltshire standing by while the priest christens the baby Mungo. Mungo no one could be called Mungo.'

'Dukes can,' he said. Dora stared after the retreating figures wishing she had looked closer. 'And part of Hope's attraction is the promise of her name. In any case one mustn't presume that every child is christened. That's very chauvinistic. Christening is naming in Christ. Remember?'

Dora looked startled. 'I never thought of that,' she said. 'What do you call it, Baptism, Christening?'

'The Naming of the child,' he said, 'and quite good enough. Names are so important. What you're saddled with becomes you, do you think? Is Dora your real name? Have you another good Irish one like Philomena or Bernadette to keep the spooks at bay?'

'Tony's not Jewish is it?' she asked. 'I pray to St Anthony still to find things and he does though I don't believe in him. I suppose it touches some nerve which makes me remember.'

'I was called Monty as a child,' he said, 'and the moment I reached the age of reason, I changed it.'

'Was Monty short for Montgomery?'

He looked at her for a long minute and seeing she was serious began to laugh.

'Not exactly,' he said. 'More like Montague, wouldn't you say?'

During that meal Dora learnt that at the outbreak of war his father had chartered a yacht and sailed it to Dubrovnik, again and again, picking up escaping Jews.

'Most of them were sent, on arrival, to an aliens' camp on the Isle of Man. When he'd run his last rescue mission, he joined them in the camp and was an embarrassment to the authorities who kept trying to chuck him out.'

'And where were you while all this was going on?'

'I was in my last year at Eton,' he said and she stared at him in astonishment.

'I thought only English boys went to Eton,' she said.

'Well, I was,' he said. 'You can change nationality, you know Dora, though I doubt you'll get an Anglo-Irish passport and I didn't need to change mine. I was born in England. We moved to Ireland after the war. I suppose it seemed the last refuge in Europe to my father and there was, ostensibly, no anti-semitism there.'

He began to tuck into some moist labia-like scallops. 'Of course it helped that there were no Jews.'

'I seem to remember a Jewish Lord Mayor of Dublin,' Dora said, looking at her grisly whitebait, separate, spiky.

'Yes but in that sense they were no longer Jewish – the Jews in Ireland. They became grand. The Irish look up to them.'

'Not always,' Dora said. 'There was quite a violent boycott of Jewish merchants in Limerick around the turn of the century. As I remember.'

'Your memory goes back a long way.'

'Genetic, by now,' Dora said.

He laughed. He told of the times his father had sat in the camp for aliens in the Isle of Man sketching his fellow internees, showing solidarity, his protest quite unpublicised, his deprivation endured for no tangible results.

'You can't measure it in tangibilities,' she said.

'I think I worked that one out myself quite early on,' he said, 'and decided against it as a way of life. And wherever did you get that idea about Eton? There were lots of Irishmen there and some French, a man called Guerlain I seem to remember. Had a moustache. When he stood up in church all the mothers clutched their left bosom and fainted.'

'Not what I would call Irish if they went to Eton,' she said.

'Oh God,' he said. 'Not again. Eat up and we'll get on to the tangibles.'

When they came out of the restaurant, she felt as pink and moist as the scallops. They set off in the opposite direction from her office, he moving as fast as ever. She panted alongside him.

'Where are we supposed to be going?'

'We're not supposing,' he said. 'We're going home.'

'What, we're off to Ireland are we?' she asked ironic as anything.

'My car's in the next street,' he said, and she followed him towards a taxi rank. A mini was parked behind a taxi like a baby elephant behind its mother.

A policeman was standing beside it.

Dora, embarrassed at the idea of the contretemps, turned away, and when she looked around again, the policeman was becking and nodding and moving away.

'How did you do that?' she asked. 'I thought you'd be arrested.'

'Don't be so silly,' he said, and as they climbed in: 'Do you always think the worst?'

'No I think the best but the worst happens. I thought I was only going to look at some nice snaps this morning when Thomasina called me in. So now I'm a pessimist. Nicer to be surprised than alarmed.'

The car had wicker-work sides and a steering wheel made of stitched leather, and when he switched on the wireless the noise boomed out all around. It was the first stereo she had ever seen or heard. The tiny car reeked of luxury though it was not a word she had much truck with.

'Now home. Where is home?' he said.

'I thought we were going to your house,' she said and he laughed.

'I live in Montague Street,' she said. It was her turn to laugh. 'Home from home.'

'My God,' he said, 'where's that?'

'It's in Bloomsbury,' she said, waiting for the accolade of recognition.

'Bloomsbury,' he began to laugh. 'Call it Holborn and have done with it,' he said. 'No one lives there. It's all museums and offices.'

'It's where Diana Cooper lived, or near it, for years after she was married,' Dora said crossly and then, added, honesty getting the better of her: 'Her mother lamented about it though.'

'I should think so too,' Tony said, 'marrying a nobody and moving to nowhere.'

'Virginia Woolf lived near here, she didn't think it was nowhere,' Dora said as he skidded into the Tottenham Court Road. 'Wherever you live is the central place. Everyone else lives somewhere else, more or less inconvenient, not the other way round.'

'No darling,' he said, 'some places will always be nowhere. And wherever *one* lives is the central place. Not you.'

'It's the one semantic absolute in the English versus Irish language debate,' Dora said. 'All that about whether English is our mother tongue and Irish our native language. Or the other way around. I can never remember. Anyway the one give-away is "one" – no real Irish person ever uses one. Ever. Ever. One. One.' She mimicked him angrily.

'What you said earlier only made sense if you used the word "one", Dora,' he said. 'Unless you mean that I am the centre of the universe which position I am happy to occupy. For someone so concerned with words as you, I should have thought that making sense was the point.'

'Pompous as well,' she said.

He drove the wrong way down the many one-way streets that lay on his route. Dora was shocked by this lawlessness. He parked on the pavement and she let him in, and as he walked down its dark length and looked into its rooms Dora saw that not only was it not the most desirable flat in London which she'd tended to think before, if only because of its location, but that it was not even going to be a permanent base.

'Do you live here alone?' he asked.

She told him about Henrietta though not about her money.

'And the furniture?'

'Hers,' she said as they went into Dora's bedroom. 'I'm going to have shelves put up,' she said defensively. Where she came from, bed-sitter land, having shelves put up was a significant and committing thing to do. You had to leave them behind when you moved.

'I shouldn't bother doing anything to it at all,' he said, 'it's perfectly all right as it is, you'd either have to spend a fortune or leave it and you won't be here that long.'

'Why won't I?' Dora asked surprised.

'Oh you'll move on,' he said, casual, his eyes alert. 'You've got ambition.' She was pleased to have it stated. 'It's a character defect no one should be without.' He looked down at Henrietta's carpet. 'This is nice,' he said. 'Where did you find it?'

She looked at the rug. She didn't want to tell him it wasn't even hers, never mind that she hadn't really noticed it, after all his strictures on the Irish visual sense.

'Why is it a character defect?' She was shocked. People were meant to have ambition, it was a virtue. Her teachers had urged it on her, even mad Sister Scholastica.

Behind her she heard Henrietta come into the flat with a jangling of keys, and she came out of her room, hurriedly, in case Henrietta thought she was up to no good, in there with a strange man. He came out behind her and Dora introduced them, tentatively.

As they shook hands Dora knew Henrietta well enough to know there was something ambivalent in her manner, curiosity, disapproval certainly, but something else which puzzled Dora whose famous intuition was beginning to fail her badly. She was fearful, though also somewhat hopeful, that Tony might be diverted from her by Henrietta's looks, her sophistication, by what Dora now realised was a kind of grandness.

She questioned him about Henrietta, hoping to be subtle about it, after Henrietta had gone into the kitchen. Tony saw through the supposed subtlety.

'I don't fancy her,' he said. 'There's nothing there to interest me.'

Dora was shocked. 'She'll hear,' she said but Tony went back into her room and pushed her unceremoniously onto the bed and took off her clothes. 'What lovely big thighs,' he said and Dora was furious. He didn't care. What Dora found extraordinary was that angry as she believed herself to be, she enjoyed love-making with him more than she could have ever imagined. It was all so appallingly pleasurable that she could be disgusted with herself for behaving so badly. After a time she forgot about good and bad and just felt what was happening with an intensity of pleasure she had no idea she was capable of. To her shame, she also let the adjacent world of Russell Square know about it. Until Tony set about her, using his mouth and hands with the single-mindedness of a piranha on a tasty carcase, busying himself sucking and panting, opening and closing, until then, when making love, she had lain in silence terrified lest any sounds escaped her lips.

'What's going on in here?' her mother used to call through any closed door, when they were small and simply sitting sucking their teeth or burning bits of paper over oil lamps to see if the house would go on fire. Now Dora was actually doing what presumably everyone had always been terrified of, the bad frolic her mentors had hinted at, and not just doing it but going to the extremes of feeling where good and bad did not exist, a kind of Micomicon, and enjoying it hysterically. She'd always been embarrassed by the idea that people uttered while making love, imagine what St Paul would think, and now she could hear herself making really dreadful noises, squeaking, moaning, groaning noises, and when he had finished and she was lying there in a heap, she said, 'Oh God the noise,' and moaned some more.

'What noise?' he said. 'I wish there had been noise, the more noise the better for me, you couldn't make enough noise for me.'

'Why is ambition a character defect?' she said, and he rolled onto his back and made a groaning noise of his own. 'I knew it,' he said, 'a terrier. It gets a bone and doesn't let go.'

It transpired though that Henrietta could have enough noise.

'Frankly I can't stand it,' she said after some heated sessions and Dora, instead of dying instantly with shame, said she would try to be quieter but Henrietta would have to stand it. After all they'd agreed to try to respect each other's peculiarities. Although perhaps groaning loudly half the evening was overdoing it, she conceded, as lying in his arms in her bed, she told Tony who said, 'I shouldn't worry about it. You're too important to her to do anything serious about upsetting you.'

'Important?' she said. 'Me, important to Henrietta?' And as she said it she was overcome by a wave of nausea for herself, for her breasts, for her body, for the boring realisation that she felt she was important to no one under the sun, and her eye-lids hurt and her throat ached as she stared away into the distance trying to think of something funny or prosaic, Buster Keaton on the edge of a skyscraper, her sister Iris, doing a little dance while singing 'Fly Me to the Moon', anything to stop the deluge which if started would engulf her, Tony, Henrietta, the flat and the British Museum.

'If you hear me groaning I shall be writing poetry,' she said, at length, refusing to look at him, knowing her voice was squeaking past the boulder of pain in her throat. 'Proust said it, not me.'

He put his arm out in a strange, isolated gesture and said, 'For God's sake hold thy tongue and let me love,' and she whispered, 'Who said that?' and he said, 'You're the literary genius round here – you find out.'

Later, before she fell asleep, Dora remembered Henrietta's first look when she'd seen Tony and realised that what she had seen was jealousy.

From the very first day Tony recognised Dora's ignorance of the world he moved in, not just in the names he threw out, but of the significance of the names. She knew nothing of the interlocking circles of kin and kissing cousins, none of the do-you-know games he could play so well, tracing accurately the swollen growth of the English aristocracy, its convoluted roots, trees, branches, sprigs. He was, he said, besotted with the English upper classes, in love with the Arabellas and the Sophies and the Lady Marys and mad about duchesses but never found any of them erotic. An Irish refugee looking for the magic realm laid open endless possibilities for diversion. 'I'm not a refugee,' she said, most indignant. 'Talk about the kettle. I've got a good home to go to if I wanted,' and then settled to fretting as she submitted to his pleasurable corruption of what she thought was her innocence and was in fact pudeur and timidity.

Dora did not move out of the flat. She did indeed put curtains up in her room and shelves, and rearranged Henrietta's furniture but she spent less and less time in Bloomsbury and more time with Tony on the fringe of Belgravia. His house in London was near the Munster, one of the great hotels of London, and most evenings they would slip in through an unused side entrance to which he had a key. At first Dora hated this act of daring and feared that if they were caught they would be jailed or beaten with napkins. She soon found out that anyone who mattered in the hotel knew that Tony used the entrance and tolerated it. He had made it into a custom which Dora could see would become part of the hotel's tradition, part of the legend of the handbook of the future.

It had started after he had painted a portrait of the Chairman of the hotel group. 'The old queen got it free.' Tony said. 'I get hot dinners.'

It was the sort of arrangement he lived by and after a while she also had no doubt that the magical house he lived in in London was his by some kind of barter. It was a series of rooms spread over the top floor of four houses, linked up by steps, concealed entrances and small stairways. In a big landing on the first floor, two middle-aged secretaries sat, who never seemed to leave and who organised the mechanics of his life. Dora's appearance on the scene affected them not at all. They had obviously seen it all before. Dora felt she should bring them little sops to gain access to Tony's kingdom beyond the doors and up to the passages and false doors and narrow tunnels, along which you had to stumble, head bowed, past mansard windows where pigeons roosted and turned a disaffected eye, into pale yellow rooms crammed with idiosyncratic treasures.

His father's sketches hung in one of the passages.

'I value them,' Tony said portentously once, 'more than I value those big bints in their Turkish knickers.' He was looking at his Matisses.

'No wonder the Irish are joked upon if they talk faddle like that,' Dora said. 'I wonder which you'd seize up if there was a fire. No I don't wonder.'

'Quite right you disagreeable little brute,' he said.

She began to notice things though, in retrospect, she knew she had not noticed enough. Among the things she remembered were shelves of Wemyss ware, ebony boxes, silver eggs, turban pins, a crystal crucifix with a dark stone at its centre, a coco-de-mer bean shell, giltwood carvings, a pair of painted chairs with masks and ribbons, four elaborate figures with the names of continents painted underneath, a chinese screen in gold and black, gold coins with the etched profile of Alexander the Great, looking as fresh as a daisy, the two Matisse drawings, a small Vuillard propped against a book, a Paul Nash watercolour of a Suffolk landscape, a painting by a Thomas Spencer of a horse who never failed or fall'd her master, and a linen poster by Picasso for the Festival Mondial de la Jeunesse et des Etudiants pour la Paix, Berlin 1951. This last Dora coveted. It was somehow within her means and ken. A plump white dove of peace sat in the centre bearing its sprig of olive and four outward-looking profiles on each side, pink, brown, yellow, white, to represent the races of the world. Whatever way you turned the poster it looked the same except for the plump pouter-breasted dove who remained snared and which, when the white profile was facing downwards, seemed to be lying on its back. He remarked on its resemblance to Dora when she was under him or indeed at any angle and one day he gave her an identical poster which she had framed.

'For your jeunesse,' he said, 'may it never grow older.' It was still in pride of place in her dressing room and her children lay on their stomachs to look at it from every angle, and she watched them remaking her history.

Dora knew from the beginning that Tony's form of second sight was not unlike hers, though it worked to different ends. As she could see behind the lineaments of the person, towards the persona lurking in the shadows, so could he. But he made a more profitable use of the knowledge. His vision was tempered by age, knowledge and experience, what he called cynicism. He used his intuition to further his own ends. Dora watched and learnt.

She took to Tony's life and style as though she had been practising for it all her life. Indeed the two words came together for the first time under his aegis. Everything slotted into place, a place far removed from the other places she'd known and those desires she had divined through literature. She was fascinated and frightened by his energy, how he rode slipshod over everything and everyone. His way of life had a society, history, genealogy, of its own, a phantasmagoria which belonged only to those who, by sharing it, created it. It was an elaborate superstructure which rested on the surface of the city and country in which those who lived their life found themselves, where they had their own passwords, patois and style.

She was still accustomed to the sliding shy, sly, ways of the people she had grown up with, and had learnt to negotiate with, where any overstatement was an assault, and where everyone knew everyone else, not through surface presentation but through their roots. In this world in which Tony moved, everything was brazen and flaunted, everything was spoken of with exaggeration and the only provenance was either price, or the deal or who had been whose wife or husband or lover, had stayed where, was going where, was planning what rout or diversion. 'At least they say what they think. The Irish only say what they want *you* to say,' Tony said when she remarked on the blatancy and emphasis of the conversations in his house. 'And no one exaggerates like the Irish. They see a leaking tap, they talk of the Flood.'

She said, 'That's odd. People usually say that the Irish only say what you want to hear, or rather,' she screwed up her mouth exaggeratedly, 'what *one* wants to hear. And if they do, and I don't, it's because that way of talking has been the only safety net in the hazardous highwire system which has constituted their way of life for centuries. You don't say, one doesn't say, exactly what you'd like to say, to someone who might kill you and certainly has the power to do so.'

She knew there was no point in trying to compress the long savagery of the history of Ireland under English rule into cursory conversations. Tragedy became petulance under such conditions.

She wanted to tell how, if you had ears to hear and the will to listen, you could have heard a different kind of talk at a different level in any era you chose in Ireland. She thought of the historian Douglas Hyde, standing by the elbows of scythers working in the small fields of Connacht in the eighteen nineties, taking down courtly verse preserved over centuries in the secret memories of old men and women, their tongues speaking of a sunken culture; she thought fleetingly of the old story teller in Roscommon who had been taught poems from ancient manuscripts but who, as a boy at school, had a stick put around his neck and a notch in it for every word of Irish he spoke, and a beating for the number of notches; she thought of the croonings of gaels and she held her tongue.

Tony's power came from manipulation, bribery, obligation, from his knowing enough powerful people and knowing enough about powerful people; from his accommodation of the best and the worst the world had to offer. He was a fixer, a new word to Dora in her life. She thought the word meant to repair, a kind of journeyman plumber but she learnt that it was a cross between an international butler, a chaplain and a procurer to a household composed of the rich, and sometimes the famous. He gave people what they wanted which Dora later realised, even in those comparatively innocent early days, included drugs, in return for what he wanted which was not only money but diversion, prestige, escape from boredom. He did it because he enjoyed it, enjoyed having a finger in many pies, if pies was the word, which Dora doubted.

He turned a blind eye here, a beady look there and an anticipatory glance there, bought and sold, took notice of everything and did nothing hasty, but everything at amazing speed. There were always cars waiting at airports, reserved seats in the train, champagne on the aeroplane. Her wonder was that he got any painting done at all.

'That's why Ireland,' he said; 'they come to me there and there's nothing else to do. Best studio conditions in the world.'

The more she was with him the more she became fascinated by him, and the less frightened. She began to resent his assumption that she would always be available when he wanted her, which she was.

Increasingly, as he spent more time with her, she began to grow more confident and it was a short step to cultivating the first tasty feelings of contempt. He could not be such a big deal if he wanted her. She began to behave badly.

One night he took her to a ball in a house in Chelsea, not an area much in her realm, nor had she ever been to a ball. She went to the finance director and borrowed enough money to buy herself a dress and then couldn't find one she liked in any shop; she panicked and wept and told Henrietta of her distress and to her surprise Henrietta too was going to the ball. She'd have no problem with a dress, Dora thought, half a million pounds, she can go to Dior but Henrietta had no such plan, no indeedy, she was wearing the same long blue silk skirt and dark ruffled blouse she had worn to many a dance before. Not exactly inspired by this costume but, given an idea, Dora went to a Mexican shop in Lower Sloane Street and bought herself a long pleated and tucked skirt, with a white lace top that came off the shoulders. She looked at herself in her room, and went to show Henrietta.

'I look like Carmen Miranda,' she said hopelessly.

'You do a bit,' Henrietta said, 'or Belle Epoque. Your paramour will like that.'

'You mean fat drunk La Goulue,' Dora said. 'Not even Carmen.'

Her hair looked wrong and her face looked wrong, her exuberance seemed to her vulgar and when she saw Henrietta elegant and modest, waiting for her escort, she became even more depressed. When Tony arrived she flounced out ahead of him and threw herself in a heap into the front seat of the car.

'Does she know I'm coming?' Dora said, whined.

'Are you?' he said, 'such excitements.'

'She'll turn me away at the door.'

'Are you talking about Georgiana?' he said. 'Of course she knows you're coming, you're my guest.'

'She doesn't like me.'

'She doesn't know you,' he said patiently. 'She thinks of you – if she thinks of you at all, which is highly unlikely – as a friend of mine. And when she has met you, she has, if anything, liked you.'

'Oh great,' Dora said savagely. 'If anything. If anything, I don't want to go.'

'Dora,' Tony said, suddenly serious. 'Behave yourself.'

'I don't look good,' she said. 'Henrietta looked good. Henrietta,' she said in a loud voice, 'Henrietta looked upper-class.'

'Henrietta looked dull,' Tony said. 'And certainly you have never looked good. You look either innocent, or a big bold bad girl. So don't start trying to look good on me now.'

'I don't mean good good,' Dora said, 'and well you know it. And you'll nestle into this ball like a cuckoo and leave me alone hanging onto the edge.' She was only a little mollified.

They drove to Chelsea, up a narrow side street near the river. Unusually quiet and verdant the street seemed, a silence and greenness brought about, Dora realised, because one side of the street had a high red brick wall surrounding a hidden park of some kind and the other side was lined by houses with gardens. Her mouth opened as she looked at the lovely façades, the balconies, the porticoes, the french windows, the air of benignancy. Tony turned into a wider street and parked in front of a garage on which was written in enormous white letters, 'Positively No Parking Day or Night.' They walked back to the house, Dora clutching and pulling at her clothes under her coat fearful of having to shed it, functional, tweedy and unsuitable as it was. She stood in the dark shadow of the trees at the gate, shivering.

'Dora,' he said patiently, 'your clothes don't matter. They only matter if they're very grand or very eccentric and yours are very ordinary. The point is that you look like something out of Toulouse Lautrec and should point that up. All you need to do to have a success is to walk around holding your breasts, with your thighs coming out of long black stockings like white ice-cream cones, white thighs with long black suspenders.'

She looked at him quickly but he appeared to be serious. 'If I took you seriously,' she said, 'I'd be more of a fool than I am. But you are serious. That's what you're like at heart. That's what you want. You're so predictable. I said so to Henrietta. Why don't you chop your legs off at the knees so you can really get down to the right level for your proclivities.'

'You don't have to be so frightened of being sexy,' he said. 'It's what you're here for.'

She thought best how she could punish him, and thought to leave and try to catch a bus or even a taxi but he pre-empted her and grasped her arm and brought her into the house. A stairway hung with paintings cascaded upwards, divided, and flew further towards a waterfall of a chandelier hanging from an enormous cupola storeys above. In the drawing room the flowers were such as she had never seen, strange grey and white encrusted bouquets, and vegetables and flowers entwined like pictures by the Dutch masters.

Already there was a conglomeration of people gabbling and laughing and Dora saw, yes, that the clothes of the women were either very grand or eccentric and that they either looked as though they were about to sing in an opera, or act in a Regency drama or had lately come out of a cathedral crypt. Through the huge glass doors which opened onto a balcony, she could see below, tables in the garden, with swags and garlands of flowers arching over them, each table with a fat bunch of roses spilling onto the damask cloths and then the hostess was upon them, hair like a lioness, but curiously without lustre, streaming tawnily around her shoulders, and her face was tawny too, cracked and old, left out too long in the sun. A great lioness smile which, though it seemed impossibly wide, mysteriously excluded Dora. The woman kissed Dora like a moth at a flame. Instant recoil.

'Lovely, lovely Doreen,' she said. Her eyes were unsmiling; unlovely Doreen.

'Dora,' Dora said.

'Thank you,' her hostess said, 'so are you.'

Dora looked across at Tony. He was bowling out into the garden with a drink in his hand, a great grin on his face. Dora looked around. Everyone seemed to be smaller, or bigger or blonder or more limned than she was. She felt cruelly exposed, gripped by the dogma of anxiety though no one so far as she could tell was looking at her; then she didn't know whether to sulk or look animated. She moved onto the balcony and looked down at the garden and saw Henrietta crossing the garden, past the tall flowers parading in their prime, in the half-light, threading her way between the tables, determined, intent in her navy-blue habit like a grand mother superior, and come to rest in front of Tony who, surprisingly enough, and wonderfully slowly, as though he had all the time in the world, traced the outline of her lips with his tongue and then kissed her. Dora remembered that first kiss under the Hockney and was most put out, and thought how ugly Tony was, a large round bee really getting down to some common or garden pollen, Yvette Guilbert, ice-cream cones, spilling breasts, all of it spurious; Henrietta's thighs were like hockey sticks, how could he, Dora raged. There was honeysuckle on the wall beside her, it smelt of unguent and her idea of Greece and she looked obliquely towards the couple and refused to attach the importance of her mind to the back of the vision.

She thought again to try to go home and how foolish and melodramatic that might turn out to be; she clutched her drink and cursed these comparatively harmless acquaintances with oblivion, annihilation, actual bodily harm. Then, when a man she knew stopped and talked to her, she arrested the swirl of words in her head and swirled other ones through her mouth. She could not think what she was doing in this alien place, in these alien accents, aping another race. She looked at the faces around her and could see only death's heads, misplaced arrogance, a dullness of eye allied to a smugness of demeanour. When Tony came back to bring her into dinner she was sick with rage. 'I'm sick,' she said. 'Why were you kissing Henrietta? You don't even like her. Why were you kissing her?'

'Because I like kissing beautiful women. Now get your nose back in joint and go to your table.'

'I'm sick,' she said again. 'I want to go home. She's not beautiful.'

She knew people were watching them, amused.

'I'm going to vomit.' She knew she sounded like Violet Bott but she was beyond caring.

'Go to your place,' he said.

'My place?' she said flouncing. 'Who are you to tell me about my place, Monty, you get back in yours.'

He took her by the elbow with a strength that she knew better than to resist and he sat her down at the place marked by her name. She hoped he was watching her as she sulked and grew even more sullen so that the other people at the table were forced to ignore the lumpen creature in their midst and talk across her bowed head.

After dinner he came over and began to make light of things, to try to amuse her but she pulled away and he took her into the hallway and got a maid to fetch her coat and went outside with her. She was frightened not to obey him. When they came under the shadow of the trees he hit her across the face. He walked ahead, she followed, her jaw rattling and there was a row of cars up the street, some with chauffeurs leaning against them, talking and smoking. She saw him nod at one who detached himself and came over, and she saw him pass over a bank note and then somehow without argument she was in the Rolls and being driven off. As the car passed the gate, she saw him going back through the door, and beyond, in the glittering hall, under the extravagant urn of flowers she caught a glimpse of Henrietta, advancing, smiling. The car sped on.

He telephoned the next morning.

He said, 'It was the worst evening of my life.' He began to laugh. 'You were odious and downright rude. You didn't speak to any guests, you threatened to vomit which is frightfully sophisticated, were rude to your hostess, and in general gave a performance of which Sarah Bernhardt would be proud. But that's over now. We won't take any notice of that.'

'You hit me,' she said.

He said, 'You asked for it.'

'I didn't ask for it. When I want to ask for something I use my voice. I don't want to see you again. You and your palaver.'

'Come to Ireland next week,' he said, as though she hadn't spoken. 'I'm going there for a month. I've got an old biddy from Philadelphia coming to be painted and friends staying.'

'I wouldn't go to Ireland with you if you were the last man on earth,' she said. 'My face hurts. Anyway, I couldn't. I've not got holidays and the office is frantic.'

'What do you mean you've not got holidays?' he said. 'You're not still at school. Just take some time off.'

'I can't,' Dora said and indeed, the idea of taking a holiday when and as she wanted, seemed impossible, as unthinkable as say doing so at her old school, marching up to the madwoman who had been the headmistress and saying, 'I want some time off.'

'Of course you can,' Tony said and then hearing that indeed she could not, he telephoned Thomasina who was more than pleased that Dora should go to Sligo and do a story on the old biddy from Philadelphia and who, as it turned out, was an Italian princess.

'You'd be hard put to find an Italian who isn't,' Tony said.

Dora had avoided Henrietta since the ball and Henrietta too had been curiously evasive. When Dora told her that she was going to Ireland, Henrietta, Dora was thrilled to note, was not best pleased.

'We're supposed to be so busy,' she had said. 'You somehow always manage to get what you want and make it seem as though you're doing the favour.'

'So I am,' Dora said. 'I don't want to go to Ireland. I've just got away from the place. Thomasina wants a story.'

'But you want Tony,' Henrietta said.

'No I don't,' Dora said. 'It's him that wants me.'

'So it appears,' Henrietta said. Dora looked at her, wondering if something was being said that she didn't want to hear.

'Do you think he doesn't?' she said.

'Who knows what he wants?' Henrietta said. 'I don't know him as well as you do. But I know he's very devious.'

'He's not the only one who's devious,' Dora said.

'He certainly isn't,' Henrietta said. 'Anyway enjoy yourself. And don't forget to leave the rent.'

V

Dora, born and bred in Ireland, knew nothing of the country outside her native county, save what she thought she knew through instinct. Her curtailed philistine education had not been a kind one and had not included the history of her own country though she knew the dates of the Tudor Kings and the Stuarts and the Hanoverian Succession. The Irish Question for her was merely an examination one, centring on Gladstone. But because she was so deeply passionately Irish in her idea of herself, her nationality seemed to her, as is often the case with exiles, her most precious possession. And though factually, geographically, she knew so little about Ireland, her love for it made her proclaim herself its mistress and an expert on every aspect.

So nothing had prepared her for the country to which Tony introduced her. For her it was a guise of Ireland, a country she thought, that did not exist for most of the Irish who lived there, an Ireland far more beautiful than she had ever imagined, though this she found hard to admit. She hated it that the Ireland he and his friends had made their own, apparently without permission from those with rights to refuse such requisition – me, Dora thought, and the likes of me – was so much more delightful than her own, the one she knew and thought of as the only authentic Ireland. The inhabitants of this Ireland, as far as she could see, existed without drinking the lees of guilt or shame or pain that had drenched the rest of Ireland and she wanted the inhabitants of the enchanted and flowery demesne to choke on the bitter brew, as her kin had had to choke on it. She begrudged these privileged people their existence when she thought of how the tribe to whom she belonged had had to retreat from their native soil, to accommodate these interlopers and scratch out their starved existence like hens in a coop. She chose not to see that this body of people, the Anglo-Irish, moving over the surface of what she called the real Ireland, had created a world, which to the rest of the world was as Irish as any other aspect of that country; and that, whatever the pros and cons of its creation, they had sacrificed a deal to keep it in existence. Such a vision would not have squared with her anger.

They stopped at houses whose existence she had never suspected and where a way of life still obtained that she believed had vanished for ever, a world which, if she had known about it, she might have thought as fantastical as pre-revolutionary Russia. After they came off the ferry they drove down the coastline and he brought her to a house with a pale classical façade. Dora looked at it through the windscreen. It was grand, symmetrical, handsome, a passionless palace among the woods. 'Hold hard,' said Tony and they climbed out and he made her walk stealthily, so as not to be seen from the windows, to the other side of the house. She grew irritated, imagined he wanted her to look at the view, and she'd had enough of views; but when they'd reached the other side and he spun her around, the classical house had vanished and instead, a high Gothic exterior, with arched windows, curlicues, finials stood against the sky.

'Who was it said that when a nation left its old buildings moulder and moved into nasty new ones it had become barbaric?'

'You I shouldn't wonder,' Dora said.

In the course of this voyage through her native land, she was led to see that other Ireland, the Ireland of her enemies, a world she had believed to be hard and cruel, as an enchanted demesne, like the one she had glimpsed in literature, which was as closed from those who had not learnt or been given the secret passwords, as was any other secret realm. She saw too that although Tony knew the entrances to this world and the password, he did not wholly belong. He came in by the entrance reserved for the artist, and the Jewish artist to boot. Dora remembered the story of the great bard Carolan who was made to eat in the kitchen of a great house after his recital and sang there a curse that reverberated down the years.

The curse had come to pass. Many of the houses in which he sang, golden beehives beside the midden, had perished, their gardens scorified.

'Good riddance,' Dora said, when she had finished telling the story and was ashamed of herself.

'All they did in burning houses,' Tony said, 'was to get rid of their own heritage. Have you read Burke?'

'Of course I have,' Dora said. He was Irish so she must have read him.

'He wrote – he was writing about the French Revolution but he could have been writing about The Troubles, that those who make a revolution should not think it among their rights to commit waste on their inheritance, leaving those who come after them to live in a ruin instead of a habitation.'

'It wasn't their inheritance,' Dora said. 'Those big houses were excluding palaces, teasing the people, like the Raj. The English did that wherever they went, excluded the people whose country it was and made them into inferiors by creating a class above them. No Indian could go into the clubs of the Raj and no Irishman could sit in the drawing room of a big house without twisting his cap in his hand.'

Tony said, 'A lot of Indians didn't want to go into those clubs. You hardly need to spell discrimination out to me. You are missing the point. The people who lived in these houses were Irish.'

'No,' Dora said. 'They weren't. There was a poet who lived at the same time as Robert Browning, only this one was called Oscar Browning and he rushed up to Tennyson, all excited and said, "I am Browning" and Tennyson said, "You are not." Just because they claim they're Irish doesn't make them so.'

'I see I've brought the terrier along again,' Tony said. 'Just let go Dora.'

They drove through the villages of Sligo. The landscape, as it unfolded in front of her eyes, reduced her to maudlinity. She discoursed on how poverty effectively killed aesthetic appreciation, on how raising your eyes to the hills was a luxury when you had to work to keep yourself alive and your eyes were bent anxiously on the ground. He let her rave on and forbore to mention that as far as he knew she had never actually tilled the lands of Sligo. She thought of herself hurrying through the streets of London hoping to find a lost coin, the great monuments silent above her.

'The Irish don't deserve their country,' Tony said.

'Do you realise how racist you are?' Dora asked. 'You complain about the Irish as though they were a lumpen mass. You should know better than to harbour prejudice. Who do you think it was kept the light of Europe alive in the Dark Ages? Showed the stone masons in Ravenna how to make those interlocked circles and crosses? It wasn't the fucking English I can tell you, daubing themselves with wattle.'

'Woad dear,' he said mildly. 'The Irish made small cabins and nine-bean rows with wattle.'

'Woad, then. Nor was it the Jews, doing everything in their power not to get themselves noticed, they weren't out proseletysing you may be sure.'

'You think proseletysing is admirable? You blame us for not doing so? Jews don't set out to convert, horrible word for a horrible concept, or make images. That's why it's such a civilised religion, the great religion. You never presume to put a human limit on God. It's impossible to enter almost any Roman Catholic church in Ireland, for sheer ugliness. The gore is so dreadful.'

'At least we didn't leave our beautiful old buildings to rot and move into new ones. We didn't have old buildings. The Anglo-Irish had them: and left them.'

'Hardly darling,' he said. 'It's difficult to sit in a burning building. And show me a beautiful building, built by those you call the native Irish since they took over – just one.'

'Show me a beautiful poem or book written by an Anglo-Irishman,' she said. 'Anyway, Francis Johnston was an Irishman and he built the Bank of Ireland.'

'An Ulsterman?' he said. 'Two hundred years ago. A different thing entirely.'

Dora began to laugh. 'They are,' she agreed, delighted. 'They are. Where do you think they come from? Some fall-out from outer space? They're supposed to come from Scotland, the original charm school of Europe. Whatever they are, there's no Irishness about them.'

'What do you think of as Irishness?' he said.

'Jewishness,' she said. 'They're alike – impulsive, given to fantasy, addicted to associative thinking, wanting in rational discipline.'

'Sheer prejudice,' he said laughing.

'Sheer Joyce,' she said. 'He thought we were completely similar, you and me. And he thought Jews were a womanly race, who all the same despised women: clever old Joyce.'

They had reached the sea and were driving along a narrow road twisting between hedges of whin and banks of moss, studded with fuschias and set with pale boulders. The effect was of extreme natural beauty and extreme human poverty. Below, the brown sea beat at a series of craggy grey and white rocks that jutted out from the waves, and the road twisted, climbed and plunged, following a ridge connecting two headlands. To the left, clouds meandered above a moor.

A man was leaving the road to cross the moor in clothes which reflected the colour and texture of the landscape; knobbly faded tweeds, knobbly knitted wool, a hat with a feather in it. Dora stared. Leather brogues. He had a beard, a russet complexion. There was nothing about him that was not natural save his overall appearance. To Dora he might have been dressed in stainless steel; he would have blended as well or better into this background in a country where the deliberate use of natural fibres for artistic effect was something unheard of.

'There goes a fellow who's had a brush with the arts,' Tony said amiably.

'William Morris himself,' Dora said scornfully, but she had to admit that she admired his wholehearted ethnic commitment, his tramp across the moors while she was whirled by in a large car. She pondered on the people she had grown up with who wore versions of such clothes, but theirs were unspeakable, shapeless, moulded by years of stains and grease into a body language that had nothing to do with this man's confident assertion. For Sunday best, for a tramp across the hills – she stopped the train of thought: none of the people she was thinking of would ever go for a tramp across the hills. They would (as they said) have more to do. Their idea of heaven was a spin in the car, and why not – who wanted to commune with Nature when you had toiled and wrestled with the old bitch all week? She began to look carefully at the people who sat in the cars they passed on the road. They were few and far between; and women in those cars, even fewer, and always passengers. They wore bright unnatural colours – polyester pink, turquoise blue, a curious shade of fawn. Dora, in her own pale gooseberry bouclé, copied from Chanel by a chain store, saluted them. She respected their choice, their grasp of colour, though she imagined they would not respect hers.

The road led down to the shores of a lough, which lay in the circle of indigo and purple hills rimmed with gold at the edges. The water was blue and green, edged with sand the colour of ochre. The trees that grew down to the edge of the foreshore were black in their denseness with serrated gilt edges.

Tony stopped the car on the hill above the house. The long garden sliced up the valley towards the hills, spilling with a foam of roses and foliage like lace out of a vast cleavage. Sitting among the ripeness, reminding her of a ravishing illustration from Hansel and Gretel, was the house. Encrusted with light, it was painted much the same colour as her suit, but wisteria hanging from the walls and enormous climbing roses almost cloaked the colour which glimmered through in patches. She knew if she'd seen the house not long before she might have wondered when the owner was going to do something about changing the colour – she felt a slight regret for that time, so shortly gone, but so utterly vanished.

'How did you find it?'

'Twenty years ago,' he said. 'I was on my way back from staying with Desmond, and decided to explore. There'd been a fire, not in the house, but on the peninsula. No, not The Troubles,' he said seeing her look. 'An accident. Oil lamps. An old woman who had lived here by herself just became forgetful. Half the trees were gone, the other half black, and gaunt, I thought they were gone too. There'd been a boat house, its rafters were burnt, the stones were black, the garden was derelict, but I bought it immediately. The walls were black but you could still see the colour. I found tins of it in the shed and re-painted it. I dread trying to get it again. It's a kind of rash colour – John Betjeman wrote a poem about it, it moved him so much, all about cucumber sandwiches and gooseberry fool, and Edwardian winceyette knickers.'

'Directoire we call them in the trade,' Dora said.

Tony looked at her and began to put his hand up her thigh; and to stop him scandalising Sligo she said hastily, 'How do you mean, a rash? Like scarlet fever or shingles?'

'A wash,' he said, 'a wash, not a rash.'

'Oh I see. Like bleu de travail? As green as it's blue.'

'Blue de what?' Tony said.

'Bleu de travail, like in France, workman's uniforms. . . .' Dora lost her nerve.

'Oh bleu de travail, I see yes. That's very Irish, as green as that's blue.'

'It isn't Irish at all,' she said giving him a thump, 'it shows how removed you live from the world. It's a variation on a famous fashion statement. You know nothing from nothing.'

When they drew up outside the door, on gravel that was uniform in size and colour, like burnished hail, two women came down the steps in a flurry of flowered pinafores and from around the corner a man with a pair of shears lurched into view, like an extra in a bucolic French film. They greeted Tony with cries, murmurs of pleasure and welcome and Dora was borne along, in a welter of good-will, up to a room with pink roses on a polished dressing-table and a bed with a painted bedhead spilling with roses and birds.

The young woman who showed Dora to her room was Kathleen, the daughter of Tony's housekeeper, Josie the queen of the house. Dora already knew of her from Tony, her brilliance at cooking, her threats and tantrums, her sweetness of nature when she wasn't in a rage.

She had arrived at the same time as the house, with the house, a widowed woman with three young children, who had long since grown up. Only Kathleen her daughter still remained in Sligo. At certain arbitrary moments, Josie threatened she would go and live with Kathleen and her husband, in their new modern house in the nearest town.

'Of course she hasn't a notion of leaving,' Tony said, 'it's just a way of making sure that I realise how indispensable she is, her way of keeping me under threat.'

'But she is indispensable,' Dora said.

'Nothing and no one is indispensable,' Tony said. 'If Josie leaves then I will get someone else or dispense with the house.'

As Kathleen, a woman not much older than she but already mother to three children, unpacked Dora's suitcases she learnt that she lived in a housing estate in a small town near Shannaglish and when Mr Flaxmeyer returned to the Big House, Kathleen came to help her mother.

'I miss the wee ones,' Kathleen said, 'but I see them at night.'

'Who looks after them during the day?' Dora asked.

'My husband,' Kathleen said. 'He runs a taxi business but there's no call for taxis. He had a job in a carpet factory but it closed. He comes to fetch me in the evenings with the children in the back. It's a great soothener for them, by the time we're home, they're well asleep.'

'Don't you get very tired?' Dora asked. She saw as she looked around the room a bunch of tiny yellow flowers in a little round green pot, their colour so minor, so modest that it made her tone down her voice.

'It's a rest for me to be here,' Kathleen said. 'It's a great change. We can be very busy mind, when there might be ten or twelve people staying, and as many again for the dinner and all the nicest people you could hope to meet.'

'Have any of the others arrived yet?' Dora asked.

'There's ones coming on Friday,' Kathleen said, 'but till then you're on your lone. Are you getting your likeness painted?'

'No,' Dora said, 'but I'm writing about someone who is.'

Kathleen looked at her, trying to place her in the scheme of things. She held up Dora's nightdresses and murmured in admiration. Dora had bought them on borrowed money the day after Tony had asked her to Ireland. She wanted to give one to Kathleen, in a rush of love but forbore. She bathed and changed and brushed and pomaded and then roseate, fat and scented as one of Tony's little Weymss' pigs, trotted along the corridor for an explore before going down to find him.

It was like walking through a casual litter of time. Everywhere there were delectable objects, pictures hanging frame to frame, furniture with all the surfaces covered, more crowded even than in London, and Dora had thought that prodigal. The atmosphere had a different quality here, the rooms and passages were imbued with exhalations of earlier history, the objects frail as though pulled back from the edge of decay. She went down a small flight of stairs beyond a door with glazed panels, its white paint peeling, and found herself in a back hall. A large red setter full of good-will came wriggling on its stomach across the flagged floor. The hall was rimmed with thick coats and boots, baskets and benches and creels of woods and turf and horned trophies on the walls. The largest of these reminded Dora of an elk's head she had once seen in a house near her parents' house, and she climbed onto a bench the better to look at the horrible ornament. As she peered up, it slowly toppled forward, a frowsty hairy avalanche with a faintly sulphurous smell and she leaned back, caught it and remained transfixed, in an absurd permanence with the thing poised above her head so that she looked like an incipient Bottom or a duped Salome. A door at the other end of the hall swung open and Kathleen put her head around it.

'Are you lost?' she asked.

'Not lost,' Dora said, 'but I'm a bit stuck.'

'Bring her on in,' Josie called.

Kathleen came down the hall. In her white apron she was small, neat, vivacious. She was quite unperturbed. 'They're desperate things,' she said, 'big dead heads looking down at you and them here from before the flood. Give it here and we'll get Packy to put it up again in the morning.' Together she and Dora levered the disintegrating head to the floor.

As she followed Kathleen into the kitchen Dora saw that the red setter was wriggling towards the head with a certain ecstatic intensity, but she kept her counsel.

Except for a big white gleaming Aga and electric ovens built into arched alcoves the kitchen appeared to have been quite unchanged for a hundred years. It could have come out of an illustration from Brobdingnag or the cellars of the Escorial. A wood and wire meat larder hung high in the ceiling, alongside dark steel gibbets and iron racks. The top half of the vast areas of walls were painted an institutional green and cream and where the paint finished green tiles took over. A glade of chains hung from the ceiling and hooks swayed at their ends, and trivets, and curious tripod trays, brass and copper coil lamps with vaseline glass globes, and circled sconces of candles. Massive cupboards with wire fronts lined one wall, dressers filled with bowls and plates and mugs another and a maze of pipes criss-crossed and swivelled and back-tracked at every extremity. Alongside the cookers, on each side of the alcoves, were slate shelves ranged with glazed crocks, and griddles, pans, and above in black Roman letters a legend warned 'Waste not want not.'

Josie was at the stove stirring. Behind her on a central block with deep drawers were bowls, boards, vegetables, the gizzards and giblets of fowl, onion skins. On another block some distance away at right angles were fruit cakes, meringues, and bowls of raspberries and strawberries, a jug of cream.

'One of them old heads nearly brained her,' Kathleen said.

Josie made commiserating noises. 'That's a lovely dress you have on you,' Kathleen said. Dora plucked at the dress. They were smiling at her with such sweetness that Dora who had just been about to say, this old thing, blushed, stopped and turned around and around slowly the better to be admired.

'I got it in London,' she said. 'Do you think it's all right?'

'God, it's great style,' Kathleen said.

'The belt needs tying, right.' Josie said. Dora stood obediently while Josie tied the knot at the back.

'Do you love cooking?' Dora asked her.

'Oh Jaysus, do I love cooking she asks.' Josie tightened the knot. 'I hate it. But what am I to do. There's nobody else would work in a shanty like this. I'm going to live with Kathleen.'

'Don't listen to her,' Kathleen said. 'She loves every stone, and what would she do in my house after this? She'd eat her heart out. Anyway we'd mow each other.'

Josie laughed. 'It's the God's truth,' she said.

Dora looked around the kitchen and at the women and sat down.

'Would you like a cup of something?' Josie asked.

'I'll wait for a drink,' Dora said. The two women discussed dinner, the day's affairs and Dora felt at home. She was not romantic, our Dora, though she was frequently misguided and even soft-hearted and she did not think a hard and primitive life was more virtuous than a soft and sophisticated one, nor that being in the kitchen or backstage was preferable to being in the drawing room or centre-stage. What did seem to be true was that occupying the front of place seemed inevitably to fill the occupier with a stout self-importance. In Josie's and Kathleen's kitchen Dora felt the existence of something that was lacking in the drawing room, something obscure and undignified, and ready to be disregarded in her own life, but something that was, all the same, necessary and even perhaps precious. None of the people habitually in Tony's drawing room would have thanked Josie or Kathleen for these commodities. She knew as she sat listening to them talk, that she was listening to the sound of good women, women with compassion, with that imaginative and tender consciousness of another's condition, and that these were women who believed in fidelity at whatever cost. And the more she listened, the more she discerned the quality of innocence and knew that to recognise it she must have lost it.

'Do you do much cooking yourself?' Kathleen asked. She was laying up a coffee tray for two.

'I don't,' Dora said. 'I would love to do more. I love food, the taste of food, I hate tricked-up food, and different tastes all together.'

She stopped in case Josie was of the pineapple and gammon, or raspberry and mutton school of cooking.

'So do I,' Josie said. 'I'm a plain cook. I can't be bothered with all that.'

'Don't listen to her,' Kathleen said. 'Wait till you see.'

Tony came into the kitchen. He looked less glossy, easier, as though accommodating the spirit of the house. As he talked to Josie and dipped his finger in the sauce on the Aga, it became apparent to Dora that Josie loved him.

'Come on,' he said. 'I want to show you around before dinner.'

Dora rolled her eyes conspiratorially at the women and followed him out to the other side of the door.

In the drawing room he opened a bottle of champagne and carrying their glasses they went into the garden, brushing past shrubs that shook out a waft of perfume.

'Elaeagnus,' he said. 'Wonderful smell. A wedding or a death. I try to grow everything that smells delicious . . . tobacco plants, stocks, daphne.'

'Tobacco?' she said. 'You can't mean it.'

'It doesn't smell like someone who's been smoking, ninny,' he said. 'Here, smell.'

The white faces of the flowers magnified and glimmered in the dusk.

'Champagne and smell,' Dora said, 'and Sligo and me.'

'Well don't mind me,' he said. 'I only live here.'

They walked through the garden and she was enchanted by its diversions, by the decorum of the black yew-lined paths that led to the small gardens with tumultuous fountains, garlanded urns, lichened statues surrounded by weeping silver trees.

'Everywhere you live,' she said, 'is full of secret places.'

'I inherited it,' Tony said. 'When we cut away the undergrowth the bones were there. I have a great respect for my predecessors. They carried most of these plants on the packet from England and up here by train. I found notebooks in the house, albums, photographs of the garden, and did it as I think it once was or was meant to be.'

She felt a surge of rage that he should have been here first. He had no right to it. She turned her back on the dark yew and looked down to where the water glinted between the green trees and the heather, and thought that there was nothing she wanted more than this house and everything in it. She turned back towards Tony, leaning against an urn surrounded by some tall plant with a silvery sheen that matched the low glint of the lough and saw him watching her, noting her expression. Across the garden came a muffled note and another and another, mysterious, resonant, unreasonable.

'It's the bleeding Cherry Orchard,' she said.

'The gong for dinner,' he said, and they went back to the house.

Dora recognised as she ate that Josie's cooking was of a quality other than she had known. After the meal they went into the library and Kathleen brought in coffee and said goodnight. Dora was in a welter of well-being.

'She's so lovely,' she said sitting down suddenly on a chair. 'She has the most beautiful face. A real Irish face.'

'Nicely fuddled,' Tony said. 'Time for bed.'

'She's never,' Dora said. 'She looked steady enough to me.'

'Not her, you,' Tony said.

'It *is* time for bed,' Dora said and stood up. She was indeed fuddled and she made an ardent prayer to herself not to bump or ricochet like something out of a bad comedy. She was gracious in speech as she threaded her way to the door, hoping to divert him, thanking him for the delicious dinner.

'One has enjoyed it so much,' she said. 'See, not fuddled, I didn't say you.'

'You don't need to tell me I enjoyed it,' he said. 'You say I enjoyed it in this case, if that is indeed the case. Come over here and kiss me.'

'It is the case,' she said. 'But I'm trying to divert you.'

'Dora,' he said, not moving, 'you have been diverting me since I met you. Come over here.'

'No,' she said. 'I don't feel at all well. I might vomit again like that other night.' She managed to walk straight to the door and went down the hall carefully, tripped over the red setter, which had, she noticed, a lot of shaggy hair around its mouth and a certain sulphurous smell. She negotiated the stairs and fell onto the bed with relief. After a while she got up, drank great quantities of water and peed great quantities and began to feel more sloshed but less drunk. She climbed into bed, happy and at home, wishing that the way of life of this night might be hers without paying any price for it.

She thought of the barrenness of the west of Ireland, of the talent left mouldering with no possibility of negotiations with the future, and was thankful that she had fled such places. By leaving, by crossing to the other side, she had stepped into a place where people took negotiations with their future for granted, where possibilities were part of their transactions with life and where prospects were a matter of forseeable options rather than happenstance. In her new world good fortune meant wealth, innocence was only cupidity, and fidelity was a matter for constant negotiation.

She drifted off into sleep well pleased with her line of thought, and the feeling that the lines were still open to that lunatic in her glass cradle, so that when she felt his hands on her, between her thighs, she was at first bewildered and then once she had fought herself awake, so violent that she was out of the bed and across the room in an instant. She felt like Mrs Rochester on the edge of the parapet, insane, dishevelled. Tony was at first astonished, then amused, then angry. She saw again the steel glitter of his temper.

'I won't,' she said. 'I don't want to.'

'I'm not interested in what you think you want,' he said. 'But in God's name why not?'

'I won't,' she said, in an adamantine rage. 'I don't want to.' She was in tears. 'That's reason enough.'

'No it's not,' he said. His eyes were like pitch.

'Josie and Kathleen might hear,' she said.

'Listen, you stupid bitch,' he said, 'you never make any noise anyway. You're like a deaf mute, it's like fucking a koala bear. Kathleen goes home at night and Josie sleeps in her rooms at the very back of the house. She wouldn't hear you if you were screaming blue murder. Which you will do if you don't stop this nonsense. They know you're with me if that's your problem. Do you think they think you're here for the scenery? Such utter nonsense.' But it wasn't nonsense to Dora who evaded his angry lunges and sped out of the door and down the passages into the flagged hall where moonlight streamed through the fanlight over the door. She stood holding her breath, listening for his pursuit and heard him come stealthily into the passage above. The red setter began to bark and Packy the gardener appeared from the back of the house with a strange brown overall wrapped around his person, perhaps as protection against the goings-on of the night. The dog ran from behind, bounded up the stairs, just as Tony started down and tripped him up, so that Tony slid down the steps, the dog barking joyously. Dora, in a state of nervous hysteria, felt laughter surging up and the more she tried to suppress it the more it curled out like smoke from a bag. Tony sat on the stairs and looked down at Packy.

'We're going for a walk in the garden,' he said; and Packy without speaking went back through the door to the flagged passage. The dog looked at Tony and then thinking the better of it followed Packy. Dora thought to do the same but Tony had risen and turned and was walking back up the stairs. She gauged, from the set and sound of his footsteps, the intensity of his rage. She pulled open the big front door and went outside. The smell of the garden was the more astonishing in the stillness and the roses were moon-watered down, leached of colour, so that they glimmered pale in the moonlight, as though a line-up of Edwardian barmaids had been turned into a Quaker choir by a trick of the light.

She walked down the paths, dark and silver as the moon fell, and down the steps and down to the shore of the lough. She put her foot in the water, felt its cold pierce the skin as though slicing it and walked in till the water came over her ankles, and stood there shivering, as if doing penance, as though the water might shrive her, and thinking garbled thoughts of the days when Nora had waded along the shores of her childhood, looking for fool's gold, submerged treasure, with the soft, cold water lapping her ankles. She felt repentant, but only in a certain way and one that stopped her doing anything about it, for the blow across her face, on the Chelsea night, was throbbing still. She shivered. Considering it was summer, the water was freezing, and she could see her feet under the immaculate quavery water, like flat sea creatures, waiting for the move from the attachment above. She waded out of the water and felt the warmth of the earth and began to think that perhaps he had a right to be angry and she had a right to be punished. She was reneging on the contract between them.

He hadn't just brought her here halfway across Ireland for the good of her health or the scenery. She went back up and into the house resolved to have done with her resentment, her ridiculous anger and accommodating superstition but she knew better than to go near his room until his anger had simmered down. She crept along the passage and into her bed and thought, as she went to sleep, how delightful a companion she would contrive to be on the morrow.

She was awakened by Josie drawing her curtains and bringing her breakfast on a green and gothick, wood and wicker tray with legs that made it stand proud of the bed. It was a still-life of starched linen and sprigged china, with tiny slivers of toast in a muffin dish, an egg in an egg cup under a small flowered cosy, a coffee pot painted with roses, butter and marmalade in little china pots, orange slices under a dome, a frill of buds of pinks in a glass vase. Josie watched Dora's reaction with pleasure. 'It was Mrs Pell from New York who showed me how to set it up at first,' she said. 'She brought me the breakfast set and one every time since. They come from Tiffany's, the place in the film.'

'The tray cloth is wonderful too,' Dora said.

'I embroidered that myself,' Josie said. She was as proud of her transient installation of a breakfast tray as Tony was of his house or any of his paintings and with as good reason. Dora looked at her, her flowered cross-over apron tied tightly over her body, and saw, without irony, the representative of a timeless line of unsung artists who gave their genius and their generosity to beautify and aggrandise the lives of others.

'It's so perfect Josie,' Dora said, 'that I'm almost afraid to disturb it.'

'It's what it's there for, to be disturbed,' Josie said. 'You eat up.'

She stood smiling at Dora and Dora thanked her god of superstition and her saints of yore and gore that there was no sign of Tony's occupation in the room. She could not have looked into that good face if she had made love all night to a man who not only wasn't her husband, but a man whom Josie loved. To Josie, she knew, she would never be a rival or a danger, but she might well be an occasion of sin.

She knew full well that Tony had had countless women and how and when he'd made it with them, in his bed or theirs, this room or that, was none of her business, or not for the moment. But her own behaviour was her business and she would not be a whore, which was what she would be here. Other ages and other tongues had fancy euphemistic names: poule de luxe, just good friends, companion, mistress, grande horizontale, courtesan, but in this old Ireland where Josie and her parents lived, if you went to bed with someone to whom you were not married you were a whore, and she knew she would be entered into the lists under that subscription.

It was not just Josie's good opinion that she hoped to earn and keep, and not only because Josie and Kathleen were representatives of the people among whom she had spent most of her life though that way of life was no longer relevant to her. It was because their world was so open to bruising and corruption, was so liable to disappear, and she did not wish to add to the decay. And perhaps also, it was because when she set foot in Ireland, like it or lump it, the creature in the glass coffin stirred and opened one eye and watched. She was outside the reach of that vision in England but in Ireland she was subject to its survey. Josie propped the pillows up behind Dora, and when she had gone Dora plundered the felicitous tray with delight. She thought of the kitchen of her childhood, and remembered Ellen, their own maidservant, a left-over from her grandparents' days, an unhappy blighted woman put into service when she was twelve with no other future. She had set about making an accomplice of Dora from an early age, and the fear that her parents would hate her if they knew how she had to betray them every time Ellen made a joke at their expense, how she had to smile to keep Ellen happy, haunted her and coloured her relationships with them. Iris, her sister, would have no truck with Ellen and Dora found her sister's moral courage and indeed physical courage in resisting Ellen both enviable and unattainable. She had been frightened of it, and fled, even now, the thought of it. The very waft of such memory made her want to cram something into her mouth. Silly Dora, she thought as she nibbled at the toast, you are a sentimentalist who will get fat. You do not want to have any truck with women in kitchens, fidelitas or innocence be damned, Ellen lurks in there alongside bleeding lumps of meat and dead chickens with their necks singed, and dead birds swinging from the gibbets, and fish with staring eyes, and sticky dough and clammy pastry and washing up. You will choose.Tony's drawing room is in another time, where money is the sacrament, and the surface of things is the religion, and the only immorality is bad taste and being boring, where staying in the same place for your lifetime is not a matter of continuity but an admission of defeat, of being left behind.

She spread her marmalade with a silver spoon, stuck it in her mouth, and thought of her parents. They might as well have been in a different age and a different country as in the here and now, and not so far away either.

There was nothing to prevent her, their daughter, driving across the little lanes of Ireland and arriving at their doorstep but there were no means by which she could drive there and remain the person she was choosing to become. She put her tray carefully to one side of the bed and climbed from its deep lace-trimmed sheets and went into the bathroom, where wisteria clouded the window.

Whilst she was in the bath under a rime of foam Tony came in, silent, his dressing gown open. Safe in her own resolves and Josie's benediction, she lifted her arms out of the water in greeting, the foam falling away like the white wings on the dove and he reached towards her and yanked her by the hair out of the bath. She felt the pain of her scalp, her hair tearing as he slung her against the door of the bedroom so that it swung open, and they both fell inwards. He disengaged himself and hauled her, by her feet, face downwards, her arms scraping the furniture, her nails gathering a horrid fur as she tried to crawl away, clawing at the carpet but she could get no purchase. She was mute as she fought, determined not to make a sound lest Josie or Kathleen hear and misinterpret or, worse, run in to the rescue and find her naked, dripping and bleeding, being reversed like a wheelbarrow across the floor. He crashed her onto the bed and as she struck it she felt the coffee pot crack, felt the scalding heat of the coffee, felt the cup crush under her spine, the slivers of china spike her skin, heard the arches of the tray splinter under their locked weight, tasted the bilious egg as the thin vomit rose in her throat. He wedged her under him, she thought what would she tell Josie, how could she explain the destruction to Josie, and as the breakages went on, the crashing, the splintering, the ruination of her still-life, she cried for the journey she had made, the journeys she could no longer make, for the place she found herself in, and above all for the loss of the gift of the breakfast.

THREE
Select Amusements

I

Dora put down her pen. It seemed a long time ago and Tony would be no more than a memory, were it not for the living fact of Thomas. She missed her children with a terrible pang and was, for a moment, shaken by a knowledge of her own mendacity in leaving them even for an instant. In doing so she exposed them to the vigilant malignance of Fate, while she tried to escape the fierce addiction of infatuation, and she thought she must try to get the first plane off the island in the morning. She tried to telephone England but it was impossible and after a while she gave up and went out of the hotel room and down to the beach, again.

She felt surfeited by her own selective memory. No matter what routes you took through your own past, you were never going to get it right. What was appalling, Dora thought, was what a good gloss she put on her own bad behaviour. There was something indecent about dragging in decency to justify your own expediency. The fact is, she said, you were, are, a coward, someone who does not fulfil the terms of a contract, who cloaks her twists and turns with fine words, who wriggles on the point of a pin, canting about morality and choices and childhood innocence.

She realised she was muttering as she walked and knew that to the people on the beach she must appear increasingly eccentric, except of course to the importunate room-service boy who was waiting for her, by the bamboo grove. To him she must appear increasingly in need of sexual solace. She knew all she had to do to be rid of his overtures was to complain to the manager, but to do so might mean he would lose his job. She would be leaving here soon enough, he would not get his job back. She thought, I will tell him that I am going to report him if he comes near me other than in the course of work. After that it will be his choice. She felt she had arrived at a solution. She turned and walked a long way up in the opposite direction and rounded a spit of land.

She waded into the water, a different texture and a different temperature from that at Tony's house or from that which lapped the high green mound of the graveyard at home – at her parents' house, she corrected herself – where she had waded as a child, and where she still waded when she returned, as though checking in, to make sure that there was still a possibility of getting back. She heard someone calling, Miss Miss, and she turned round and a man was running towards her. She was furious and began to stride out into the water and he called more urgently and she saw coming towards her out of nowhere a great curling wave that lifted her and smashed her down and lifted her again; panic-stricken, she opened her mouth to scream but the wave lifted her again, the noise of the water covered her and swept her under, and as she struggled and thrashed she knew she was drowning, but when she came to her senses she was lying on the beach with brine eating into some cut on her face. She moved her bruised arms and touched her cheekbones. She felt embarrassed, an absurd clumsy woman, and, refusing the help of the solicitous man who had tried to warn her, she got to her feet and fell down again. She looked at the sea lying placidly off the white beach and saw another huge wave gathering force out below the spit, saw it rear and break and crash and draw back and crash again and thought herself lucky to be alive. She picked herself up and hobbled to the shade of a grove, the man walking beside her trying to help. In the grove they were joined by children and a woman who hovered anxiously, and offered her a tin mug of water but Dora refused it, grateful but afraid to drink it. Eventually they left. She thought that the skin on her face must be grazed, but there seemed to be no wound as far as she could feel, no gushing of blood. She got up carefully, testing her ankle, and went back to the hotel dreading to pass the interested parties on the beach, but by the time she got back the sun was high and the beach was empty.

Inside her room she swabbed and dabbed and the damage was far less than she'd feared though she knew the next day she might be covered in green bruises. She lay down and tried to rest but her face hurt and she got up and went back to her desk and returned to Sligo. Or thereabouts.

She telephoned from a public telephone in the hall of a small hotel in Shannaglish where Eddie, Kathleen's husband had driven her. There was a public bar just through the door and two men propping the bar were delighted by the diversion of Dora's appearance. There appeared to be no one in charge of either the bar or the hotel. After a few rings her mother answered. 'Who is it?' she asked.

Dora told her.

'Who?' her mother said, her voice rising.

Dora was beginning to panic. What name could she say? 'Your daughter,' she shouted. One of the men tiptoed behind the bar and pulled himself a Guinness with elaborate stealth so as not to miss a word. She lowered her voice, and whispered so that her mother couldn't hear either.

'Remember, the lump who wouldn't wash up? Who kept bringing flowers into the house,' and then, louder: 'It's Dora.'

There was a pause. The men moved nearer towards her end of the bar. 'I didn't hear,' her mother said. 'I didn't know it was you. Where are you?'

'I'm in Dublin,' Dora lied. She wasn't going to break old habits now.

'You're in Ireland?' she said. 'What brought you over? Are you coming home?'

What brought me over, Dora thought, well might you ask and as to who, better not to know. She thought of Tony and her mother, their mutual incomprehension should they meet, the strain it would cause her mother who found any new encounter a source of terror. And the sheer enormity of the scale of knowledge that Tony would glean about her from even the most fleeting moment with her parents on her home ground was unthinkable, so she stopped the thought. Another contingent one surged in. Tony might ring Thomasina to find her home address and follow her. She felt panic stirring in her. 'I'll ring you back,' she said to her mother. 'I've run out of money. Don't go away.' She rang the operator and asked for London. The operator was astonished. 'London,' she said. 'You'll need a fair bit of change by you, a pound or more.'

'I'll have to go and find it,' she said. 'Don't go away.'

'I'll hardly,' the operator said. 'I'm rooted here for the day.'

Dora went down the hall to try to find someone who could help and went through a door into a kitchen. Deserted. Then though she had resolved at all costs not to appeal to the audience in the bar she decided that the stakes were too high and went in there.

'It's change you're wanting,' one of the men said. He went round to the back of the bar, rang open the till and gave her a handful of change. He put the pound note Dora gave him in return into his pocket. Strange book-keeping she thought. She dialled the operator again and after a long delay the woman came back on the line. 'I had to go after all,' she said, 'but I'm back now. So. Hold on tight till I try to connect you and have the pound and half crown ready.'

Dora held the receiver tight. She heard the office switchboard ring and the brisk voice of Renee at the other end. The Irish operator said, 'Are you Holborn oh two oh two?'

'We are,' Renee sang out. 'Who did you want to speak to?'

'I don't want to speak to anyone,' the operator began and Dora called down the phone, 'Renee I want to speak to the editor,' and the operator said affronted, 'She can't hear you, you wait till you have the money in.'

'Well, when can I put it in?' Dora screamed and the men in the bar came and stood in the doorway, their drinks in their hands, well pleased by the cabaret.

'Put it in now,' the operator said, 'and then press button A,' and Dora set about inserting coin after coin after coin every second one of which rolled or stuck or dropped to the floor and did everything but go into the slot. Finally she was through to Renee. 'I'm in Ireland,' she shouted. 'Renee if I get cut off will you ring me back.' 'Sorry,' Renee trilled. 'Who did you wish to speak to?'

'To the editor,' Dora shouted, 'or her secretary. Tell her it's Dora and I'm in Ireland with no money for the phone.'

She heard the extension ring and Henrietta picked it up, thank God for Henrietta, for all she had been so cross. Dora was stuttering with angst. Henrietta was soothing. 'We'll ring you back if you get cut off,' she said and Dora shouted, 'You can't, I'm not at Tony's, I've left Tony,' and Henrietta said, 'Oh,' followed by 'Oh really,' and 'Well where are you?' Dora realised that there was no identification of any kind on or about the telephone. 'What's the number here?' she asked the man who had taken the money. 'It's . . .' he stopped. 'Sure I know it as well as I know my own,' he said. He appealed to his companion. 'What's the number on that yoke?' 'Isn't it three four eight?' the man asked. 'No, that's my own in the house, it's two six three here, I think, hold on till I ask the wife.' Dora had given up. 'Is Thomasina in?' she shouted.

'Hold on,' Henrietta said. 'I'll put you through to her.'

When Dora heard Thomasina's voice she was immediately transported to a place where things worked and plans could be made, where life was not a series of arbitrary uncontrollable happenings and people you had tried to love did not beat your heart into a pulp. Never mind your body.

Thomasina's deep round voice with its undertones of priorities and humour calmed Dora, so that she thought she might somehow get back to firm ground.

'Thomasina, it's Dora.'

'Darling,' Thomasina said. 'Are you having a lovely time? How is Tony?'

'I'm ringing about that,' Dora said, and the operator interrupted, 'Your time is up please insert more money,' and Dora shouted, 'I haven't got the change,' and Thomasina said, 'We'll ring you back.' Dora shouted, desperate, 'I'm not at Tony's,' and a woman came from behind the bar holding out a pile of change; Dora pushed it in without a hitch and said, 'Thomasina, Thomasina, I have to go and see my mother, she's not well. But I don't want Tony to join me there, so if by chance he rings would you please not give my address or number. Or even say where I am.'

There was a silence. Thomasina asked, 'Are you all right Dora? You're not doing anything rash?' Dora said, 'No, not at all, but it wouldn't do at all for him to visit me at home. My parents wouldn't understand.'

Thomasina said, 'I'll have to tell him why I can't give it to him. He'll know I know where you are.'

'What will you say?' Dora asked.

'Well that you asked me not to, you fool,' Thomasina said. Dora was silent. 'Are you sure you're all right Dora?' Thomasina asked and then as though remembering, 'I'm so sorry about your mother.'

'She's not very ill,' Dora said, superstition making her wince at thus using her mother. She knew from experience that if she said someone was ill who was not, then more often than not, that person became ill within days. Perhaps her mother was a bit ill already. God knows she sounded as though both oars weren't in the water. Then it wouldn't count.

'I see,' Thomasina said, in the voice of one who sees too much. 'Good. Well, keep in touch. Let me know what's happening. What's the Queen of Philadelphia like?'

'He hadn't arrived,' Dora said. 'Nor his wife,' remembering that she had gone to Tony's house ostensibly to write a story about her for Thomasina.

'Watch it Dora,' Thomasina said, and the operator said, regret in her voice, 'Your time is up. Do you want to go on with the call?'

Dora made truncated goodbyes and went into the bar to pay back and thank the woman who had come to her rescue. The men at the bar nodded and smiled, glad to have been in on the whole story and, to their obvious pleasure, Dora got more change to continue the saga. She went back to the phone and rang her mother.

This time her mother's voice sounded even more vague. Dora wondered if something really was wrong and then dismissed the idea. Her mother never got ill. She got what she called bad heads but rarely took to her bed except when she was sulking, when the whole house would be hushed.

'Is that you, Mother?' her mother asked. Dora began to laugh.

'That's my line,' she said.

Her mother said, 'I don't know what's wrong with me. I can't remember anything.' And then in her usual voice, 'I wish you were coming home today.' This was unlike her. She never voiced any wishes. Dora wished she would, it would be a way towards the hidden creature behind the wall.

'I don't know what's wrong with your father,' her mother said. 'He's in a filthy temper. If he knew you were coming it might sweeten him up, if anything could.'

There was a silence. Complain. Complain, it had always been like this, the eternal declension, an endless series of complaints, mute, spoken, gestured. Complaint, the action of complaining, an expression of grief, an utterance of grievance against, a statement of injustice suffered, a bloody whining habitual noise made by my mother, complaint compliance pliance pliant, and I've got the habit too, lying below the skin of the tongue, articulate, complete, just waiting for any kind of aggravation to be released.

Dora stared at her reflection in the little foxed glass on the wall.

'He only loves you.'

Surely that couldn't be what she had just heard. Surely not.

'What?' Dora said, startled out of her scrutiny.

Her mother said, 'You're the only one he loves.'

She heard the statement with incredulity. It was what she had been waiting to hear all her life; and waiting for it to be uttered by this person. That it should even have been said was a reversal of all that was possible and natural. Dora's world rocked on its hinges, the scaffolding began to pull away. To come to some kind of accommodation with what had just been said, to keep the balance, to try to get back to the perpendicular, to pay her back in some wise for the painful anomaly, to try to ease the wrench in her head that it must have cost her, Dora extemporised. She listened to what she was going to say.

'That's not true,' she said. 'He loves only you. You're the one he loves.'

Neither of us has ever spoken of love before, Dora thought. Christ what's happening here?

There was a silence. A silence that was not full of question, reproach, complaint. The first full silence, it seemed to Dora, that she had ever heard from her mother.

She asked the first real question: 'Is that true?'

It seemed to Dora that there was no target for the question to land on, or that she had no equipment for receiving such questions from a woman who had brought her up never to ask them. Her world rocked again, getting up power. She had told her mother he loved her, knowing profoundly as she said it, that it was a lie, the consolation prize from the victor to the vanquished. *He* must love her, Dora, far more than anyone else and that was the first rule. If she had thought, as she told it, of the consequence of the lie, she would have said it could not affect her. All the same, as she had said it, she had made a little obeisance to her silvered foxed reflection in the chrome-framed mirror, an obeisance to placate the furies, to protect her from sinning in the name of love, from taking love in vain. But, as she listened to her mother's silence, it was as though in some deep tunnel, in a Hamelin she had never known, a great door had thudded shut and a child was incarcerated for ever. She knew what she had told her mother was indeed true.

'Yes,' Dora said. 'He loves us all, because he has to. But he loves only you for no reason at all.' There was a silence at the other end. Her mother said, 'When will you be home?' but as Dora explained that she would ring from the station, she could hear that her mother was no longer listening. She put down the phone, the tears tripping her and the reverberations of what had been said seemed to echo around the little phone box. The three people in the bar were talking animatedly about the weather. She saluted their delicacy and gave the woman money for the change.

She went outside and spoke to Eddie who had taxied her thus far. There was a train from Sligo to Dublin and thence she might catch a train to the north. Kathleen's husband had been a source of enlightenment on the journey and had none of Kathleen's inhibitions about working out Dora's position in the hierarchy. If she was leaving she was not permanent. He was thus wonderfully indiscreet. Dora learnt of the many women who came to the house with Tony, sometimes the same ones, some different, year after year. Mr Flaxmeyer juggled it all. Some, Eddie said, were dying alive about him and would have married him the morrow, and Josie wished he would marry so he would come and settle in Ireland and then there would be children.

'Would Josie like to have babies and children there?' Dora said. 'I thought she wanted to retire.'

'That's what would keep her,' he said. 'Wee ones. Are you married yourself miss?'

'I'm not,' she said. 'Though I must say I would love children.' It was her day for lying to please people and finding out the truth in so doing.

'There's nothing to beat them,' he said. 'But they're a drain in the pocket, mind.'

He dropped her at the station, and she found she had an hour to wait for the train. Whether it would get in to Dublin in time to catch the Belfast connection was not, the station master said, something he would care to hazard a guess about. She sat on a seat on the empty platform. After half an hour a long train pulled in. She watched it. It was surely uncommonly long for a local train but it was not yet time for the Dublin train. There was no one on the platform whom she could consult. The train gave a jerk and the engine started up and in a sudden spurt of desperation Dora climbed in and ran along the empty carriages. The engine stopped again with a whistle. She found a man in a corner of one of the carriages gazing out at the empty platform.

'Could this possibly be the Dublin train?' Dora asked.

He brooded for a while. Dora thought to shake him till he rattled and then thought it might be counter-productive.

'I take it to be,' he said, and she rushed out and collected her bags and rushed back in. The train settled itself on the tracks like a tortoise. After twenty minutes people began to trickle onto the train. It left ten minutes late and Dora settled herself for the journey ahead.

II

Dora knew of her mother's life just before her time, through the relics of legend, and photographs taken before some party. In these she had worn a long dress with narrow straps that bit slightly into the round flesh of her bare shoulders, and lay long and shining against her thighs. There were other photographs of her in tennis clothes, bathing costumes, tweed suits. She had tiny ankles, wide calves and small feet, and had learnt to dance in the spick church halls of the town where she had grown up, where clean young men, and women with bobbed hair, played the piano or the wind-up gramophone and where she whirled in her crepe-de-chine dresses to the sound of the 'Wedding of the Painted Doll'. She was like a little painted doll herself, with her big eyes and burnished looks, her way of looking up from under her waved bangs. Her hair was biscuit-coloured, or the colour of sand, like sun filtering through honey, or the stooks of wheat in the stubble. Once when Dora was Nora she looked into a covered blue china bowl and saw a coil of gleaming hair lying there, like Rumpelstiltskin's gleanings coiled in the bottom of the bowl, glimmering like moonlight or flax, the colour wildly alive. Her mother looked at this relic without interest; it was her hair, she said, saved from its first cutting when she was three. Nora was confounded both by the hair and by the idea of the immutable creature in front of her having been younger than she was and this creature having stood still in babyhood whilst her mother, Nora's grandmother, snipped at her hair.

One day when her mother was still a girl and walking past the cathedral, she heard a noise such as she had never heard, an enormous crack, and a man walking at a diagonal down the steps toppled slowly and fell, and rolled bump by bump down the steps, a stream of red liquid smearing and pumping as he rolled towards her. She had no idea what had happened to him. She knew nothing about guns or shooting. She was a child reared in the town and had only been to the cinema twice, in the newly built Picture Palace. It was 1922, the year of The Troubles. The figure toppled in Nora's imagination and continued to topple more violently and vividly in Dora's, perhaps more so than in her mother's memory.

At nineteen her mother went to teach in a small seaside town where the swimming baths were white and green and there was a bandstand in the middle of the park, where a band played on Saturdays and to return to her own mother's house she had to take a train halfway across the top of Ireland. When she heard of a job in a remote country district which all the same was nearer to home – a journey of forty miles rather than sixty – she applied for it, was given it and found herself utterly translated. Within weeks, even though she continued to return home at weekends, her previous life began to seem something from a dream, a dream that lay somewhere not in the past or in the present but far away in the future only reached by the time machine that was the train.

In the school district she lodged with an old woman in one of the very few houses that had more than one bedroom and which lay at the end of a long boggy lane. The other two houses belonged to the priest and the head teacher.

Her strappy shiny shoes became soaked as she walked up and down the muddy lane to her lodgings, a lane that she too, soon, called the rampar and she took to wearing wellingtons and changing at the school.

She came back to her lodgings exhausted from teaching forty children of all ages, but revived after her tea and would have gone out, but there was nowhere to go. Her landlady cooked her meals, potatoes, fried bacon, fried eggs, fried cabbage. She grew fatter. When she went back at the weekend she felt left out of her friends' lives. They were working in offices, typing, or in shops selling clothes and artefacts, or in the local hospital as nurses. They seemed glossy, sharp, defined; their preoccupations depended on a dailiness, a plethora of things and possessions, a timetable of minutiae, occupations and amusements. She found she was living in her place of work, not just working in it and in that place there were no amusements. The word hardly existed. Time was measured by seasons, by births, by deaths and holydays of the Church, by feasts of abstinence. As she cycled from the station back to her lodgings every Sunday night, down past the tiny cottages, further into the bogs, the silence became profound, the darkness palpable; she cycled into a country that lay a century behind the one she had left. There were no cars, no electricity, no telephones. The people wore dark fusty clothes and, though they never changed, seemed only to cast off clothes in the summer and to add more in the winter without touching the basic swaddling layer, they did not smell of anything other than smoke from the fire that burnt perpetually on the hearths of the central room in their small houses. She thought of her friends in her home town taking their daily baths, showering after walks and their tennis, washing their hair after swimming, their fear of bad breath, their reception of visitors in parlours and sitting rooms, and wondered why her life was getting beyond her grasp.

The women in the district were modest and deferred to her, the men respectful, the children timid. She did not know it but she was a central topic of the conversations within the houses as was the fact that she taught songs to the children by singing to them. She sang 'My love's an Arbutus by the borders of Lene', and 'Slieve Trostan's in shadow and Glenaan's in tears', her pure true voice rising above the children's heads and floating out through the window, over the school yard to where a passer-by would stop beguiled, amazed, scandalised, by the voice, by the soft ways of what they had hoped would be a hard teacher needed to beat sense into the children.

There was no veneer, no dissembling, no mode of manners in the parish beyond simple hospitality. The people called her The Mistress and she set the standard. She knew they were sorry not to see her in church on a Sunday when they could have gauged the state and style of the outside world by her hat, her coat, her shoes, her handbag. But they knew she had to visit her mother and admired her devotion as right and natural.

Later as she grew to know the people, to distinguish one shawled full-gathered long-skirted woman from another, she discerned that there were more fierce and rancorous hatreds and jealousies among these apparently peaceful and communally minded people than any she had ever known. Every family was inter-related but kinship seemed only to add to the rancour. The longer she lived there the more she learnt that poverty and hardship bred spite. All the same, except for actively feuding families, at hay-making or potato-picking time, people helped each other on a barter basis. She discovered too that no one was judged on their own merits but on the merits or otherwise of their forbears. She would mention to the only other teacher, the headmaster, that some child was rough or sickly or not attending school regularly and he would say without surprise, that that was to be expected, the child's breed seed and generation had been the same.

He would warn her about one child and say that thieving was in the family, or tell her that another would have a mathematical gift, and she found that she was beginning to identify the children by their family nicknames, often descriptions from the Gaelic, rather than by the names in the register.

Soon the people in her home town began to seem transient and though she still returned home every weekend they seemed to recede as they made liaisons and arrangements that precluded her. She was devout and believed fervently in the potency of prayer and she began a Novena in the small chapel beside the school. To make the Novena she had to attend Mass on the first Friday of every month for nine months without a break. If the continuity was broken then she had to begin all over again even if she had already made eight Fridays. She did not know what she was making the Novena for, nor why she was beseeching Heaven, so she called it a Novena of Good Intentions.

She began to go to the ceilidhs that were held monthly in the small Hibernian hall beside the chapel. The women stood at one end, the men at the other. When the fiddler started a reel or the jig the men were bashful about coming forward and were especially paralysed at the idea of dancing with the Mistress; so, left alone on a bench at the end of the hall, she stopped going.

One day the headmaster said to her that his nephew was coming to visit. He was to meet him off the train in a pony and trap, would she like to come? She always cycled to the station to catch the train and was excited by the idea of a different kind of transport. She sat in the trap, bumping over the boggy road with a feeling of real pleasure. She told Dora about it in one of her rare moments of recall, looking out of her new windows as though she were back on the bog road. Dora, unaccustomed to confidences from her mother, felt a rage of resentment rise at such moments since her mother seemed to have a perverse knack of delivering them at unpropititious times. But she had been moved by the idea of that young woman, who even in her drabbest moment had a quality of illumination, of something about to blossom, sitting tight in the sprung seat of the trap, as it cut through the country lanes, the people they met or passed standing to one side, respectful, pleased by the diligence.

Dora's mother – as she was not then – did not speculate on the master's nephew, as they drove to the station. The journey was an end in itself. Dora trying to establish anticipation, insisted that her mother must have imagined him a bit, surely a bit, but she said no or if so, then she would have thought of him as the nephew, a child much like the ones she taught. She might have been nearer in her speculation than she thought.

Nothing, thus, prepared her for the creature who climbed off the train, cool, blue-shadowed, raven-haired, with black and speckled eyes and brilliant irises and a manner both bashful and confident. She sat opposite him on the narrow seat with the little gallery at her back and the headmaster shouted over his shoulder, comments about the weather, about his sister, the nephew's mother, to which he answered in a way she had never heard before. He spoke in reluctant, short answers, in a voice of melancholic good-will with, behind it, the hint of something he was remembering that might make him laugh. His long legs were crossed, and on one long-fingered hand he wore a ring. She looked at the dandy with astonishment. She did not know how to test his reality.

As she climbed off the trap at the end of her rampar he did not help her out, but smiled at her, a smile of charm and sweetness tinged with a certain ironic confidence. The next evening he came to her lodgings and asked her to a dance being held in a town ten miles away and she sent a telegram to her mother not to expect her home that weekend.

On the Saturday night he took her, in a motor-car taxi, to a dance in Portadown. The road crossed a high bridge over a canal and he asked the taxi-driver to stop on the crest and the driver, clutching his hand brake, as though reining in a horse, did so. The nephew pointed out, far away, the long glimmer of a line of water and told her that there, straight ahead of his finger, on that shore, was where he lived, where his family house was. Dora, as she listened, heard the haunt of prophecy.

The hall where the dance was held was like nothing her mother had seen before, a white-pinnacled temple with an elaborate mantled doorway set in a brick arch, studded with small elaborate windows. Under a large rose window was written 'The Temple' and underneath that the words 'of Liberty, Learning and Select Amusement designed, erected and endowed by John Carey, a free gift to his country.'

Dora got up and walked to the mirror, agitated. Why was she resurrecting her mother? It wasn't, surely, within her rights to take her mother to pieces in order to try to find out how she herself worked. Rights or wrongs, Dora thought, no one has a monopoly but we may have a duty, though my dutiful equipment is so thin, so worn with disuse, so failing, and the signals are fainter by the day. Soon they will have gone for ever.

They had erected their Temple of Select Amusements with its

own arcane rites and rituals, presumably painfully, Dora thought, over the years. Brick by brick they had built it, embellished it here, stripped it there, filled in a chink there, so that it began to look seamless. Year by year they added more camouflaging and more coverings, so that it looked to the outsider, the child born within the edifice, as though it had grown out of nature, aeons before, at the time of creation, when in reality the foundations had only been laid a year or two before that child's birth. Yet here she was, stout Dora, come to reckon it, measure it up with her inexperienced eye, pace it out with her flat feet, gauge its density with her inadequate callipers and announce her findings to a long immortal silence. She wondered what other such observers, her own daughters Laura or Alice, say, would in their time make of her marriage but suppressed that line of thought, scowling. She sidled in, closer to the edifice, not seamless at all she now saw, as she poked and peered, but riddled with hairline cracks, with gaps and missing pieces covered with tendrils and strange bulging growths. And yet parts of it were like the pyramids or Machu Picchu, where one could only stand amazed at the accuracy of the fit, the sheer weight of the masonry locked together by honing and gravity, all done with block and tackle and rudimentary instruments.

Only in their ruins, when the builders had long gone with their secret, could observers analyse how such monuments were made but they could only speculate on how the inhabitants had lived and endured and rejoiced inside them. It would fit her better, Dora thought, to set about mortarising her own house, than to go prodding her coarse fingers at the walls of their marriage, hoping to find the fatal chink so that she could stop it up.

All the same her mother couldn't have known what she was letting herself in for when they began building their select foundations. But then for that matter, what bride or bridegroom could. When she married him, she moved into a dispensation that had elsewhere vanished,and not even her six months in the school parish in which she had tunnelled backwards in time, prepared her for what lay ahead, if ahead was the right word for a way of life that seemed to have no direction or inclination towards the tilt of the rest of the world. Her dark bridegroom came from an earlier dispensation in more ways than one. Sometimes Dora thought that he must have died a kind of mind-death when he was a child, which had left him rooted in that certain age. In her mind's eye Dora saw him finding his mother lying face downwards on the red-tiled floor, as she saw that other man topple down the cathedral steps. He had thought his mother was dead but she was in a stupor of drink. It was a time when women never drank, when the Virgin Mary ruled the roost in Ireland. Dora wondered how he had dealt with that image of his mother, but whatever else she rampaged over, it wasn't in her gift to go hauling out her father's dreams and ask him for an explanation. Ellen had told her about it when Dora was still a child, coarsely, with enjoyment.

'Drank herself paralytic every week. Imagine. The Mistress, till she couldn't stand.' It seemed to Dora looking back that her female forbears for generations had been teachers, presumably all suffering that hardening of the heart that seemed endemic to the profession. Dora tried to imagine the woman's, her grandmother's, unhappiness. Whenever he mentioned his mother, tears sprang into his eyes. She used to watch him. He was a fabulous creature. Mysterious, fleeting, a creature in the forest. She could not go in to find him. He must be lured out.

The unicorn was an intelligent and dangerous animal. The only sure way to catch it was to use a virgin as a lure. The unicorn bewitched by a pure young woman would become docile and kneel beside her laying its head in her lap. Thus entranced, the moon-coloured horse was easy prey for whoever wanted it or its horn. Save of course for the virgin who was trapped like a slavey, under its heavy head.

Dora read this information in a book on myths and fairy tales she had picked up at the station in Dublin. The head seemed still to be in her lap for all her deflowering. The train rocketed along the coastline, passing stretches of beach wreathed with wrack and seaweed at the tideline. On one strand of sand two children, their skirts puffed, tucked into their knickers, walked out towards the line of water slinking along the horizon, waiting to make a dash for the shore. They ricketed past a small town lying across an estuary linked by an iron footbridge, and a woman with a shopping basket stood still and watched the train rumble by. Dora remembered a story about a German woman during the Second World War, watching one of the mysterious cattle trains rattle past her garden and seeing two planks in one of the wagons suddenly jolt apart. For a split second a woman in the wagon looked out at her, a woman with blonde hair, an exquisite face whom, the watcher thought, could well have been her sister. The train swayed on.

When Dora got to the other end she could either telephone him to come and meet her or take a taxi. If there was a taxi. Thirty miles. She'd never have enough money and he would come so willingly to pick her up and drive her back into the place she felt she could never really leave. She was manacled to it. Already Tony was a world away, an impossibly ludicrous figment.

She telephoned her father from the station. It would take him an hour, on those small and twisting roads and he would cross the high bridge. Dora wondered if each time he drove over it he remembered pointing out to her mother the place of her future before it had even been mentioned. Dora remembered it every time the car crashed over the join at the top of the bridge but then, mythology was often stronger than the event.

She went out of the station, and into the forecourt. There were enamel advertisements pinned to the railings half-chipped away. IROL for Health; Sweet Afton; a something, a hen and a Waverley pen. They're worth a guinea a box.

In earlier times, of course, it would have been unthinkable to look at him clearly, to perceive him as another morsel of man. The centre would have collapsed and she would have been dragged into the vacuum.

All her life she had worshipped him. She still had the habit of grinning with anxiety throughout his interminable stories which she had heard a thousand times before. Grinning and smiling to show pleasure and amusement, though the stories gave her neither, and, by the time he had reached the end and the climax, she was quite exhausted with the effort of producing sufficient reaction to satisfy herself that she had satisfied him.

She had loved him without reservation, knowing that he was not perfect, but unable to find fault with his imperfections. The characteristics that in any other man would have made her dismissive, contemptuous, became in him mere foibles, necessities for his well-being. His gambling, his refusal to look at the present or the future with any kind of reality or concern, his perpetual retelling of incidents from the golden domain of the past without, apparently, any recognition of the desolate context of the incidents, the drunkenness, the squalor, the ignorance, finding in them only material for amusement and something perhaps parallel to pity, his disavowal of responsibility. She had protected him from her own hard-won knowledge, refused to judge him and thus judged other men the more harshly.

Looking back, it seemed that half her young life had been lived vicariously for him, in his place. If a sharp word was spoken she felt it keenly and tried to deflect it. If someone seemed not fully to appreciate him she felt a livid anger lick around her heart; she defended him in her own mind against the knowledge that was impossible to resist. For her he was cloaked, she could not discern the lineaments of the real man under the cloak she had to have him wear. Her power could not, must not, reach to him; if it did, he would be scorched, and she would burn. So she kept her distance and circled around him, never taking her eyes off him, while her life went on about her. The erotic feedback of his presence made her frantic. And it seemed to her that everyone colluded with her in making him marvellous, in making him the magic creature in their midst; an old unicorn who had sired creatures with fontanels instead of horns.

There was an old barn with high rafters on the farm. It was a two-storey building with cows and horses in the byres and stalls, the machine for veal below and barley grain stored on the floor above. It had a fine wide-planked pine floor and an intricately raftered ceiling. The crossbeams, spanning the spaces from wall to wall, were like a series of gargantuan parallel bars. When he was a youth he could swing the whole length of the barn, his body swooping through the air like a marten, across gaps that seemed too wide to be covered even by the impetus of his launching hands, his lithe, swinging body. And yet, there he was, winging through the air, through which the other boys were falling, dropping short of the beams, fingers scrabbling, while his arm hooked itself, almost nonchalantly across a beam, like a greeting across a shoulder. It was on sustenance from such feats that the legend lived and shone around him, though all the rest of his life might be lived down on the ground.

Dora had been told casually enough about that quicksilver flight across the rafters, by one of the young men who had followed him wherever he had led, a young man now old and grizzled but who still saw her father through idolatrous eyes.

'He was the best footballer,' he said, 'the best high-jumper, and the best long-jumper, too, a racing cyclist who would cycle forty miles to a dance, dance the night away and ride home without weariness. He couldn't be beat. You'd never hear tell of such a spree now.'

The man who spoke told her of his brother finding a giant elk's head in his fishing net. He had felt the big resistance, enough to fear it would break his net, and had been alarmed when he saw the great spread of the antlers break the surface. Dora asked to see it and her father drove her to a little two-room house down by the lough shore. The old man who opened the door greeted her father with a cry, and they swayed towards each other and beat each other's shoulders. Dora realised they were contemporaries.

'You come on me too early,' the old man said. 'I haven't the house redd up, nor the floor washed. You come on me too early. I would have liked to have redd up before you came.'

They set about reminiscing on how long it had been since they had seen each other, bandying names and dates, and Dora waited listening to their cadences. He led them across the garden to a shed full of the paraphernalia of fishing. It was laid out with the votive offerings of his craft, ranged, impeccable, the sawn hemi-boxes filled with swaddled mounds of twine, a stone garden of speckled pebbles of one size and shape, and rows of hooks in perfect symmetry, jabbed into the wooden floor of the boxes, all of it the accurate expression of the means and skills of a lifetime on the lough. Above the boxes, hanging high on the wall, was a scoured skull, the colour of hardness, the planes and angles of its bone skimmed with white striations, and branching from the brow, antlers, like the skeletons of giants' hands, frozen in an imploring moment. The lower half of its jaw was missing and the convex roof of the mouth tilted upwards so that it looked agape.

'We snagged it in the net,' the old man said. 'Oh, a lifetime ago.'

'How long ago?' Dora said.

She thought of the unimaginable age in which it had blundered through a countryside now under water.

'It must be over forty years now,' he said. 'There was people came from a museum to see it, but they never came back. They say the animal might be a thousand years old.'

'Older than that,' Dora said.

'Older than that?' he said. 'Couldn't be.'

'Twelve thousand years,' Dora said. 'It walked the plains.'

'A lifetime,' he said.

'They went out of the shed. Dora watched the two men walk up to the house, one hobbling, the other still limber. After a suitable amount of obeisances they parted. She walked behind him on the narrow path looking at his body, bent to one side now, the line out of true, but invested with obdurate elegance.

She went back into the waiting room. She thought she would freeze. The weather had been warm at Tony's, the air like balm. Here there was a whipping wind. She sneezed.

She heard his car drive into the station yard, ran out to save him from climbing out and he waited in the car while she threw the bags in the back seat. She kissed him.

'How did you get over?' he asked. 'Isn't it great to see you.'

'I was doing an interview in Dublin,' she said, 'and said I was taking a day or two off.'

'Will they pay you?' he said.

'Oh yes,' she said. 'I'm paid anyway.' Over here the pittance didn't seem so small.

All the way home in the car he smoked. She thought she would never get rid of the smell of smoking. She wound down her window. He opened his, humbly.

'I have the head blown off you,' she said, laughing.

'And I have you tormented,' he said.

'And I have you terrorised.'

'And they'll ultimately kill me.'

But he smoked on. He had never made a sacrifice in his life.

By the time she got home she could hardly breathe. Her head, her nose, her eyes, were stuffed with some nameless liquid, thicker than oil. It was as though the smoke from his cigarettes had liquidised inside her head and her mind felt slow and lost in the smog. The inside of her mouth became covered in ulcers, she had a cold sore on the side of her lip and her respiratory system sounded like something wheezing under a door. She felt an obscure satisfaction in the midst of this discomfort. Dora who tried to eschew superstition, felt that her body was manufacturing a residue of years and was now pushing it out, the lubrication, the oil of blind love. God knows where she thought the reservoir had been stowed, in the heart or the head, or nasal caverns immeasurable to man. But the evidence was there, as anyone who might have been in her company, listening to her snuffling, blowing and wheezing could testify, or saw the paperchase of handkerchiefs around her, a kind of Himalaya of cotton and tissues.

Within twenty-four hours her whole being seemed filled with a potent mixture of impatience and boredom and fright. The boredom was the worst. She began to eat as though she were a loose cushion or eiderdown that had to be filled, stuffed, every nook and cranny, with soft white bread and buns and old apple tart, biscuits, potatoes – what she ate looked like a chart of forbidden foods for dieters. Food for thought, but she was too bored to think. She tried to talk to her parents together or separately but they were elusive. She wondered if the conversation with her mother on the telephone had actually taken place but her mother refused to acknowledge it and sidestepped, as though vaguely attempting to shy at it. Dora felt as though she were burying her hands in dry sand and trying to lift handfuls of it while it slipped and trickled away. Soon every time she opened her mouth, inertia slipped in and lay down and curled asleep, around her vocal chords.

In such a short time, she had slipped back into place, like Carver Doone going under into the quicksand. The house in Sligo, the houses that Tony had shown her, no longer existed. So must her mother have felt as she cycled down the dark lanes into her future knowing that she was cutting herself off for ever from life in that sunny seaside town with its clipped grass, its privet hedges and high houses, sunny pavements and bakeries selling meringues. But this is *her* past, I'm living, Dora cried to herself, Christ, how do I get shot of it, to get back to my own present wherever that is.

Soon only her arm would be waving above ground towards her life in England, and she would be sucked into the defeating swamp of damp, rural, vicious Ireland, yawning as she went under. Yet she knew well that when she returned to England she would be overwhelmed by a grief, about what she was doing there, in an alien place, feeling displaced, neither one thing nor the other. There was something gaping in her life, some emptiness at the centre which was to do with her displacement. And yet God knows she would suffocate if she remained here, where there were no gaps at all for a person to slide through to escape, a place where people were bored to death without ever having had the opportunity to put a realisation or a name to their disease. She thought of what Caroline or Annabel, or even Henrietta would have made of the place and she began to laugh; and her mother, hearing the laugh, volunteered to go for a walk with her. This was so unexpected that Dora was immediately galvanised and, swaddled against the wind, what her father called the Black Blowing, they both set off.

'I have to leave tomorrow,' Dora said.

'I wish I could come with you,' her mother said.

'Tell me more about before you were married,' Dora said.

'There's nothing to tell,' her mother said. 'But I can remember it better than the things I did yesterday. My memory has got very bad.'

III

Before they were married, he came to see her two or three times a week, a ten-mile cycle journey to the station and then a wait for the train. When they met, all they could do was to walk along the road, or visit his uncle's house. They were never alone. His father resented him leaving the home ground to go courting a foreigner and the headmaster feared that his nephew might become a permanent fixture in his house, a penniless lodger. Their amusements were walks down the road, ceilidhs at the Hibernian hall, a stilted talk by the fire in the company of the headmaster and wherever they went they were watched. She was the cynosure and he was famous for his looks, his sporting achievements, his advent from another parish, his capture of such a trophy.

One weekend they took the train to Belfast and he led her to a huge showroom, with glittering plate-glass windows, and there he showed her his heart's desire, a small green car. It cost four hundred and eighty pounds and might as well have cost fifty thousand. He yearned for it without expectation, as he yearned for her. There was no way in which they could get married. He could not earn a living away from his territory, from the farm, from helping with the ramshackle business. She could not stop work; without her wage they would be penniless and she could not find a teaching job nearer to his house. There were few schools and many teachers. She sought Divine Intervention and became convinced she must finish her Novena, started so long before but always interrupted. She forbade him to come on the first Friday of the month and began, again, the long haul towards its consummation.

Soon after, the man who sold tickets for the Irish Hospital Sweepstakes came around to the farm on his old high-frame bicycle. The tickets were expensive, five times as much as the train fare to get to her, but he bought one and when he arrived off the train gave it to her. She put it in the little crocodile handbag, yes, she agreed, that same little crocodile bag that Dora as a child had carried around with no idea of its miraculous provenance.

There was a custom in the country then to use a *nom de plume* on a ticket in the hope it would bring added luck, a talismanic name tallying with something of personal significance. The nom de plume he chose was First Friday and when the sweep was drawn months later, the day after she had completed her Novena, the ticket was drawn. They had won five hundred pounds and both parishes were alight with the news of their luck.

The wedding was held in the same cathedral where, as a child, she had watched the man, who had been shot, roll down the steps. They drove back from the wedding to his house in their little car.

Her mother stopped talking.

'It's cold,' she said. 'I have to go home back to my mother.'

'Your mother's been dead years,' Dora said, amused.

She went back to London the next day.

Years later she told her father the story, and he listened, his speckled dark eyes still glowing intense in his parchment-coloured face.

'Did she tell you the rest of it?' he said. He lit a cigarette and began to talk and showed her, in the telling, of how a hole had been burned into the fabric of the marriage, a hole that had continued to smoulder. Dora felt that she had always been wary of its heat without knowing the source.

The parade of the bride and the groom was always on the first Sunday after the wedding, at second Mass. The crowds waited for the beholding outside the church and the newly married couple walked along the road and into the church watched by the congregation who then followed them in. For many of the modest women of the parish the ritual was both the high-spot and the ordeal of their lifetimes, a moment when they became divas, swept centre-stage for a huge moment.

But she surely had nothing to fear. She had made the best match in the parish. He was as strong as a lion, as fearless as a champion, if not a god, then the darling of the gods and he was hers.

They left his father's house in good time and set out on the road to the chapel and the scrutiny and benediction of the congregation.

Dora watched him as he related it. He did not speak of himself as a god but he had his ways. She interrupted, and said: 'But you had won the car, you had won the car, why didn't you drive?' And he looked at her, amazed by her lack of comprehension, 'You wouldn't do that, drive up in a car the first Sunday after you were married with everyone waiting to look. You wouldn't think of it. We'd never have even considered it,' and by his tone he conveyed what a solecism it would be, and conveyed, though he did not mean to do so, for he was unaware of it, the infinite tact of his sensibility. She knew as she watched him and listened to his threnodic voice that part of his charm, which now she resisted as though it were truly a charm in the sense of a curse, came from the fact that he was unaware of his charm. It was as natural to him as breathing.

They walked along the road in their finery, the livery of wedlock. The road curved and beyond the curve was a short strait, and at the end of it the crowd waited outside the open dark door of the chapel. To reach this final swerve in the road they had to pass a small house, almost a hovel, lived in by an old man, a rumpled reprobate, dirty in his habits, and scourge of the district, sententious when sober and contentious when drunk, a man who spat great gobbets of slime at his own feet as he walked. As they passed his door, she in her navy-blue and white suit (and Dora had a photograph of her in these same clothes, hung in her dressing room below Tony's pouter pigeon), the old man came out of his house in his caked and soiled clothes, and swung into place beside them. She waited for her new husband to get rid of him, to detach her from his company, but he greeted the man, who, thus encouraged, continued to walk with them and to talk to them in a way that she found incomprehensible. She did not understand what he was saying, nor why he was saying it, nor why he was with them.

She whispered to her husband to tell the old man to go away, to fall behind, to go ahead but not to walk alongside them, as though he belonged to them, was part of their marriage but he, embarrassed, did not like to offend the man who had been a neighbour all his life, and chose to offend his wife instead.

As Dora listened to the story, as he related it, in that elegiac unresisting voice that her mother had heard as they rode back from the station in the trap, she hoped that it was not in his gift to perceive the extent of the tragedy, in that short walk to the chapel, when a young woman had begun a long walk on her own, with a family straggling after, hoping that one day they might hear her voice, lifted in song.

Sitting at her dressing-table, Dora began to cry. The bruises on her face were hurting. She spread some ointment on them so that she looked like something from a stone-age tribe in a lost jungle. The shifting blanched shadows made by the fan slowly stirring the white net made her uneasy. It was dark outside, and she was hungry but she could not go to the restaurant looking like this. She crossed to the window. The lights of India were on the horizon or perhaps it was a ship glittering in the far darkness.

She turned back to her papers, for a last look at the edifice and saw that, though light glimmered there too, somewhere within it was closed and secret against her and her impudence.

It was to counterbalance that place and its ways, to escape its effects that she had set about so obsessively putting her own house in order and had so intently sought a man who would not be charming, feckless, reckless and who, when the moment came and the monster came out of the woods and walked along the road alongside the young couple and asked for the ransom, would not give away the bride instead.

FOUR
The Fossil Resin

I

Anyone walking around the edifice of her own marriage would not need a magnifying glass to find the cracks, Dora thought, and lately the more she chipped them open, the more Simon filled them in, trying to make a new bond without either of them acknowledging what was happening.

In coming to this island she had banished herself to an anonymous room perhaps knowing that she could not receive a sign until relieved of some of her property. At home, she lived in a house that was full of things and textures, as though gathering up enough things would make a different kind of glue.

When she looked out of her windows in Suffolk she saw an archetypal English landscape, a park with oak trees standing in pools of green darkness, and in the distance another sea divided by unskeined dense hedgerows studded with wild oaks, with moss and lichen creeping up their bark. In the spring, in the shadows underneath the boles, bluebells floated, their colour skimming over the surface of the fields as though the earth underneath, shifting from its sleep, had sent the colour flying.

There were generally sheep in the fields, curiously immobile blobs, like stones on sticks or enormous mutated mushrooms and these were separated from the garden proper by a haha, so that it looked as if the sheep could wander at will, and in the park horses grazed and neighed and galloped and kicked up their heels. Immediately below her bedroom window was a small intricate garden that she had planned in a somewhat over-ambitious reach but which she loved, however short it fell of its concept.

*

Once sitting in Tony Flaxmeyer's library (of course, for all the melodrama of their first parting, she had often revisited his house in Sligo and made love there too, though not always to him), she had opened a book and read about the spring carpet that a certain Persian king, Chosroes, had had woven in the sixth century for his palace, to celebrate his defeat of the Romans and his victories in Arabia. The design was that of a garden, and made on such a scale, four hundred feet long by a hundred feet wide, that he could walk down the paths and stand and gaze at his flower-beds. The carpet was studded with jewels woven with gold and silver and silk and, as Dora recalled it, had been cut to pieces when he'd come a cropper. The idea of such a carpet stayed with her and when a rose garden to one side of the house contracted some dread disease, she thought to make a garden based on the description. She read what she could find on the subject. Persian carpets were made so that a garden could be invoked indoors, and she set about reversing the concept. She tried to create a Persian carpet outdoors, evoking the sophisticated asymmetries, the medallions, the interlocked borders, with box and privet and rosemary and yew. The crowded fields of each section she filled with flowers and sprays, with asters, coreopsis, evening primroses, irises and flowering shrubs. She had to forgo water courses, but she had made two long narrow ponds with fish, and planted weeping willow to signify sorrow and death, and two sycamore trees. At least that was what she said she was doing to anyone who would listen. They hadn't done too well, the sycamores, they were at the far end and looking stunted.

In fact as she looked out over it, the whole garden far from looking like a wonderful Persian carpet looked more as though some giant sluggard had flung a torn embroidered eiderdown to the ground and stamped around on it for a while. This, if anything, pleased her. She loved the look of quilts and eiderdowns, paisleys and patchwork, tatting and brocade, guipure and lace, fringe and gimp, tassels, galloon and passementerie, goffered linens, appliqué, and crewel work, and in her house were all of these as well as tapestries and samplers and stump-work, Berlin work and needlepoint embroidery, smocking, laid-work, all the myriad lovely weavings that female human skill, ingenuity, patience, expertise, strained eyes and craving for order had contrived over the ages. Dora conceded that men had occasionally done some good needlework but only as a remarkable hobby.

For years Dora had done her best to build a refuge of ornament and softness around her, tried to infect herself with the constancy and patience of the seamstresses and knitters in the sun but the cracks and gaps in her life seemed to widen and she found herself living in the wind's blast, found herself, too, to be inconstant; and found that the plethora of possessions were beginning to seem to her to be the encrustations of a mad woman or a miser or of someone storing up hostages against a day of dread and barter. She feared too that her mania for collecting was, at its base, a joyless search for a tourniquet on her life, or a manifestation of greed, but even these defeating and masochistic interpretations did not prevent her from daily adding another object to her collection. Simon turned his head and let her get on with it, in the hope she believed that it might keep her, if not happy, then at least occupied. Which it did, in between times.

She got up and went over to the windows and pulled up the blinds. Dusk was falling and a cat was running along the side of the hotel in the long curiously green grass. There was no hint of hurry in its alert triumphant lope towards the quiet place where it could play with the small creature in its jaws. Dora thought, perhaps their heart simply stops beating, perhaps their nervous systems are less acute than ours, perhaps each time they are put down they think they are free, perhaps they just give up and stop feeling. Her body was aching. She remembered reading an account of the sale of a woman into slavery and how, as she stood on the block, she had simpered and pursed her lips and blown kisses at the bidders.

The cat disappeared round the corner and down towards the beach. Dora opened a drawer in her dressing-table and took out the necklace and held it against her neck, as the boy had held it, as Laura had held it while Dora had been packing to leave. The big central nugget had almost reached Laura's waist. She had said carefully, 'Mum, I've got an image. Things come down out of the corners. They frighten me. I hear noises.'

Dora noted the word image. She said, 'When they come down shout for me. We could look at them straight on together.'

Laura looked sceptical as well she might and Dora fastened the necklace around Laura's neck. They both stared at it in the glass remembering its provenance. Dora said, 'What are the images like?'

Laura hesitated. 'They're like bloody eyes and arms separated from bodies and things like that.'

Separation. It's not just the three of us who are throwing the ball, Dora thought, Laura is in the game too and is watching the fuse burn.

Laura said, 'What will I do when you're away?'

'Shout for someone else,' Dora said briskly, refusing the question. 'They'll come straight away.'

'No,' she said. 'I can't tell anyone else about them.'

Dora thought about how simple it was to tell someone to look at something directly when the thing you were supposed to look at was complex and convoluted and horrible and the only other person who could see them was a world away. She hoped that this evening Laura was not lying staring at a nursery ceiling that could, at a blink, turn into an abattoir but, even as she hoped, trying to concentrate the hope into a chain to circle the world, her lover's face and voice filled her mind and memory, and she fastened the amber necklace around her neck and took the stopper out of Stella's tonic. It tasted like cold coffee and syrup of figs with a bitter underlay and she hoped that Stella had not decided to end the lunches once and for all. It was almost dark but the air was still humid and the blades of the fan turned lazily above her head. She lay staring at the weary ceiling hoping the tonic was a sedative or a lure to pull the images across the world so that Laura could lie easy.

Simon sometimes spoke of his beloved old house in affectionate terms as something that needed endless shoring-up and took all his energy and resources. Listening to him made Dora think that he might as well have been talking about their marriage. 'You patch up one end,' he said, 'and stand back because something is finally secure and right at the other end a great lump of plaster or a chimney begins to unhook itself, so you rush down there with the ladder and bandages and on the way the middle begins to sag and you begin to wonder about the foundations.'

There were so many saws about marriage; Dora had listened to them all. One partner was the aristocrat, one the peasant; one the giver, one the taker; one active, the other passive; one the punisher, one the punished; one faithful, the other not; one the worker, the other a drone; one the wrecker, the other the salvager. The game could be endlessly played and the roles reversed depending on who was doing the allowing, the depending, the demanding. Not that they ever seemed to reverse in hers, Dora thought guiltily. She was always the baddie. Both partners suffered though, who ever played what part, of that Dora was sure.

She tried to think about her marriage as a fact, as something that existed, something built up of countless moments when two people, together, had learnt something about themselves, about each other and about their life that they could never have learnt in any other way. That presumably was why divorce was so painful, cutting through the forged moments that linked two people together and to their past. Never mind the children.

She lay on the bed separated from her husband and children by thousands of miles and remembered with an ache that made her hunch her shoulders and pull up her knees an episode from her marriage, before she had met Theodore, when she had still thought that affection and effort were enough to keep a marriage going.

She had been cooking, something she didn't often do since she paid someone else to do it, or rather Simon did. But Karen the New Zealand girl who was working her way around the world and was the cook of the moment was on her day off and Betty was upstairs with Thomas, so Dora started putting the food together, feeling, she thought, quite happy. Mother Nurture. But her back and shoulders were sore, had been for a week and though she had spent a good part of the day with her children, she felt at her nub a sense of deprivation for work not done. When she did force herself to sit at her desk she had to stop herself from making more obsessive lists.

Dora wished that there could be a way of wiping the grooves of guilt and pain etched so deeply in her psyche. Her conscience seemed to have become a kind of stylus, moving smoothly in those narrow spirals, sending messages, felt rather than heard, messages that turned life upside down and delivered falsehoods; that time spent away from her work was somehow wasted, that the small repeated tasks that constituted the rearing of children were trivia, when she knew in her heart that they were the true and valuable stuff of life, its very constituents. But she could not accept such currency, issued from such an unreliable source and her own early life seemed to have taught her that childhood was fundamentally worthless. She told herself – and well she knew without being told – that any day filled with the dailiness of her children's doings and emotions was priceless, irreplaceable, unrepeatable, but even as she spent the days with them some voice within her nagged, a tiny persistent fishwife, saying she was neglecting something more important.

Dora was hardly so unschooled that she did not realise whence sprang this profound feeling that childhood moments were of no account. The jesuits had got her early. She knew that the intricate and beautiful entwining of her life, and her children's lives as infants, was as shortlived as the flowerings of morning glory or convolvulus, and that they would too soon separate themselves, tendril by tendril, so that she would slip into the past as they flourished into their unclaimable future. Simon was late. She hoped he was not caught in traffic. In the years since their marriage, traffic to Suffolk had increased immeasurably, all the roads becoming increasingly engorged. He was going away for two weeks and she always felt a great surge of love for him when he was about to disappear.

The week before, he had told her a story, which had made her look at him with a sense of surprise. He related it as though at face value, without reference to it as a parable, but she was never sure whether he pretended this simplicity or chose it. His company was investigating the possibility of buying out a rival company which used low-frequency radio signals to locate buried cables. 'Like water divining?' she said and then seeing the slight shadow cross his face added, 'Water divining's not magic – it's high tech, is water divining.'

'Of course,' he said, colluding. 'Anyway the boffins in the company were trying to find a very-low-frequency band that they could call their own and whilst they were searching across the air waves they discovered that the frequency they would most like to use cut across a low-frequency emitting signal that was regular constant, and universal. Wherever they went the same message was being transmitted on the same wave length. They found it in India, they found it in the Antarctic, they found it in Cornwall, they found it in Ballarat. . . .'

'What you tells me, Brother,' Dora said, 'They's tuned into God's heartbeat.'

'Quite,' he said. 'Do you want me to go on or not?' He looked at her with an odd little smile. 'They set about cracking the frequency and very soon they found some very large bruisers from the Ministry of Defence on their doorstep.'

Dora felt the old ravening terror that lay in the cave below her heart stir with pleasure at the prospect of a good stalk. She looked across at Simon but he was apparently pre-occupied with rolling some spilled grains of salt onto his finger. 'The message it transmits twenty-four hours a day, seven days a week is don't fire, don't fire, don't fire.' He looked up. 'It comes from an underground tunnel in Boulder, Colorado. The tunnel, incidentally, is twenty-seven miles long.'

'Throw that salt over your shoulder at once,' Dora said but it seemed to her that she had slithered deeper into the strange trap where now she lived and scrabbled, a place of doom in which her children would not flourish at all but would meet naked pain and she would not be able to raise a hand to cloak it. Don't fire. Don't fire. Whatever next.

She looked at the vegetables piled on the chopping board. The gardener had brought them in and a sorry bunch they were, dark and squalid quite unlike the brilliantly coloured ones piled in Marks & Spencer with their skin gleaming, polished and impeccable, like the women she saw when she went shopping in London. These vegetables were dingy, full of protuberances and deformities. Little gnarled knobs and secondary growths sprouted and clung to their surfaces and there were holes and black rings where nameless things had gnawed. Their skins were dull and they had follicles and hairs and blackheads in odd places. Yet to get these sorry objects onto her draining board required monumental effort and riches and diplomatic skills more suited to a modern ambassador than to an ersatz housewife. Finding, keeping and paying, not only the cook and not just a gardener but a gardener who would bring the vegetables to the larder rather than guarding their existence as a deadly secret, was a business not to be undertaken lightly. Dora had employed many a gardener in her time and had become accustomed to finding in her kitchen garden, towards the end of the summer, enormous, long, rough-skinned objects, like huge withered balloons which she discerned or rather surmised were mange-touts or green beans, or small blackened cinders which once had been raspberries. She looked at the little crisp uniform mange-touts in the supermarket with rancour.

From the room down the hall she could hear 'Jackanory'. A beguiling voice was telling the story of the little mermaid.

She thwacked a long white hairy foot off an albino carrot, and called into the room where the children were sitting to ask them if they wanted supper now or when their dad came home. They didn't answer. She went down the hall. On the screen danced a small animated creature with long blonde string hair and rickety legs and points where her feet should be.

Where the points entered the sand, small red circles appeared. Laura was pushing crisps into her mouth as though she were feeding a machine. Tears were streaming down Alice's face. Talk about comfort and violence, Dora thought, Grimm is, as Grimm does, and went out again and back to the fruits of her garden. The carrots were strange shapes as well as a strange colour, joined in the middle so that they looked like truncated mannikins: no, truncated wasn't the right word it was the opposite, it was as though they had lost their trunks, and on each carrot there was a little bulging cod piece and growing out of the waist a green feathery body. Dora sliced the mannikin in half. The sobs from the TV room got louder. Presumably the red shoes were hurting the mermaid something terrible and her children were about to be abandoned. Dora called again and then went in and stood in front of the screen to get their attention, and the children allowed that they would rather wait till their dad came home and have their meal with him. If it wasn't too late, Dora warned, and heads craned to see around her; they agreed, if it wasn't too late. But Dora could see that they had no idea of what they were saying. What was late and what was early in their world was something she couldn't fathom. But she knew well enough in her own sphere and she got their dinner ready early and they obediently came in and helped her bring it into their room, making no comment about its arbitrary appearance or about wanting to wait for their father.

She ate as she prepared his meal so that she was sated with

nibbling but her appetite was unsatisfied and, when he arrived ten minutes later, she said in greeting, 'You're late.'

'I know my darling,' he said. 'I had such a lot to do, all the clearing up. And I can't tell you what the traffic was like.'

She repented. 'It's lovely to have you home,' she said and kissed him.

The children surged in and greeted him with kisses, with little noises and titbits of news, with hoarded confidences, and they went upstairs to the nursery, to kiss Thomas; she went back into the kitchen to get Simon's food and gather up the remains of her own furtive meal. She tried to refuse to think about why she had prepared the food for different times, in different stages, but the thought slunk along her mind like a lurcher. It was as easy, easier, for them all to eat together, to make a celebration. So why had she set up separate meals? The lurcher began to move out into view. Eating together was a ritual, a celebration or, she thought, tipping the sliced carrots onto his plate, an institutionalised practice, a practice among those incarcerated. She heard them come down the stairs and go into the dining room and heard him say in a confidential voice, 'I've got a dreadful decision to make. Perhaps you could help me make it.' She stopped moving about the kitchen and listened. Laura and Alice were silent. 'It's whether or not to give your ma her birthday present before I go away.'

Dora could hear them tumbling, twittering with excitement like starlings.

'Oh Dad. Where is it? What is it? Can we guess? If we guess right will you say?'

She came into the dining room with the dishes and they were, as she knew they would be, entwined around him, he besieged by their beauty.

He said, sotto voce, but so she could hear. 'I don't know whether she should get it now or later.'

'She should get it now,' Dora said. 'And not only should but will.'

'Well, that's decided it girls,' he said. 'She doesn't get it until I get back.'

'Oh please Dad.' Laura had her arms around his neck.

'Oh Mum,' Alice hissed. 'Why did you say that, now he won't.'

She rested her head on her father's shoulder; his arm was around her waist.

'Oh yes he will,' Dora said, going back into the kitchen. 'He'll do exactly as I want. He always does.' She was smiling.

The children were silent.

'You see, girls,' he said confidently, 'you do see what a monster she is. There's no question of her getting it now, or ever, the way she's going on.'

They squeaked and chirruped, delighted at the conspiracy, at the affirmations of love in his voice and something voluptuous, gelid, black began to rise in Dora's body. She stood still, waiting for it to slither up to her brain where it would convert into a torpedo, and she drilled through the air into the dining room, and flung herself into her chair.

'For Christ's sake will you stop this obscene game. I don't want your presents. And I can't bear to see you two slavering all over him.'

There was a thin white silence at the top of the table. He looked down at the table; it seemed as if the air had withered. The children's arms dropped down from his neck and shoulders like ivy that has been lopped at some root far below. They went to their chairs, sideways, angling themselves on to the seats, keeping their faces averted from where she sat in her chair.

'I can't bear to see you going on like that,' she said. 'Having to seduce a man to get what you want.'

'My darling,' he said, his voice full of pain. 'We were just having fun. I'm sorry if it has upset you. It was just fun. And it wasn't seduction – all those things you read into it. It wasn't for themselves. It was a game.'

'It was an elaborate tease.'

'It wasn't an elaborate tease. It was a game, truly Dora. We were having fun and I'm sorry that it's upset you, but I can't think why.'

'If you can't think why after ten years of marriage there's something wrong,' she said.

'And if, after ten years of marriage, you read such things into a game I'm playing with the children, there certainly is.'

'It wasn't a game, it was an elaborate tease.'

'It wasn't a tease.'

'It was. What else is saying "Oh, I've got something for her but I won't give it to her? No let her dance for it"?'

She listened to the hissing words, the spleen, the spite, tried to stop the horrible launch of anger but jammed the effort with the white snow of anger, the obscure pain of violation, with the desire to punish. One part of her mind watched as she screamed, apparently because he had brought her a present and had not delivered it, and the other part whispered that it had nothing to do with what was happening, that the present was merely a trigger detonating bigger grievances. Caught between the two voices was a passive, somewhat stooped figure, shielding itself against the blast, a figure she knew so well, loved so much, despised so dearly, hated so clearly, a figure only of her imagination and memory, the figure of that mother who had had to reject affection to survive, who had lost her father, who had watched her daughters adore her feckless husband. That misshapen figure was, she knew, also herself, the shrew who had to keep tryst with that earlier mother, redeem her by authenticating her behaviour, by repetition, by actions not words, and who was now the mother of these two white-faced children, stricken, silent and learning their lessons well. She raised her head and looked at the man opposite whom she loved as much as life itself, that life that seemed to be breaking her or grinding her down into particles which spun around a hollow at the centre, down a long dark tunnel reverberating with a negative message that, when it was stopped, broke up the world.

He looked down and began to try to eat, to bring normality back into the room as though it were a creature waiting outside the door, but Dora kicked it out. Calamity could never be left well alone when she was on the rampage and though she could not give it the good name, her courage drove her on.

His not punishing her for her badness was surely a form of violence, the worst kind of punishment. Her mind ran back and forwards scrabbling, weeping, seeking for redemption, punishment, penance.

'I don't want the bloody present, especially after all this song and dance.'

'Well, let's forget about it, or try to,' he said.

There was another silence. Alice sniffed and wiped her nose on her sleeve and looked at Dora, who said, not looking back, 'I mean, you do what you know drives me almost mad and then wonder why I'm angry.'

'Oh stop it, stop it, stop it,' Laura screamed. 'We're trying to forget it and you start all over again.'

Dora got up and carried her plate to the kitchen. The children followed with theirs. They cleared the table while she washed up. They cried silently, modestly, as though their tears, wrung so deeply, were of no account in the scheme of the tragedy. He helped clear up.

She looked at herself in the glass over the sink, saw her mother looking back at her, saw her shapeless, angry, craving face, saw the lines between her eyes deepen, saw her skin grained grey and dull. She thought of herself, on many an evening, sitting, glittering, animated with pleasure in the company of people she loved far, far less than those now around her angling their bodies against her storm. She thought of her own image of herself, of the woman she knew she could be and sometimes was and saw herself now, angry, malevolent, brooding like a succubus over the people who had been locked in a circle of love which she had torn apart in order to enter, or to make them bring her in, to try to stop them making her into the totem, to stop them placating her. The reasons went around in her head, she kept heading for the real reason like the rat in the cage and saw herself and Iris within their father's arms while her mother left the room to lie down with a bad head and they watched her go. Tragedy she thought? Tragedy? Tawdry, helpless farce, this is. She remembered her mother and thought of her battles, battles she had never won because the earlier situation of the man being loved more, existed, because the situation stretched back to the crack of dawn, the circles were linked so tightly, she could never break them, didn't want to break them. There was something authentic about this grim gloom she had cast over the evening, something tyrannically wonderful about her implacability.

She cast, as though throwing a stone, her mind and imagination back to when she was a child and her mother had behaved as she was now behaving and remembered the impotent sorrow and grief she had felt at her inability to sway or soften her mother, her anguished question: Why is she like that? Why can't she stop. Yet

Nora had not been able to take a step outside the magic male circle to help her mother. It was too much to ask of a child. She plunged her hands into the water in the sink and, looking at herself again, she heard why, why can't she stop, and staring at her own eyes, she asked herself why, why can't you stop? And it was like asking a swimmer in heavy seas, finally exhausted, to swim another few yards to safety. It seemed to the onlooker on the shore such a necessary little thing to do, but to the swimmer, impossible. She could not do the stroke. She saw her children disappear through the door and she rode the dark undertow of her anger and she remembered herself looking at the bulwark of her unforgiving mother before the waters had closed over her head and it was what she, Dora, here and now, was, whatever the reasons, an ill-mannered, shrewish, unhappy woman bulwarking against the light, a woman who had the means to contrive to be joyful, and would not use them. She took a breath and gathered her exhausted limbs and turned around and swam to a rock, pulled herself up though her feet were giving way under her, and said to her daughters as they carried in the last of the dishes, 'I'm sorry.' She began to cry, as they were doing, openly now, the tears splashing. 'I'm so sorry.' And she kissed them, her hair streaming. They put their arms around her and consoled her, without reproach, and she went in, barnacled by them and hung her head and said to Simon, 'I'm sorry,' and she knew it was not true but she had to believe it because if she did not she would have to think again and start the questions game; and her anger would be justified so why was she bearing the blame?

He kissed her. 'What happened?' he asked.

She was weeping. 'I don't know. I do know. I hate being teased. Something old. I don't know. Some trigger. I was jealous.' She could not tell him the truth since she did not know it, could not know it, had to refuse this knowledge if the marriage, and tenure on her family, was to keep going. He held her in his arms until she pretended to be consoled and when she looked up the children were watching them. She wanted to go under the waves again, to refuse him his role as saviour, to kill this false restoration before it began but she struck out again, a kind of dog paddle, reached another shore and dragged herself up there, thinking she surely must be wearing shoes by now but there were still the points of pain where she walked.

She said, smiling or trying to, 'Can I have my present now?' and he whispered the secret into their ears and they whooped off. They came thundering back down the stairs and she heard the present go crashing down, and hoped it wasn't glass or ceramics. There was a silence and whispering and then they came in, red-faced and anxious, desperate that she might start in again, but she took the parcel from them with a smile and felt its shape through the tissue paper. Small round connected shapes.

'Ah,' she said. 'A big fat square book. Scribble scribble scribble.'

Alice looked at it, twisting her head, puzzled. 'It's not, Mum,' she said, anxious lest Dora be disappointed. 'It's round.'

'Shut up,' Laura said, 'she's teasing,' and then hearing the word bit her lip.

Dora ceremoniously opened the layers of tissue paper and looked at the beads of amber and silver, tawny and gilded, bound together by a leather thong. Some of the amber was cut square, some round, like solidified lumps of honey. It looked as though it had just been untied from a neck and an emanation came off the necklace as though gusting in sound waves to a receptor. She looked at it with woe and saw the children looking at her, and masked her face into a smile.

'It's wonderful,' she said looking at Simon. 'I've never seen such wonderful amber. Where did you get it? It's like someone's heirloom – someone's really cared for it.'

He said, 'I got it in a shop in Great Russell Street on my way to the meeting last week.'

'The high-tech diviners? The don't fires, don't fires.'

'The same.'

'What shop?'

'A shop that specialises in African jewellery. It came from the famine region.' He looked across at her. He knew her so well. 'Yes,' he said, 'probably someone sold it for food. They've been getting a lot of jewellery lately.'

'How do you know?'

'I asked. He told me.'

'You asked if they'd been getting more jewellery because of the famine?'

'I asked how old it was. How long they'd had it. He said it had just arrived.'

She lifted it in her hands and she saw a woman with a child crying at her old breast, though her blank, hopeless face was young, and saw this woman raise her arms and unthong the necklace and sell it to the carpetbagger. She put the necklace down on the table. She would have no truck with it. That was why she had quarrelled, the necklace had been at the root of it, the canker in the bud, a golden snake coiled in a hiding place in her husband's dressing room, sending its venom through the halls of her house, carrying the unhappiness of a woman who had had to sell her dowry, to keep her children alive.

'You don't like it, Mum, do you?' Alice said. 'You think it's bad luck.'

Dora looked at the intuitive eyes in the small face already meshed into gear for another crisis and lifted the necklace again, caressing each warm weighty bead. One more trinket in your engorged house is a matter of life and death, Dora thought. A woman sold this for her children to live and you with your acute and precious sensibility deign to baulk at the gift.

Laura said, 'Might they have died, the person who sold it?'

'No,' Simon said, 'the money they sold it for would have bought a lot of food.'

Dora said, putting one foot in front of the other, 'She would be pleased that someone who has children too will love her necklace and take care of it.' She watched their faces clear and relax and thought, what a ridiculous irresponsible woman you are to believe even for a moment that the reason for your quarrel was because of an emblem hidden upstairs. And how more ridiculous would you be if you did not know that what you embarked on as a lie, to quell their terror, is surely an assertion of truth.

The children lifted the necklace and Dora looked at the tops of their heads bent over it, their small hands feeling each dense apricot fossil.

'Is it stone?' Alice asked. 'It's not heavy enough to be stone.'

'It's amber,' he said, 'which is a kind of resin. A fossilised resin.'

'What's resin?' Laura said.

'It's a sort of juice in the veins of a tree,' Simon said, as though reciting, 'which seeps out – at times naturally, or you can get it by incision, by cutting, so that . . .' he stopped.

Alice said, 'So that it cries?'

'I was going to say seeps,' he said. 'But yes, so that it cries.'

'It doesn't cry,' Dora said sharply, and the children looked across at her, apprehensive, disbelieving, and she softened her voice.

'Trees don't cry,' she said. Everywhere there seemed to be traps of innocence and sentiment. 'Only humans cry. But amber heals. When we were children, when we got a cold or cough we had to wear a set of amber beads around our neck to help to cure it.'

'And did it?' Laura said.

'Who knows,' Dora said. 'It's what you believe in.'

'And there's something more about amber,' Simon said.

'I'll tell you what it is,' Dora said. 'It's the best way to see if you like it. Look.'

She held the necklace under Alice's chin. A round yellow sun shone on the white skin of the neck, a little pool of energy, beating too fast.

'She loves it,' Laura said. 'Can I try it on you?'

Dora tilted her neck and hoped that her skin would lie. She looked down at the children, at the intensity with which they were staring at the oracle of her neck as it radiated its message. Their faces were gleaming with pleasure and they held it against each other's throats to verify the love.

'But there's something *else* about resin,' Simon said again, 'a most curious characteristic. If it is rubbed it becomes electric.'

'Perhaps that's how it cures,' Dora said and looked down at the many pairs of hands hovering over the amber ornament, at the unmarked starfish hands of the children, at the steady hands of her husband, and she saw the veins in her own hands beginning to rise under the skin where before her hands had been round with dimples at the knuckles. She thought of the seepage of pain that kept her at her work and the negative signals that broke the peace and made her release her fire and knew that the least she could do for the starving woman, for the women who were still her children, was to try to be ordinary, to quell the electricity, to shape the seepage into ornament.

II

The fan above her head had given up the ghost. The amber necklace was heavy. In the distance she could hear the sound of a party on the beach. She climbed into bed and fell asleep to the mechanical tinny beat of a disco record and dreamt that she was caught in traffic and listening to a broadcast that was issuing important information which she could not catch.

When she awoke her face was still painful and although she could only dimly remember the dream it brought back the memory of a broadcast she had listened to at home, whilst ostensibly working, in her room, and which might well solve the problem of importunate men on the beach.

She dressed and went down to the hotel foyer, and gave the necklace to the clerk behind the desk to put into the safe deposit, and walked along the drive to the gates of the enclave that surrounded the hotel. She was surprised at how far the hotel lay from the road. Arriving at the hotel in the dark, she had had the impression of palm trees, of lawns, but not of isolation. By the time she got to the gatehouse she was sticky and sweating, and her face felt like a balloon. She had not left the cocoon of the hotel before and was amazed and ashamed at what she saw beyond the gates, the numbers of people on the road, the traffic, the animals, the swirl of vivacity and colour, the variety and scale of the houses some makeshift, some venerable, built right up and attached to the pumice walls of the gardens of the hotel. The road looked as though it were carnival time, with a moving throng of people in white and coloured tunics and sarongs, weaving in elaborate patterns to melody she could not hear. She stood under the fronds of the tree at the gatehouse to the hotel wherein all was quiet, enervated, geared to people whose idea of a holiday was to escape, and watched the multitude and felt helpless and hopeless and white and clumsy, like a kind of daddy-long-legs in a colony of ladybirds.

A man spoke to her softly at her shoulder. 'Miss.' She turned around fearing that the room waiter had tracked her down but it was a security guard in a khaki uniform. 'Where do you wish to go, miss?' he asked, and she said, 'I was hoping to catch a bus into Trincomalee.'

He said, 'The bus will be very crowded when it happens along. It would be better to get a taxi.'

'I suppose it would,' Dora said. 'But I don't want to go back to the hotel,' and he said, 'No problem,' and went into the gatehouse. Dora was relieved at this easy solution and by the time the jalopy arrived she was doubly relieved. The heat was defeating. They drove at high speed in the way that Dora had often read about but arrived in the town without incident, though with a good deal of head banging and horn blowing from her driver and a good showing of white knuckle from Dora. She asked him to take her to a pharmacy and to wait, and she bought a quantity of bandages and a cane walking-stick. They returned to the hotel at the same speed, the sides of his curious vehicle grazing animals and people. The drive up to the hotel shrank under his accelerator.

She went to her room and took a shower, shrinking as the water poured over her face, and she wrapped her knee and calf in the bandages, gathered up her writing things and hobbled down to the beach. On the way, women who had previously moved closer to their husbands as she walked by, men who had looked at her speculatively and then looked away at her furious glance, spoke to her commiseratingly. She made little mutters and moues to show how silly she felt at being knocked over, silly not to have seen the signs, such a pity, and when she went and sat under a canopy it was as though some sour chaperone was at her side and she was left alone in peace.

Well, peace might be too strong a word for it she thought, ataraxy might be a better one for the emotional limbo in which she was anchored. Even under the canopy, the sun was intolerably bright and she closed her eyes.

Time after time, no matter what she did and how she fought, she felt helpless, passive, as though suspended at the end of a pulley, hoisted on both sides by equal pressures. One side pulled harder, she swung away from him; one relaxed a bit, she swung towards the other; when both pulled together, she felt as if she were being torn apart. As she pulled back and forth into the threatening haven belonging to one or other of the men, she longed to be able to get back even to that time before Theodore, when she had lived in no man's land, a Gilead, it seemed to her now, though it had been a barren red desert where women with grizzled hair and lion bodies and friendly faces had lain on the rocks and looked at her as she stood on the side on the dock and watched the ships pull away.

'What can I do?' she had said to Stella. 'I have clung to the knowledge that the only real thing I seem to have in all this indecision and stalemate,' (and she dared Stella to take her up on her description) 'is that if Theodore should leave me, my life would be intolerable. Yet when I think of telling Simon or leaving everything I can't do it. I sometimes think that the only answer is that Simon must die and I'm throwing the death ball. Thank God, Simon won't catch it, because I'm also not fool enough not to see that, if he did, everything would change and I couldn't go to Theodore. But if I have to go back to Simon,' she said, beginning to cry again, 'I can see it all . . . affectionate, settled, a paragon couple, rich, devoted, tolerant, lots of affection, even passion occasionally, and what fills me with horror is the idea of my continuing search for passion afterwards, the love affairs. That future appals me, to be one of those voracious women with an amenable husband.'

'You're trying to weigh it up,' Stella said. 'Taking away the passion and ecstasy and bringing it down to numbers like a child. There's no joy. You weigh things up, this on one side, that on the other. On one side your marriage, its establishment, fulfilment, security, affection; on the other being a social outcast, and having a passion, being hopeful.'

Dora said timidly, 'Why did you not use hopeful about my marriage?'

Stella began to laugh. 'You're making lists.'

'It's no laughing matter,' Dora said.

She knew she must try to decide what she was going to do when she went back. That was why she had come here, to make up her mind in the sun but all she had done so far was to search through fragments of her own archaeology as if she could construct a path to the future from spoil. She watched as the swimmers left the water and the beach emptied and she began to doze again and knew what she was doing was dangerous, that she would burn even more, but so she should, practice for frying in hell. As she lay in the swamp of sin and heat and sweat and memory, she dreamed that she was in a room full of people dressed in swathed purple and red and emerald clothes, trimmed with fur, plumed with ostrich feathers. They swarmed around, talking animatedly, and with large affected gestures in a grotesque parody of a cocktail party – gestures which, she realised, in their larger-than-life extravagance, were to do with the Edwardian age or the dancers of the Moulin Rouge, and that under their elaborate dresses they had white thighs and black stockings. They welcomed her joyously, jabbering at her and it seemed proper that they should be so grotesque, that their clothes and finery, decorations and adornments should be so detailed, and lush, that their faces should be so unlike the faces of human beings, desiccated with layer upon layer of crinkly dry skin as though made from old papier-mâché or like the fabric of wasps' nests, but as she sought for the proper description she realised that they had the faces of ghosts, frail, porous, decaying hollows, the inside flesh eaten away, so that they were like Chinese concertina lanterns.

She was both archaeologist and archaeology, searching for her shards which, dusted down with puffs of breath and memory and fitted together again, would show her a history full of conjecture, interpretation, assumption, lacking in colour as a broken Greek statue. She moved around the dump, among the dust, about the broken limbs of her own foundations, turning over a memory here, a phrase there, a pair of curtains billowing in the breeze, the barking of a dog across the lough shore, her mother shouting, her father revving the car, Ellen in the kitchen monitoring every sound through her strange filtering ears, the sound of a child crying with hunger.

She was startled awake in a panic. Two people, the older woman and her young husband, were running up the beach shouting, and she thought there had been another accident, someone else had been knocked over and gone under and she tried to rise but as they ran nearer she saw that they were playing a game, so engrossed in each other that they were hardly aware of Dora. They ran past and into the hotel.

She watched them go and tried to come to her senses. It was all alms for oblivion and the wallet at her back she was busily filling with her worthless past, a personal currency.

She thought of how she had to aggrandise every detail because of her hunger to prove that she was loved and was not a figment, consigned to a wind that had already blown past.

Dora believed that the jigsaw life she was trying to turn over bit by bit as she sat and wrote was the only material she had or ever would have to put that life together again. In this belief she was not unique, as she was not unique in so much that happened to her. All the same it happened only to her. Among the things that to Dora were both unique and general was her sense that her life had already been lived even while she was still living it, that its essence had somehow been sucked from it before she had savoured it, that there was some watermark under her life that held the secret and which she could never hold up to the light. She lived in a landscape where everything was blackening up for rain.

She felt too that she knew it all, although she knew only what she had experienced, and believed that her future, in many ways, had been ordained by the actions of the blonde scorched stranger who was her mother, who once was a fair and frightened child, or the feckless gallant hero who now appeared to her still to be a child and was her father.

At the beginning of her descent into depression, Dora would not apply that word to her state. Indeed words such as depression suffering, pain, loss, were avoided by her as being too important and diagnostic. She used words like anxiety, tenseness, irritation, cross, words which undermined and diminished and blamed. She had no awareness of her own moral probity. In that mad early dispensation any awareness of, or acceptance of, probity was labelled presumption and the habit had lingered on.

Henrietta had told her that what had struck her about Dora was her self-confidence but since that time, somewhere along the way, she had mislaid this peerless attribute and not all her searching could find it and nothing she could do seemed able to bring it back. It had edged so slowly out of her life, inch by inch, that for some time she didn't realise she had lost it, or indeed what she had lost, merely that some gift that had been hers, without her acknowledging it or being thankful for it, had disappeared as though sick of her ingratitude and that ever since it had gone, life had become more difficult. She knew she had been arrogant and spoiled to use it so carelessly as though it were her right.

Or perhaps it had all been a mirage, a Fata Morgana, and she had never really had it and only the impetus and courage of youth had carried her through. Whatever the truth, a void had opened in her life and into it had swept, or crept might be a better verb, a shambling new occupant, immovable as a sleeping elephant, this lack of feeling called depression, when everything seemed to roll away from her and disappear into the cracks in her life. In that grey time between the arrival of depression and meeting Theodore she had watched lovers and couples caress each other, share jokes, laugh spontaneously and had felt as though she were watching some kind of hurdy-gurdy spectacle or peepshow that had no connection with real life.

She rose and hobbled back into the hotel and realised that she was really hobbling. She had wrapped the bandages too tightly and when she unbound them her veins tingled and she could see their marks all down her leg like puttees. She wondered how long it was going to take her to do herself serious injury. She opened the folder to keep the destruction at bay.

When Dora lost her confidence, she found that she had also lost her energy. She put on weight, and went about losing her looks. She began to neglect herself, to bite her nails again, to cancel appointments and when Stella tried to help her it sounded as though her voice were coming through water. Dora began to stay at home, to turn down work, and everything that she had once thought interesting was no longer worth the effort. In the mornings when she woke, the first thing she saw was her bedside table groaning with books, and magazines, she could almost hear its joints buckling under unread *Country Life*s, popular philosophy, new novels, books on art, articles on painting, reviews of books, books on the Irish landscape, on Georgian houses, amazing interiors, social history, poetry, belles lettres, essays, and manuals on how to paint cheap furniture, so that it looked like painted cheap furniture instead of cheap furniture. On top of the nearest pile there lay an old Penguin copy of *A House In Paris* by Elizabeth Bowen.

Women writers, poets, Irish historians were the only writers Dora could bring herself to read. The popinjay heartless mediocrity of the male writers of her generation was anathema to her. She knew that in that yellowing incipient avalanche on her painted table was much material on these men, and in the review magazines there were reviews by them of each other's work. In the newspapers she conned she saw mutual interviews, congratulatory, complacent, and sometimes she even saw them in the flesh, though there seemed little that was fleshly about these mean-faced carrowarrys, preening along in their tight grey trousers. They all seemed small, etiolated, even the tall ones, whey-faced and full of a knowledge of their own artistic imperative and importance.

It wasn't just the males of the artistic bent who suddenly looked so different. A whole sub-species of men had sprung up fully-fledged while she had been in purdah. They were unlike any men she had hitherto noticed. The telephone engineers who came to mend the telephone, the Ministers of Parliament she saw being interviewed on television, the interviewers, the salesmen behind counters, or driving down the motorways with their coats on hangers in the window all had a similar look, perky, cheeky chaps often with moustaches, flat unspirited voices and eyes that did not soften their expression whatever the provocation. Wherever she looked there they were, talking loudly at gatherings, often in a curious transpontine accent, occupying the width of the street as they walked, driving fast towards women pushing pushchairs across pedestrian crossings, and playing their car radios so loudly that everyone else in the street must needs share their choice of music.

They all seemed to share a common confidence.

'Feminists are all so ugly,' she heard one say on television, his eyes asking for collusion from the woman who was interviewing him, and who did indeed smile back perhaps through reflex or perhaps simply secure behind her flaming blonde cowl.

Because she felt invisible Dora felt that she had been given other ways of seeing and began to notice other women she had not noticed before, and whom she assumed also felt invisible; women who did not dress well, or looked defeated or tired or were old, or sad, or had abdicated from the race and thus had been edited out of the world's vision.

In her house she played with her children and tried to work and waited for Armageddon. The house was silent, save for the sound of birds outside, the low distant hum of a house oiled still with money and considerable help. Outside in the long walk lined with pyramidal hornbeam and beyond, where the sheep grazed on the sward behind the haha, the enemy was gathering; the priest, the nun, the freezing woman with ice in her veins, the postman, the teacher, the old man in the road, spitting.

She waited for the man with the black mask and slit eyes to appear at the window, waited for the woman with the tussore hair and the papier-mâché face to float over her but the jasmine hung unparted. She waited for the sound of crackling and rasping, the smell of searing heat, from the rooms below, waited for the postman to ring and look at her, in her dressing-gown, with contempt and hand her a prettily packaged parcel.

She saw herself as one of those frogs which blow themselves out and then deflate, and she shrank into deflation when Simon tried to touch her: as soon ask her to blow herself out again as tell a paralysed person to walk. Only with the children did she remain inflated not because their uncritical love kept her buoyed but because for them she was the source of confidence.

She felt that she carried within herself a binary liquid mixture which, if tipped, splashed, tilted, spilled in any arbitrary movement would combine with the elements in her body and soul to make a poisonous, overcoming gas which would fill her head and senses with the unspeakable images that increasingly were taking over her imagination. She had never seen the sights that swarmed into her head, the things that had happened within her lifetime and therefore could happen again, though they were etched into her imagination as they surely must be into that of any sentient human being.

She could not believe that she might have been among the perpetrators of the horrors visited on mankind in the twentieth century.

Dora had read Jung or snippets thereof and had memorised a passage: 'Even if, juristically speaking, we were not accessories to the crime we are always, thanks to our human nature, potential criminals. In reality we merely lack of suitable opportunity to be drawn into the infernal mêlée. None of us stands outside humanity's black collective shadow.'

I do, I do, Dora said angrily to the woodpecker and the starling and the shrill cry of the nightjar. If it means sending children to their death then I stand outside.

She heard people admitting to the possibility of culpability as connivers if not perpetrators and knew they did this to show their recognition of human frailty and cupidity, to admit that they shared in the weakness of human nature and thus shared in the crime.

She listened to them confessing their awareness of the possibility of the failure of every human heart, saying mea culpa, to show the extent of their understanding of how ordinary human beings, as they put it, could descend to such depths. Such caveats filled Dora, not with sympathy, no more than repugnance, though the ghosts of such feelings were there in her response, but with a vast impatience. She felt that outright condemnation was the only appropriate response, and that the victims deserved at least that their slaughterers should be savagely condemned for what they were and what they had done. She refused to pay service to the idea of mass-responsibility, to collective guilt. She thought of the people who, because they had lived before such things had happened, had been able to enjoy the dream of Arcadian innocence, of Wordsworth say, sitting in a green shady place listening for the fall of a walnut, slackening his thoughts by choice and settling into gentler happiness. Christ, the luxury of it, Dora thought, when she sat in the woods and seemed to hear the echo of falling bodies in the distance. She tried to hold her thoughts and imagination tight, to stop them loosening at the edges because at that unravelling the images began, but the pressure became intolerable and she would let go and begin to weep. She knew what was happening to her might be helped by doctors, by medicine or pills but she didn't want to take the step towards admitting she needed them or towards forgetfulness.

Thomasina telephoned her. It was obvious to Dora that Stella had spoken to her and warned her of Dora's state. She asked Dora to interview a film director Dora had long admired, and offered her so much money that Dora for whatever reason could not refuse.

On the day of the interview she got up early and helped Betty get Laura off to school. Simon left the house, relieved that she was going out and she kissed Alice and Thomas goodbye with a certain lightening of the heart. She would be back before evening and they accepted her going with a distinct lack of interest since they were engrossed in setting up home in the staggering, ugly plastic Wendy house that flapped in the draught in one corner of the nursery. Thomas, she was glad to note, was the homemaker while Alice bossed him around. 'Have you lessoned what I teached you yet?' she heard her ask, really quite crossly, in what, Dora hoped, was an imitation of Betty's voice and not hers. She made her final check of the vital things she needed in order to leave the house for the day and heard, as she went through the door, Thomas saying, 'I wish it wasn't morning, I wish it was night all day,' and thought that the worst about indiscriminate wishing was that someone else might be granted your wish.

III

She and the film director walked down the street after the interview. Dora was wearing a brown beret and two passing boys looked at it and her and she took it off, surreptitiously dreading that it might have slipped into some strange dangle on her head and was making her look like the bag lady she now felt she had become, at least internally.

She looked at his enormous ill-shod feet as he strode along and felt desire run along the veins in her body and was relieved. At least it was a feeling.

They reached the car just in time to thwart a traffic warden who was circling it like a jackal at a carcase. Dora climbed in and watched him lope off with a certain regret. She drove towards Hyde Park. Almost immediately she was stuck in a traffic jam, at a standstill. The man in the car immediately in front of her began to signal that he wanted to change lanes. The kind of manoeuvre he was trying to make normally drove Dora almost frantic with rage. Stuck behind a driver who hadn't the foresight to get into the proper lane, and without the nous to get out of the wrong one until it was too late, she would mouth impotent threats and curses and often shout aloud into the air. Now because the interview was over and she felt relieved and was in no great hurry she watched with a certain prim sympathy as the drivers in the lane on the right edged their cars ever more closely in tribal stockades against the alien from the other lane. The little orange blinker flashed, as persistent as it was useless, and the driver began to twist his torso, crane his neck, hunch his shoulders and roll his head, as though, by behaving like a lunatic, he could coax or threaten some other driver into letting him change lanes.

There wasn't a chance. Nothing was moving. There was nowhere to go. Hundreds of people were sitting in powerful machines, anticipatory feet hovering over pedals. Unless the driver in front had an ascension, a day of judgement for cars where all would be taken body and soul upwards, he wasn't going to get anywhere. Dora's careful placidity began to shiver into cracks. She resented the insistence of his flashing lights, the rolling head movements.

The local radio station, wise as ever after the event, was warning its listeners with considerable relish that traffic was heavy in the Hyde Park Corner area, right down through Knightsbridge. Traffic lights had failed, sheer weight of traffic. Dora was pleased to hear this official verification of her plight. She wondered what opaque weight looked like.

A man not three feet away, behind the glass windows of a Rover on her right, was picking his nose, laughing, banging his steering wheel with the flat of his hand. At any other time, in any other society, such a public display of lunacy might have meant committal to a madhouse. Here, now, it was unregarded. The man was more likely than not listening to a radio station broadcasting less disheartening material than hers, which seemed wholly committed to imbecilic interviewers and doom-laden messages about weather and traffic or local and international rumour-mongering.

She thought of the apocryphal medieval countess in Siena whom Henry James had conjured up, as he had lumbered to a slow astonished stop in the narrow steep streets of that jewel-like city, bemused by the proximity of the palaces and their lack of privacy. Any woman having her hair dressed beside her windows must have been a wonderfully near neighbour to a cavalier in the palace opposite being shaved by his valet. She thought of James edging his bulk sideways down the streets, and of his image of art as a great glazed tank into which he must dive, and wondered what he would have made of these streets and the proximity of the cars.

Everyone around her was sitting in a glazed tank but there was very little art. She switched to Radio Three. A woman was reading an account of a sojourn in Sicily. The seamless unregistered voice flowed over the fiery words, almost extinguishing them. The writer was being harassed and pestered by the gallants of Palermo; she was angered by their incessant attentions but helpless to stop it. If she protested, reacted at all, they seemed the more encouraged. She did not know how she could solve the problem.

The reader paused for a moment. 'Pretend you have a limp,' a male friend advised her. All attentions ceased. She became an object to avoid. The friend had read Joyce perhaps, Dora thought, and everyone cried, O! O! in raptures O so lovely O soft, sweet, soft, tight boots? No. She's lame. O!

Far ahead the lanes of cars began to move, hesitantly, jerking forward. Their red lights came on again, move, brake, stop. Perhaps four cars had got away on that spasm. The cars on the left lane were still crawling forward, their escape route up ahead not quite so blocked.

The man in the Rover was scratching between his shoulder blades and still laughing. No doubt by the time they parted he would have pared his toenails with his teeth.

Dora waggled her gear to check neutral and resolved to keep her temper there too. Sitting in a car could stretch your patience to a new boundary of human extremity. We have no choice, she thought, we're surrounded by glass or Perspex and life is exposed, shivering, except the bits you want to know about, they're still behind the glass darkly, obscure and varied and old. She waggled her steering wheel as a token gesture of control. The man in front switched off his orange blinker and hunched over his wheel. Now that the orange light had stopped signalling, Dora felt less anxious. The man in front wound down his window; cigarette smoke drifted out.

Dora thought of her parents in Ireland who, in a sudden attempt at modernity, had replaced the windows of the house of her childhood with great sheets of double glazing. Now one could see clear through the rooms. My picture windows, her mother had called them, when she could still remember names and she had waited for Dora to make suitable noises of envy, approbation and delight, all of which Dora had done, whilst she thought with sentimental affection of the lost dark windows behind which the mother she had always known had bulked indomitable and eternal. Standing between those new sheets of glass which made such an exhibition of the life within the house, the old woman whom her mother had suddenly become seemed too frail, too human, Dora thought, to be her mother, and then began to laugh at her own demands and conceit. The man in the Rover grinned back. Dora hardened her face and looked ahead, and the man in the car in front looked around beseechingly as though sensing some kind of contact. Dora pretended not to see him either.

Far ahead, the front row of cars trundled forward like acolytes to a ceremony, and she could see now that there were policemen on duty at strategic points around Hyde Park Corner, waiting like priests, to give admittance to the cult. Policemen. That made sense. Traffic policemen had only to appear, confident, booted, gauntleted, for the whole area to get snarled up and grind down. Left to its own devices the traffic surged violently around the huge roundabout and devil take the hindmost. There might be a few near misses, horn-blowings, the occasional accident, but not this sullen waiting, stuck in limbo. Dora scowled and revved her engine in lieu of her own growl.

The man in front threw his cigarette out of the window with a shower of sparks. Dora was amazed that the combination of petrol and tossed cigarette did not cause an immediate explosion. What was that story about the astronauts in their space craft, hurtling hundreds of miles above Australia who saw, against their windows, the bonfire sparks blown up as benediction by the aborigines below, sitting around their fire?

She looked at her watch. She had been in this jam for hours, for hours, yet her watch told her it was a matter of minutes.

Aboriginal, from the original. Why was it such an odious sobriquet? No wonder Joyce had had such play with words. And he had been called an aborigine in his time, quoted as the living argument against establishing a separate university for the aboriginals of Ireland.

She thought of her mother, caught in the pewter light between her windows and wondered why people in northern countries had suddenly started putting such huge windows into their houses. It's unnatural, she thought, we're a people used to huddling, to darkness, not just for warmth's but for safety's sake. It can't be a sudden aesthetic interest in light for its own sake, light in this place is a necessity, for grass and growth; it was what happened when the darkness drew away, lacking the dazzling and positive quality it had in other places, where it added a new property to the thing it touched. The light in these islands was a limpid and furtive light, stained by use, coming through plate-glass panels reluctantly, like a governess on a music-hall stage, not knowing where to turn. And well might it be shy, Dora thought, remembering the rooms in Ireland and looking out at the scene around her. The cars inched forward again, the man in front sprang from his slump over his wheel and his light began to semaphore again. She inched forward and stopped, bloody policemen, she'd have been on the road home by now if it hadn't been for them with their great shiny white helmets like albino wasps. She revved the engine. Well might that Irish light be shy, slinking towards such a house and objects, revealing rather than illuminating. Her first visit to Greece had altered her ideas about light and made sense of the things she had read about Cézanne. In Greece everything the light touched had been changed and charged by its extreme brilliancy. The light there seemed the most real thing, more palpable than the buildings, the ruins, the people, the land and seascapes which shimmered under it. The brilliance there had little in common with this substance, sliding along under the swollen clouds, creeping past the buildings, and stopping short of the stunted shrubs on the park opposite, like a tinker with a torch.

No wonder we're all so depressed, Dora thought, living in this grey flat matter we're pleased to call light. On the other hand what was there to illuminate? That sad arch sitting dumpily among the crocuses, an empty hole with marble around it, England's answer to the Arc de Triomphe with Victory on her chariot lashing her horses up on top, or the square and unmannerly hotel on the left where older and prettier buildings had once stood, and not so long ago either.

The thing about light was that you had to live up to it: no wonder great things had been done in Greece. Perhaps there was a new law waiting to be discovered. Light shines in proportion to the merit of the object to be illuminated. And if all you've got is an acre of stalled car, a man picking his nose, a bad copy of the Arc de Triomphe and the Hilton Hotel, the wattage is bound to be low.

'London's traffic news.' The announcer chuckled. 'Well, bad news this afternoon for drivers. A couple of trouble spots. Traffic isn't moving so freely around Highbury Corner, a burst water main there; and Hyde Park Corner, there's trouble there, a tailback right up Park Lane, with traffic at a standstill, in Piccadilly and Knightsbridge – a lorry shed its load earlier but that's no real reason for the hold-up, just sheer weight of traffic so avoid that area if you can.'

She inclined forward. The man in the car alongside had wound his window down, and was looking across at her. She stared ahead pretending she hadn't noticed him or the man in front, who was twisting around, intent on making the eye-contact that every driver would go to any length to avoid. She looked upwards as the safest place and saw the sun-roof. It wasn't just the expanse of window in her parents' house that she hated, and the light was well enough in the summer. It was the lack of security. However did they think they'd protect themselves in danger? Not so much the thrown brick as the lack of protection after a bomb attack or a nuclear war. What protection would panoramic plate glass windows be to them then? I wait for it daily, Dora thought, perhaps that smiling man does too and his smile is one of despair and good-will. How many of us trapped in these tin machines, are waiting for the crack of doom.

The policemen were waving her column of cars on, but hell's bells, the car at its head was stalled. The cars all the way back, synchronised like the Rockettes, signalling and edging out, past the obstruction, except the car immediately in front whose light continuously jabbed right, right, right. The policeman put his hand up. The traffic stayed at bay, growling while the passengers from the stalled car pushed it out of the way, in an intricate manoeuvre around islands and shoals and interstices. I want tiny mullioned heavy intricate sections of glass fitted into iron stanchions and all of it behind heavy shutters, Dora thought. I want to be barricaded in and to barricade danger out. Perhaps being born during the war has something to do with this endemic insecurity, rather than the given wisdom about us being the first children of the atomic age. I always thought I was too young to know about the war but surely, even a baby, perhaps most of all a baby, would have been aware of the tension, fear, excitement in the atmosphere, and day by day throughout infancy, the wireless must have broadcast a never-ending message into our uncomprehending ears, waiting for the Rosetta Stone of our future to decode it, fire, fire, fire, an irreversible conception of the world as a place where death tumbled in from a clear sky.

When Belfast had been bombed, her parents had seen the horizon burn; they had carried her out in their arms to see the image of war reflected in the water. And the news on the wireless, normally so remote that it might have come from another planet, had synchronised with their lives. As the announcer spoke of the raid on Belfast, they could see the leaping red water bearing out his words. Her father had been as pleased by that verification, as I am, here, learning from the traffic news that I'm stuck in traffic and which of us is the more affected.

She tried to visualise her parents on their doorstep, and then thought of other stricken people standing on other doorsteps, watching, first, their horizons burning, and then the foreground scorching and then the ground burning under their feet. They did not ask in Belfast now for whom the fire burned, they were getting their own time-bombs now, planted by themselves. What was it that nice Belfast lawyer had said, the one she'd offended because of her own assumptions – that because he was a lawyer and a Protestant, he was a Unionist. Prejudice, not assumption. He'd said that if the Unionists had met the Catholic grievances in any spirit of fairness or generosity, without the slightest risk to their entrenched positions of power, there would never have been any troubles. She thought of the hard-faced brutes, the B-men, who had frisked her father and demanded his name though they knew it as well as their own. The magic in the naming of things B-men.

The policeman waved at the line of cars impatiently. One more lot and it would be her turn to go. A couple on foot negotiated the road, the man with the baby in a papoose, its head lolling between his shoulder blades. The idea of such intimacy with a father appalled her.

Her parents had never carried her in their arms or between their shoulder blades and the idea of scooping her up to show her the excitement of destruction was too far-fetched, not because of their sensibility but because of their indifference. They wouldn't have held me up for the Second Coming, she thought, as she edged past the signs pointing to Victoria. Yet she knew she had watched something burning from her doorstep. She pressed the accelerator, the engine roared. At least the proximate grinning lunatic had disappeared, his car surging away on the last exeat.

Her father had told her of the memorable night when instead of hearing 'Here is the nine o'clock news and this is Alvar Liddell reading it', the broadcaster had gabbled, 'I'm going to read you the news and there's some cracking good news coming.' Tears filled his eyes as he told her, but then his eyes were rarely dry, his tear ducts were the most essential piece of armoury in his emotional arsenal. The traffic began to move on her right, slowly then with increasing speed, filtering towards Knightsbridge and the man in front swivelled his head and edged his car slowly right, the blinker still going. Dora was beginning to feel proprietary about him and the footless toil he'd got himself into, but a car revved furiously on her right and edged up to keep him out.

She glanced at the car now edging up on the right. A low expensive car, it was, foreign-made, with a left-hand drive, so that the hands gripping the wheel were just within Dora's vision. She saw them as though they were lit, vivid, golden, their long broad fingers moving restlessly over the wheel. Another hand rested on it for a moment, this one with glittering nails, a narrow wrist, a bracelet of bright gold about the bone. Dora looked ahead, gorging on anger and jealousy. A rich, young, stupid, uncaring, arrogant, extrovert car she thought, and why should she care? Jealousy perhaps, or fear or the knowledge that she would never sit in the passenger seat of such a car. The fact that she might sit in the driver's seat was another thing entirely. A man who drove a car like that had no truck with reality, with the primary things. She bent her head surreptitiously to look in, and saw his profile. A rich young extrovert indeed. Or a tinker or a tailor. Why was she so angry? His engine was thudding and reverberating, the exhaust spewed out a great cloud of fumes. Because his advertisements for himself deliver a horrid message, Dora told herself, her lips moving; he has chosen to present an image of himself by driving such a car, an unacceptable image, or unacceptable to me and I don't like him. The anger that she had held in check began to seethe. Anger at his arrogance, his assumption that he could, or should, own such a car in a world where other people hadn't enough to eat. I hope he crashes or it breaks down or he is scrunched up in it and has to be cut out, Dora thought, muscles and steel welded together in a bloody concaulescence.

She bent her head to see if she could glimpse the owner of the hands beside him, her silly beautiful face. She felt angry for the women to whom she now belonged, the street-furniture women, made invisible by their own pain, while vacuous bitches like her – Dora's car jerked as her acceleration foot twitched – had the world in their laps, laps, those weren't laps, those little pointy pelvises, narrowing like cleats, those were man traps. Your own car, Dora told herself, trying to pull herself together, to stop herself actually foaming, is foreign and has cost a great deal, if not as much as the flashy piece of machinery on the right. She wiped her mouth and glanced to her left and caught an alarmed stare from another driver. I must look mad, she thought, twitching and talking to myself and dribbling. Why the fuck can't the traffic move. The blond young cadet with the golden hands edged his car more closely to the one ahead, determined not to let the man in front of Dora in at any cost. The anger that had been bubbling just below the vent swept up and over her. She hated both of them in their ostentatious car, their greedy smug whittled faces, one of which she'd not even glimpsed. She pressed a button to make her window slide down, leaned out and smiled ingratiatingly. The young man glanced up, his eyes alarmed, and then reassured by her smile, slid his window down too.

'Can't you see,' Dora said, smiling and smiling, 'can't you see that he's trying to get in?' She nodded her head at the car in front.

The young driver, glanced up, following her gesture. 'That's all he's trying to do,' Dora continued still smiling, her voice above the traffic still mild and reproachful as a nun's in catechism class. 'He's not getting at you, he's not trying to make you lose points in the great game of life, he's not going to steal your . . .' she paused very slightly, 'your crumpet, he's not going to take your job, bend your car, question your manhood if that's the word, or cut off your cock. He just wants to turn right. That's all, you horrible little prick.'

As he caught her words, the expressions on his face flickered, always a little behind what was being said, as though programmed by an out-of-kilter control panel. From anticipation, to surprise, to dismay, to hostility, the expressions merged at last into incredulity and anger.

The policeman waved them on, the traffic started up and began slowly to move forward and the driver in front, unaware of Dora's advocacy on his behalf, whipped his car into the sudden space that had opened up where the Ferrari should be and was off with a roar, ready in his turn, to refuse to let drifters, idlers, slackers and unwise virgins who found themselves in the wrong lane get in front of *him*.

The young extrovert's face had gone a most peculiar mottled colour. Rather frightened, Dora pressed hard on her window switch. His lips began to move as he got his breath back and she heard him scream as her window glided shut, but she caught only the word fascist echoing repeatedly as she moved off, circling around her head, like a halo that fitted her condition. She was round the corner in a trice, and heading for Knightsbridge and she thought no more of light or luck or the unhappy faces of mothers but only that she must get home.

When she had finally arrived home, the house had been peaceful, a refuge into which she scuttled, thankful to be on her own territory surrounded by her things. There was a note from Simon; he was down in the lower fields. The telephone was ringing but Dora remembered that she hadn't even been vaguely curious. Betty would answer it. There was no one she wanted to speak to.

She started to climb the stairs to the children's rooms when she heard Betty call out to her. Since Betty never raised her voice, Dora had been perturbed. She went to the phone and listened to her father's voice. Tears had never been far away even when they were inappropriate but now they were in order, his voice was hard and dry.

FIVE
The Ferryman

I

Dora stood on the deck of the ferry and watched as Dublin pulled back and the sea raced between her and the land as though it couldn't wait to get rid of her. The gulls had already gathered, gliding on their crests of air, beaks snickering the space ahead, bodies tunnelling into the parting.

Dublin was a foreign city, as foreign as Paris or Genoa. She had visited it for day trips when she was a child on holiday in Greystones and when she was a student she had sometimes hitchhiked down to it, the dream-like sinful city of the south, but she had never been there long enough to be familiar with it, though she had loved it at sight.

She understood the language but didn't speak it well, she used to say, and got the occasional laugh, yet there was truth to it. Wherever she went in the city she looked into the faces of people and saw only what she wanted to see; one day, faces borne down by the strain of living, stained with the weight of another morality, faces connected to goodness and saintliness as nowhere else in the Western world; another day, she saw only the faces of pinched and braggart youth.

She felt she had to make an effort not to be misunderstood when she spoke. Her accent sounded in her own ears like a brass instrument, a cornet, heralding certainties and when she tried to take the native note she sounded to her ears eager and false. Dublin most of the time, seemed a city so overwhelmed by its own corrupt sadness that it shimmered in a miasma. Histories of the city told of how it was built on an outcrop of rock known as Standfast Dick –

Dubliners had ever been ambivalent especially in another tongue – but its atmosphere was more as though the piles of its foundations were hollow, like ventilation shafts, and had been driven into the sump of damage and cruelty which had been ducted over the centuries, and which they siphoned up so that the air was damp and moulded with memory.

When she walked through a Dublin street she was stricken by the immediacy and vivacity of the response in the faces around her. There seemed none of the anonymity of other big cities where the likelihood of meeting a friend or kinsman was not part of the diurnal currency and where hurry was a quality. Here people looked at you as though they might know you and who your people were and, though she knew it for a cliché, it was no such thing to her, who had lived her adult life among a race which assumed that everyone else was a stranger. She looked back into these Dublin faces, faces full of sentiment and feeling, to try to fathom the secret of their continuous gallant curiosity, of how it had been kept alive in the other face of Dublin, of indifference and poverty, and she saw, besides curiosity, the marks of the abuse of daily city living.

In other cities when she looked into faces she rarely met another's eye. Here people looked straight at you and glances forever met and locked and fell and met again not in any flirtatious optical tango but in examination and speculation and almost bewilderment as though another could exist and be so unbeknown.

The ferry steamed on. On the deck below a young officer in a shiny white peaked cap was slowly pushing the aerial of his transmitter back into its little black hole watched by three crew men, their huge red gloves like hands from a grim fairy-tale lying on a capstan behind them. The red and white chimneys of the power-station slid past into sight, stripy candles on a mud cake, the low plum-blue sky turned to darkness and the lights of Dublin and Howth began to mark the places they had been.

It was in Dublin, years before, that the first intimations that her mother was not well had been brought to Dora. She and her father were to meet her, after shopping, in the foyer of the hotel in which they were staying. Her father loved staying in hotels, the grander the better, the more expensive it was the more he purred into place. Her mother hated them, felt displaced, uneasy, made the beds before she left the room, and fretted about the chambermaids. Since Dora's marriage she could afford to give them these tricks and treats. It was an admirable ploy, she won on all fronts and she could see them without having to go back to the quicksands. Dora and her father waited in the foyer but her mother so obsessively punctual did not appear. Her father began to be impatient which always made Dora uneasy and she went into the big salon and saw her there, looking strangely out of kilter, sitting on a red banquette by the door, her mouth quivering, like a lost girl.

Dora went across to her, laughing, for once loving her wholly, for she looked nothing more than a defenceless child but, as she walked across the room, Dora perceived that she was indeed lost, that the million-petalled flower of being which was her mother was ceasing to bloom and that she, so permanently in control, so impatient of weakness was in a state of trembling panic.

She waited for her mother to look at her with rage or relief, some reaction to being lost, but her mother had stared puzzled as though trying to place her, and then her face had cleared and she had got up and walked past Dora and she heard her whisper to her father, 'Who is that woman looking at me?' Dora looked around. Her mother was staring at her.

The wind was beginning to be bitter and the gulls were blanched bunches cruising alongside the bulk of the ship. The couple of passengers still on deck went down the steps to the deck below, to the public rooms and the smaller cabins.

Dora's cabin had a bathroom and a carpet, a bowl of fruit and a ticket for a complimentary breakfast, but she dreaded its narrow proportions, its wooden sides, its low-lidded ceiling, so she stood on. A heavy swell of smoke and chips lurched downwind. Her stomach buckled. It seemed inconceivable that this ponderous boat making such heavy weather of every slough and rise would ever reach Liverpool. It moved by inches and the escort gulls only needed to give occasional glimmering flaps of their pinions to keep them abreast. She remembered reading an account of travel in Elizabethan days in which it transpired that Sir Walter Raleigh in Ireland could receive messengers and missives from the court of Elizabeth, the day after they had been sent out or issued, as quickly, bar telephoning, as they could be sent now.

She thought of her struggles to escape her mother. It had never occurred to her, in her solipsism, that her mother could ever wish to escape her. There had been a time when Dora had felt that without constant vigilance she would metamorphose into her mother, replicate her stealthily, and wake up one morning to find that she was suspicious of beauty, frightened of pleasure, unable to be joyful. Everywhere she looked now she saw symbols and signifiers, and each signifier, every word became an elegy. She felt she had lived a life of talisman and ritual, making sacrifices to the future as though there were some malign deity waiting in the darkness ahead, with the integument of her mother, waiting to drop it over her head and only by diversionary tactics and disguises could she slip by her.

Whenever she applied lipstick, she leaned closer to the mirror to see if she had yet been smitten with those tiny lines, hoping to find a way to outwit the pursuers; and by trying to live her life so that it bore no resemblance to her mother's or its patterns, she had hoped to circumvent the obstacles and jump the traps that had snapped shut on the young dazzling people who had been her parents before her time. Their struggles to live together had coloured and shaped the pattern of her own childhood, a convoluted, intricate, serpentine pattern like an initial letter in majuscule print, the Book of Kells, so complicated that you had to trace with a finger to see where the letter ended. In poring over the letter she failed to see its beauty or the joy in its making.

She watched Ireland recede into a dream, a dark low lump candied with lights while she stood on the reality of a B & I ferry carrying its cargo of human beings and fried potatoes and container lorries to the other side and she allowed herself a vision of her own bereftness. She had watched her mother dwindle, trying to disappear, and Dora had looked away. Perhaps it had been kinder to do so, though Dora no longer cared to question her own motives.

Twice in her life, her mother had gone to Summer School in Edinburgh and only lately had Dora understood what an enormous effort it must have been for her mother to heave herself out of the swamp of the family and the place and get herself on that ferry which took her there.

As soon tell a Victorian matron, swaddled in bombazine and braid, to slip into a beaded flapper dress, as disentangle the women of her parish from their atavistic lives into the lives of other places a ferry journey away. Yet her mother had struggled out, and taken the ferry from Larne to Stranraer. It was called the Princess Victoria and later it had sunk with a great loss of life, and her mother had repeated, for the rest of her life, in awe at her brush with death, that she had been on that ship, that very ship, with that very name, the Princess Victoria. She had stood on its deck and watched its great doors close, the same doors that had broken open in the storm and through which the waters had rushed in, closing over the heads of people who might well have been with her at the Summer School.

She thought of her mother on the ferry steaming towards Stranraer and tried to imagine her leaning on a rail, watching the gulls, liberated, alone, the woman who must have existed under the peevish carapace that she and Iris and her father had each seen from a different angle.

Dora recollected something which when it had happened had made her laugh. Her daughter, Alice, sitting on a window-seat in her room, was brooding and scolding over a wrong-doing on the part of her mother, Dora, who listened quite unmoved. Laura had come in, in the middle of the keening, and Alice had stopped whining, leaned forward, and said to her elder sister in a voice full of curiosity, of search for knowledge: 'Laura, what would you do if you had a mother like mine?' Now the memory was like a stab. What would you do, Alice, if you hadn't a mother like mine.

Dora imagined her mother standing beside her, watching the lights of the south disappear, a young blonde woman with an inviting body, borne modestly, with slender ankles and rounded calves, a woman with all her beauty and wits about her, shining with innocence, wearing the blue and white suit. Her skin would have the sheen of unbruised fruit, her smile after its first hesitation would gleam out with a signal to the world; a signal that Dora knew had too soon been freighted into silence.

She looked out across the horizon, the tears from the whipping wind staining her eyes. The lights shimmered faintly in the glaze. The furl of the wake of the ship gleamed as it fell. She had never seen her mother put her hand in friendship or love on another's body, but she had felt its weight and she wished that she could now take it in her own hand, gauge its strength and tensility and hold it with love. She conjured herself beside the young woman on the way to Summer School, imagined them linking arms and, without words, walking around the deck of the boat together, delighted to be setting out on the adventure to the future, protected from each other's timidity by intimacy and proximity.

A door banged and a seaman came out to the deck below and picked up the dismembered red gloves, looked up and called, 'It's a raw night the night,' and she nodded and raised her hand and he went back into the body of the ship.

She stood on the solitary deck, her arms by her side, her eyes a foment of tears. The wind whipped her hair across her runny nose and dragged the moisture over her stinging skin, and she wiped herself up with her sleeve and scarf and went down the narrow stairs of the gangway to the deck below. Though it jutted further out on the boat it was more sheltered. Behind her a few feet away, across the deck, the curved glass doors and windows of a lighted saloon threw an arc of light on the steel deck. Through the steamed windows she could make out men and women drinking and laughing in a glow, and she leaned against the rails and looked long at the glow, and after a while turned round and looked back at Ireland, at the place where her mother had left her behind.

The place where her mother lay, lodged beyond any of Dora's shifting, was on a prow like this, and with unceasing water lapping its sides, but the prow was the gentle thrust of a high green hill which had stopped in its geologic slide to the water millennia before and the waters were those of the lough lapping and curling around the sedge and the boulders at the foot of the mound, and changing, lap by lap, the decaying bones of an old boat into petrification.

Beyond where Dora looked, the sky and the land were still marked by an occasional will-of-the-wisp twinkle, a faint swerve as some powerful light turned a corner. Where her mother was, the sea met the sky without any collision of textures so that there was nothing to mark their meeting, no telling where one ended and the other began. Only at night the lights of the parish sprinkled a sign.

*

As she waited in the terminal, the woman sitting beside Dora had said, suddenly, 'It's a terrible thing not to love a child,' and Dora had looked at her, startled into alarm as though an emissary had finally, too late, tracked her down, but the woman shook the newspaper she was holding, and Dora saw the small bruised face, familiar through ceaseless reproduction, of the child who had been starved and bitten to death. Dora had nodded, unable to contribute even a mite of energy to the woman's indignation. Such things were beyond agreement or tallying, were not to be borne, so Dora did not bear them. The child sitting in a pushchair on the other side of the woman began to whine for attention. Her rusk had fallen to the floor. Her mother rattled the newspaper impatiently and told her to hush. The floor of the ferry building was none too clean and Dora was exercised as to whether to reach over and give her back the rusk or to leave it be. To the woman reading a newspaper stunned by the descriptions of cruelty and neglect, the lack of love that Dora's mother had suffered as a child would surely seem trifling. It could not be her, Dora's, duty to try to redeem the pain of her own mother's past, especially since the fruits of that pain had been visited upon her. Surely to God, children of an unloved child cannot trek back beyond their own beginnings to repair damage, literally beyond their conception.

But Dora knew since she had become a mother herself, and had learnt of the demands and disciplines of maternal love, its extremities and needs, that she could have tried to console her mother when she herself had begun to learn the craft of motherhood and some of its arts. But by that time old slights and angers had become packed in salt and ice, the resentments had become preserved – held in store against an empty day.

And then, she hadn't known where to start, or where to find the time, where to look for the buried markers at the crossroads. She couldn't see the banks where the roads ended and the desolate moors began and her heart had none of the charts of her mother's topography stored away, and everywhere there were tygers. Yet Dora's own heart was a marvel of the cartographer's skill when it came to knowing how her own children were at any time of the day or night. Indeed then it was no longer antique methods with maps, but radar constantly turning, picking up the faintest distress signals from no matter how far away. She knew her children's needs and moods and she made for them without thought, without planning, driven only by the irrefutable codings of love. She reminded herself that her children were still in her gift, she didn't have to travel far, since they were still lodged in childhood and she might not find the journeys so easy when they grew older and learnt to muffle the signals, to erect diversions in her path.

What she does not want to do, Dora has warned herself, is leave a trail of tears for them, by which they will have to find their way back to her later.

She wondered how children whose father or mother died when they were young managed to come to terms with their adult life, how they worked their way out from under the magical giants, people who might have hurled clods of land out to sea to become islands, if those same giants had done a disappearing act at their children's beginning. Without them blocking out the light so that you had to find a way around to a new source, how could the future ever be anything but a reflection; without them pulling against you, how could you ever be sure of your own strength? They got you coming in and going out, did parents. If they were always there, they loomed too large and, by the time they could be put in perspective, they had so shrivelled that you were undone and angered by their vulnerability.

The blonde with the pretty legs on the forlorn deck swirled into the darkness, and the reality nudged into the void; a memory of her mother sweeping away a rose petal that had drifted down from a bunch of roses which Iris had put on the kitchen table, her mother muttering that she couldn't see why people had flowers in the house, they died so quickly and were too much bother for what they were worth. No wonder Dora tried to cultivate a garden that would bloom all the year round, and filled her house with roses in November.

She remembered as a child colouring the vivid complexities of patterns in a painting book on Tutankhamun, which she had won for some bit of showing-off at school and how her mother had scoffed at the simplicity of a people who could believe that by placing artefacts in their tombs they were equipping themselves for the journey to come. Her mother's belief in plenary bullion seemed no less amazing to Dora. She prayed long litanies regularly to secure some favour, or to lay up credit on her account in heaven, went to Benediction to gain indulgences, prayed to St Jude the patron of hopeless causes for almost any favour, big or small. Yet she had only told Dora the miracle of the car and the Novena long after Dora had left home and gone to London. If she had told us as children, Dora thought, leaning on the rail, would it have made any difference? Not to my belief, she thought, but to my perceptions, to my view of you, not as a monument beyond moving, save by irritation, but as someone capable of being touched by chance, by fate, someone born under a lucky star, instead of under a cloud. But if she had told me, then we would have been talking and that would have been a miracle in itself.

In the small parish church on Sundays under a banner text, which read God is Love, Dora had listened to horrid sermons about grace and could see nothing graceful about the sermons or the tyrants who delivered them. Slovenly men preached about sin and penance and sacrifice, and the wicked ways of women, while her mother and the women of the parish listened to them, humbly, obediently, repentantly. All the children of that parish had wanted, Dora muttered to the cruising glimmers, was to be in the only state of grace which mattered, to be good enough to be loved by someone who for ever was beyond love.

Over the years Dora's grip on her resentment had loosened only slowly. It was too important a staff to lay down easily. None so blind, her mother used to say as she attended to something they had not done, or done as she had wished it true, and Dora had gritted her teeth at the phrase but indeed there were none so blind, and Dora did not wish to see that she could not look at her mother and love her as she was, and could not imagine her. The image of her mother pleated by the pressure of Dora's baffled need into distortion could not so easily be shaken out.

The inside of her head darkened, and she was in an inconsolable cage: a fabulous blonde companion was disappearing into a beige bundle on a stick, shuffling into the scullery to clatter at the sink while her big bold blonde daughter, her legs crossed above her knees, smiled at her father in his chair, lapped him in worship, and stared with distaste and powerlessness at the disappearing back.

When at last she could look into her mother's small face without having to look away – indeed when she could look for as long as she liked since her mother would never again look back – she had seen an unknowable face. Those lines around her mouth were the contour lines of a personal history beyond anyone.

Looking at that face, a nobler one than Dora had ever granted it could be, she saw that her mother's defensive life had been her strategy against the fecklessness of those around her and that her weariness and discontent came as much from exhaustion as from early deprivation. She had worked from morning to night, and she could only marvel at her egotism in believing that she and Iris were the cause of her mother's malaise.

The ship ploughed on into mid-channel and the wind grew sharper, whipping the sea into alertness. That golden girl had become a middle-aged rebarbative woman, and then an old lost one and Dora had never linked arms with her and now never would.

She thought to walk across the deck and push open the doors and enter into the steamed and crowded saloon but seemed unable to get up the energy to move. Inside the bar, a man stood up behind the glass doors, and began to edge his way towards the counter and for a moment composed, with his bulk and blackness, a mirror in which Dora was suddenly confronted by her own reflection, illuminated by the weak white light of the outside deck bulb. She looked at her image in the saloon door and saw her face in shadow and below it her mother's body, her lineaments, her clothes, the brown and shapeless cardigan, the tussore hair, her body with its little hunched shoulders, the look of drainedness as though the life force were leaking slowly away from some tiny puncture of time.

Dora looked at the apparition, hardly surprised by the translation in the glass of her own tall strong body clad in its loden and scarves and good brown shoes, into the creature whom age had kidnapped, and then the man moved on and the image disappeared and the lighted bar shone back at her.

The door opened behind her and a woman came out and looked across at Dora and asked, 'Are you all right?'

'How kind,' Dora said in an artificial voice, for God knows where her real voice was any longer. She was still only halfway across the

Irish Sea with a foot slipping in each country and each accent only half-formed, and the woman said, 'Is there anything wrong?' and Dora said as though it were a one-liner she had been practising all her life to get the timing right, 'My mother is dead.' They were words without any likelihood whatsoever, an impossible arrangement, an incontrovertible verb with incompatible noun and here they were linked together for the first time in a new and horrible grammar. 'My mother is dead.'

'I'm so sorry,' the woman said.

Dora said, 'I've just come back from her funeral.'

The woman said, 'Were you there when she died?'

Dora shook her head. 'She waited till we were all away. We were good at being away.'

'I'm sorry,' she said again. 'I know what it's like. My mother died last year. I was in Dublin, she was in Limerick and my father phoned me; he said, "Your mother went to sleep last night and woke up dead." He was asking me was such a thing possible, had he got it right. It was a great shock. But one gets over it. With time.'

Dora looked at her, as much as she could see in the light from the door, and saw that though she was telling her what she believed, she was not telling the truth.

'No,' she said with the certainty of revelation. 'You don't get over it. It's a law of life that I never knew but I know now. You never get over your mother's death.'

'You may well be right,' the woman said.

'But you keep on going,' Dora said briskly, having cleared that misunderstanding up. 'Like Mr Plod the policeman you put one foot in front of the other and you get there in the end.'

The woman said tentatively, 'I think the better you knew them when they were alive, the more you get over it when they die.'

Dora was silent. The ferry ploughed on through the night. If she stared hard enough away from the steamed-up windows of the bar and across the empty deck beyond, and beyond that to the idea of Ireland, she might see the high green headland jutting over the water capped by a pied and emerald graveyard with its winding path down which her mother had made her last voyage; but stare as she might the light refracted and she could only see the wavering reflection of light and water.

Below was her cabin with its flat and narrow bed, and ahead of her lay Liverpool and the drive across England to Simon and the children and a life that seemed to have begun to run out into some hidden duct that she couldn't find to dam.

She turned to go down the stairs and saw that the moon was rising and the red dwarf star Bethelgeusa was glimmering. She remembered that long-held mythical, indeed almost mystical belief, that her parents had held her in their arms on their doorstep and shown her Belfast burn long before she could walk. With a pang of memory that was as sudden and powerful as though she had been transported, she remembered when she had stood on the doorstep, her hand in Ellen's, and looked across the horizon to the north and had been told to see the lights in the sky. Everyone was exclaiming as though they were looking at a wonderful nocturnal rainbow, an arch, or wash of colours which Dora, for the life of her, could not see.

'The Oory Bory Alice,' Ellen said: 'they only come every hundred years,' and Dora strained her eyes and saw a faint glow in the sky.

She stretched herself out on the narrow bed and folded her arms on her chest and she closed her eyes and saw in the distance, standing against an open door, a young woman, full of delight, her eyes shaded against a cascade of light watching a man swinging through pillars of glinting mote-filled light across the rafters of a barn.

II

There was only one thing wrong with having a gammy leg, Dora discovered, and that was that one had to go on having it, at least for a while. She hobbled out to the beach and the hard-faced woman, whose young husband seemed so obsessed with her, sitting surrounded by the paraphernalia that seemed necessary for any camp-out on the beach, greeted her.

'How's the leg this morning?' she asked.

Dora was surprised by the quality of her voice, its soft inquiry, her Australian accent. She saw as she looked closer that the impression of hardness came from the thin arched eyebrows, the high cheekbones, rather than any innate quality.

'My leg's perfectly all right,' Dora said. 'Actually there's nothing wrong with it. I was knocked down by a wave a couple of days ago and got this interesting black and blue effect and I invented the leg because I was fed-up with being accosted by a man who works here just because I'm on my own.'

The woman smiled. 'Not just because you're on your own,' she said.

Then she stopped smiling and shifted somewhat uneasily on her cane chair and looked more closely at Dora.

'The bruises are from where I was knocked down,' Dora said, 'honest.'

The woman said, and her tone was more guarded, 'Wouldn't it be easier to make a complaint. If you really can't stop him pestering you. It seems,' she hesitated, 'mad, to inconvenience yourself for him.'

'I don't want the hassle,' Dora said. 'Have you tried to get anything done here? If they do believe me, which is unlikely, it only means endless questioning and he's sacked and I'm gone. If they don't it's almost worse. And when it comes to it, it's only a matter of my word. He hasn't done anything. Not that that would stand up, as the bishop said.'

'It would stop him though,' the woman said.

Dora could see that the woman thought she wasn't in her right mind, which was a sensible enough assumption. She thought to tell her about the writer in Palermo and then thought she would probably send for the men in white coats.

'Your husband's away?' Dora asked, trying to get onto safer ground.

'Just for the morning,' she said. 'He heard you could get wonderful fish at the next bay and we plan to have a barbecue this evening on the beach. Would you like to join us?'

'Thank you,' Dora said, her heart dropping at the idea of all the smiling and talking and temporary good-will it would entail. 'But I have to work. I don't think I can make it.' It sounded as though she were brooding over the rush hour in some great city.

'Work?' the woman said, astonished. 'What on earth work can you do here? This place is just geared to vacation.'

'I'm trying to write,' Dora said.

'Well I'd never have guessed,' she said. 'Are you getting much done?'

'The best time is in the evenings, at night,' Dora said. 'If there is a best time.'

'I guess having the bandage on means that you can't swim?' the woman said.

'It did yesterday,' Dora said. 'I hadn't quite the nerve. But I'm swimming today. I bought plenty of bandages.'

'Well try and come this evening,' she said. 'You might enjoy it. It should give you something to write about.'

She walked down to the sea's edge and Dora watched her go, kind, self-possessed, but then Dora thought, perhaps that's how she too appeared to the observer. No hint of Io, changing shape on demand, fluctuating and straining between the forces of opposite attractions. She resolved to go out for the day, and go to bed early and avoid the barbecue on the beach, although she did not want to rebuff the woman who had seemed so pleasant.

She took a taxi into the town. It seemed even stranger on this visit, necromantic, squalid, its streets lined with colour, jammed with noise, an exploitable mixture of rich human interest mingled with the poorest living conditions. The air was blisteringly hot. She went to the state-run tourist shop and bought a certain amount of junk, photograph frames and fish and ducks and small palm trees made out of Coca-Cola tins and then on to the local museum, carrying her packages; she looked at statues of Buddha, and Shiva and lengths of fabrics, basketwork and semi-precious stones of different colours. She liked them being called semi-precious, it seemed a good half-measure, applicable to a lot of things she held dear. A very large lingam stood proud in a glass case. Two Englishwomen were circling it with deep interest, one looking at it over her bi-focals. Dora heard her whisper to her companion, 'He must have had a very big mouth.'

Her friend looked astonished.

'Whatever can you mean, Posy?' she asked.

'To have had teeth like that,' the woman said.

Dora moved on and looked at a stone hand bigger than herself, thumb and first finger touching in a gigantic gesture of rest. She took a taxi back to the hotel, exhausted, and lay down under her mosquito net, surrounded by her acquisitions and slept as she hadn't slept since she'd arrived.

She awoke in a sweat of terror. She could hear someone outside her door, footsteps, or rather could not hear them but in her sleep had heard footsteps approach and then stop at the entrance and the door handle creak, and she could not think where she was but only that her door was about to open and a flood of light would appear and a creature would stand in silhouette and look silently at her and fade back into the light and she knew well there was no source of such light in the passage. She lay as though pinioned, her muscles racked, her body in the shape of an X, her arms stretched aslant above her head, her legs asplay. There was silence in the hotel. Hotel, she said to herself, and then aloud, I am in an hotel, there is a telephone beside me and she reached for it and said Hello hello loudly into it and heard its silence, and heard within the silence the footsteps behind her door creak away.

She looked at her watch. It seemed unnaturally dark. She got up and pulled the blinds and saw that the sky was a strange, heavy green. Behind her the telephone shrilled. She was astonished. It was the first call from the machine. Even getting through to reception was a matter of luck rather than mechanics. She lifted it and heard echoes and crackles and then the hotel operator said in her ear, 'Miss, you have a call from England,' and she said hello and hello again, and she heard satellites whizzing around space and the tinkling music of the spheres and filaments buried fathoms deep but she heard no voice from England. Nor could she raise the operator. She juggled the telephone rest and began to shout and then to bang the receiver and she slammed it back on the rest and ran down the hall to the front desk, cursing not quite under her breath.

The men there were vaguely regretful but unsurprised. She had been cut off or the caller had gone away. He might try again. No they did not know what part of England the call was from, very sorry, madam, but you must wait for the person to telephone again. She huffed and puffed and they watched her, and she saw herself yet again angry with people who had no control over events, onlookers for whom she was a welcome diversion to while away the tedium. She went back to her room and waited by the telephone. She tried to read. The room darkened more, the sky swelled up, a sloe-green abscess, and burst. She realised, watching and listening, that sheets of rain meant just that, solid areas of rain pegging down as though hanging from a water-line in the sky.

She knew it was a sign. Theodore had got through. He was connected with water, a creature of ice and fluency, and quite dampening too when he had a mind to be, but one whose arrival had closed up the clouds.

Her heart was ambushed by a sudden painful recall of both of them running across the flooded fields of Cambridge, the meadows swampy, where the river had burst its banks. The water was dark brown, shovelling itself against the planks of the bridge and breaking over them. A swan at some distance away had reared up, its wings making an angelic arc behind its hooped neck and it began to advance towards another swan, crouched near the river.

'Look,' she said. 'Is that courtship? The ritual.'

'It's anger,' he said. 'Territorial rights, he's showing the other swan off.'

The second swan suddenly rose in the air and, cleaving a hole through the damp air, flew towards another part of the river.

'I'm not going any nearer,' she said. 'He looks very nasty.'

'I don't know why you think it's a he,' he said.

'Don't you?' she said.

They watched the brown water. Two birds rose, from almost underneath their feet and one went winging across the water, sending little plummets of spray into the thin air as it skimmed the surface. The other dived underneath. They watched where it had dived.

After a few minutes he said, 'It's drowned.'

'Birds don't commit suicide,' she said. 'It must have gone to the bank underwater.'

They ran to the other side but there was nothing there. They never saw it re-surface.

Cambridge seemed enchanted under his tutelage, under the effects of this new love. It was intoxicating to be able so to discover an Ultima Thule. He dried her feet as she sat on the stile, warbling an old

Irish ballad about sitting on a stile Maryeeee until passers-by began to give them a wide berth. She remembered walking through the warm April air towards the edge of the retreating river and his exultant shout as the stones skimmed ten, twelve times across the surface; or in Venice, watching him leaning over the bridge, by the Colleoni statue, near where she was hiding, and when he had found her, behind that superb glorification of a bandit, they had tried to bury themselves in each other's arms as the November fog had wraithed around them. In the first sparkling of attraction, need and desire, there was glory. Its point, of course, was that it was the opposite of being bored. Under his attention Dora became beautiful, so that people looked after her in the street. She listened to music she thought she would never listen to again. The songs she had listened to as original were now revivals, though a lot of the old troupers seemed to be still going just as strong. While she had been listening to Bach, Mozart and Gerald Finzi, in these latter days, the Rolling Stones and Dylan were still belting out their noises. She went roaring down a street in Cambridge in his open red sports car, listening to Tina Turner and she felt a happiness that was more intense because it was ludicrous and impossible. In her adolescent years she had craved to drive down city streets in an open sports car with a bottle of champagne between her feet, but in those days such a thing was unattainable. Now that they were being attained she thought she knew too much about what was happening to take them seriously. Or so she told herself. But she took what was happening intensely, and she took it painfully, and every day, though she tried not to think about him, was full of him.

She looked out at the white beach, the dry sky and felt the tears rise, lachrymae rerum, the falsest tears of all. She felt if she pressed her skin, tears would seep out from just below the surface.

Just before she had met him it had seemed that the world was about to be engulfed in water. She conceded that even given her own cosmic importance, it was extravagant to believe that Nature was responding to her own inner damp misery but every time she opened a newspaper, turned on the wireless, looked at television, there was another report of a deluge. Tidal waves were crashing down on Bangladesh, Venice was slipping like mercury into the sea, floods were making parts of England, the United States and Denmark look like Holland after a dyke-burst; Spain had had the highest rainfall ever recorded, and certain towns in the Po valley and Belgium had the look of Venice about them.

She wished she could do what she had once had it in her gift to do, to make sickness her decoy, and will herself ill, and in so doing, yield control and responsibility. It was an irreproachable way to gain time, to be helpless and demanding, to ask for constant attention without blame. But to make the break out of her isolated, floating anonymous pain into specific, nameable illness was now beyond her. Stella looked on this as an encouraging sign, as she did Dora's feeling that she was going under for the third time.

'At least it means you're not avoiding what's about to happen,' she said. 'And you're keeping on your feet.'

'Nothing's about to happen,' Dora said. 'That's the whole point. I feel exhausted. It's as if my life's over. That I'm a fossil.'

She looked at the waters rising not breaking, around the world, and thought that the original Flood had probably been brought on by Noah's wife. It made more sense than any nonsense about God punishing his people. Noah's wife, anonymous as all wives, had suffered a misery so intense, her power had been so fiercely concentrated that it had brought about an answer of sorts to her prayers – a deluge which, while drowning everyone else, would leave behind her husband, obviously competent to a fault, who then not only built an ark to preserve her, but, Sweet Jesus, two of everything else. When Dora looked around the house she sometimes felt like Noah's wife, and felt that she, too, could take off and float away in an ark with two of everything, except perhaps the greater mammals. Even some of those, she thought, surveying herself in the glass and seeing how she had put on weight. The only problem with adding cover is that the girth thickens. In other words the protection racket can make you fat.

Simon had appeared to be unmoved at her changed appearance and when she stood in front of the glass plucking at herself, he tried to comfort her but his comfort appeared to her to be as clumsy as her own appearance. He loved her, he said, and Dora could see that the her he saw had little to do with her surface and despised him for it.

She tried to make restitution for this and for her sadness, indeed her general lack of vivacity and joy, by pretending to be a good wifely hostess and by organising dinner parties, not such an undertaking when someone else was doing the cooking, and not something that necessarily soothes the soul.

On the particular weekend that Caroline and her husband were coming to dinner with her friends, Dora resolved to put her best foot forward. It was a long time since she'd seen Caroline's name in that announcement in *The Times* so she filled the house with roses, twitched everything into place, and went to London to have her hair done. She visited Stella, and afterwards went to the Tate gallery and was stopped in her tracks by an enormous painting she had somehow contrived not to see before: a coarse, powerful picture covering the whole of one wall, a maelstrom of water and bodies and drownings. A group of half-naked men and women huddled, on the top of a mountain, waiting for the deluge to overcome them. Just below, spread out across the rock, was a flotsam of exhausted bodies. Those who had reached the pinnacle knew, though they had climbed as far as they could climb, that they had not reached haven, the waters were still rising. And yet among the despairing faces the painter had shown the glimmerings of hope, as if some of the doomed believed there could still be some angelic swooping, which would rescue them from death by drowning which approached inch by watery inch.

She drove back through the mud and the rain and when she got home there was still time to go for a walk. Raining or not, hair lacquered into submission or not, she should have some fresh air and the dogs needed to be exercised. Laura and Alice were at a friend's house so Thomas was press-ganged into the excursion. The dogs, reluctant at first to get their precious coats wet, leapt about once out of doors, and shook and yelped, and within moments began to smell of old rope and wet laundry. Thomas joined in the yelping and jumping, his fat little heels wedged halfway down his wellingtons so that he kept toppling over. She held him between her knees and bent over him, his head jammed between her breasts, and hauled the boots on. The cavalcade spilled out, through the garden door, like porridge out of a pot, and just as they reached the side gate she heard the outside bell of the telephone. She wavered. By the time Betty or Anona had answered and come to fetch her, and she had levered her gumboots off, Thomas would be bored, the walk would be aborted and the caller paralysed with waiting. Dora heard Betty call and she went back into the house, slowly. The dogs stopped yelping and jumping, their heads began to droop, their tails to hang, like clockwork creatures running down. She left her boots on, and squelched across the hall. Someone in a pay-phone. The money dropped. Pamela's tentative but none the less demanding voice.

Dora was immediately on guard. Pamela never telephoned unless she wanted something, although it had never apparently occurred to her that Dora might work this out. And she always contrived somehow to make Dora feel as though she ought to be doing more for her than she was doing. These telephone calls usually ended with Dora inviting Pamela down for the weekend, which was why she telephoned in the first place. All the same, she never failed to make little genuine-sounding grunts of surprise and delight at the prospect. She was delighted to hear that Dora was in. 'I'm not,' Dora said. 'I was out and the children are getting soaked waiting.'

'I'm quite near,' Pamela said, 'with a friend. We'd love to come and see you.' Dora knew immediately what the sub-text was. Pamela had met a man who might do as a husband, or, failing that, a father for the child she longed for. She wanted Dora to look him over. She thought Dora's imprimatur important. It seemed to Dora very unlikely that Pamela found herself by chance in the vicinity of Dora's house which lay on the road to nowhere. To get to Suffolk was a matter of planning not happenstance. 'I've been in London all day,' Dora said. 'And I have a dinner party tonight.' She knew even as she said it that she had made a tactical error. 'I have to take the dogs for a walk. How far away are you?'

'Oooh a dinner party,' Pamela said. 'Have you lots of people staying? I'm not sure exactly where we are. We seemed to come by a totally different way. We're at a sort of crossroads and there's a pub just down the road, closed of course. It's called . . .' her voice got fainter, she heard a man's voice trying to tell her the name and then her voice came back on the line. 'Could it be The Gurney Arms?'

'I know exactly where you are,' Dora said. 'Have you got a pencil?' The pips went. 'Can you ring me back?' Pamela shouted. 'I've no more change.'

She gabbled the number and Dora tried to hold it in her memory while she dialled. A man, with a slightly foreign accent, answered her, so she thought she had got the wrong number but it was Pamela's companion. Since he was driving he thought it best if he took down the instructions. Sensible man, Dora thought. Left to Pamela she would have them both in Cardiff. All the same, between them, Dora and the man, they made the simple journey sound like an excursion into Outer Mongolia. When he had finished Dora asked if she could speak to Pamela. There was a kind of scuffle and the phone fell with a crash at the other end, Dora remembered how large Pamela was and how small the telephone box was, and wondered about the scale of the man; then Pamela's voice, breathless, excited, was in her ear.

'So we'll be there quite soon.'

'I'm taking Thomas and the dogs for a walk,' Dora said again. 'So I may still be out when you get here. But Betty will leave the garden door open so make yourselves at home. I'll be back as soon as possible.'

'Oh dear,' Pamela said. 'It would be nice if you could be there.'

'I *will* be there,' Dora said impatiently. 'If not when you come, immediately after, but I must take the dogs for a walk, otherwise they'll shit everywhere. And Betty will get you a drink or Anona.'

Dora knew very well that Betty did not approve of Pamela, ever since Pamela had outlined her plans to become, if necessary, a single-parent family.

'Oh,' Pamela said. 'Oh, all right we'll drive slowly. But Dora . . .'

'Yes?' Dora said as repressively as she knew how, forestalling any questions about staying, and Pamela said, 'I'm longing to see you.'

Dora walked briskly, the dogs running ahead, busy, impudent, their behinds wagging with the importance of being a dog and scenting that something other than a dog had had the nerve to pass this way earlier and, what was more, oh how their spines and tails quivered, left its smell behind. They were outraged and delighted and ran thither and back comparing pungencies. Thomas stumbled along behind, trying to emulate them. The rain stopped, almost on the instant, and did a vanishing trick. It was as though the misery, the clinging damp of the past season, had never existed. The clouds rushed by as though someone were rolling them up like bandages, the leaves glittered and the earth steamed. Dora could hardly believe it. She had left the house in a miasma of bad weather and depression and here was a day like a baby's fingernail, astonishing, complete, touching and just to be expected.

She climbed the hill and looked down on the house. Every time she came up here she perceived the place differently. Looking down on it now she felt intimidated by its bulk, its many-angled roofs, its crockets and pediments and lunettes. The dogs and Thomas tore around the blackberry bushes, Thomas trying to lick rain drops off the leaves. She watched him with a pang of love. In his miniature yellow oilskins and souwester he looked like a sentimental Victorian painting, The Littlest Skipper perhaps and she thought with sadness and guilt of Henrietta. He was her greatest gift and she had lost him, as she had lost so much in the life-sentence that had been her life, trying to copy what she saw other people enjoying, overcome by a festering past and apparently unable to accommodate any present happiness of her own. Henrietta's suicide had given Dora, as nothing else had done, an idea of what mental suffering might mean. That you could, through choice, however agonised, however pre-ordained, abandon your child not to his own fate but to your fate was beyond Dora's comprehension. The fatal selfishness of the idea sickened her and drove out sympathy. Yet she knew that Henrietta would have thought of this too and that she must have found the alternative – that of staying alive – more excruciating still. Dora feared that Henrietta's lasting legacy to her child, apart from her wealth, could well be not just a sense of loss, but a sense of guilt that he had not been important enough to make his mother stay alive. A nice millstone to hang around anyone's neck, Dora thought, and scooped Thomas into her arms, so that he wriggled and shouted and stumped off on his whorled legs, indignant at such babying. What a pair of parents, Dora thought, Henrietta depriving herself because she thought there was no way ahead, when a son like Thomas must be the best route to the future, and Tony depriving himself through anger because he thinks that Thomas is a piece of living blackmail.

She wondered what Pamela's friend would be like. Most of her swains were monsters, not surprising, her friends sagely agreed, since if a man was unattached and available over the age of forty there must be something wrong with him, well, not necessarily wrong, they amended, but he must be either married, mad, homosexual or quite startlingly determined not to be married. In fact there often was something wrong with them or, as Betty said, they were a coupon short of a toaster.

The one characteristic they seemed to share was that they were remarkably well pleased with themselves for no reason that Dora could fathom, other than that they had gone to a public school of one degree or another.

Pamela had certain requirements from her men. She liked them, in theory, to be well-born, rich, and famous. Preferably all three. She also wanted them, whatever else their proclivities, to be capable of fathering a child. Beyond this, she said, she cared not a hoot for their looks, habits, manners or behaviour. Dora believed that in fact she minded very much about all of these things, but desperation had winnowed her critical faculties down. She would bring down someone to stay who was, she would protest, terribly learned in some esoteric field – mixed bathing in Upper Cambodia, or leafy walks in Umbria – but not only would he send his listeners to sleep with his stories, he would go to sleep himself whilst telling them. She would produce a seedy scion of some great family, who seemed to think his name was sufficient credential to excuse his arrogance.

She remembered one such who had walked around the house examining everything. He had got badly into his cups at dinner and had said confidentially to Simon: 'Of course, a house like this nowadays could only belong to a rich merchant.'

'Fortunately,' Simon had said equably, 'I am a rich merchant.'

Simon, thought Dora, would never in a million years consider that his background gave him any passport to privilege or to bad behaviour. Occasionally Pamela produced someone who gave the impression of having a great deal of money, but there was generally a lack of fogrum about these particular men which made Dora deeply suspicious.

It was rarely that Pamela brought down anyone who appeared to be what Dora might call, reverting to the standards of her forbears, a decent ordinary man. If pressed to define such terms or asked to give the female equivalent, Dora would have been hard put for an answer. But she knew what she meant. She also meant that Pamela should settle for someone who did not try to be glamorous, have a title and who did an honest day's work. She meant too that Pamela should be grateful. Pamela was grateful for nothing. It was why Dora, finally, found her fascinating. Twice Pamela had appeared with the paragons who answered to Dora's specifications for Pamela and twice they had folded their tents and slipped away. Dora surmised that they left because they had realised that they were merely means to an end. Pamela said they had left because they bored her and she had shown them the door. For all she wanted a child, she didn't want a boring child. After her last visit, with the friend of the moment, a man who had broken two of Dora's gold-rimmed dinner plates whose match she had lately seen in a shop at forty-eight pounds each, drunk half a dozen bottles of wine and a bottle of whisky, complained of the temperature in the swimming pool, and collapsed in a stupor on a particularly narrow spiral staircase so that he had to be levered down, Dora had sworn a great oath that she would never again have a lover of Pamela's to stay, sight unseen. Simon, too, said without rancour, that if Pamela brought down another man like the last, then he would move out whilst they were there.

'Where will you go?' Dora said with interest.

'To the pub,' he said. 'They've got a very pretty red-haired barmaid, I've heard tell.'

Stella on hearing of Dora's resolve said briskly, 'If Pamela had worried one tenth as much about bringing those men to stay with you whenever she wanted a comfortable kip, as you're doing about suggesting she lets you meet them, you wouldn't have this problem.'

When it was put like this, Dora was reassured. Perhaps she was not a heartless bitch, but only a fool, a soft touch, being conned by Pamela. 'She's thick-skinned,' Stella said. 'You always think everyone is as thin-skinned as you. You couldn't pierce Pamela's skin with an awl.'

'Am I thin-skinned?' Dora asked. 'And isn't an awl an extinct animal?'

'Touchy is probably a better word,' Stella said, 'and the auk's what you're thinking of.'

'But it isn't just that,' Dora protested. She hesitated, afraid to bring Stella's ridicule down on her head.

For Dora who had hardened her heart against Pamela, as bullies often do against those less strong or fortunate than themselves, had been touched by the reason confided to her by Pamela for her fidelity to Dora's household. She brought her putative husbands for the weekend so that they could witness a normal marriage at close quarters and, perhaps, be made to see the arguments for such a state themselves. As Dora listened she could hardly believe her ears: not at Pamela's blindness, her blinkered optimism, or even the use of the word arguments, but her assumption that any marriage could be called normal, or that observers, on the outside of the truth, could bear away some stencil, half-identify the blind impress and trace it home.

'So, what else is it?' Stella said. 'If not the worst kind of free-loading? She gets a dirty weekend in the country without any hassle, or any bills and what does it cost her? A box of Bendicks? A cyclamen? And what does it cost you? She eats off the fat of the land in a household warmer than any hotel, and prettier, and I bet those friends of hers drink a lot. And that's not counting the hours I've seen her make you spend with her. And she never lifts a finger.'

It cost Dora nothing. Or not in financial terms. Simon paid the bills. And to be a good hostess made her think that perhaps she was successful at something. But, since Dora did not like to hear her generosity called, perhaps properly, foolishness, nor her hospitality being seen as nothing more than an opportunity for exploitation, she protested.

'Well then,' Stella said. 'What's the other reason?'

Dora hesitated. 'It's because she thinks faced with our married bliss her suitor will suddenly be overcome with a mad desire to achieve the same state and go thundering off to the altar. She says we're the only normal married people she knows.'

'And can't the silly bitch work out that if something is the only example of a thing, not only is it not normal, it's unique. And is she absolutely blind? Can't she see what's happening?'

'What do you mean, what's happening?' Dora said, anxiously.

'You tell me,' Stella said but Dora told her instead of Simon's threat and her vow.

'I don't suppose you'll stick to it,' Stella said. 'You'll get soft-hearted when she starts using her sad little voice.'

Dora, watching Thomas eating the blackberry leaves, now realised that was indeed the voice she had heard at the end of the telephone conversation and felt resigned. Pamela was coming to stay.

They started the journey down the hill. There were no cars in the courtyard other than Simon's and Dora's. Dora stripped Thomas down out of his oil-skins and they went hand-in-hand into the kitchen where Dora broke it to Anona that there were two extra for dinner. She and Thomas went up to the nursery. Laura and Alice were back, and Simon. The girls fell on Dora and Thomas with cries of tortured pleasure. Simon groaned when Dora told him about Pamela.

'Can I ask where they are staying?' he said.

'Guess,' Dora said.

'I suppose,' he said. 'Come on. We'd better start changing. The others will be here soon.'

III

As she bathed and changed Dora thought that surely even Pamela with her yearning for a contented marriage, her desire to find happiness in Dora's example, her refusal to believe in things going wrong, would sense Dora's misery, see that her energy had disappeared, perceive her confusion, her loss of confidence, her irritability, her inability to move. But then Dora thought of her mother. None so blind, we see what we want to see.

When she was dressed she tiptoed into the nursery to kiss the sleeping babe, but Thomas was standing rocking the sides of his bed, well pleased with himself for being so wide-awake. He was wearing a certain look, which he knew Dora found irresistible, pleating up the smile behind his face, to shake it out later if someone played their cards right. He was pink and golden and gleaming and held out his arms for fun and games. Betty, sensing a palace revolution, came into the nursery.

'I'm taking him down for one minute,' Dora said, playing the ace.

The smile appeared. 'Pamela is coming to dinner and she adores Thomas.'

'He don't adore her,' Betty said as Dora bore her trophy out, '*and* he'll get beyond his sleep.' Dora saw Thomas looking back at Betty and was shocked to see such masculine naked triumph in a glance. Already, she thought, at his age.

She went down to the drawing room.

The guests had just arrived and after the greetings, and after Thomas had been suitably fussed over, she and Caroline and Thomas went out into the garden.

'Your shoes might get wet on the grass,' Dora said to Caroline, looking at a pair of black patent pumps with petersham bows. The pearls too, she was happy to note, were still in place. Dora lifted Thomas up to play with the cherub's head, and the women stood looking back at the house, Dora listening while Caroline admired and tried to hide her astonishment at Dora's advancement.

'Someone else seems to have arrived,' Caroline said looking towards the orangery and Dora waved to show where they were: they watched as Pamela came across the lawn, breathless, beautiful.

'I'm so sorry,' Pamela said. 'We lost our way.'

They touched cheeks.

'You'd better stay for dinner,' Dora said in as neutral a voice as she could muster. She was in fact quite happy to have a leavening of more new guests into the set dinner party, and perfectly resigned to them staying but she wanted Pamela to sing a little more for her supper.

She wondered where the man was and wondered too, if he knew that he was here for the once-over.

So here she is, Dora, a difficult woman of an uncertain age, but in her prime, in her garden, standing with her back to the big yew hedge, looking up towards the house, and the garden door bangs out, and she sees him for the first time, running down the steps, her steps, and across the path and over the paving stones, where the aubretia and rock-roses and campanula congregate in spectacular and limpid coveys, spilling out from every crack. His impatience seems a quality as he hurries over the quilt of flowers without apparently noticing or caring that he is crushing their heads.

Dora, as we know, has little idea that she is difficult. She feels she is a depressed woman, hopes she is occasionally an amiable one, tries to be a kind one, and knows that she is a neurotic, and sometimes shrewish one and fears she may be a tyrant to those powerless enough to be tyrannised. She does little to change these defeating and even unpleasant characteristics, but grieves about their effects each time after she has picked her way across the wounded. She resolves then to do better, but resolve is easy after the event, when one has tapped the sump of poison and is exhausted into good-will. She has no idea how formidable she appears. So she is surprised to see how tentatively Pamela comes through from the orangery door, scanning the garden to see if she can spy Dora out, as though frightened of her, or hoping to pre-empt her mood. Dora waves as Pamela hurries towards her. Dora waits for her companion to follow, but Pamela appears to be alone. Dora and Pamela touch cheeks, Thomas squashed, squeaking between them, and Pamela is introduced to Caroline. Dora knows that the jockeying for precedence, based on tenure, on who knows who and for how long, will soon begin.

'It's so lovely to be here,' Pamela exclaims.

'You'll stay for dinner?' Dora asks and Pamela assents.

'We've got a change of clothes in the car,' she says and Dora knows it has all been planned by Pamela, no doubt in a trance, so the fact that she is ensconsed for the weekend has, quite surprisingly, just come about.

Pamela holds out her arms for Thomas, who becomes a lout and lets his eyes roam everywhere, without apparently noticing that there is a blonde woman standing dead in front of him with her arms outstretched.

'He's so adorable,' Pamela croons as he resolutely refuses to acknowledge her and Dora looks at her suspiciously, for, though to her, Thomas is beautiful beyond imagining, he strikes her at this age with his high forehead, thuglet face and blond long hair, as having a look of an attendant in Las Meninas, that strange hieroglyphic masterpiece by Velazquez.

As Dora watches Pamela trying to woo Thomas she becomes completely sympathetic to her plight. She remembers a story about Isadora Duncan asking Robert de Montesquiou to give her a baby to soothe her nerves – now there was someone getting it wrong on every count. If she did not have her children, she too would be desperate, and would be hunting men down with a harpoon in order to be impregnated. When Dora sees her children bent over some doubtful business of their own she can hardly believe that they are in her gift. Sometimes she thinks that her love is like a black cloud hovering over them or a swarm of locusts buzzing with anxiety and vexation ready to strip them to the bone, but even as she tries to be more detached she remembers the lack of such buzzing love in her own childhood and decides it is better for a child to live under, than to yearn for, love's shadow. Not that the process has much to do with thought. Dora could no more not have loved her children than a healthy tree could cease putting out leaves in spring. When she pulled the blanket up over their bodies at night and looked at the spangled perfection of their skin she felt her heart move.

'Where's your friend?' Dora asks Pamela.

'He's just gone to have a pee. You're a witch, Dora, can you believe that we've been driving through torrential rain and here it's like paradise, your own micro-climate.'

'It's been raining everywhere,' Dora says. 'All the time. Haven't you noticed.' Then she softens. 'You've brought the sunshine.'

So here she is, Dora, climbing out of adolescence into adulthood, and scanning the new horizons, a difficult woman in her prime, trying to be prim, trying to be that good woman dressed in purple linen, in the Bible, who is all that the perfect helpmate should be, standing with her back to a yew hedge with Thomas perched on the jutting edge of her hip, making conversation with Pamela and Caroline and looking towards the house, as they wait for Pamela's friend to join them before going into dinner.

The thick, dark hedge, against which they are standing, undulates and billows like a green wave and in one of these rising yew waves is a deep alcove, the result of decades, if not centuries, of pruning and the tying-up of young branches so that the inside of the alcove looks as though it is lined with thick green damask. In this alcove, welded to a hidden stake, is the head of a cherub with a sly, dimpled face. Legend has it that it is one of two and that its body and pair are buried somewhere in the garden, a legend Dora doesn't believe in. She believes in a great deal that she can't see with her own eyes, but not in headless statues under her feet.

Enclosed by the billowing yew hedge as though by a dragon's tail, lies the rose garden, its circular and oval beds girdled by low hedges of box and lavender, which are further surrounded by paths, cobbled and inlaid with bricks and shells, circling on each other, and leading to a carved seat with a frieze of lambrequins and tassels and two seated putti holding swags of sea-shells, and all of it supporting an urn carved with gadrooning, dripping water and fruit and flowers. The seat is set against a mist of fennel, artemesia and the extravagant frou-frou of fat pink roses.

Dora loves, as who does not, the prodigal beauty of these flowers, so old, seemingly so fragile, but which have survived better and longer than most old things except, she reminds herself, disease and sin. She marvels as she decimates them with her secateurs, that for all their bloom lasts only a few days, their stock has survived millennia, travelled across continents, resisted the most extreme of climates, all in order simply to delight her.

Perhaps the survival of the bad and the ugly is the thing to be wondered at, Dora thinks, as she cuts a promiscuous posy, laying Cuisse de Nymph against Doctor Raubritter and covering them both with Mrs Honey Dyson, and Nature should have stamped out the shameful aberrations of the world, the poison and the pus, if she is to deserve the name mother.

'I want you to tell me what you think of him,' Pamela says.

Caroline looks interested.

'How well do you know him?' Dora asks. She doesn't listen to her own question, which means have you slept with him, are you in love with him, where did you meet him.

'Tony introduced us,' Pamela answers and looks quickly at Dora who involuntarily holds Thomas closer. 'He asked me out and we had quite a nice evening.'

'Only quite?' Dora says.

'Only quite.' Pamela nods. 'I don't know . . . he's very impatient.'

Pamela would make anyone impatient, Dora thinks to herself. She feels motherly towards the absent man.

The garden door bangs and she watches the man's approach across the rock-rose garden with eyes and an expression that can be called many things, but hardly motherly.

The garden door banged and the man came running down the steps.

Pamela was leaning forward, startled, for all her expectations, by his abrupt arrival, hoping, one could see, by the lines of her eager body, her anxious voice, that he would do her credit. The scene took on the frozen poise of a theatrical set on which the curtain has just been raised. The man runs on stage down the steps, towards the pied grass. Caroline, Dora and Pamela and her page, Thomas, wait for him like attendants, a scene from Handel, perhaps, some early opera.

Something was advancing which frightened her. All I need, she thought, is a lily in my hand and a responsive leap in the womb and it won't be Pamela who will be up the chute.

She remembered the man on the cathedral steps tumbling over and over, the old man on the road spitting, the man like a marten among the rafters, the creature in the forest crashing and breaking. The man had reached her.

'This is Theodore,' Pamela said. Dora believed in magic, coincidences, she believed in it all, and that he should be called by a name that declared he loved her seemed to her very proper.

'How do you do?' she says.

SIX
The Shifts of the Heart

I

The rain had stopped and she could hear the sound of the barbecue being set up on the beach. She switched off her lights and when she awoke the room was in darkness, but music was still coming from the beach. She slipped back into sleep but the sleep was fitful and brought up the bad dreams so she rose to try to exorcise them. She picked up a book but the words blurred and she could not concentrate.

Dora knew that when she used to pity Stella for her love-sickness she was right, that love such as she had suffered since she had met Theodore was a disease; the knowledge didn't cure her. Sexual attraction had tapped into her latent passion and brunted something into gargantuan and greedy life which threatened to overcome all the rest of her existence. While she tried to persuade herself that what was happening to her was only banal she knew there was nothing commonplace about it. This was the first time in history. Her common sense had fled. Everything became distorted under the influence of this kind of sexual love and frenzy, thought Dora, including one's own much vaunted perceptions.

At the beginning he had been as full of joy as she had been. They had found themselves – to their astonishment – for, after all, they felt they were sophisticated, worldly-wise people, on an adventure of exploration. It was a well-worn path to others but new to them and they discovered, as lovers do before they find out differently, that even their differences brought them closer together. Nothing went without saying. They talked themselves hoarse.

They rehearsed their backgrounds and their upbringings, exclaiming at the importance of the nuggets being panned. They pretended to be philosophical about these childhood memories but each could feel the other's anger and grief, and recognised the continuing search for consolation. They tracked each other's reactions. How when she had come to London she had sent her parents money and showed concern to prove she was free but loved them. How he took money and solicitude from them for precisely the same reasons.

She divined that when she was with him, she revealed to him, as she certainly revealed to herself, his high secret self, the self that he might be in an ideal world, noble, potent and charitable and she knew that he, in turn, did not see her as an everyday woman rooted in her own needs and the claims and demands of her children, a wife in her ordinariness, did not see her day-to-day struggles, her lack of confidence, her lack of mastery of her own tantrums and tempers, her inclinations to deprecation and guilt, gratitude, her ceaseless immaturity, her eagerness to please strangers. He saw her as an angel and sage, as the perfect maternal image, wife and lover, girl and matron. He saw her as a successful woman.

From the beginning she did everything in her power to be with him, within the demands of her life. Day after day she found new reasons for driving the distances between them. When she rushed back to her children she was animated, joyous – for the first few hours. She let Simon make love to her, was gracious in her generosity. She did not, of course, dare to tell Theodore about this big-heartedness though in theory they shared everything. She explained in detail to Stella how unique it all was. Stella knew when to hold her tongue.

When she went to his house she became a young woman embarking on her honeymoon. Once, after she had crept upstairs to where he was working, and had declared in a ferment of passion, 'Oh I wish we could just be *like* this all the time,' she had stopped alarmed. 'Perhaps it's because it is illicit that we like it? If we could see each other all the time then soon we wouldn't want to. We'd become a marriage, getting on with other things, bored because we were freely available to each other.' He quietened her.

'I think not. I feel nothing illicit whatsoever. I feel as if I'm already married to you. You have shown me a healthy way to love.'

She thought of those words as she sat in her room on the island; she feared that her love might have brought her to a charnel house.

'There are certain things I must never tell you,' he said to her when she'd thought he told her everything. 'And they'll have to be blank spots in our relationship. I mean I've got to suppress certain desires because there's such potential suffering that it's simply not worth thinking about.'

She did not ask him what the desires were. She knew he was seeking a way around talking about her marriage, without using the words love or leave. 'I wish you so much well. I don't want anything to happen to you that might cause you or your children even the slightest unhappiness.'

She feared he meant the opposite and that a dark underlay was spread below the conversation with a meaning too frightening to contemplate.

'Cosi Fan Tutte' was on the turntable and she listened to the waves of images breaking over her ears and became panicked and angry. She said, feeling she was making a desperate prophecy, 'I can't think we should go on with this. It will soon be over and we'll have invested endless emotion and time, the only precious things we've got, we'll reproach ourselves and hate each other for having thought we loved each other, so let's just cut our losses now.'

He said, 'Stop panicking. There's no hurry, there's no need to anticipate what's going to happen.'

'I'm not panicking. I'm saving us time and trouble. You could be A or B or C, we're all interchangeable. We just have to find each other unique to make ourselves important enough to justify the expense and shame and energy.'

He had laughed and she had been surprised. It seemed so unexpected a response, instead of the black rage which usually greeted anything adverse. It was more like a reaction Simon might have had, though this she did not wholly admit. Such information was unpleasant, to do with an honesty that she appeared to have helplessly eschewed.

'Why are you laughing?' she asked.

'"Cosi Fan Tutte" – the very idea,' he said.

'Well they come back and their women who love them differently mix them up and it's of no consequence which one they love, there's not a cat's whisker between them.'

The music soared into the quartet. 'You must learn to live in the present,' he said equably, he who constantly negotiated with the future, who punished her for time spent away from him. 'I'm not interested in what is going to happen nor in what Mozart thought about us. I'm interested in now. And I'm simply not going to ruin things because of what might happen. I count my blessings too,' he continued thoughtfully: 'which is not like me. I generally go for more tangible assets. I've been incredibly lucky.'

'That's different from what you usually say,' she said, trying to be flippant. 'You always say you had a terrible life, that's why you expect to be treated well.'

'I'll deal with you later,' he said, taking her hand and squeezing it till it hurt.

'Hey that hurts,' she protested.

'Good,' he said. 'What I'm trying to say hurts too. I've made a decision that I am not going to ask for anything that will involve you in changes – radical changes. Your life is too bound up with how you live.'

'What? My house?'

'You *would* say, "what, my house". I mean more than your house – your friends, the society you live in. It's all too much for you to leave and if you ever had to make a choice, if it came to making a choice, I know what the choice would be.'

She looked at him, amazed.

'Oh I'm shrewd,' he said, seeing her look. 'And I never believed in the limits of possibility before. Never. But here I see limits, and I don't want to start wishing for something that I can't have.'

Yet even as she heard such declarations while still wrapped in joy, the remnants of her common sense had made her fear that such vehement declarations were pre-emptive prayers on his part against some impulse ordained by his nature.

The first time she ever spent the whole night with him was in mid-winter, and afterwards they had a day of great sweetness together. It was dark outside, almost all day, but at noon the clouds lifted and a limpid and silvery light shone through and they walked to the river.

When they climbed onto the plank bridge over the river it seemed like a narrow encampment where they could pitch tents and parley, slung over rushing water, where their emotions took on a kind of extended order to the sound of the beating water. The meadows normally studded with hummocks, tussocks, odd shingled patches of grass, tufts of weeds and rushes that looked like crouched birds or hares from a distance, lay under flood water. The main channel of the river lapped its banks and topped into little succous veins, like tributaries flowing in reverse, along which the water eddied in contrary ripples.

She was going to the opera, to 'Don Giovanni', that evening and on to a party afterwards. She said, staring at the water stretched and primed to the ground by the guy-ropes of the trees, 'I must leave in good time to get to the opera,' and it seemed an impossible concept, the elaborate magnificence of the opera and the Opera House and the party waiting.

The idea of being delayed, or of having an accident, encountering a flood coloured her thoughts with anxiety.

They left the bridge and trod gently onto the sodden path and squelched towards the meadows on the other side of the flooded river. She saw the two swans advancing and retreating from each other, their whiteness like flurried meringues of water and air solidifying just above the surface of the water. She thought of the territorial rights her husband had established over so many years and which she had yielded through attrition, because she had always been in someone's charge, someone's feifdom. She had always been someone's daughter, someone's mother, someone's wife. She thought of him waiting patiently, unreproachfully, in the foyer of the Opera House, and of how his face would light up when he saw her. There was no way out. She wanted the knowledge of his stillness, his waitingness, to be delayed, to keep its distance, to stay over there with the swans, not to encroach here in an explosion of sadness and despair, new love and old joining in a white flurry, a threatening hoop of thought. She wanted her husband's face to darken, to be angry in her mind, so she could fight him, instead of feeling she was merely violating his goodness. She wished he would give her some reason for betraying him, some lever by which she could prise herself loose and go floating off into this new life, agitating the water all around her with excitement. Instead, he stood his ground in her mind, good, absurd, inviolate but defenceless.

Soon after their first meeting Theodore had arrived unexpectedly at her home, on some crafty pretext. She had left the room where they were sitting, anticipation as palpable as a third presence – to brush her hair, make her lashes dark, and on the way back had met him in the hall looking upwards at the ranks of paintings.

'What are you doing?' she said.

'Sizing up the opposition,' he said and she had let it pass, if anything, pleased by the audacity, but as the months went on the remark kept floating up, grim, ungraceful, prophetic. It did not tally with his reiteration about his lack of ambition.

And indeed almost as soon as he had declared his intention never to ask or scheme for more than he had, he began not just to ask but to demand, to throw tantrums to get what he wanted.

He lamented his endless ultimatums even as he delivered them.

'I hate putting this pressure on you,' he said. 'I hate hearing myself. I must forget the quality of our relationship. God knows I know you are not the ideal person but I love you and I no longer have pleasure from my life when you are not with me. But I can't be involved with a married woman. I want nothing to do with a woman who needs to be with another man. Nothing. I will not see you and you will not see me.'

These passionate, bullying, occasionally vicious transactions she viewed as proof of his love, his imagination. When he said he hated being angry, resentful, vindictive, she did not say, as she would say sharply to her children, her friends, her husband, 'Stop it, then.' Indeed, she blamed herself for his condition. There was certain justification for this but little truth.

'We cannot live without each other,' he said with, as far as she could see, perfect seriousness. 'I know that I could not have this feeling without it being reciprocal. I know it, you know it, I wish you could realise it and make the choice. There has to be a choice, don't you realise? I begin to wonder if you really appreciate the notion of choice.'

Each time she produced new reasons for not making the choice and each time he demolished them effectively, triumphantly, pleased to find her foolish or mendacious or evasive or all three. In between he continued, he said, to find her lovable. She seemed every day to sink deeper into a morass. The swamp was closing over her head and both the handholds were on opposite sides and each out of reach.

With horrible clarity she remembered how Simon had stayed silent, inscrutable, unscrutinised, as she explained how she had inadvertently taken on more work than she could cope with and must needs go away almost every day. But even this was not enough for Theodore. She must come to him completely.

She had tried to jump-start him past the point where he was stuck but her heart wasn't in it. There seemed to be so much right on his side, and everything he said had seemed rational and logical. Dora felt that she too might say them, were she in his place. His voice had become increasingly distraught and angry, and the only way she knew to divert him from his wilful violent anger – to go to him, to restore him to himself, and herself to him – was closed to her by the minatory decrees he kept issuing which forbade her to see him and which hoisted them on the pulley of separation. When she ignored these ultimatums and went to him, even then the restoration of their love to a simulacrum of happiness was so temporary that it brought its own special pain, as a man who has lived in the dark for a long time may find the sun hurts his eyes.

'Things like this,' he said, 'merely make me realise how foolish and petty I am. I don't want to behave like this but you have shown me over the months that I must do it. Dreadful things are happening and we can't stop them as long as you won't make up your mind.' He put his hands over his face and she looked at his tears and thought that they were not helpless tears but tears of rage and frustration because he was not getting what he wanted immediately. The knowledge of this failure of imagination and generosity did nothing to dampen the insistent demands of her desire for him.

One night he took her out to dinner – a rare event in their sequestered, foetid life, and she sat beside a scientist who worked in the university. He told her of a new machine, a field emission electron microscope which worked with such infinite precision that it could etch an image of Marilyn Monroe onto an area smaller than the point of a pin. The precision with which the machine worked, the man said, looking at her and choosing, she could see, an analogy that would impress itself on her own infinitesimal pin-brain, was equivalent to trying to paint the window-frame of a doll's house using a single-bristle paint brush with a handle a hundred miles long. 'Why did you use Marilyn Monroe?' Dora said, missing the point to keep him happy. 'Why not Einstein? He's at least as famous an image – that halo of white hair about the face.'

'They thought of that,' he said, 'but it was either Marilyn or Jacqueline Kennedy as the international image.'

'Of what?' Dora asked. She remembered a story about Marilyn Monroe, that she had spent the first part of her career on her knees, her head in the laps of men. She thought of Mrs Kennedy climbing across the trunk of the car away from the spill of brains and blood beside her. The legend was that she was either gathering up the shards of skull and hair that had been her husband's head a moment before or was crawling towards the secret service man flinging himself across the divide that nothing mortal could span. Dora knew better. Dora knew when she saw instinct at work, and in Dora's scenario Mrs K was crawling away from the scene, escaping as fast as she could. She found that more heroic than the given interpretations. The woman was a mother. She had children at home. She was going to live. She missed the scientist's answer.

When they got home she repeated this theory about Mrs Kennedy to Theodore to see if he thought it feasible but as soon as she embarked on it she knew she was in the quicksand.

He paced around and around the room impatiently. Dora had never seen such an imitation of a caged lion act. As he sped round and round the table his trousers seemed to settle lower on his waist, his eyebrows beetled over eyes which were burning like those of a character out of a Russian novel, his head lowered itself between his shoulders so that he seemed to be drilling himself into the floor. Dora half-expected to see a kind of rough-hewn furrow of shaved wood thrown up in the floor behind his feet.

The bile in his voice simmered, etching his words with acid. 'I don't want to hear these stories which tell me what you're afraid to tell me directly. I am too grown-up, too valuable, to spend my life waiting for someone who wants the best of both worlds. I won't love a woman who is divided between two men. You must choose, I will not be a stepping stone to your future without me.'

His voice sounded like the oracle, the one that answered endure,

endure, to every question only because the wind blew in a certain direction. 'I hate it that I think more about you than you think of me. I don't like this kind of mean calculation but I'm increasingly making it. I know you. I knew the moment you began to accommodate, to reconcile your two lives. I can't accept it. I don't want to but also I can't.'

'You're punishing me for my other life,' she said dolefully.

'Yes, yes.' He turned on her. 'That is exactly what I am doing. Exactly the source of my resentment. Our love is not reciprocal and I can't bear it. I'm angry, resentful, vindictive, all the things I don't like being.'

She was alarmed by his anger. She felt she could be harmed by it when she was away from him and not keeping it in control rather as she felt that anyone with sufficient malice could nail her footprint to the ground and induce in her a limp. She wanted always to be in his good graces, to be the object of his love, and that she should be the object and not merely the cause of his anger and rage upset her, and her image of herself, more than his stories of his dreams and talks of revenge and ravings of unrequited love and pain. His pain might have been her first concern rather than her ideas of her self but she could not believe in it and was shocked on looking into his eyes to see that they were red-rimmed and brimming with tears.

Sometimes when they were making love, when his mouth moved on her, she thought that there was nothing more to life and nothing better. But even as she thought it, felt it, she knew it was not enough, that love of this kind was a luxury and something in her recoiled, something perverse, linked to a need for deprivation, a buried need that hated satiety, a small mean strong part that she had almost smothered but which she wished against the odds to keep alive. That obscure part of her choked on love and wanted to spit it out. At such times she hated him and wanted him to suffer.

Her body was wet with sweat. The bandages on her leg felt itchy. She thought of the cool watered fields of Cambridge and she unwrapped her legs, put on her swimsuit, and went down the hotel lawn to the beach.

Above was a steel-blue heaven, with stars of the keenest white, the sand a scimitar curving into darkness. She slid into the water and saw below the surface a film of phosphorescence; when she turned back she could see her own wake.

She waded out of the water. There was a little makeshift shower behind the rocks and Dora watched as the dark water rinsed the silvery film down off her skin. As the water poured she remembered the chant about Baptism, Baptism, the sacrament which cleanses us from original sin, makes us Christians, children of God and members of His Holy Church.

She reached out with her eyes closed against the pouring water for the little sliver of soap and felt instead hard human flesh. Her hand sprang back as though kicked back by voltage and he was on her, his arms around her, she could feel him pushing between her legs and she began to shout but he put a hand over her mouth and her most coherent thought was how strong he was, that skinny creature she'd not reported from misplaced consideration. Rage surged through her, she felt his hand slip on her back and she kicked up between his legs and he slid and tripped and fell and her legs seemed to buckle and snap and she fell on top of him and they rolled, the two-backed beast and she heard someone running and shouting and she was unlocked and lying on her back alone before she had come, not to her senses (for her senses had been operating at an extraordinary level, his smell, his feel, his touch, the sounds of his breath, the fire of his skin, all had pressed in on her) but to her emotions. She felt quite calm. The woman who had spoken to her that morning held her and her husband stroked and patted her back, and as they comforted her, she began to shiver. The man turned the water off, it was still splashing, and the boy was nowhere to be seen.

As they helped her to her feet, a pain, cracking and sudden as an ice cube on a hot back, ran down her foot from her ankle. She sat down again. The woman knelt down with her.

'How badly are you hurt?'

'I think I've done something to my ankle,' she said and felt it. It was fat and soft.

She began to laugh and the woman said 'Easy' as though she were a horse, and Dora said, 'I tempted Fate.'

They helped her hobble back to her room and she realised what a poor imitation she had done before of a woman with a wounded knee, now that it seemed as if she really would need crutches.

'Please don't tell anyone what happened,' Dora said. 'I don't want anyone to know.'

'We're certainly going to let the management know,' the man said. 'That little bugger mustn't get away with it. Besides anything else, he's a danger to other hotel guests.'

'Please,' Dora said, 'I'm absolutely all right, I'm leaving soon. Tell them when I've gone. I can't bear to stay here.'

She lay down on the bed and the woman said, 'We should get a doctor to do something about that ankle.' They all looked at it. It was a most odd mottled colour.

'Please don't report what happened,' Dora said again, 'or not yet.' A scenario formed in her mind of her being detained on the island for months while a court case dragged on. She considered the figure she would cut, the sorry defence she could put up, a married woman on her own, and surely asking for it, swimming alone at midnight.

The man said, 'I really think we must. He should be put away. He's a danger to any woman.'

'You're more shocked than you think,' the woman said. 'We'll try to get a doctor. You try to relax.'

The man lifted the telephone and dialled reception.

'You won't get through,' Dora said. 'How did you know what was happening? I haven't said thank you. I've never been so grateful in my life. How did you know?'

'We were over in the grove, and we saw you coming out of the water.' He held the receiver away from his ear. Dora could hear a loud ringing tone, where she had always only heard silence. 'Then we saw him climbing across the rocks and I pointed him out to Elena and she started to run.'

'I remembered our conversation about the bandages,' Elena said.

'You won't be able to get a doctor at this time of night,' Dora said again. 'I can't even raise a receptionist during the day,' but as she spoke, the phone was answered and the man asked for a doctor as he might order a coffee and the woman patted her hand, cocooned in the security of a marriage where the man was in charge and things were taken care of, even love-lorn women foolish enough to go for a swim in an unknown country late at night.

The doctor arrived soon after, accompanied by the security guard, whom Dora looked at with a certain scepticism. The doctor seemed unsurprised at such goings-on in the middle of the night and was not at all the voluble, impatient medical man, scolding about carelessness that Dora, in her prejudice, had envisaged. He was gentle, had been trained in a hospital in London and he bandaged the sprain and looked at her bruises, the new ones and the old, and took her temperature; after he had felt her pulse he said, 'Is there anything else you need to tell me about?' and Dora shook her head feeling the foam of a wave of hysteria just about to break over her eyes.

'Keep the bandage dry,' he said. 'And get some rest.' He gave her some pain-killers and a sleeping pill and she was grateful for his reticence and competence, and the discretion of her new friends who had sent the security guard off, allowing his assumptions about moonlight strolls or high jinks to account for the accident. The doctor left and the couple went soon after, reassured by Dora's insisting over and over again, that she was all right. When they had gone, and only then, was she seized by anger, shaking and gusting with rage.

She hobbled into the bathroom and perched like a heron under the shower, trembling and wheezing, opened her eyes and reached out for the soap and scrubbed herself as the water ran, wet bandage or not.

II

The fact that she was hobbling around on a stick the next morning caused little comment. Anyone interested was by now so accustomed to the accident-prone woman crashing around, that a stick here or there made little difference. She found it difficult to use; she could not master the trick of balancing her weight and every so often would collapse onto her bad foot and yelp with frustration and pain.

Elena and her husband came to her room to see how she was and she asked them again not to do anything about what had happened or at least not until she had gone.

'It's more trouble than it's worth,' she said. 'If the hotel presses charges or whatever, I'll have to stay here, and I must get home.'

Dora could see that they thought she was behaving irresponsibly in leaving the man unpunished, but Dora was beyond caring. During the night, between terrible dreams, she had realised that she must leave the island as soon as possible, that it was a madness to remain on the island, trying to decide something about her future that could not be solved by rationality. Actions, she knew, were no guide. She had thought to escape from the pressures that made her life so misshapen, the levers that prized her emotions open but she had carried the weight with her and the fulcrum was gone. Actions are transitory, she said to herself, a step, a blow, the motion of a muscle this way or that, 'tis done and in the after-vacancy we wonder at ourselves like men betrayed. Sometimes having a good memory could be a curse: suffering is permanent, obscure and dark and shares the nature of infinity. She wondered how Wordsworth had known so much about the human heart whilst appearing to know so little. She tried to telephone the travel agency but as she was holding onto the void at the end of the line, she heard the familiar little tap-tap of the room-service boy on the door and her hands began to shake, she stared at them in disbelief, at the receiver quivering like a dowsing-rod over a spring of emotion. The door opened and a young woman in uniform looked in smiling and, seeing Dora on the telephone, began to retreat, but Dora put a hand over the mouthpiece and beckoned her in.

'You have had an accident,' she said looking at Dora's huge white bandaged foot propped on a chair. Dora agreed. 'Your room waiter is ill,' the girl said, with no hint of embarrassment or disingenuousness. 'So I have come to do your service.'

Dora put the telephone down and hobbled out, down into the foyer, and got another knuckle-showing, leg-banging drive into the town. She went into the large American-owned hotel, to the office of the travel agent, and wrangled and argued and finally, to her absolute astonishment, found she was bribing her way towards a ticket. She would have to wait for confirmation. She settled herself in the telephone booth in the foyer and began the telephone calls.

When she got through to Simon, it was the middle of the night, but he was immediately wide awake and when she told him that she was going to try to come home earlier than planned, there was immediate pleasure in his voice as well as surprise.

'I'm so pleased darling,' he said, 'we've all missed you.'

'I might have to pay some kind of penalty on my ticket,' she said, 'or push some old lady or child overboard to get on. I have to get out of here.'

He caught the note in her voice.

'Are you all right?'

'Not really,' she said. The line jumped and crackled and whirred and gave her time to steady herself up.

'Soldier's daughter,' he said as he might say it to Laura or Alice or 'Steady the Buffs' and she swallowed and steadied herself and said, 'I hurt my leg.'

'Oh Dora,' he said and she could hear the genuine concern. 'Shall I come and get you?'

'Are you mad?' she said. 'It's only a sprain. But it's a bore and it's sore and it's too hot.'

'Well come on home,' he said. 'I'm missing you, the children are missing you, Betty is missing you, the dogs are missing you and I can tell you the garden's missing you. When might you be here?'

But even as she spoke she had become horribly resolved. She must go to Theodore, she had to see him, she knew that if she went straight back to Suffolk, to be surrounded immediately, even by her children, by the trappings and accumulations of married life, a house full of rooms and possessions and people but absent of the person she desired with such a fervent passion, she would not be able to sustain even a modicum of pleasure or happiness.

She did not want to have her children learn about impotent sorrow and grief, their inability to sway or soften their mother, to look at her squared shoulders and think, why is she like that, and even thinking about it, and about her arrival into that clotted house made her whole body behave as though matching up to her ankle, becoming bloated with anger and tension and pent-up sexual energy and she wanted to cram something into her mouth.

'I don't know,' she said, 'they're still working out what flight I might be able to get out. It's all charter and tourist group and booked months ahead.'

'I'll see what I can do this end,' he said, 'and when you have any luck, let us know so I can meet you.' His voice got fainter.

'Please don't, Simon,' she said wildly. 'Please don't bother. It would be much more practical for me to hire a car.' 'That's dotty, Dora,' he said, his voice back on line. 'You'll be exhausted by the time you arrive. Why don't I meet you? Much easier.'

She said quite mildly, keeping the alarm down in her throat, 'Don't arrange anything yet. I don't know when I'll arrive and I can't telephone easily. I had to come into the town to make this call. The best thing might be to take the train to London and you meet me there.'

'Even with your bad leg Dora?' he said. There was a silence. She wondered what he was thinking.

'If it's any worse I'll call from the airport,' she said.

Her actions were the only prophet, since certainties did nothing but fluctuate. Words, resolves, were futile. She might long to return to her old superstitious, unconfident ways when, although cocooned in comfort, she had felt lonely, left behind, abandoned in the game of life. But she was in the middle of the game now and she knew as soon as she set out for England she would be drawn towards Theodore like iron filings towards the lodestone, responding to an imperative programmed into her own nature. It was beyond her own internal power to prevent a crash into completion.

As she waited she justified having Theodore come to meet her. Everyone benefited. Right, Dora? Simon, the children, me, him. It was like being a drug addict, Dora thought, you got your fix and could face the rest of the day in a state of normality; but it needed a bigger fix each time to get the same effect, and you want it more often and you take more risks and in the end you do anything to get it. You leave your husband and your children, you convince yourself it's all for the best, that the children wouldn't have been happy in the atmosphere of unhappiness and need you were carrying around, that your husband deserved more than the half-marriage he was getting, that contempt and revulsion for yourself was not a diet to live on. You saw that many of your friends had done the same and survived, and were sophisticated and lived with the cost, or, Dora supposed, avoided ever finally reckoning it up, refused to acknowledge the betrayed and abandoned. The ticket clerk called her over. If the gods smiled, if his colleague in head office was correct, if the money was forthcoming, she might get a seat out on the evening of the following day.

She telephoned Theodore. 'About time too,' he said. 'I'll meet you at the airport.'

When she telephoned her house, Simon was out. She was relieved to hear it and left the message with Betty. A couple from Stowmarket were on the same flight home and would give Dora a lift from the airport. Expect her when they saw her in two days' time. She put the phone down, slightly calmed. She had given herself, by however paltry the means, a time with Theodore when something, surely, might be resolved.

She drove back to her hotel and limped over to the men at the desk who waited expectantly for her new crisis to flare out but she asked mildly for her amber necklace from the safe and brought it upstairs and buried it at the bottom of her suitcase, under the rest of her belongings.

That evening she suffered as she knew she deserved to suffer. She remembered Laura's closed face, how Alice had sobbed and begged her not to go.

'I beg you,' she had cried, her voice plummeting into her throat and rising again, 'please don't go. I beg you.'

Where had she got the phrase for God's sake, surely it wasn't common parlance among her age-group.

Now, as Dora packed, her heart thumped and in the heat she was cold with fear. She felt she was goading fate to an irresistible degree, by being such a bad and wicked mother in choosing not to go back to them first, by signalling so clearly to the listening spirits that *he* came first. And what was so terrible was that whether she was punished by the aeroplane crashing, or whether the children were visited by pestilence or fire, it was they who would suffer.

The more she and Theodore had been together, the more Dora noticed that historical events had begun to take on a new gloss in the light of what he had shown her about heroic behaviour.

Dora had always been suspicious of what was deemed to be heroic behaviour. It was too romantic a concept, and indeed she had begun to think that even to believe in romance was a sin. Bravery she admired and courage and daring and these were deemed to be the ingredients of heroism, the stuff of pectorals and high jumps. But for Dora, and, she imagined, for most of those who were in the business of developing the crazy little muscle called the heart, the real stuff of heroism was the art of putting one foot in front of the other when the road was rough and the way ahead was dark and there was someone relying on you who could only meet you halfway if you had undertaken your half of the journey. She had learnt, had timid Dora, that all halves were not the same and the steps that children took down their minute and lapidary lanes were immeasurable in her adult trigonometry, and when she remembered in her dreams or caught a glimpse of the places they had to pass to reach her, she realised that they knew as much about bravery as she had forgotten. She knew too that no matter how she stood four square to the blast to shield them, a harsh wind would blow on them from another quarter.

She believed the plane would crash, and she equally knew that this belief was necessary, since it might placate the avenging gods who were flapping around the walls of her room like invisible bats. Her scalp tingled as though they had become entangled in her hair.

'Pull yourself together,' she said sternly, 'you melodramatic bitch,' and she did; she pulled herself together but she rehearsed the words for her condition in her head. Living on her nerves, astray in the head, highly strung, at her wit's end, away with it, distracted, going round the bend: all the terms down the years used to describe the condition of those under pressure from their intolerable surroundings and what made her condition so ludicrous was that her surroundings were all geared to her best comfort.

Before she had met Theodore, Dora had sometimes wondered, when reading fairy stories to her children, what would have happened if the prince, having spurred himself to dare the great encircling hedge, had found that after the first deceptive wilderness had been broached, the hedges within were topiary, the door of the castle opened at a touch, and inside were not mouldering rooms sunk in a century of stillness, nor a virgin princess, waxen and chaste in her long sleep, but a castle swept and garnished, a bustling Madame with a protective husband, a household retinue, food in the larders, blazing fires in the hearths and on the tables mead and champagne and strong tea, a place contrived for the comfort of the bourgeois couple and their offspring who lived there. What would have happened to the prince if the princess he thought he sought, had earlier been claimed by an older man, wise in the ways of spindles who had married her even before she had climbed the tower steps?

Dora thought of the black prince clanking into the great cosy room in his spurs and fancy dress, red silk and black velvet, programmed for rescue and innocence and gratitude, while she, or the likes of her, alarmed by the noise, would spin round from dealing with some domestic detail – wiping a child's mouth or straightening the paisley shawl – and would look towards the door and see him, silhouetted against the sunlight, the tangled-haired tardy hero, Prince George, Rumpelstiltskin, Lancelot, with his rimed curls and his absolutes and his single-minded romantic, old-fashioned idea that she would leave all the comforts of the castle behind to go into the forest with him.

Would the true matron, bred to the job, Caroline for example, pull herself together and graciously invite him to the spread? Hardly. The king of the castle would be standing, watchful, in some corner in the shadows on a balcony. If he was absent he would soon hear tell of the visit. What would she do? Tell him he'd got the wrong address? Go to him who should have been her deliverer, her awakener from the long sleep, go with him, into the dark woods, leaving her golden children by the fire? Hide him in the wardrobe? She would watch the man, who might have been her true being's heart and home, leave the great hall and go back into the darkness while she turned heavily back into the light where everything was familiar, the beds were made of goosefeather and what went on in them tolerable, and there was nothing to fear in the shadows and she was pinned in parenthesis.

If Dora had imagined the scene more closely and without her blind egoism she might have noticed that after his first astonishment at the expected scenario being so out of true the Prince might well have looked beyond the woman with her yearning gaze and set his sight on the virgin behind her, for whom the spindle waited, her daughter with her fat little legs in her red-strapped shoes.

Dora thought of her house as a fortified and protective place built by people who understood that the enemy was without and must be kept there. It was the undulating massive walls of yew as much as the thick walls of the house which had made Dora so passionately want to live there when she first saw it, that same craving first awakened by Tony's house. The yews spelt centuries of human tenure and tending. But for all its crenellations and fortifications there was not a time when she drove back there after she had been away that she did not expect to see it in mouldering blackened ruins, or to fix a marauder in the beam of her headlights, climbing its steep walls near to her children's windows.

In that vivid and passionate time leading up to what Theodore called his final ultimatum – Dora sometimes wondered if he had ever heard of any other kind – she had listened with a sinking heart to his hopeless reiteration of his belief, that he was only a stepping stone in her life. He had repeated it like an incantation over and over until it was evident that it must become self-fulfilling. To disprove this he required that she undertake to leave Simon by a specific date. If she did not, he said, he would have to do something irrevocable. She thought this meant that they would have to separate for ever, but he derided this notion. It would be more terrible. They both took all of this completely seriously with the monstrous egotistical pain of adolescents.

'I won't tell you what it is,' he said. 'It's too degrading for me to have had the thought, that I could or would use it. And if I did it wouldn't even be a pyrrhic victory, it would be like using the atom bomb. There would be nothing left.'

'Oh come *on*,' she said.

'No, it's true.' He appeared to be crying again; his face was turned away. She looked at him with distaste.

'You mean you would hurt the children?'

'No,' he said. 'No, this is a weapon that would leave you wishing you had never been born.'

'Would it hurt Simon?'

'Well, yes, but not through physical violence,' he said. 'It's far more shocking and would ruin any semblance of life in the future.'

'Do you mean you would kill me?' she said.

'I'll not ruin my life for you,' he said.

Reassured, she dropped the subject, though increasingly it came to prey on her as she wondered what secret weapon he had. She feared to return to the subject in case she precipitated something, but it was precipitated anyway. One day she arrived at his door and he was standing waiting, leaning against a wooden pillar, his face sullen: he was unshaven, his clothes slack. She knew he had been looking out for her car and had run downstairs to position himself as though he had been there all morning, brooding, but she allowed no hint of humour in her expression. He barred her way.

'I don't want you to come in,' he said. 'I love you, not through longing or affection or appreciation but through bitter resentment. I have struggled to free myself of what I seem to believe and yet what is obviously untrue, that life without you is worthless. I have taken a step away from you.'

'Well I'll just have to take one nearer,' she said.

'I can't bear it,' he said. 'There is no use saying you understand my suffering. You do not and cannot. You don't know what it means when I say I have reached my limits. I can't take any more.' She looked into his face and saw that he was certainly not going to take any more whether he could or not.

He saw the look. 'Have you ever been on a long march?'

She looked down at herself in her high heels and began to laugh.

'Well might you laugh,' he said. 'And you'll pay for it. On a long march you're told you have to do twenty miles and when you've done it you're exhausted. Then they say you have to do two more miles and you do it. At the end you feel more tired than after the twenty. Then they say another mile and you stagger forward. Then you realise they want another eight hundred yards and you suddenly can't do it. If you do, they'll want a bit more. You give up. You've reached your limit.'

'And I've reached my limit,' she suddenly screamed, astonished at what was issuing from her mouth, an enormous wall of angry sound. 'I'm sick and tired of you complaining and bloody whining, you never see that anyone else is suffering, you're the only one who has ever felt anything, you're the only one who has done anything or had anything done to him, you walk around showing off your grief and pain, it seems a very portable pain to me. You wear suffering like a nun wears a habit – look world, look hard, I suffer. Well other people are suffering too, but they don't scream and shriek about it. I'm risking not just my life but the other lives in my keeping. Your life is full of deadlines like trip-wires and if you suffer any inconvenience . . .'

'*Inconvenience?*' he interrupted, his voice trembling with something she did not recognise.

'Inconvenience, or if things don't suit you, you cut through them and a pity about anyone who gets sliced up. Well, I'm not cutting through my life for you. My life isn't on that kind of single line, only you're so spoiled and single-minded you can't see that, if you don't get what you want, when you want it, you scream and shout and yell like a spoiled child. Well you can yell your fucking head off, I know about your sufferings. They've been pushed down my gullet often enough.'

'My darling sweetheart,' he began but she screamed, 'Oh shut up shut up shut up I don't want these easy demonstrations of what you take as love. I didn't cry and shout to prove my love, I didn't lose my temper to show it. You're so pathologically selfish you don't even see that my real anger has nothing to do with loving you. I'm angry because I'm angry, not because I want to feed your feral streak.'

'Feral?' he said, wrapping his arms around her; she felt her body shiver, as though if he let go she would freeze.

'Don't you know there's a war on?' she said. 'It's time to get out of your turret and make me a coffee. I've driven long hours to get here.'

'When I even put one leg out,' he said, 'you shoot it down, you'd kill me. The hero.'

'I'm not shooting at him,' she said. 'I'm just trying to measure him up for socks.' But she knew he was standing at some brink and wanted her to teeter alongside him so that if he jumped in he would take her with him.

She took a step back. She said, 'I am going away for a while. For a holiday to try to sort myself out.' She hardly dared look at him. When she did she saw his eyes were black and sunk in his face. 'It's you who is taking the step away from me,' he said. 'If you go away, do not come back.'

A feeling as though a sliver of ice had entered her heart stabbed at her. Perhaps this was how heart attacks began. She was aware that he thought he had said something talismanic and damaging and was drawing a line between them, a kind of equator over which he feared she would not be able to step. She moved towards him and laid her cheek against his and as their skin softly and shockingly met she remembered what she had been forcing herself to try to forget, that she loved him.

III

To her embarrassment there was a wheelchair for her at the airport and a message from Elena. She had rung the airport and cajoled the airline. Dora was wheeled onto the aeroplane first. She felt a fraud and grateful to Elena. The truth was, she thought, Elena is right. I am not in my right mind. I ought to have my hands tied behind my back in a straitjacket.

On the aeroplane she thought what would happen if Simon discovered what plane she was on and decided to meet her. The idea of a situation where two men converged and planted a kiss on each cheek, like a comedy sequence from a sixties movie – Jack Lemmon and Walter Matthau perhaps, their swivelling eyeballs meeting over her nose – filled her vision. In the midst of this tableau Dora realised that Theodore would look out for Simon and she was then haunted by the image of Simon arriving, Theodore seeing him, stepping back into the crowd and watching them, the two halves of a marriage embrace into a battered whole. Dora squirmed in her seat, knocking the arm of the dozing man beside her who jerked awake, in alarm, mumbled, glared at her and then looked embarrassed as he remembered she was disabled. Dora could see he dreaded that she was going to twitch all the way to London. She knew better. She was going to sit rigid, keeping the aeroplane up.

In the early days when she had first met Theodore she had had a dream in which she was sitting at a high window talking on the telephone and saw Simon outside, on a high branch of a walnut tree, a blasted rotten branch; he was not far away, but unreachable, since a chasm a hundred feet deep separated them. As she looked, the branch began to creak and then to tear itself leaving a white gash on the trunk, and she watched horrified as his body crashed in slow motion to the ground. She saw the ankles and knees imploding into ossified marrow, knees telescoping into thighs, a silent human concertina of destruction. On his face Dora saw a look of silent endurance, the look she had seen in certain paintings. She had woken filled with terror for his pain and an apprehension of what his loss would mean to her.

She held tighter onto the edges of her seat and drifted in and out of sleep.

The world on the other side of the world was a wholly different world, wrapped in a crepuscular shifting light that seemed to make every face and every object leaden. The aeroplane came down through clouds and mist, just missing being diverted to Manchester, the pilot said and, Dora thought, what ho plans then? On land, the mist turned to ectoplasmic fog: it seemed like the spirit of the place, an ooze of England.

When he met her, his black hair was rimed with frost, his face was like a lamp in the dark. He hardly spoke – no wonder, she thought, he could hardly have imagined he was going to meet a middle-aged lady in a wheelchair, surrounded by packages and flight attendants. She waited in a state of apprehension while he got the car, and knew her love was obsession, the same thing that had made Stella mad, a white glow which needed to have the object of its passion within its range. As they drove she put her hand out to caress him, and felt such a surge of desire that she was sure it must be mutual – but as she later discovered, it was not. He was too absorbed in meeting the pain of absence now they were together, he said, to feel anything else. In any case, he said, he wasn't sure he did want her. She knew she was back.

'I couldn't relax,' he said, 'I was so frightened when I saw you that you wouldn't be the person I'd thought about continually. And the pain of your absence which I'd kept in one separate part of my mind suddenly percolated all the way through when you returned and released it.'

And, as he told her, she remembered that it was the same cause she had attributed to her mother's staunch grimness.

She felt light-headed, verging on the hysterical, as though a peal of trumpets should be sounding in the distance. To accustom themselves to each other, before the appalling intimacies, they went for a walk through the streets of Cambridge, she leaning against him, her stick tapping beside them like something out of T. S. Eliot, and the people looming out of the mist had faces from paintings, marked, strong, northern faces, as if they were in Flanders. The street lights made blobs like wasps' nests in the liquidised air and the lights of King's College were on, the windows ablaze with such sparkle that she was pulled towards the church like a Brunswick child to the sound of the piper. From within, came the sound she was searching for, the high exquisite noise of the choir boys' voices, chiming like the spheres.

'Can we go in?' she asked.

He shook his head.

'Not even you?' she said.

'Perhaps me,' he said; the guardian let them in and they listened to the heartless voices with spikes of mirror at their core, singing of love, and the lowliness of heart which takes the humbler part and o'er its own shortcomings weeps with loathing. When they were outside again, she said, 'They'll lose those voices putting them around like that, or they'll be broken. Yeats said that everything personal must be packed in ice if it is not to rot.'

'Yeats isn't God,' he said.

'He is to me,' she said.

They walked through the college: everywhere they passed had famous associations. She listened to the astonishing roll-call of luminaries and scholars. The mist rose a little higher and they could see the swards on the opposite bank lying like pelts drying in the pale cold air. She looked up into the branches of an enormous yew tree.

'What are you looking for?'

'I'm trying to find the branch where Charles II hid,' she said and he looked up at it amazed and then at her.

'How do you know that's the tree?'

'It's a fact,' she said, 'it's famous. The wood for Queen Elizabeth's state bed came from that tree, too. And in that church,' she pointed back towards the direction of King's, 'is where Alfred watched the spider spinning over and over again and told the burning cakes, if at first you don't succeed try, try, again. A lesson we must all learn.'

She began to lose her nerve under his scrutiny.

'I don't know why you're in such good form,' he said. 'When you've been away from me for so long.'

Dora said, 'Every time I come to Cambridge I think it's parodying itself. Did I ever tell you I once followed two dons hurrying ahead of me and I got as close as I could to catch the pearls, and as they swung around the corner, I heard one say: "And tenthly?"'

They had reached the weir and the old pump house and he began to climb the steps that clung, as precariously as ivy, to the walls. She tried to follow him, leaning in against the old brick, but putting her true weight on her ankle was painful. She turned to go down again and slipped on the wet, creeper-covered stone and in trying to save herself scraped her hand. He came down the steps, light-footed, and tied up her hand with his handkerchief.

'Every time I'm with you I have to do this,' he said. 'I've never known anyone so good at banging themselves around.'

'It's punishment,' she said. 'No one else will punish me so I have to punish myself. I get more like the curse of the mummy every minute.'

He said angrily, 'Why do you have to be punished? I see you haven't left the superstition behind.'

They set off back to the centre of the town and on the way to his rooms stopped in at the old pharmacy to buy ointment and plasters.

'I wrote to you about this pharmacy,' she said.

'I never got the letter,' he said. 'I didn't get any letters.'

'I didn't send it,' she said.

As he put the plaster on her hand he asked, 'What are you thinking about?' But how could she repeat the ancient litanies of infatuation, the declensions of enchantment, how could she tell him of her time on the island or the fact that within hours she would have to make a life-eclipsing effort to start her journey back to Simon. She was filled with despair at the prospect and could not countenance the idea of her betrayal of the man at her side. Yet being with him meant defection and betrayal of the man with whom she had forged her contract. They went through the archway of the courtyard and climbed the old curved staircase to his room.

IV

There was a winding staircase in Dora's house, as well, the one which led to her workroom at the top of the house, one of three and which in the house's grander days, had once been the servants' staircase. It was narrow, winding, with a ship's mast for the central newel and small doors at tiny landings which gave on to the bedrooms on each floor and was not used, save by Dora. On the pale flaking walls were long lines of graffiti, written by Dora over the years, pieces of poetry and fragments of thought that for her had a renovating virtue, and each time she climbed the stairs she noted which inscription leapt forth with its message as though a moving finger had written her poetic horoscope in the night.

First step: *Love survives; but for such purpose flowers no longer grow*. Second step, and on the curve: *Action is transitory, a step, a blow, the motion of a muscle this way or that; 'tis done and in the after-vacancy we wonder at ourselves like men betrayed.* Past the little turret window and up two steps: *If I make the lashes dark and the eyes more bright and the lips more scarlet, or ask if all be right. From mirror after mirror, no vanity's displayed, I'm looking for the face I had before the world was made.* Above the lintel of the small window where Thomas liked to stand glaring down at the lawns and hedges below, repelling the unsuspecting gardener: *The heart is a small thing but desireth great matters. It is not sufficient for a kite's dinner yet the whole world is not sufficient for it.* A kite's dinner. She didn't know what a kite looked like, all she knew was that her heart was a bloody great gannet. Two steep steps and a phrase written when she was fed up with something or other, or someone had given in their notice (all her previous worries and preoccupations seemed in retrospect to have been of no moment whatsoever): *In order to climb into the depths one does not need to travel very far, no, for that you do not need to abandon your immediate and accustomed environment.*

She remembered her conversation with Stella when she had asked for what she was now receiving in full and had wished to feel the force of passion. When she'd written that snatch of Wittgenstein down, pleased with its portent, during the days of her depression, she thought she had reached as dark a place as she would ever penetrate. Around the curve and immediately above so that she had to tilt her head: *Not in Utopia, subterranean fields or some secreted island Heaven knows where! But in the very world which is the world of all of us, the place where in the end we find our happiness or not at all.* And at the top outside her door, the great fragment: *Civilisation is hooped together, brought under a rule, under the semblance of peace by manifold illusion; but man's life is thought and he despite his terror cannot cease ravening through century after century, ravening raging and uprooting that he may come into the desolation of reality.*

When she was first pregnant she had written down one that spoke of joy: *Mark it, Cesario; it is old and plain. The spinsters and the knitters in the sun And the free maids that weave their thread with bones Do used to chant it. It is silly sooth, and dallies with the innocence of love like the old age.* And as she copied it out she had known what it meant. The babies in the nursery, the tender-hearted solicitude and patience of their father, her ordered home, all had been innocent. Now she could not only not comprehend the meaning of the words she could not even see where it was written on the wall. The inscription appeared to have sunk into the plaster. She remembered leaning against the newel post and seeing before her *Thank heaven, fasting, for a good man's love* and felt ravenous. Love wasn't innocent. It could scorch the heart and burn the edges of other people's lives, and make one fan the flames and pretend there was nothing burning.

Ever since she had come back from the island they had all been tiptoeing around as though the earth were crust and she had not seen Theodore for three weeks since he had delivered, he said, his final final ultimatum.

No matter how she tried she could not stop obsessively retracking their time together, trying to find hope or guidance from what had happened, trying to get synoptic wisdom in order to anticipate what was going to happen and to build a drawbridge against the calamities ahead.

She had walked the streets of Cambridge after she had left him, talking to herself, her lips moving, her eyes staring, but a normal enough looking woman, with tanned skin, persuading herself that it didn't matter, that nothing mattered, that we were as dust, that it would all be the same in a hundred years, but, all the same, blame had to be dispensed, because if it wasn't it accrued in compound mass in her psyche, a bile that choked her, and she had promised herself she would not cry again. She wondered that the very word promise was still in her vocabulary.

She climbed the spiral stairs past the poetry. When she was not with Theodore she could think of little else but him. She knew with a foreboding born of experience that today her emotions would find themselves released in great gusts of blame and rage against whoever tapped the sump first, through some inadvertent remark by someone of whom she wasn't frightened. Her husband, her children, Betty, all the people who helped her in the daily round. They would suffer. Her sweetness and her light would be kept for the undeserving.

Her body was heavy with a feeling she feared to call pain, it was such a grand name for such mean, grey, tasteless gruel that seemed to lie like puddles in the channels of her life. Pain was epic, to be kept for mourning and gravity, to describe the pangs of the starving, not applicable to this selfish and overwhelming sense of desideratum, emptiness and boredom. But no matter how much she tried to put everything into perspective, a miserable pain predicated her day. There is no chance of renewal here, she thought, as she clumped around trying to summon up enough energy to get to her work, the work she tried to make her moral imperative, and which if she could but know it, had nothing to do with moral energy at all but everything to do with her creativity, the misplaced energy of the restless and unhappy, and which now was directed towards assuagement of another kind. The work she was trying to get at was, relatively speaking, unimportant. She had grudgingly, though gratefully, undertaken it for Thomasina whose kindness took the form of making Dora feel that only she could write what Thomasina wanted.

She took some attenuating pills which in those days were still quite easily come by – many doctors would shovel out such pills at the hint of a plea – to kick-start her into work. The pills had a quite different effect almost immediately and fretfulness became heightened to vexation, her flesh and nerve endings felt as though they had been flayed. She went back down to the nursery. She felt the heat from her body would surely keep even her children at bay, but no one appeared to notice the kind of saturn in their midst.

Betty was dressing Thomas. Laura and Alice wandered around buttoning themselves erratically into their garments and struggling with thick small woollen tights that frequent washing had turned into stiff mouldings of their limbs, things that gnomes might have worn on their heads. She began to help Alice to button her OshKosh jeans but the child resisted fiercely. 'I could do it myself,' Alice said, 'if my arms were trusty enough. I can do a lot by myself.'

'You're the white hen's chicken,' Betty said.

'Am I?' Alice said. 'I thought I was the white cow's calf.'

'You're that too,' Betty said. 'Button those straps and remember what thought did. It stuck a feather in the ground and thought it would grow a hen.'

Alice said, 'Or thought it would grow a white chicken.' She fell down on the floor overcome by mirth, her ribbed red legs waving in the air and clutched at her stomach with pleasure.

'Away on down with your mother and give me peace,' Betty said, and Dora and her daughters went down to breakfast. Simon was already there and Alice embarked on an ecstatic version of her own wit in the nursery.

When Simon and Laura had gone Dora and Betty set about dressing Thomas and Alice like Sherpas for an excursion to a local pond to collect frog spawn. Their faces became flushed with the effort of pushing arms into puffy jackets, of inserting pliable unresisting floppy feet into wellingtons, of easing recalcitrant hands with numberless thumbs into mittens but finally the small convoy left the house. Dora remembered with an anguish that was like a stoat in her stomach much the same kerfuffle the day Theodore had first come into her house, ostensibly to have drinks and had stayed to dinner.

When Simon came home in the evening she could hardly bring herself to greet him, never mind embrace him, and while he ate, she kept her eyes fixed on his lower lip, so that he said 'What's wrong with my face?' self-consciously, brushed at his lower lip and blushed. She looked away, and said nothing. He manfully kept on eating and trying to make conversation and his demeanour was so mannerly that she wanted to hit him for his lack of reaction, his refusal to meet her anger. She knew his behaviour came as much from ingrained manners as from a desire to do good, as much from courtesy as from avoidance. She no longer believed that he could rescue her. That would require a feat of imagination beyond him. *That* she believed was her prerogative. *He* had married her for such things, it was part of her dowry, her only dowry, if it came to that. Nor did she consider the possibilities that he was trying to keep the balance, that he did not wish to precipitate things or, most unthinkable of all, that he was frightened of her. But he was – all the same – courageous and when he said, 'What's wrong Dora? What is wrong?' she said, 'Nothing,' and moved away. He said, 'I know that there is something wrong and I wish you would tell me.' She said, her voice making a trench of frigid air between them, 'There's nothing wrong. We must do dates. You must keep half an hour free to do dates.' She left the room but then thought, if he can ask me then I must tell, and she went back in and tried to start, and found instead that her mouth was making peripheral conversation and so was his, desultory sincere conversation about the family, about work, about catching up with work, about the various disasters that somehow seemed to be overtaking them but not about the biggest disaster of all.

He got up to answer the telephone and she took the chance to leave, and climbed the stairs and went into her bathroom where she sat down in front of the triple mirror and thought that her heart would give out on her at any moment, explode like Henry VIII's and spatter all over the ceiling. Her face, as she looked at it between her splayed fingers, was red-veined and congested like the face of someone who has been drinking for years. She thought of the cholerics of other days, the spleen and congestion that had affected our forbears, and knew that her horrible humours might be the death of her. Humours. She shook her head. He had given her, as far as he was able, all her heart's desire but her heart's desire was beyond his gift, down in the woods with the raggle-taggle gypsies.

She heard him come upstairs, his tread slow, and she went into his dressing room and beat about the subject and he beat busily with her. Then he rose to his feet and said wearily, 'Well, I'm off to lock up,' and as he slipped out she said in a high hysterical whisper, 'You won't talk to me, you won't even try to begin to find out what's wrong.'

'That isn't true, Dora,' he said. 'I asked you tonight and yesterday and over and over again since you've come back and you say nothing so crossly and won't tell me.'

'I don't say nothing,' she said turning away and banging the sides of the chair, 'and I don't because you don't want to hear, you don't want to know, you're hoping if I don't tell you it will go away.'

'That's true,' he murmured and she was amazed at his admission and wondered if he had heard the cry *I don't*, over and over again. He sat down. 'Why are you so unhappy Dora? I wish I could make you happy.'

'What's the use of saying something like that,' she said, sobbing, 'as though you were a child. I'm not your mother. I'm not your mother. You avoid cross and angry women because you think they're your mother. But I'm not. I'm Dora. I'm your cross and angry wife.'

In the morning when she woke up, he was already awake and he tried to comfort her with an embrace but her muscles tightened in recoil and he lay back in such a way that she felt defeated, never mind what he felt. He did not question her. She was left with her own refusal; it filled her body with a message that could not get out, as though every pore had been stopped up. She felt that her skin might turn from biscuit brown to livid yellow to blue as the pressure inside increased.

She left the bed and went into the linen room and began to weep at the place she found herself; he found her there and put his arms around her and said, 'My sweet and lovely Dora,' and she looked at him and said in a whisper, 'Sweet and lovely? Are you mad? Are you mad?' And went into her room and got dressed in the best raiment she could, given that there was no sackcloth and ashes.

*

The next morning she climbed to her workroom, feeling exhausted, as though she had been on some horrible odyssey during the night and sat listening through anxious habit for the sounds of her children, though she knew they were out with Betty. The house was silent in their absence, and she became alert for the ringing of the telephone in the rooms below. She made lists of what she had to do and when she looked at the lists she saw that, among the trivia, she had written the name Theodore over and over again.

She endured what was left of the morning, as though time were palpable, constituted of formaldehyde petrifying her inch by inch. She remembered with guilt and pain how Simon had cupped his hands gently around her and she had felt herself shrivel. When Theodore touched her, however roughly, it was as though her skin had a million minute suctions so that his hands would remain clamped to her flesh.

She looked around her workroom with everything in it chosen by her and paid for by Simon and thought of him, his kindness, his refusal to become angry when she wanted him to be.

'Where *are* your black spots?' she had shouted. 'Why can't you just once raise your voice back? Are you so bloody timid? Or terrified.'

'Dora,' he said, 'I refuse to get angry to satisfy your demands. And I don't have black spots.'

It appeared to be true. He was courteous, quiet, unflamboyant. She knew that part of the reason she had married him was his own sense of himself, his quiet confidence.

She got to her feet and crossed to the window and craned to try to see if Betty and her children were in sight. She wondered why she wasn't with them, why she was incarcerating herself, reeling and racking, pretending to work. She went back to her desk and read over what she was supposed to be writing: a piece about myth, the functions of mythology: a piece of plagiarism for readers like herself. The first function of a mythology is to waken and maintain in the individual a sense of wonder and participation in the mystery of the universe; the pedagogical one of conducting individuals through the passages of human life from dependency of childhood to responsibilities of maturity, old age and ultimate passage of the dark gate.

She lifted her pen, laid it down, pulled out a reference book and laid it down, switched on the wireless. A brass band was playing a specially commissioned piece. She turned it off with a surge of rage, thought to write to the Controller of Radio 3 who seemed to live only for Percy Grainger and Northern Brass Bands. She then abandoned work and left the room, went downstairs and hauled out a great many ingredients and began to make a large sponge cake though she knew full well it would be uneatable and that Anona would have left half a dozen sponge cakes in the freezer.

She heard a noise at the courtyard door and thought that perhaps Betty had come back early – but there was no eruption of dogs or children or the slap of gumboots on tiles and the breathless cries of excitement that heralded the return of the wanderers. Suddenly there, the air shaking around him, eyes blazing, was Theodore and she was in his arms before she had moved and she stood within that circle and felt the anger and tension flooding out, so that there might have been an iridescent pool on the floor like petrol in the puddles on the way to school. She felt his mouth on hers and her teeth, that had been so sharp and ferret-like, with grating edges that serrated the day, had become part of the oyster of sensation that was her mouth. Their mouths parted, their bodies still moulded together and they looked at each other.

Dora was shocked by the change in his looks, the flesh stretched taut over the bone. The spirit that informed his face had receded like sap from a cut tree. She felt plain, prosaic and she pulled away embarrassed, gesticulating at her apron, the floury hands and the paraphernalia of the kitchen, of the domestic woman and he smiled at her with great tenderness. 'My darling,' he said, 'seeing you like this makes me know something I thought was no longer possible. We will be together for thirty years.'

'Why only thirty?' she said. 'You mean you'll dump me when I'm in my old age and go off with a young blonde bint?' He kissed her again, nodding agreement. She was appalled and delighted at his wholesale breaking of the taboos – his arrival on her territory out of the shadows, his rescinding of his vow, his assumption that they would be together, his apparent dumping of the unspeakable atomic ultimatum, the oaths and tantrums, all seemed to be forgotten.

They went out into the garden and sat on the wet bench by the pond and the yellow water reflected the glittering daffodils, and two ducks and a drake paddled about in the water. The violent place that was Dora's life became tranquil and her shoulders dropped so that only then did she know she had been living in it as though hunched inside a cage.

She had not known that rest from such anxiety could exist. There were no journeys to make between her and her lover. She had not abandoned her children to get to him, they were not at the peril of fire or the marauder. Surely if Simon were suddenly to come walking down the path and find them there, he would have to recognise the unstoppable force between them and would in an instant's grand realisation of the binary magic that made their perfect whole, give them his blessing.

Cynicism was not allowed into this radiant scheme of things, love justified all and she sat at peace in the circle of his arms watching the ducks. After a while the spell was broken by anxiety. At any moment Betty and the children might come back, and from her changed appearance – for changed it was, of that she had no doubt – would know what this stranger meant to her. He said, 'What's wrong?' and she, fearful of damaging their circle, fearful that he would get in one of his rages, said, 'Betty and the children will be back soon.' He said in an equable tone, 'At all costs they mustn't find me here,' and her heart filled with gratitude. He left in a great flurry of noise, exhaust fumes and a swirl of gravel. Nothing had been said but it seemed to her that she had been given her future.

When her children came home they were delighted by her exuberance and greetings as she swung them in the air, by the posy of yellow flowers, by her chatter. Betty looked suspicious, but said nothing.

Dora felt that the very air was sparkling. She could not for the life of her see why there had been a problem about where she was going to spend the rest of her life. She ran up the stairs to her workroom and saw as she ran, the words, *being your slave what should I do but tend upon the hours and times of your desires*, and felt that the time on the island had been a testing time to make her sure of the staying power of the life she now knew she must undertake.

The glow of Theodore's presence sustained her all through the afternoon and evening and she coaxed Betty into smiles and played with the children until they were peaceably in bed. After she had kissed her goodnight Laura said, her hair like spun sugar on the Magic Roundabout pillowcase, 'Did you speak to Theodore today?' 'Yes,' Dora said calmly, though she was shocked by the child's prescience.

'I knew you did, you were in such a good temper.' Laura sat up, alert to the possibility that in this mood her mother might reveal more. She thought on. Dora watched her as she changed tack to gain a better advantage. 'Can I not go to school tomorrow?' 'Yes,' Dora smiled. 'Or no. I mean, yes, you must go.' Laura reverted. 'It must be hard on him being a bachelor and loving you,' she said.

Dora began to laugh helplessly at the idea of her demon lover as a bachelor and after a moment Laura too began to laugh and Dora held her and rocked her and said, 'It's only the word bachelor, it's a word I haven't heard for so long. There used to be a group called The Bachelors who sang like this,' and she began to warble in a pronounced brogue, with much vibrato, and Laura and Alice began to sing and climbed out of their beds and capered and tottered about, intoxicated with the noise, the released tensions in the air. 'You'll waken Thomas,' Dora warned as Simon walked in and, seeing the scene, began to smile and the children ran to him to embrace him. Dora said sharply, 'To bed, into bed, it's far too late for this gallivanting,' and the children climbed into bed and Dora went out of the nursery leaving him alone with his children.

She went into her room, trying to rehearse in her mind what she could do, what she would say. Perhaps he would say it, give her permission to go, and continue to love her. How could he not fail to see that there was no possibility of redemption in their union? 'All there is between us,' she would explain, 'are things, hundreds of things; objects, pictures, books, bricks and mortar. We've built up this edifice around emptiness and roam around inside it hardly touching, never talking.' A nice lot of codswallop that is, her conscience, such as it was, reminded her. She remembered, while she was at it, some other home truths. That it was she who needed edifying; that it was her own gambling streak that sent her out to collect anything that took her magpie fancy. That things are unspoken because they need not be said. That marriage, if it works, becomes a free-holding in which to live with someone in peace and rear children as best you can. And that it was she who had crammed the house to the gunwales.

'Being married to Dora,' she had overheard Simon remark, 'means that we need a fleet of pantechnicons to go on a picnic.'

'You always know married couples in restaurants,' Pamela had once said. 'They never speak.' Dora did not say that you do not need to make small talk when you have made children together and nor do you need to say more than three or four words if some of those words are the names of your children.

She was at her dressing-table again where only this morning she had looked through her splayed fingers holding her blotched face together, and this time she saw a woman with skin like a child's, still tanned, freckled, glowing. She looked at a photograph of Laura in a tiny spotted swimsuit and remembered how, almost immediately after she had learnt to swim, she had waded out into the sea and set out gamely for France. Dora had become alarmed and had run down the beach screaming, 'Swim sideways to the shore, swim *in*,' and Laura frightened by her mother's shouts had begun to flounder and slap the water and gulp. Simon, showing an astonishing turn of speed, had swum out to her and had stayed in the water with her, gently coaxing her back to confidence.

She went downstairs, hearing the murmur of his voice from the nursery and knew that if the children had understood and sensed her rejection, he would, through his own unchanging behaviour, do his best to repair it. She busied herself, yet again to ward everything off but, as she heard him come downstairs, his pain arrived ahead of him, with a huge silent announcement, and met hers, and under the combined onslaught she rehearsed her choice. She wanted him to be less unhappy and she wanted to be happy. She would try to be honourable in at least one small thing, by telling him at once, so that together they could face it. But how could she tell him that she had tried to do her best when the worst was the result?

He came in and sat down. She looked at him and he looked back, and smiled, and she hated the unfairness of what was happening, hated that he still loved her, hated how he made her think of the cardinal virtues, justice, fortitude, temperance and obedience to duty, old cant words to do with the pathological religion of childhood. They were never wrong about sinning either, the Old Masters, she thought, except in overstating their case; they did not need ten commandments. They needed only the one injunction *you shalt not* and they also knew very well that the punishment was not in the hereafter but in the consequences here, in the accustomed environment. She tried to speak but her throat seemed to seize up into an ache of muteness. The inside of her head was like a tangle of hay where small sharp-toothed rodents scraped around trying to settle. He rose and put his hand on her shoulder – as he had so often put it, consistently, tenderly, through thick and thin, a good man with a tender hand, and said, 'What is it, Dora. Can't I help?'

'We need to talk,' she said.

'Is now a good time?' he asked. She was surprised by his equanimity.

'It's never a good time for a talk like this,' she said and sat mute. He turned his head and walked back to his desk and sat down again; she thought *Ite missa est*.

The silence went on. Only the big grandfather clock chimed and chimed again and she dreaded the messages her dumbness signified. She got up and went up to their bedroom, lay on the counterpane and tried to imagine the reality of her actions, and remembered a story she had read about Cézanne painting till his eyes bled. She tried to imagine the consequence of what she was going to say. The upheaval, the wounds, the ripping apart of the grafts that she and her husband had spliced together so many years before and which had taken so well that no one could tell which was the parent and which the graft, the damage to the children.

All this lay ahead because of her own needs, some early slippage of her foundations of life which needed shoring up at any cost, because she said to herself, because of your own selfishness, your own turpitude, because you are a wicked woman, because of desire. Such a mild little word which turned with so little warning into want, dying by inches for lack of nourishment, the soul withering while the family grew. As she lay, pitying herself, the creature in the deeps stirred again, lazily, the creature that had stirred so many years before when she had sucked baby food in Stella's kitchen, and she knew, as though something had surfaced, that her hunger as a child had not been metaphorical and that she and her sister had literally starved. But this knowledge brought only acknowledgement whereas she knew at any other time she would have pored over it like a witch over entrails.

She thought of the dissolution of a family, the centrifugal forces flying out from the central core of her desire and her hunger. And for what? For a chimera, a succubus given the name of love, given the name of Theodore. Dora adores thee, Theo adores Dora, Theodora Theodore the name was like a loop in her brain.

She feared that when she had finally surrendered and told Simon that she was leaving, she would find that the prize was not worth the candle and that Theodore had been elevated by her craving for adventure for sexual love, for excitement and for escape, into something more than he was. She dreaded that she had invested him with strength and daring because of the growths of anger and grief infesting her spirit, looking for any suitable stake around which to entwine. She feared that the love which seemed to them like a beacon, if it were allowed to blaze, would turn out, after all the dismay and destruction, to be a candle to the sun.

She crawled into bed and pretended to sleep and heard Simon climb in and murmur goodnight. She lay silent, frightened but thankful, and slept, finally, and dreamt. Her dreams were to do with the rescuing of an obscure precious object, but no matter how she strained she could not see what or who was precious. She awoke in alarm, instantly alert. Laura was calling and she could hear the soft slap of her feet in the passage and then she was there, her round blonde face at the same level as Dora's on the pillow, her features reversed by the panic of nightmare into babyhood again like Verrocchio's angel. She clambered into bed, helped and hauled by Dora and immediately fitted herself around Dora's body as though she had never left it and began to babble a story about horses and dreams and fish. Dora smoothed and soothed her and the heat of her body met her own. It was years since Laura had been a baby like this and she fell into a fitful sleep; and Dora slept too. She awoke to feel Laura crying silently.

She held Laura in her arms and rocked her, trying as much to console herself, as her child and not allowing herself to believe that her wise daughter was grieving for what was going to happen. It transpired that Laura's grief had a more immediate cause. She dreaded going to school. She said she was afraid of her teacher. How much of it was true and how much a ploy and plea to stay at home Dora could not judge, but her instinct was to let her stay at home. Old wives' tales, ersatz wisdom passed from one age of mothers to the next, crowded in on her, saws about sparing the rod and facing up and precepts and proverbs, and she knew that she must send Laura to school in order that in her future she should be able to face up to the difficult and demanding situations she would undoubtedly find throughout life. Dora turned her face away from the crudeness of her own failure to do exactly that. She comforted Laura as much as she could until she stopped crying. By now she could hear Betty in the nursery and Laura left the bed and went towards the noise.

She followed Laura to the nursery. She could see that Laura had repeated the story of the Evil Teacher to Betty and that Betty was going to disapprove of the decision to send her anyway. Dora and Laura dressed in Dora's room away from Betty's mutters and Alice's anxious and placatory smiles.

As they began to go down the stairs Laura said, 'Where is my school book? I lost it last week and Mrs Lear says I must have it,' and Dora's heart sank, because there, laid out in front of her like a horrible ordnance map, was the course of the morning; whichever route she took there were going to be rows, tears, tension. To lose things induced a terrible panic in Dora's breast. Things going missing left her at her wits' end. The book was lost, how was it ever to be found?

She thought of all the rooms in her house, filled with so many books, and a huge anger surged through her, against her greedy accumulations, against Gutenberg and the written word, against Simon, against Betty, against her life, against teachers who sent books home with children, books that then were mixed up with the thousands of books all over her house. If it were ever to be found, it must be by accident when she was looking for something else and not as a result of a search. She wanted to scream at Laura, push her face up very close to her tear-stained one and shriek dementedly, '*If*, if the bloody book was lost a week ago why have you left it to the last minute to look for it, you little pillock?'

Instead, she sent Laura down to breakfast and turned back to look doggedly through bookcases. She catapulted from nursery to bedroom to playroom while the house grew more hushed as the hysteria built up. Laura came back upstairs and began to follow her, her voice thin and high and watery. 'It doesn't matter,' she said. 'I'll go to school without the book,' but Dora went on slamming, throwing, searching, crying, reproaching herself and the child, knowing how useless, wounding, shameful this was but quite unable to stop it. Everything was going missing in her life. There was an emptiness which she couldn't fill, not with food, not with children, not with work, not with possessions, not without Theodore, and the world would end if the book weren't found.

She wondered how the tempest of emotion had not whirled Simon to its source. She found him in the shower and beat on the glass. He turned, startled, the water pouring over his face, and she hammered at the door and he reached for the taps but before he could get out she ran off and into the nursery. Betty was there with Thomas comforting Laura, and Dora was out of the nursery, a streak of rage, and back up to Simon before she could speak.

He was almost dressed and she felt her anger like a blade glinting, a blade that would cut her own body open if she didn't turn it on him. She went back into the nursery before she could slice Simon up with the scimitar in her mouth and knelt by Laura's bed and put her head into her hands and began to cry. Laura was suddenly there, her face like a younger version of the one Dora had seen from behind her splayed fingers, an eruption of grief and bad drainage, and she tried to put her arms around Dora, sobbing, 'I'm sorry, it's my fault, I'm so sorry.' Dora said, 'Just put your bloody book where it's meant to go and none of this would have happened.' Laura ran to the bookshelves and began frantically to search and Simon came into the room fully dressed and watched her and she thought: He cannot love me or my daughter if he can so calmly dress himself as though nothing has happened. He is doing this on purpose, standing and watching, when all he has to do is to help me, run his hands over the books, make finding noises, just show willing and it will be all right, it would be all right, but all he does is make himself presentable to the world and let me suffer without helping, let me get myself into it and watch me not get out. She bent her head to the bed and he asked, 'What is the name of the book?' and Dora said, and, to her disbelief, almost laughed, '*Piggle.*' '*Piggle*?' he said, and her daughter from behind said, 'I've found it,' and Dora said in a matter-of-fact voice, exactly as if nothing had happened, 'Oh good, clever girl, you go on down and finish your breakfast.'

Laura said, 'Will you take me to school, like you said you would?' and Dora said, 'Of course. Go and have some breakfast and I'll be down in a minute.'

The child went reluctantly, not wanting to leave her parents alone in case of what might happen and Simon started to go back to the bedroom. Dora followed him. If he hoped to avoid a row by continuing his hateful passivity, he was quite wrong. She could think of no epithet that was unworthy enough to suit him and she whispered, her voice coming out in a sibilant hiss that she hadn't heard in her own mouth before, 'All you needed to do was to help me, or not even help, just pretend to help, instead of which you stand watching me, thinking what a fool I'm making of myself, when all you have to do is help just a little. You always do it, wait till I've got into a state where there's no way out and then watch to see what's happened. Why can't you open your mouth instead of just standing there? No one can lead a blameless life, that's what you try to do, and so the blame goes into a void and comes back on me. No one can lead a blameless life. No one, no one, no one.'

Justified now in her anger as she always needed to be, she went to the kitchen and Betty, playing the game as gallantly as ever, said, 'You found the book. I told Laura the bogey had its foot on it.' But Laura, Dora could see, was more determined than ever not to go to school. 'Please, please, I'll be sick,' she said, her fingers gripping her dinner money. She is her mother's daughter, Dora thought, I am mistress of her fate. And then, looking into her daughter's face, saw that Laura believed the same, that she held her parents' fate in her hands and feared that if she abandoned them even for a day, they would fall apart, Simon disappearing into loneliness, Dora tumbling through space towards the horrible man.

Dora took Laura's hand and Betty, muttering, angry, but too loyal to the children to scold Dora in front of them, helped Laura into her coat. Once in the car Dora ignored Laura's tears and blackmailed her into cheerfulness with chatter but when Laura said, sniffing, 'Daddy says that next year we might all go to Switzerland,' Dora found it impossible to collude with the child's hopefulness.

'I can't go to Switzerland.'

'Why not?'

'Because I don't like skiing very much or snowy holidays. I feel sure you and Daddy and everyone will have a lovely time together.'

'You're everyone,' Laura said, and Dora's peripatetic heart lurched. They went into the school and Laura's teacher walked past. Dora said, 'Good morning, Mrs Lear,' and the teacher without glancing at either of them, said, 'Good morning.'

'You bitch,' Dora thought. 'The very least you could do would be to acknowledge her presence even if you can't smile. I wouldn't much want to be in a room with you all day.' She thought of the many teachers she had known throughout her life who should never have been in charge of children, the small cruelties they indulged in, women who presumably were angry because they were left in charge of children who were not their own.

She left Laura in the hall with the other children and went into Laura's classroom, but Mrs Lear was not there. Dora could see her through the partition talking to another teacher and she hung on, hoping that she could speak to her before the bell rang and the children came flooding through, but, though Mrs Lear glanced through the glass door, she did not come in, almost as though hoping Dora would go away. Dora determined not to think like this. After all, she never came to the school – she was surely the archetypal non-interfering parent – there was no reason for her to be paranoid, to believe that Mrs Lear meant to snub her. But the morning's work had left its toll and this woman, hostile for no reason that Dora could think of, was adding her mite to the pile of pain and angst in her life. When at last Mrs Lear came into the classroom looking pointedly at her watch, Dora took a deep breath and said, 'Mrs Lear, Laura is not feeling well. I thought she might just want to be at home after yesterday's holiday but I saw as we came in that she is unwell. I think I'm going to take her home.'

She looked towards the teacher for a modicum of good-will, for permission, but there was nothing but frigidity on her pinched face and Dora slid her eyes away, thinking, Mrs Lear, Mrs Goneril, more like. She thought again as to why it should be that so many of the people in charge of children were stony-hearted, and wondered if perhaps she could simply ask Mrs Lear. 'Mrs Lear,' she would say simply seeking information, 'why are you such a cunt?' It would have to wait till Laura had left school, of course. The thought struck her that someone, one day, could well ask her, Dora, a question or two about the children in her charge.

'If children are sick we do think it's a good idea to keep them at home,' said Mrs Lear. 'I know it's a bind especially when you are away so much but we are so overcrowded and have so few facilities that if a child is sick we haven't got anywhere to send her.'

Dora wanted to hit her. The only reason she was standing here at all was because her daughter didn't want to come into her classroom for reasons that were becoming clear to Dora. The bell rang and the children came in a blue flood and Dora saw Laura sidling in, white-faced probably from fear that Dora might suddenly start in about Piggle and that the whole terrible drama of the morning would be repeated here on her territory. Dora took Laura gently by the hand and closed the door quietly behind her and all the way home talked in a matter-of-fact voice as lovingly as she knew how. Laura chattered back, timidly endearing, hardly able to believe in her escape. All Dora could think about was Mrs Lear's words: 'Especially when you are away so much.'

When she got back the house was quiet. Betty was hanging out clothes. She was delighted to see Laura, and Dora could see she was forgiven. 'All over, is it?' she asked. Thomas was trying to pin a clothes peg onto a dog's tail and Alice was trying to stop him. Dora and Laura walked around the garden to feed the ducks. She felt a lack of urgency as people must feel when their house, having been up for sale for too long, has finally been sold. Those cracks in the fabric, the leaks in the attic, no longer a responsibility – someone else could take care of them.

She heard Betty calling, her voice urgent, 'Someone on the telephone,' she said. 'I said you were in the garden but he says it's urgent. He didn't give his name.'

She knew that Betty knew. She tried to stop Laura coming with her while she took the call but Laura stuck by her. She lifted the phone, listened and said in a brisk social voice, 'How nice to hear you, I can't talk now, I'm busy. Perhaps you could ring back this afternoon?'

His voice was quiet. 'I want you here. Tonight.'

She said, 'That will be fine,' and put the phone down.

Laura said, 'Who was that? Who is going to ring back? I'm not going out this afternoon. I'm sick.'

'Theodore,' Dora said.

Laura was so startled by the plain truth that her shoulders dropped, the planes of her face tilted back again into babyhood as they had done that morning. 'I knew it was,' she said. 'You don't speak to anyone else like that.'

'How did I speak?' Dora said. 'I thought I was quite sharp.'

'In a really soft voice,' Laura said. 'It doesn't sound sharp. Anyway I hate him. I always will hate him. Nothing will ever make me like him.'

'Why do you hate him?'

She raised her head and looked directly at her mother. 'Because I do. I don't like him and if anything happens to Daddy and he died and you married him I would never ever want to live with you. I would see you if you wanted to see me but I would never live with you.'

'Where would you live?' Dora asked.

'With my Dad or my Granddad,' she said.

'Why do you hate him?' Dora asked. 'Because you're jealous of him?'

'I am jealous,' Laura said looking at her steadfastly. 'But I hate him. And he doesn't like me.'

'He loves you.'

'Well I don't love him and I never will nor even like him, if Dad died.'

'But Dad doesn't need to die for me to be with Theodore,' Dora said. 'It doesn't mean that something awful has to happen because I love Theodore.'

Laura gaped at Dora. 'How?' she demanded. 'How do you love him? In a husband sort of way or a brotherly way?'

'A husband way.'

'Oh.' She began to cry. 'You don't love Daddy.'

'I do love him,' Dora said. 'You must see that I do. But I also love Theodore. But if things changed, I mean if we moved from here, things would change anyway. And if I was with Theodore you could be with me or Daddy at different times. We would still be the same parents, the same love would exist for you . . .' Dora listened to her own mendacity with shame. But wicked or weak, stupid or practical, cruel or kind, whichever she was being, talking thus to a child, she could only do what she thought best, and what she thought worst was being in the dark, not knowing what or whom to believe, listening at doors and weeping in the night, and losing trust in the only people you had ever learnt to trust.

Laura said, 'It mightn't be too bad. Some of my friends have divorced parents. I think what I'm feeling now is as bad as it would be. Sometimes I think I could cope with you being dead.'

'This has nothing to do with my being dead,' Dora said. 'I have no intention of dying, nor has Dad. We like being alive and we're not ready to hand in our meal tickets. We have far too much to do looking after you for a start.'

Laura walked over to the door and turned. She said, 'Is Theodore a good man?'

Dora was startled. 'Yes,' she said but even as she said it, she knew that whoever else was good she herself was not. She thought with longing of the vivid small face of her lover brimming with energy and rancour, his glittering eyes, rapacious mouth. She thought of his fierceness, the lunging grasp of his own reactions even in the face of what he called her nonsenses, her belief in the great sea of human consciousness binding those who felt for each other, the common run of people together.

She thought of his passion, the way he fell on her body so that her flesh seemed to combine with his in a smelt at the edges, their skins fusing, and she remembered him lying with his mouth on her stomach as though loath to leave it, his hand on her thigh and she looking down at the thick curly black hair, knowing that he was the man she had always feared, and had never thought to meet – and knew that goodness did not come in such guises.

The afternoon went slowly. Wherever Dora went, Laura followed. Dora got out the jam jars and the painting books and the crayons and settled down to 'Blue Peter' and making things out of lavatory rolls. The telephone did not ring and Laura relaxed as the day wore on and, by Thomas and Alice's bedtime, Laura was worn out too. Betty and Dora bathed them, tucked them up and Dora sang to Laura until she was asleep, an endless lachrymose song about sheep going over the hill, then one to Alice, one made popular by Nina and Frederick about two-eyed birds clinging like foam, till she was hoarse. Just when she thought she had got her over to sleep Alice raised herself up out of her bed and asked her what four-eyed birds looked like and Dora had to start in all over again.

When they were settled she went into Betty and told her, trying not to look at her, that she was going to London, to Stella's house for the night. She would leave a note for Simon. Betty, tight-lipped, said nothing but looked at her in such a way that Dora could feel herself blushing, and she left the nursery angry and fevered.

She drove down the road towards Cambridge, liverish with apprehension, longing to turn home, but being pulled towards where he waited as though she were on the end of a tether.

The door opened. He must have been watching for her arrival. He pulled her into his arms. He was gaunt, with a thick dark stubble and an old torn shirt, and he wrapped her in his arms and rocked her and she felt as Laura might have done, at peace, listening to the voice of the only person who knew the secret tones to reach the heart.

She lay in the bed where she had so often lain, and looked at the cherry tree and the glint of the rising moon reflected in the old glass. Outside the window the cherry leaves were beginning to bud, the season was just on the turn. She could see the outline of the branches under the leaves, as they had been when she had first lain there, until he rose above her and blocked her vision of everything but him.

She remembered how, when she had sat on the stile and looked down on him, standing in the flooded sedge, it was as if the gates of passion soldered with ice around her heart had juddered and a section of old ice had cracked and fallen, leaving a jagged hole, and along its edges had appeared a faint line of melting ice, a tundra of feeling, a new spring.

She lay soaked in his arms and fell asleep. She could hear a bell and knew it was the bell beside her ancient oak front door, a door which had hung on its hinges for more than four hundred years. There was a green mist on the spiral stair and, at the bottom, a postman was standing, familiar and smiling and holding a well-wrapped parcel, the shape of a shoe box. Dora saw, as she looked at the name on the parcel, that it was not for her but for someone called Kitty Joyce and she tried to give it back to the postman but he said 'Nice kitty' and Dora knew it was for her. As she untied the silken ribbon and lifted the pleated tissue paper, her instincts were already agape, her skin gelid, and when she saw that the edges of the tissue paper were soft and fretted with bright scarlet specks, her heart began its free-fall down some abyss in her body and she saw what she had known from the moment she had heard the bell: her daughter's baby feet still buttoned neatly into their patent sandals. She had been so proud of their shine. There was no shine now; you could see that it had been an untidy business.

It took Dora a while to make sure that the heart hadn't crashed, to get the marrow of her knees strengthened, before she could claw her way through the constraining air to being fully awake. Beside her, Theodore feeling her distress, put his arms around her but she climbed out of bed. She didn't want to share such turmoil and nightmare from her other life that she had so jeopardised by being with him. She was overcome by a feeling of such fear and desolation that she began to dress hastily. He watched her from his pillows.

'Something has happened,' she said.

He said, 'You're being superstitious. God I hate these messugahs.'

'No,' she said, 'this is real. I must get back.'

She telephoned her house. There was no answer. She telephoned again and held on – the bell rang so long that it cut itself off. She redialled, in tears, angry beyond words, seething, hectic. At last the phone was lifted; she could hardly get her voice to start and before she gusted out the anger, Alice's voice said sleepily, 'Who is it?'

'Alice?' she said. 'Alice. Aren't you in bed. Where's Daddy? Where's Laura? Is Daddy home? Where's Betty?'

'I don't know where Betty is,' the child began to cry, hearing her mother's agitation. Dora lowered her voice. She mustn't panic herself or the child.

'Darling, can you just see if Daddy's in his bathroom? I'll hold on.'

'I won't put the phone on the white thing?' she asked.

'No, darling, just put it on the table.'

She put the receiver down gently. There was a long silence and a strange crackling then Alice's voice again.

'I found Daddy.'

When Simon came on finally, she wanted to slay him with her voice. He interrupted, quietly, 'Please don't shout at me like that, it does nobody any good . . . I didn't hear the telephone.'

'It does me good,' she screamed, 'it does me good, so you can hear how I feel. I thought that something had happened. I've been phoning for an hour. . . .' He interrupted. 'Look, I've said I'm sorry,' he said again, 'we were all asleep.' Dora was silenced. She felt ashamed.

Theodore climbed from his bed without a word and wrapped himself in a dressing-gown and went downstairs. She crept downstairs. He was sitting at his desk. Without turning he said, 'If you ever came back here I'd kill you.'

She closed the door quietly behind her and ran for the car, afraid to look behind.

It was a pearly night and the streets of Cambridge were empty.

The roads glittered and the little towns along the way were like ghost towns with the traffic lights changing for her and her only.

As she came to Bury St Edmunds the light indicating that she was running out of petrol came up on the dial and she drove more slowly, though her instinct was to put her foot down to reach home before the petrol ran out. She drove towards the garage where she knew there was an all-night self-service pump and her heart lifted as she drove into the forecourt. An out-of-order sign was draped across it like a sash of triumph. As she drove back onto the road she tried to calculate whether she could get home on what was left in the tank. It seemed unlikely. Yet if she were stranded anywhere along this road and had to call Simon he would know she had not come from London. He would be surprised enough at her returning at two in the morning. She drove along slowly, talking to the car as though it were a sentient creature with her fate in its keeping. She counted the furlongs, whispered old incantations, as though performing a rite, as the car continued to glide between the hedges.

As she drew nearer the house, she watched for the Manderley glow in the sky but all was darkness and as she turned down the little hill towards the lodge she heard her engine give a final splutter and jerk, a kind of tiny orgasm. She switched the ignition off, and the car glided and swerved silently down, till she came to the last stretch of road to the gates. She turned the key, the engine fired and she drove slowly up the long drive. The trees were sharp against the silver and black rolling sky and in the distance, across the hills a light was flickering through the woods, a poacher or the gamekeeper or both, or the will-o'-the-wisp leading someone on.

She went upstairs. Alice was in her bed, wrapped in Simon's arms like St Christopher halfway across the Rubicon. Laura was on his other side. They all looked as though they were surrounded by steam or a miasma of some kind. She took Alice from him and stroked her and soothed Laura and, when they were settled, brought them both back to their own rooms and they fell asleep almost immediately. She looked at Thomas sleeping the sleep of the energetic and went back to Simon.

'What was that telephone call all about?' he said angrily.

'A dream,' she whispered. 'A nightmare.'

'Going off like that,' he said, 'and doing it in *such* a way. Do you think I have no feelings? To go off to your lover like that.'

She looked around the room to try to find herself a buffer and saw the book *Piggle* on the table; after all that, they had forgotten to take it back to school. Her brain crept towards the word that Simon had uttered. She looked at him standing in the light. He was not avenging, nor glittering, nor wielding weapons nor hissing threats, not advancing towards her to kill her, not shimmering with rage in the back of the cage. He was an angry man in pyjamas. He was her husband.

She said: 'I came back.'

Simon said, 'If you can't go on without leaving, at least plan it in such a way that everyone knows where they are.'

She wanted to whisper, 'I don't know where I am. I'm in no man's land,' but had sense enough, just, to keep quiet. Then she said, 'I'm sorry,' and Simon said in a tired voice, 'Oh go to bed. You must be tired.'

She turned away, trying to get her mouth into some shape before it slackened into a huge black hole of sound and he said again, gently, 'Come to bed, Dora. You must be tired. God knows I am.'

She said, trying to by-pass the word lover, 'I would have been home much earlier but I was afraid I would run out of petrol. The tank's empty.'

They climbed into bed and she set about trying to pray, not to any god but to the lacuna where he used to be but praying was precluded, since she remembered that those in limbo cannot pray. A violent current seemed to surge through her arms pouring out at her fingers, she expected to see forked lightning glittering out from their tips and she hung one hand over the edge of the bed to try to direct this malevolent force away from their field. He was on the walnut tree an inch away but she could not reach him.

She tried to concentrate fiercely on an external object as she had learned to do as a child when the pain in her throat choked her and she did not wish to cry. Now, as then, she could feel the tears rising up in her body, passing various levels until they reached her orifices where, if she didn't stare, frozen, they would spill out, eyes, ears, nose, through holes and spouts in her skin she didn't know she had.

She sat up and said, 'I'm sorry, Simon. I can't stand this. It's no good for either of us pretending like this.' She dried her tears and was ashamed of herself and for herself but she persevered. 'I must leave.'

'I'm not pretending,' he said. 'You can't mean you're going back tonight.'

She said, 'I can't stay here.'

There was no point in trying to redeem anything. She knew she was a foolish, bad, miserable woman who wanted to have her cake and eat it and did so and still felt starving. She knew she was a miserable young woman trying to find her happiness before she died. She knew she was behaving like something that had had its head chopped off and was still running. She remembered a story about the axe not quite cutting Mary, Queen of Scots' head clean off and that between the first and second stroke she had whispered 'Sweet Jesus'. She remembered a lot to aggrandise her squalid little story, did Dora.

He left the room. She saw him disappear as her lover had disappeared earlier but she felt none of the fright she had felt earlier as Theodore's vivid body had flashed from the room like a comet leaving a trail of rage.

She went into Laura's and Alice's room and stared at them, their eyelids creamy, shadowed in the half-light, their perfect skin, the lines of their bodies under the counterpanes. She dressed and went downstairs and through the oak door into the prospect beyond. Simon was nowhere to be seen.

The silvery sky had vanished, disappeared under cloud and it had begun to rain. She looked across to where the light had flickered but the rain had extinguished it or the poacher had gone or the will-o'-the-wisp had done its job for the night. The car was not at the door and as she looked around, Simon drove it up and climbed out without a word and, without looking at her, went back into the house. She switched on the engine and drove to the gates. She looked at the petrol dial. It registered half-full.

She turned off the engine. She thought of Theodore's reaction as she left him to save the children who would be in his keeping if she went to him. She knew that imprecations and a spore of ill-will had followed her on her journey home and well she deserved them. She thought of Simon climbing out of bed and taking her car to the stables and filling up the tank and bringing it to the door grim and silent, his face set against the storm. She looked at the wet road ahead, winding towards Cambridge and did a three-point turn, went back up the drive and felt that her body was making a mute call, a howl of pain squeezing its suffocated way out before she reached home, protesting against what lay ahead, against taking the arid road that led from the woods to the castle.

She crept through the door, her shoes in her hand and climbed the stairs to her workroom determined not to look at the walls but saw *in order to climb into the depths one does not need to travel very far* and thought, bugger you, Wittgenstein, and sat at her desk and heard the creak of the stairs, like the creak of the universe. Simon stood at the door. She said, 'Why did you fill the tank with petrol?'

He said, 'I could not have my wife wandering around the lanes of Suffolk in the middle of the night.'

She said, 'Did you know where I was going?'

He said, 'Of course.'

'How long have you known?' she said.

'It was obvious,' he said. 'And I knew when you came back from that holiday someone had met you.'

'Why didn't you say anything before? Didn't you want to?'

'As you say: having said it, means you have to do something about it, and I wanted to postpone that as long as possible.'

He was standing in the full light now.

'If I had a reproach,' he said, 'it would be that when you thought that this might affect our marriage you continued with it.'

'The Temple of Select Amusements,' she said.

He said, 'What?' Suddenly cross.

'I did once think at the beginning, that it might affect the marriage but I dismissed it. It was out of the question. When I thought it again, it had happened.'

They sat silent. Her marriage was like a fortress from which there appeared to be no escape. And not just because of the blocked-up doors, the mullioned windows, the sheer drops, but because outside stretched vast forlorn deserts where only demons called in the mists.

Simon stretched out his hand and took hers. She let him hold it, passive, without surprise and she knew that her life was infected with a further disease, the disease of gratitude.

She thought of what Theodore had prophesied, that she would use him, that he was only a stepping stone in her life. Step by step she had gone towards him, through the torrent, but when there were only a few more yards to go and the stones had been swept away, the person she was leaving had blocked her dream of a different future with the reality of charity. He had given her the means to continue the crossing, or, she thought, refusing the implication, given her permission to go. She had hoped, as she stumbled towards Theodore, that she would find the promised land but the promised land had lain around her, hidden by a fog of pain and anger, the place she had entered when she made her vows.

She felt nothing but rage and age and knew that from now on instead of living her life she was advancing towards death and that part of her was dying already and singing a dirge for what she had abandoned and she loved Simon more, worst fate of all, more than she wanted to love him.

Time after time she had asked him to betray what she had given him, and which she had to punish him for taking and keeping. Trust. Betray it so that she would not have to finalise their transaction, complete the vow taken long before she could know what such a vow would entail. Time after time she had made him walk the last eight hundred yards hoping he would fail so that she would not have to recognise that he would always be able to read the word that could never be seen in the mirror, the word that Rumpelstiltskin hated, the word that made the black prince ride away.

She thought of Theodore in the churchyard with the lake behind him, his glinting eyes, his curly black hair, the muscular body in his big army coat caressing her, saying this *is* my business, or running towards her as the swans swept overhead and he hurried her into his arms, of him rising above her, tender, triumphant, and knew that it was finished; the manifold illusions were waiting to be shattered by her own hands, the hooped semblances to be rusted by disuse. It could never happen again, never never never, when a gusher of love had sprung up in her heart and watered her life and her soul. The flowering was over, only duty remained.

She thought not to cry, to keep the tears in check and the anger, a normal enough looking woman, whose skin no longer shone, persuading herself that it didn't matter, that she had done her best though it felt like the worst, and she followed Simon down the spiral stairs, down, down round the dark tower.

V

One evening, some time later, when the house was quiet, she was up in her little attic room working. She had climbed the spiral stairs in the darkness. These days the steps were familiar and she had no need for graffiti, such aleatory devices were behind her. The house was still, had been for hours. Simon was in London as he now often was. Laura and Alice and Thomas were asleep in their rooms, and Betty was out with an old friend who would fetch her home from the whist party with a crash of gears. From far below her room she heard a noise that made her heart stutter. The house should be silent. She leapt from her chair and ran out onto the little landing, switching the light on so that she could scale the stairs more quickly, and as she ran down, round and round, spinning downwards, the old scrawled legends came singing out like a magic lantern show, *a kite's meal, his glory was he had such friends, it is necessary to descend, a hooped semblance, such a dance of images, being your slave, as free maids do chant it, perserve the Venice treacle in the bone*, her eyes scanning and conning as her feet sent her arched body flying with fear through the door towards whatever had made the noise in the dark sitting room. She saw them as though they had been coated in phosphorescence, holding hands, their heads bowed, the puff-sleeves of the nightdresses looking like the details from a painting by Piero Della Francesca, tender and divine, their pale arms shining in the moonlight coming through the big windows. They had made this journey through the darkened house, down their separate staircase, through the echoing hall, the children of her heart, in a journey that treated with nightmares to where their mother should have been and was not.

They were alone in a house, murderous because suddenly empty, where the ticking of the big old painted clock had lost its neutrality, and they clung together in the timeless calamity of being alone. They could not raise the curtain of darkness and fear and find their mother or father beyond it, by a fire reading or writing, or looking surprised because they were out of bed. The house was in darkness and would be for ever, and all this Dora saw, as she came hurtling through the door and saw too, from the edge of her eye, the last inscription, streaming behind her and, for an instant, the worst was upon the children, the dark shape from behind the turret; and then she had her arms around them, their faces pressed against her, their bodies animated by need, and there was such movement and terror in those bodies that she was weak with remorse, with longing, with love, and she knew to her bones that what she was seeing was the pain of loss, of departure, the pain of separation which she could never have gauged if she had inflicted it on them.

Their sobs became cries and then dropped into snuffles and then rose again into little curlew cries of explanation, the delight of relief, of how one had woken up the other and shapes had started out at them.

Dora on her knees just inside the big oak door that had once swung open on her dream, and closed again, her arms around them, showed them through the tall windows reaching almost to the floor, how the dark yew hedges and the sycamore trees were not yawning caverns, full of shadows, but real things, familiar shapes in a light they had not seen before.

As she knelt with her arms around them she thought of the last inscription: *man's life is thought and he despite his terror cannot cease ravening through century after century ravening raging and uprooting that he may come into the desolation of reality*; Yeats, who had always spoken what he perceived to be the truth and so she had believed it, humbly credulous, because her betters had said it and it had the imprimatur of her religion, literature. But she knew that he was wrong, that he was fallible, that man's or woman's life is not all thought and that they can cease ravening and raging and go quietly into the active universe in an act of love.

She had lopped herself off from her own world to enter a world that she had longed to believe in, a world of incompatibles, that the terrible deceits of infatuation had tendered as true. She had sought and entered a world of manifold illusion, of conceit and delusion where the cardinal virtues played no part, where duty and piety were strangers. She remembered Josie smiling at her in the kitchen and she was ashamed of herself, for it was her duty to be joyful and knowledgeable and not to be an innocent, not to be the first woman on earth, not to be a woman to whom things happened, but to be a woman who recognised the worthwhile, a woman with children who had a father they loved as much as they loved her; and she must lead her life as best she should, and not as best she could.

Dora hoped that what she would remember of the sounds in her life which would ripple outward would be not what she had copied onto the curving walls, nor what he had whispered as he loved her, but the sound from two pale children, their hair silvered in the moonlight, as they stood within her arms and looked outwards on a landscape that had turned from dark to light, towards the silver yew trees in the garden.

SEVEN
The Gazebo

I

Dora sat in her little sitting room doing her needlepoint. Over the years she had become a little more skilled. She was embroidering a present for her sister Iris, a cushion which she hoped she might find diverting. She had drawn out the central pattern on the graph of the canvas with care: three birds, a nightingale, a swallow and a hoopoe perched in a bay tree. At least, that was what they were supposed to be but they all looked much the same, except for the hoopoe's distinguishing erectile crest which seemed more like something obscene in slow motion. The design was based on a legend Dora had read in a book on Greek mythology, the usual tale of rapine, incest, murder, and interference from the gods. A Greek princess, Philomela, daughter of a king of Athens, had been raped by one Tereus, her brother-in-law, married to her sister Procne. After the deed he had cut out her tongue to teach her to hold it, but Philomela still had, after all, the use of her hands and had embroidered her tragedy, stitch by stitch, in tapestry, spinning a yarn with a vengeance. As a result the gods had changed them all into birds; Philomela into the nightingale, as befitted someone who had been robbed of the gift of song, Procne into the swallow and Tereus into the hoopoe. Dora felt sorry for Procne; a sister could hardly be held responsible for a husband's criminality. She looked up the hoopoe in a book on birds and noted that it got its name from its peculiar double cry. The gods too had their little ways.

She thought that Philomela must have been a brilliant needlewoman which was more than she could say for herself. Even when she explained what she was embroidering people tended to look at it upside down.

She looked around her room. The walls were painted with trompe l'oeil panelling so artfully done that the colour looked as though leached out by time. It had taken two skilled people a good deal of time to achieve that effect. Surroundings were important, a part of the aesthetic of life, and how one lived was an advertisement of oneself, for good or for ill. Taste as a pointer to sensibility, taste as bulwark against an upbringing where taste was the unknown factor. Ho, hum, Dora thought, you really ought to be put down, Dora; what you like is Owning, being deceived by ornament. Yet for as long as she could remember ornament had meant credibility, extras which added authenticity to a bare life, whether it was an old handbag hung around her neck as a child, or getting herself up with kohl and jangling metal belts and gold lamé to try to look like Hollywood's idea of Cleopatra when she had first come to London, or collecting like a lunatic as an adult so that as the years rolled by, her house became ever more filled with objects, layer upon layer, so that the rooms seemed encrusted, and even the attics and lofts were barnacled with wrack from the wash below.

It was as though she were trying to compose and construct the semblance of a heritage, the aggregations that undisturbed or unvexed families had passed down through generations, to their progeny, or epigone more like, Dora thought, looking around her sitting room at her assembled guests.

In earlier days, Dora had thought of her instinct, indeed mania, to collect as accidental, energetic, genetic, and that she was asserting her rights by filling the house, that there was a kind of restitution to her accumulations, and that by plundering she was reaching back.

She did not say this to many people, as she had a whit of sense, and when apologising to Stella about her surroundings she was more inclined to attribute the inchoation of her greed, her desire to have one more thing, to the fact, or her belief (much the same thing now in Dora's book, as she grows older and harder) that she was starved as an infant by the mad housekeeper whom for years she had thought of as a Mrs Poole in reverse, a raving slut who kept the till of food closed. Now she thinks that Ellen in fact had been perfectly sane but reared in a hard school where crying children should be left to cry for their own good, that they cried as they might breathe, a natural reflex, not necessarily attributable to grievance or need. Betty had had shreds of the same attitude. 'It clears their lungs,' she had once said, when Laura was in the middle of a bawl and Dora, affronted, had seized Laura up, who had then, as Dora recalled, vomited down her back. Betty had been well pleased. Laura was her pet.

She lived most of her life now in Keep Hall, possessor of all she surveyed, or joint possessor, but she had chosen for years to think of herself as dispossessed, an outsider, against the evidence, the facts, the conduct of her life. It was only as she grew older and discovered, without falling into despair, without the world seizing up, that she was an ordinary woman, that she had begun to make an effort to feel a part of things, wherever she was, if only as a matter of manners, and out of consideration for other people. Simon had taught her the value of that and she thought it a kind of modesty.

But the sense of being on the outside was a difficult feeling to yield. She had cultivated it for so long and it made for a kind of self-importance. She had of course supposed that being an outsider had been thrust upon her, and, that had she had the choice, she would have been a part of every circle or at the centre of the ring, instead of circling it watchfully. But in a certain sense, choose it she did, if only because it was a strategy by which she could come to terms with herself. So long as she was an outsider, she did not have to apply the ordinary rules of living and be found wanting. Though she did not necessarily recognise this intaglio under her life, its sunken shadow ran through her days and coloured her actions. Then too, she had read often enough at an impressionable age – and with Dora that age is every stage in her life – that being an outsider was the only position and stance suitable and proper to the artist, which was what she wanted to be.

When she was younger she had thought of herself as emblematic of her tribe and creed who, though declassified, stripped of their possessions, had never been reduced to serfdom. Certain lists had swirled in her head like mist on a bog, a toneless sentimental lament for what had been lost, for her permanently impoverished stock. But to have something to lose presupposes possession and Dora and her ilk had not for generations possessed much, other than their powerful energies and memories, so it was not loss she grieved and raged over, but absence, the absence of things that should have been loved, from their collective life.

This grief had odd outlets. She never climbed a great stairwell hung with portraits without feeling a heady sulphurous mixture of rancour and resentment, rage mingled with admiration and pleasure, which made her haughty with the owners, if they were around, or touchy with the National Trust staff, who dealt with too many capering loonies as a matter of course, to notice one touched woman sending out sinusoidal messages about how she had been robbed.

These philistines in their golden frames above her, jowled, bewigged, long-necked if they were women, without necks if men, with spaniels on their laps, and crops in their hands, or crops of another kind stretching golden and green behind them, standing beside potent-looking hunters with little truncheoned tails, had, all the same, composed, by the force of money and tenure of place, an enviable and splendid aesthetic of living. She did not allow that they were masters of the art, or that they might have plundered Italy and Greece in their own version of an effort to reach back to their antecedents and history. She could not grant them sensibility since they had everything else that made life worth living.

She thought of her long-fingered, long-legged father with his raven hair and high nose and excellence at all sports and his passion for horses. He had never had the chance to ride and had watched as the hunt, strayed far afield, had jumped the hedges of his tiny farm. She knew to her bones that he would have been a champion. She grieved for his loss and raged against the hard-faced red-jacketed brutes who had ridden past their door. They wouldn't ride there now, she thought, or their jackets would be stained a different hue.

She remembered with relish what Elizabeth Bowen had written: 'a past that Ireland still too much dwells on, is still by England not enough recognised. My family got their position and drew their power from a situation that shows an inherent wrong.' In museums and great houses as Dora walked past the oak furniture, the satin wood, the burr walnut and the mahogany, with their labels of provenance, she thought of the sentences she had read in a history of Irish furniture, slipped in casually, informatively, among facts about carving on coffers or elm chests, representative of the kind of chest furniture found in Irish castles and lower houses until the Georgian period. 'Of course the ownership of such articles or indeed the need for them, was confined to the landed classes.' Then came the zeugma. 'The destitution of the peasantry rendered storage boxes superfluous.'

The landed classes. How did they come by their land, Dora had wondered, even as she walked down the lawns at Keep Hall, and over the paths and through the yews, across the lawns to the gazebo and dovecote. By appropriating what wasn't theirs, she thought aloud, startling the dogs.

The destitution of the peasantry rendered storage boxes superfluous. In other words there was nothing to store. By Christ, Dora thought, no wonder I fill coffers and carve my name on them. Destitution, restitution. With one bound Dora was incarcerated in acquisition.

'So it's compensation now, is it?' Stella said, looking around her for somewhere to sit down.

'No,' Dora said, 'it's restitution.' She began to laugh at her own brazenness. 'To myself, for the rest of them.'

'Oh very good,' Stella said. 'But compensation could be the favourite?'

'Compensation is paying you for what you had. Restitution is giving you what you should have had. Making good.'

'Making good,' Stella said. 'You always had a way with words.'

Once, years before, when waiting for Theodore to finish a lecture, Dora had followed the signs to the mysteriously named Kettle's Yard, and discovered one man's resolution to the dilemma of possessions. In those simple unsoliciting arrangements he showed there was dignity to possessing, that what mattered was the inner worth of the outward show. Dora was delighted. Permission and an imprimatur. Theodore who had never visited Kettle's Yard and who could have loaded his possessions into the back of a mini said, 'You're talking rubbish, Dora.'

Dora had not laughed at the instinctive use of words.

'No,' she said. 'I am talking the proper end of art.' But she knew that what she had meant was that she simply wanted to have.

She started to try to tone down the crest of the hoopoe, and listened to her guests, her eyes travelling around the room. Simon's forbears' possessions were hidden under the influx. The house was like a palimpsest of a life that at one time she would have stared at with derision and envy, indeed had done so. Tony Flaxmeyer might have been proud of her; or then again he might not.

Her guests had strewn themselves around the room, the biggest people somehow choosing the smallest chairs, the men with the longest legs crouching on the smallest footstools. She was sitting in a large chair near the fire, the coffee-tray at hand. At her feet, his knees drawn up, his feet sporting a pretty pair of embroidered slippers, sat a large man who was more at home on a large horse. Still, he seemed comfortable enough as he declaimed to a playwright on the eccentricity of his wife's Anglo-Irish ancestry. The long low fender stool he was sitting on was covered in a needlepoint unicorn, tethered, drawn and executed by Dora and she noted, without alarm, that where he sat, it sagged. She had researched the unicorn and found that it had a white body, a red head and blue eyes, a colour scheme that fairly defused the magic. On the long sofa Elvira was talking to a neighbour about the possibility of borrowing his horse-box. She had heard he had a new one and she had promised to take a likely hunter to Ireland to her sister. Could she borrow his old one? Perhaps she'd got it all wrong, she said, and he hadn't got a new one at all. There wasn't a problem, the man said all gallantry, save that the said horse-box was rather old and rickety so she'd better have the new.

'You can't possibly go on your own,' James said. 'It's far too tiring – how are you going – Fishguard to Rosslare?'

'Stranraer to Larne,' she said.

'And you can't go tearing up England and halfway across Scotland alone with a horse-box. If anything happens or you break down you can't leave to get help. And you realise that if there's any kind of sea running, the captain won't let the box on board. The number of times I've sat on that quayside with a ton of horse kicking the sides in.'

'Which means I'd have to unbox Vulcan,' Elvira said.

'Which means you'd have to unbox him and that's a doddle compared to getting him back in.'

'But I've promised Pooky I'd bring it over,' Elvira said.

'How is Pooky?' someone asked from the other side of the room.

'Oh as well as ever,' Elvira said. 'Hunts every day she can.'

'Isn't it dangerous?' someone said. 'With all the troubles and shooting over there?'

'No.' Elvira shook her head dismissively. 'They're all terrified of horses.'

'Where do they live?' Dora said.

'In Tyrone,' Elvira said and Dora, her needle poised, thought again of her father and, for the first time in a long time, of the virgin Nora, petrified into effigy by now, she shouldn't wonder, or else still frightened of unicorns.

'I'll go with you,' she said to Elvira, 'I should visit my father anyway.'

'How is he?' someone asked.

'Remarkable,' Dora said. It depended, she thought, on who was passing the remarks.

A week later they set out.

II

Vulcan had not been best pleased by the journey or by the rattling across the gangway and Dora thought he might stove his box in. She and Elvira watched the gangers on the cargo deck fasten it down with chains before going up to the extraordinary orange and yellow cafeteria on the middle deck.

A man sidled into the banquette opposite them though there were many empty places where he might have sat and Dora was astonished by his nerve. He had round glasses and a fine face under the thatch of hair, the unkempt eyebrows. There was a very faint smell of old badger about him. Without much preamble he asked them would they be interested in subscribing to pamphlets on Irish history.

'Clandeboye,' he said. 'They sit up there in Clandeboye and use the name and it was stolen out from under us. O'Donnell. Antrim. O'Neill. Tyrone. Lord Tyrconnell. How in God's name could you be a lord and be an Irishman? It's a contradiction in terms, it's worse than that it's an insult, imagine if the Afrikaners called themselves Lord Matebele or something. Lord Tyrone, my ass, if you'll pardon the expression.'

'It's all so long ago,' Elvira said. Dora admired her reticence. She wondered how he would react if he knew the woman on his right eating some limp lettuce was Lady Tyrone's sister.

'It happened yesterday,' he said.

'It's still happening,' Dora said.

He looked at her without warmth. 'It's still happening because we collude,' he said, 'or some of us. Names are important, it's all we had left and they took those too. This Anglicisation of our place names, I live in a townland with an Irish name meaning the wooded hill. Now I get a letter saying I'm to be part of a road out of Dungannon fifteen miles away. Three two five Dungannon Road. I'm not using it.'

'I shouldn't think you'll get many letters then,' Elvira said, clearly bored.

'Oh I'll get them,' he said, 'the postman knows me.'

He was head of RATH, the Restoration of Ancient Titles, Hereditary, and wrote fierce pamphlets on the illegality of anyone holding an Irish title to which he believed they were not entitled. A rath he explained was the place of residence of the chief of a Celtic tribe and the acrostic had come to him in his sleep.

'I know exactly what a rath is,' Dora said. He ignored her.

'The proper descendants of the great Gaelic noblemen lived in Portugal, France, Spain' ('Hennessy Brandy,' murmured Elvira greedily, 'Chateau Haut Brion, the Irish always liked their drink') 'whence they had fled on the night of September 14th, 1607, the Flight of the Earls.'

'I know all that,' Dora said, 'I'm Irish too.'

'Where did they go from?' he said. 'And how many went?'

'Hundreds?' Dora hazarded. 'From Derry.'

'From a boat in Lough Swilly,' he said, 'ninety-nine of the noblest men in Ireland.'

'They abandoned their country,' Dora said and wished she hadn't.

'They knew if they stayed, they would be arraigned and hanged, and they knew well too that when they left, a dispensation that had lasted since the mists of time, would vanish as though it had never happened.'

He talked in what Dora thought of as the Irish environmental voice: it created a moral and social landscape – revealing the world in which he lived, in which he had been brought up, as though its climate had steeped the chords. It's because you know every nuance, Dora thought, as you will never know what's behind the big ringing tones of England.

There was something else about his voice. It set the tone, the level of the debate between them. She resented this and tried to resist, as she now tried to resist so much that she saw as Irish, the treaties that he set up by his tone and expression of voice. No wonder the Irish were great talkers: their voices were their instruments.

'None of the titles left in Ireland is the real thing,' he said. 'And they give their children Irish names and send them to England to be educated. My name is O'Neill and if Hugh O'Neill, the greatest patriot of them all, hadn't been betrayed history would be different.'

'History is made from ifs,' Dora said, 'and in any case Hugh O'Neill was educated in England and was much respected there and was described as being more English than the English. Baron of Dungannon he was called and he walked the streets of London as a lord, that is, knocking down anyone who got in his way.'

He looked at her with surprise but rallied.

'All the same he sloughed all that when he got back here and became The O'Neill,' he said. 'The hereditary King of Ireland. I'll tell you what he said when that whore Elizabeth tried to subdue him: I care not to be an Earl unless I be better and higher than an earl, for I am in blood and power better than the best of them, these new Irish earls, and will give place to none but my cousin of Kildare for that he is of mine house. My ancestors were Kings of Ulster, and Ulster is mine and shall be mine.'

'That's more or less what Edward Carson said when he was fighting to make Ulster a separate state,' Dora said and he looked offended. She said to make up, 'Did you ever read what was found in O'Neill's castle, what was left, when he was finally run to ground?'

He shook his head. She recited: two old chests, two forms, one pair of taffeta curtains, a brass kettle, two baskets with certain broken earthen dishes and some waste spices, a box, two drinking glasses, a vessel with two gallons of vinegar, two glass bottles, a little iron pot and a grate spit, a frying pan and a dripping pan. Not much fit for a king.'

She did not say, for she might be called to pay a fealty, that her own ancestors had been The O'Neill's bodyguard and hatchet men. Over a thousand of her small tribe had died for him, slaughtered in their efforts to keep the enemy at bay, away from the old golden lion who represented the last of his race, the last of his order. They knew that with his going the light of the Gaelic life would be extinguished and they fought like madmen to keep the flame flickering.

'What are you doing living in England,' he said. 'What do you think you're doing there? Every Irish person owes it to their country to come back.'

'That's not true,' Dora said. 'I owe the country nothing. A feeling of moral superiority on your part just because you live there is hardly justified. It's always used as emotional blackmail. Have you ever thought that what's so often presented as moral courage is fear of the foreign landscape?'

He stared at her over his glass. 'No,' he said.

'And of course those who leave – like me – advance precisely these arguments in order to justify their desertion. Circus animals all, whether we go or stay.'

The boat gave a lurch. 'I'm going down to look at Vulcan,' Elvira said. 'I hope it doesn't get up any rougher.'

'Bringing horses over are you?' he said, looking after Elvira with a kind of angry admiration. 'I thought the traffic was all the other way round and she'd be bringing them back.'

Dora wondered what he would say if he knew she was delivering an eighteen-hand hunter to Lady Tyrone. Quisling, probably, if he didn't think they were all some horrible figment of his worst imaginings.

The sea did indeed get up rougher and Dora made her excuses and fled. She spent a bad night.

The boat docked and as they descended to the car deck an announcement came over the Tannoy asking Elvira to go to the purser's office. Elvira ground her teeth. 'Some bloody slip-up about Vulcan's jabs,' she said. 'I've been dreading this. You go down to the car and get the box off. I'll be as quick as I can.'

The horse was quiet in its box but as she opened the door of the car it kicked and whinnied. She hoped Elvira would come back soon and take over, and drove to the side of the docks and waited. Soldiers circled the quayside. When Elvira did arrive, she was small and pale and frightened. 'Robin has had to go into hospital,' she said. 'Do you think you can manage the rest of the journey? I'll fly back from Belfast. We'll unbox here to give him a stretch. Or I could try to get Pooky to send a groom down. . . .' Her voice trailed off and Dora said briskly, 'Of course I can manage,' and as they drove slowly over the ramp she tried her best to comfort and cheer Elvira.

When they had manoeuvred away from the quayside, Elvira roped in some of the soldiers to help back Vulcan out. He looked bigger than the Trojan horse, snorting and blowing out his nostrils and jumping around on his silly fragile legs, glad of the diversion. One soldier nipped inside the box and nipped out again sharpish.

'Strewth,' he said.

It was a harder job getting Vulcan back in but under a combined assault of soldiers and dock hands it was done and Dora set off, somewhat nervously.

She thanked heaven for the good road. One always knew when one was in a Protestant area of Northern Ireland, because the roads were decent. She thought of Tony and his strictures about 'one' and 'you' and smiled.

The journey was remarkably short. But then she knew the road well enough though she had never been headed for this particular destination before.

When she came to the main gates, they looked very shut so she parked just outside and rang at the door of the lodge. The bell played a tune, 'Home Sweet Home', and through the frosted glass door Dora could see a woman approaching. A cat came into the porch and, as the door opened, oozed through into the house.

The woman looked Dora up and down, but Dora in her jeans, sweater and pearls was as confident and safe as a citadel. Her hair was piled on top of her head, and for all she had been sick half the night her skin was glowing, and what she had to ask was in the woman's gift to answer and answer well and civilly. She greeted the woman, who responded without pleasure and looked suspiciously at the car and the horse box. Dora felt a surge of irritation and amusement, familiar, though she thought she had forgotten it, at the surliness of the woman. She knew her own smiles cut no ice with this descendant of the imported Scots who had displaced her forbears but she felt superior to them. She quite saw why these Presbyterian descendants clung so fiercely to their rigorous way of life. Anything to protect themselves from the encroachment of the enemy on the doorstep, the turbulent natives, with their imagination, their anger and their endless quelling of their need for revenge.

Dora was put in mind of her mother. In some ways this woman's attitude reminded Dora of her mother's inclination to suspicion, her resistance to charm, her husband's chief weapon. In any marriage the characteristic that the outside world finds appealing is often the one which the partner finds most unbearable.

'The pleasure gardens isn't open to the public the day,' the woman said, delighted to be able to thwart Dora.

'I'm not going to the gardens,' Dora said. 'I'm lunching with Lord Tyrone.'

The woman, silent for the moment, made a move to one side as though to catch Dora at more of an angle, but Dora turned more subtly against the light.

'Follow the road alongside the wall about two miles,' the woman said reluctantly, 'and you'll come to the other gates. If you get to Dungannon you'll have got too far.'

'Not far enough for you, my girl,' Dora thought as she drove alongside the demesne wall, as in Ireland she had driven so often, mile after mile, along wall after wall, built to contain the misappropriated acres and keep the dispossessed out, with not even a gate, a grid, an eyehole to give the stolen perspectives back to the land.

Beyond that wall flowed the Blackwater, a river that threaded its ways through Irish history. There The O'Neill, the Lord Tyrone of his time, the ancestor of her shipboard companion no doubt – weren't we all descended from kings? – had laid siege to the English garrison. The relieving army had been routed, its commander, Bagenal, killed. Half of Ireland had lain open to the rebels. All Tyrone had to do was march. Ah, why did he not march?

She turned in at the gate, drove past pretty cottages, through a farm yard, through an archway and down to where she thought the stables might be. A groom came out and backed Vulcan out as easily as a knife out of butter. He was like a tank on legs, blasé enough about his journey. Dora and the man stared at him, the sheer scale. 'Pooky will be pleased,' he murmured and Dora realised that he was Lord Tyrone. They shook hands.

'Have you heard from Elvira?'

'Not yet. She's not back I think. But Robin will certainly live. He's a tough old boy.'

They walked through another arch and into a courtyard. On each side stretched long buildings with small paned windows above double doors which had once accommodated carriages, gigs, wagons, carts, diligences. Above the archway was a clock tower with, on the clock face, the letters of TYRONE CASTLE marking the hours. Joining the two wings was a solid unadorned building, decent, with handsome proportions. It faced across the courtyard, towards the park with its enormous trees throwing dark circles of shadows on the grass.

'This was where the old house stood,' her host said. 'The place was a ruin when I bought it. A madman lived in it for twenty years and did nothing but drink champagne and throw the bottles in the corner. As one room filled up with bottles he moved into another. And then at the end when there were no more rooms to go to he set fire to the whole caboodle. He stood outside watching it burn. He said it was one good way of cracking a bottle.'

'Was it a beautiful house?' Dora asked. 'Was anything saved?'

'Very beautiful, at least from photographs. Of course the original castle was knocked about in the seventeenth century.'

They went through into a large hall beyond which was another inner hall, flooded with light. Gum boots, waxed jackets, dog baskets lay on the floor and benches, a Louis XVI settee with exquisite needlepoint stood under an enormous Reynolds, the drinks tray was on a large ebony and *pietra dura* table. Underneath two empty enormous dog baskets were piled with hairy tartan rugs. Lady Tyrone came down the stairs in jeans and a jumper, her small vivid face like Elvira's, though younger and with more spirit. She made Dora welcome. Would she like to see the garden before or after lunch? 'We might go for a walk along the shore after lunch,' her host said. 'Elvira mentioned you'd been born in the province.'

They had drinks in the felicitous drawing room. This was the Ireland Tony had showed her, the Ireland she had told him she wished to enter in their first conversation a lifetime ago, before she knew what she was talking about.

She looked at the paintings with their little name plaques on the frames. The sulphurous mixture began to move. Quell it, she said, you don't break bread with people and then grumble; well, actually you often do, she reminded herself. The pictures were all of his ancestors, he said and Dora peered at the labels and they none had Irish names.

'My grandmother's family,' he said. She looked at the charming picture of ruddy-cheeked children in muffs and bonnets and buttoned boots and lace fichus and silken shoes, at two beautiful Misses Fortescues on their way to some wonderful rout. Where was the connection with Tyrone in God's name, how had they fetched up here, how had he come by the most ancient Irish name of all?

As they went into lunch she saw a portrait of Pooky as a young girl and stopped dead in front of it. She bit her tongue. 'It's Flaxmeyer,' he said. 'What do you think of his work? People say it's gone off but I must say I've always liked it.'

'Me, too,' she said.

She helped herself from the hot plate; casserole, apple crumble. Perfectly good. When O'Neill had set out to regain his country, his fiefdom, he had reinstated the practice of coshery, whereby a king exacted hospitality, at whatever cost, from his dependants, or whosoever he chose to lodge upon.

Throughout lunch Dora set out to please. The persona she had constructed, cell by cell, filament by filament, was in its element. She was slightly embarrassed by the tendency of this persona to insist on its attractiveness. What was she trying to prove? Everything. Everything.

She thought of the delectable food her cook was, with a bit of luck, putting on her own dining-table, for her family and whatever guests were there in her absence. No casseroles there. Though Thomas would have eaten an ox, spitted, Laura and Alice liked their meals pure, precise, green. All that striving for perfection, all that effort on her part to recreate what she thought had been lost, stolen, strayed, abandoned, wrenched away, leaving an open wound that could never be staunched, no, no matter how much she stuffed it, for the materials she was using were the wrong ones, they were only trinkets and geegaws, the outward signs of riches of another race and the bleeding she sought to staunch was internal. It would need a different kind of poultice from a bit of cash.

She hardly thought of where she was going afterwards, to where the last of the hatchet men for The O'Neill sat with his memories behind speckled intense eyes glowing in a parchment face.

In a thousand years she could never explain to her host, this nice pretender, with his shy and mannerly disposition, where she had come from and where she was going, if she ever found out herself. Not in the long run, for she no longer knew where that route was leading and Nora had apparently long since been smothered into silence, but in the short run beyond the wall, further down the lough shore where the aborigines of Tyrone lived in their enclave, as mysterious and enclosed as was this man behind his long brick barricades.

She had learnt to speak two languages, not the native one spoken in those fields of Roscommon, the old Gaelic tongue, but another kind of native one, with code words and language as different from the one she had learnt from Caroline and her ilk as Cyrillic from Romance. One gave her the passwords and access to the world she entered at lunchtime, the other to that world she had left behind long ago and which pulled her back because of its effigies hidden in the heartland.

After the walk she took her farewell and drove along the wall until it turned away into the woods, and the fields became smaller and the roads rutted. Everywhere there were bushes and houses and little stunted trees covered in ivy. In the distance the waters of the lough gleamed pewter and she could hear the gulls mewling. The rooks rose and circled as she drove up. Her father was sitting in his high-backed chair dozing but he rose to his feet, suddenly limber, to greet her with a cry, tears springing in his eyes.

She told him about Vulcan and where she had delivered him. 'And you took your dinner at the castle?' he asked.

'I did,' she said, 'and it was lovely. But it was more a house than a castle.'

'You were always mad about castles,' he said. 'Even as a youngster. You were always drawing them.'

'And I was always running between the woods and the castle,' she said, 'being a good girl or a bad one.'

'You were always the best best girl,' he said and she stared hard at the rooks flapping lazily onto the tops of the trees, the trick she had learnt as a child to keep the tear ducts dry.

'They start building their nests on the first of March,' he said, 'you could set your almanac by them. I would have liked to have seen them do it just the one more time.'

The rooks rose, flapped, and settled on the tops of the old trees grown long beyond their strength. When he had gone they would have to be felled.

'Have they always been here?' she said. 'It's nearly the first sound I remember.'

'They've always been here, daughter,' he said, 'and if they leave a house it's bad luck.'

She looked at him. She had never walked into his house but he had not been there to greet her. She had never done wrong in his eyes and whoever she was, she was all the same to him. 'That I can well believe,' she said.

She went down to the lough shore and climbed to the hill and stood beside her mother's grave, the darkest thing in the mercuried landscape. Below the waves slung themselves gently along the soft line of the shore and the sunken bones of the old boat frozen in decay. The swans dipped their black beaks in the water. She climbed down to the shore again and took her wellingtons and stockings off and put her feet into the soft cold water. She bent down and began to pull at the small rocks as if to find the hidden casket.

'You'll be foundered in that water,' a fisherman said as he walked past to his nets on the sally trees, 'and catch your death.'

So she straightened up and left off looking.

As she drove to the ferry a man by the side of the road was hitching a lift and, as she accelerated past, she saw that it was the RATH writer. She stopped. He climbed in.

'I didn't know you were from these parts,' he said. 'I'd have said you dug with the other foot if I didn't know better.'

'When the English were looking for The O'Neill,' she said, as they pulled away up the road that led to England, 'a reward of £2,000 alive or £1,000 dead was put on his head but his name was so reverenced that no one could be induced to betray him – even for so large a sum.'

'Boys oh boys, the times have changed,' he said.

Dora stood on the deck of the ferry and watched as Dublin pulled back and the sea raced between her and the land as though it couldn't wait to get rid of her.

She went down to the cabin and lay on the bed and slept. She dreamed she was in a room with her mother and another woman whom she could not see but thought was Stella. Sun was floating through the windows and the room was warm, golden, drowsy with the hint of something jungly in the air, rank and powerful. An enormous bee flew up to the window like a huge golden mayfly or scarab, but full of warmth and sun, bumping and glimmering, and the strangers who were suddenly gathered in the room began to hit at it to bring it down, to be rid of it, to destroy it. Dora, wide awake in the dream, could see that for them it was only a threatening insect, yet if they could but stop and let it be they would surely see that it was mysterious, fecund, generating.

They struck out in a frenzy and Dora shivered with despair and turned towards the woman in the shadows as the great golden bee broke up, drifting into dusty fragments in mid-air and turning into a gossamer which floated downwards. The woman moved out of the shadows and Dora saw that she had tussore hair but Dora's face and had a cartridge belt around her waist. She said, 'You must let it be.'

The boat dipped as the sea swelled and Dora awoke and lay waiting for the boat to reach dock so that she could start the journey home.

The Present

One day Dora was walking along the street carrying a needlepoint cushion which she had just had made up, when she heard herself hailed. There was no one in sight save a man on a bicycle skimming to a halt. He was wearing a huge crash helmet and shorts so that he looked like a child's drawing of a space alien. He waved at her and turned the bike and pushed it back towards her. She could tell he was smiling but the helmet so much obscured him that she could not think who it was. He propped the bike against his body and unbuckled the head gear and smiled at her, dark, speckled, glowing, and she gazed at him astonished, at this creature from her dream. She was suddenly filled to the lip with nostalgia for the shape and smell of the room in which passion had blazed out and flowered, for the branches of the cherry tree at the window, blooming without her, for the heaps of books around the bed in which she had, during that season of her heart, found lines that described what was happening to them in exultant language, for the days when they had peeled themselves apart, astonished to find that they were separate. He said, 'How are you?' and she said, 'Fine, thank you.' He asked, 'What's that?' and she said, 'A needlepoint cushion,' holding it close. He said, 'Still at it are you?' and so they parted. And she thought as she walked away that the heart is a small thing but desireth great matters and great matters are small and good and daily.